NINE LIVES

Also by Geoffrey Mehl...

Fiction (Tommy Kane/Mandy Owens)
STRAY CATS

Landscaping/Sustainable Design
PENNYSLVANIA NATURALLY

PERENNIALS: HABITAT AND CULTURE

A GARDENER'S GUIDE TO NATIVE PLANTS
OF NORTHEASTERN PENNSYLVANIA

Learn more at www.geoffmehl.com

Nine Lives
Copyright 2016 © by Geoffrey Mehl

ISBN-13: 978-0-9862766-2-0
ISBN-10: 0-9862766-2-6
Printed in the United States of America

NINE LIVES

by Geoffrey Mehl

CHAPTER ONE

West Twenty-third Street and Sixth Avenue, New York City

Benny looked up at Mandy, his eyes filled with hope and excitement. Tufts of hair snuck out from a greasy blue baseball cap to flutter in an October breeze. The same breeze carried the scent of his tweedy jacket to her nose, the kind of scent that comes from dark corners of a parking garage. He rocked back and forth, lifting each foot in turn.

Kind of like a duck that stepped into a wad of chewing gum. Mandy winced at her own metaphor. Poor Benny — the personification of pathetic, the epitome of hopeless. Benny was Benny, but the tug of manners, courtesy, compassion of her upbringing and causes arrived anyway to confront the impatience of running late. That as well as the cool objectivity of being a respected journalist in a city of blue chip media people. Objectivity. More like jaded cynicism sometimes. More like the honed edge of New York.

"But I got a really good tip today, Miss Owens. A really, *really* good one. You'll see."

Of course he did. As usual. Impatience won. "As good as the secret chemical the hot dog vendors sneak into the buns by Columbus Circle?"

He fluffed out to full-blown pride, but his eyes flitted left, right, up, down, never stopping. As usual, *they* were watching, something about special scanning equipment, probably government issue.

He scrunched his face and squinted to keep thick eyeglasses perched high on his nose. "Better."

Okay, occupational hazard, like gnats in summertime. The tipsters, the guys who listen to way too much A-M radio, the lonely little peo—ple with an urban rumor to share. Cynicism was flowing freely now, on autopilot.

She glanced at her watch. No time for Benny today. Her schedule a mess. A couple of bills coming due. Three pitches out, no callbacks. "Like the mayor's secret plan to tear down Rockefeller Center and build a giant fast food museum?" *Ouch. He's become the target for my own frustrations. Not good at all. Not who I'm supposed to be.*

His head bowed. He shrugged into a wave of arms, like a chubby little duck impatiently flapping its wings. "Aw, Miss Owens, it was for hamburgers and fries. Everybody knows that. Of course, all the news—papers are in their pocket, which is why — "

Well, maybe a little time, to be decent. Her voice softened. "Yes, that's right. I forgot."

But Benny's expression had already tumbled into disillusionment. "I suppose you don't care about the secret deal the United Nations made with the governor to put millions of refugees in Central Park. I bet Carl Jorgenson would listen. He's that big TV guy, you know."

Patience, patience. Benny wore a stained t-shirt a couple of sizes too large and the filthy jacket, a size too small. No socks, ratty sneakers, and a baseball cap that had been lined with plenty of tin foil after it was discovered in a dumpster. In any other city, Benny would attract the attention of a police officer. Especially near a school. But this was New York, where everyone looked past, walked around, avoided. *It's so hard to keep a straight face. Be nice. Any other day, I'd buy him a coffee, let him rant a bit, be on my way. Today, he just had to mention Carl.* "I know. Mister Investigative Reports. I wouldn't mind... But... I'm very sorry, Benny. I'm late for an interview at the Federal Reserve."

"But Miss Owens..."

"Benny, you have to understand. I'm a freelance business writer now. I don't have all the editorial resources of a powerful newspaper at my disposal." *Never did, really, but he'd never comprehend it.*

Benny stared straight ahead. The tempo of the rocking picked up.

A reprieve. The beep of a text alert.

Nice concept, but not for us at this time. JWC.

A reprieve, maybe, but not a good one. Her shoulders drooped at the rejection.

C'mon, Jack. Need a sale. Anything. A mental step back. *Okay. It happens.* But nothing makes the day quite like a rejection in the middle of another encounter with Benny.

He leaned wide left, right, and turned in both directions. "You'll see, you'll see. They know all my secrets. But now I have one of theirs!"

Yeah, right, I'm sure. Patience. Compassion. "Benny? Do you think you might want to get a little help?"

Eyes tracing the customary imaginary demons across the faces of buildings, his expression shifted from hope to despair as they appeared and vanished. His jaw dropped and his eyes went wide. "There!" He pointed past her. "There they are!"

Mandy whirled.

Nothing but the traffic, the buildings, the people of the neighbor-hood, going about their day. Not even the guys in black, with spotting scopes and directional mikes on the roofs. Plain old West Twenty-Third Street, same as always.

She turned back. "Benny..." Her words dissipated into a long sigh. Benny plodded away, back to Sixth Avenue, toward the subway en-trance from which he emerged a few minutes earlier. More like wad-dled. Like a duck. *Such a gloomy set of emotions.* Guilt. Annoyance. And pity, too. The phone's cheery ring tugging her from a plunge into shame. *Alan Rothstein. Federal Reserve Bank of New York.* "Hi, Alan. Just in the nick of time."

Benny, the proverbial sore thumb, stood out in a flock of pedestri-ans waiting at the curb for the light to change.

"Beg your pardon?"

"Never mind. What's up?"

The traffic light changed. Benny fumbled with something in his jacket pocket. In moments, he was alone on the curb. Alan said some-thing about the interview, the chairman delayed, no need to rush to the financial district downtown.

"Mandy?"

"Huh? Oh. Yes. Got it, thanks. Twenty minutes late. Otherwise we're still good."

Benny stepped off the curb, still preoccupied with whatever was in his jacket pocket.

"No, I said twenty at the earliest, more likely thirty. You all right?"

Focus. "Thirty minutes. Got it. Thanks much."

Benny had taken several steps. Alone in the crosswalk.

A blur. From the left. Truck. *Ambulance.*

And it mowed Benny right to the ground.

Tires screeched. Hundreds of heads turned. Jaws dropped, eyes widened. A wispy cloud of white, acrid smoke. The scent of burned rubber. Somber silence crushed a frozen moment of shock, terror, horror.

"Oh, my God..."

"What? Hello? Mandy? You okay? You still there?"

A deep, full breath. "Yes. Still here. I just saw a guy get run over by an ambulance. On Sixth Avenue."

"What? That's terrible. Awful. Is he...."

"No idea, Alan. Gotta go. I'll see you in a bit."

Bystanders closed into a ring. Arms went high with cell phones. A few decibels at a time, city sounds crept back on a tide of urban impa – tience. Cars honked. Humanity hummed again. An October wind pushed trash along the gutter. Muffled music floated past in a jumbled symphony of noise.

A notepad appeared in Mandy's left hand and a pen in her right while she pushed through the thin crowd of onlookers. Her eyes roamed to sift the scene. Words flowed from the tip of her pen.

Guy gets out of ambulance. Directs driver to back up. Benny's laid out. Not looking good. Three other guys all uniforms rush forward. Stretcher-thing. Surround Benny.

Rewind, the last few minutes of her morning. Running late. Looked up, there's Benny, near the entrance to the subway stop. No. He was coming up the steps. She wrote, *just arrived. Crosses street.*

Conversation.

Mandy glanced up to take in the evolving scene. Her pen contin−ued to write. *They were watching. Who?* Like always. Benny was con−stantly under surveillance, especially when off his meds. *Points some−where, somewhere W on 23. Turned to look. Nothing. Walks away, to Sixth. Something in pocket.*

She had drifted close and strained to see through the uniforms and quickly gave up on a bad perspective. She wrote, *signal changed. Lingers. Walks. Struck.*

Mandy's shoulders slumped again, her pen on pause. Good notes were crucial, objectivity essential. *Concentrate. Details matter.*

She looked up to observe and wrote, *NYFD Ambulance. Load Ben−ny on ambulance. What hospital? Check. Lights, no siren.*

She glanced up at the street sign, to be sure, as the ambulance made a right turn, onto Twenty-third.

Wait. Something's wrong with the truck. Use the phone. Take a picture. Another. The guy in front sees me. Take his picture. Darn...missed the number.

The ambulance picked up speed and rolled away.

Flipping a page on the pad, writing fast, but calmer now, impres−sions of the ambulance and the guy in front. The first police siren. *Check time. Write it down.* Onlookers drifted away to resume their lives, their pace speeding up as the sirens got closer. A few lingered to watch uniformed police flood the scene. One by one, she harvested the numbers on the patrol cars. An unmarked car. She stretched high, all the way up on her toes, to see. Phil Donatello himself. Mandy tapped the pen on the closed notepad.

Slip away, catch a subway downtown? Should have taken a little time. Been more cordial. Maybe listened. Then Benny might... No. Maybe not. But there was still time to get to interview at the fed and Donatello was always okay. She could be a good citizen, a witness. And stay with the story.

CHAPTER TWO

230 East Twenty-first Street, New York City

Detective Phillip Donatello opened a scuffed leather-bound notepad on the table separating them. An assortment of folded sheets and business cards stuffed pockets on the left, a lined yellow pad of paper on the right.

He gestured to the chair opposite while pointing to a surveillance camera in the ceiling. "Miss Owens, thanks for coming in. Take a seat. You doing all right?"

No need to hide from the camera. We're friends. "Good, Phil. Very well. Things are going great."

"Yeah?" He brushed his tie flat against the bulge of an older cop's belly and sat. "You look a little frayed around the edges, maybe."

"Wow, thanks. You've really added to my day."

He chuckled. "Not goin' so good? Me? I remember that cute little kid that come into the precinct — how many years ago was that?"

She reached into her bag for her notes. "More than I care to count, Phil. And you'll have to pardon me, but I haven't seen many people get killed lately. Out of practice, I'm afraid. It's been a while since I worked a cop beat."

He centered his materials, like always, on the table with precision into parallel lines with the edges and laughed. "I remember some of those days. You asking all the pushy questions from your social justice agenda, the others going for the gore. Still into all them lefty causes?"

Yes. And he still knows how to make me laugh. "I still care, Phil. But these days, I'm just trying to pay the bills. Tough times in the busi—

ness. A lot of cutbacks."

"Too bad. Used to be you'd make a good collar, there'd be twenty, thirty of you guys, cameras clicking, shouting questions. Now it's a few kids who don't know what do to with a handout from the P-R guys downtown."

She sighed. "One of these days, maybe I'll pack, leave the city, go find a nice, quiet country town with a little paper, cover the PTA Cupcake Contest or something. Days and days of yawning."

He straightened the pen next to the pad. "You could maybe buy your own newspaper, have a little job security."

"That'd be a laugh. I'd actually have to work. Heck, I'd probably wind up going all the way broke."

"Yeah. I hear ya." His eyes took an unabashed survey. "Still dress—ing very sharp, though. All the guys always admired your, uh, style."

She flipped through notebook pages for a blank one and looked up. "I just bet they did."

His face reddened.

"It's all right, Phil, especially in your case. And yes, when it comes to wardrobe, I'm still addicted... Sorry, that came out wrong."

He smiled and fussed with his notepad. "No offense taken. Part of, well, moving on, is learning to not take things the wrong way."

His face was lined with aging that had come too fast. All the trials of life itself. Plus a steady parade of corpses. It had to be terribly wear—ing. Yet he also appeared calm, even serene. "How about you? Lose a couple of pounds? Working out? You look well, more relaxed than I remember."

He grunted. "Same old waistline. But, yeah, coasting to the finish line now, so the pressure's off. Coupla days from hanging it up, grab—bing that city pension."

"Wow, really? That's a surprise." Donatello was one of those cops who she expected to be around six or seven years beyond forever. "Any special plans?"

"Yeah, me and a buddy got us a little charter fishing business in the works. Florida. Panama City Beach or something. I caught this case because all the hotshots are working an organized crime thing and they figured the old fart oughta earn his keep with one last call."

He moved the ball point pen to the center of the notepad. Social banter done. He was getting down to business.

Donatello's organizer was the most interesting object in a room that longed for memorable but languished in interview-room efficiency. Two metal chairs with gray seats, one metal table, nondescript paint and the obligatory mirror with the unseen faces on the other side.

Donatello began to write and scowled. "Dammit." He scribbled with more force, but the pen left no trail. Tiny beads of sweat blossomed under thinning black hair, combed straight back in retreat from his forehead. He patted his shirt pocket again with a beefy hand, large and calloused. A metaphor for the man himself in size, reputation and personality. Bigger in an interrogation room than on the street or even at his desk, in a place with too much noise and too many ears.

"Sorry, I gotta get a new pen. City pens. Always running out of ink." His face flushed as he began to stand.

Homicide detectives were all the same, hating to be caught off guard when focused on process. "Hold on, Phil. I think I've got a spare." In her bag, her fingers navigated through the familiar. Everything where it should be. Spare notepad. Phone. A tiny flashlight. The extra pen, beyond... Something odd. She rolled it over on her fingertips, took a guess and dropped it. A little further for the extra pen, out into the flat, fluorescent light.

He said, "Great, thanks."

"Keep it."

Donatello nodded appreciation that was little more than an exaggerated breath. "So. Yeah. Your coming in gives the uniforms more time to canvas all the people who, as usual, saw nothing but got pictures for their social media crap."

"No trouble. Anything for you, Phil." Time for a favor, one leg of a *quid pro quo*, to keep a working relationship in good order. *May as well. Everything else is going sideways.*

Donatello fired up methodical, prompting questions, hoping to prod loose a scrap of memory to yield a clue. A hit and run, he said, because the ambulance guys weren't supposed to leave the scene. And so he needed not only details, but impressions, too.

Poor Benny's coming off as a bonafide nutcase. I have to get Phil to understand he's a sad, harmless little guy.

Another question, different direction, but on the same path. The phone hummed an alert. She looked at the screen apologized for the interruption. A text message from Alan at the Fed. Indefinite delay. Chairman unavailable. No time to explain, more later. *Aw, c'mon, Alan, I really needed the fed chairman piece. Bergdorf's likes to be paid on time.* Mandy took a deep breath and leaned forward. *Where was — oh, yes. Bennie. Check the notes.* "What did he say? Oh, right. Okay. He said 'They know all my secrets. Now I know one of theirs.'" She paused to read her own handwriting. "No. That's not right. He said 'Now I *have* one of theirs.' Exact words." She closed the spiral-bound tablet. "They're good notes, Phil."

The object in the bag. A flash drive. Benny was sharing some sort of files on a flash drive. *Think. I reflexively turned to look. Nothing. When I turned back, he was walking away.*

Phil scowled and drew a line through the incorrect phrase and replaced it with the corrected version. "Okay, good. You're doing great. And then?"

"He looks up, really abrupt, sort of past my shoulder, the right one, and pointed. He said, 'There! There they are!' in a certain kind of voice. But really, Phil, if you knew Benny — "

Donatello nodded. "I get what you mean. And...?"

Flash drive. He had to... Stay focused. Stay calm. "All of a sudden he gave up and walked away. He paused at the light, at Sixth Avenue. I got a phone call. He was standing on the curb, like he was trying to find something in his pocket. The light turned. Other people went across, but he was still looking for something. He started to cross and, bang, down he went. The tires screeched when the driver hit the brakes."

Donatello continued to take notes, looking up when she paused.

"Phil, any idea how long those skid marks were?" *It would be nice to know how fast that ambulance was actually going.*

"Not yet. Uniforms'll get it in their report."

"Other witnesses?"

"The usual. By the time the uniforms got there, most of them were gone, and by the time I got there, everybody had the same story, that they saw nothing, couldn't remember a thing except it was a city ambulance."

"Another one of those finer New York moments." *The flash drive. What was Benny trying to say? Why the diversion? Should Phil know? Pay attention.*

"Yeah, exactly. So that's why you hanging around, coming forward is a good thing, Mandy. I appreciate it. But what I don't get is what you said about the ambulance, the tags. Maybe we can find out for sure from your pictures."

The Jersey plates. Pictures to prove it. Maybe.

Donatello leaned back and rubbed his jaw. "Okay. In as much detail as you can recall, describe the truck again. Everything you remember."

Mandy verbally painted a portrait of a standard New York Fire Department ambulance.

Donatello rummaged through the left side of his notebook and produced a photograph. "Like this one?"

"Exactly like that one. I don't remember the unit number on it, but I swear it had a New Jersey license plate on the back. A regular plate."

"Could have been the way the light caught it? I mean, reflections, sunlight, whatever?"

"No. It was a Jersey plate. You don't believe me, do you?"

He drummed his fingertips on the table.

"What? C'mon, Phil. I know you too well. You know you can trust me. What aren't you telling me?"

Donatello reached for Mandy's cell phone. "Let me have the boys downstairs pull the images, see what we got."

"Can I come along?"

"Nah, it's a restricted area. But I'll bring you copies of whatever you took. Something to drink? Water, soda, maybe coffee? I wish I could offer you something stronger, but you know how it is."

"How long?"

"Five years, three months, six days."

"Bravo!"

"The day's not over yet."

"I'm your number one cheerleader, Phil. Yes, I'd love a cup of genuine cop coffee," she answered. "After all that fancy stuff from Starbuck's, some really outstanding cop coffee would be perfect."

"Regular?"

"Can any civilian handle it any other way? I mean, really lean on the milk and sugar, okay?"

Donatello mustered a laugh, gathered his notebook, tucked it under his arm and promised to return in a few minutes.

The moment the door closed behind him, Mandy checked the time, stood, stretched, walked around. She sat down, got up, paced. The stick in her bag. *Can't risk taking a look at it, not with surveillance cameras in the ceiling.* She looked at her watch every few minutes, circled the table every few minutes, sat for a few minutes.

Just after the twenty-five minute mark, the door opened. She turned to tease Donatello about taking so long to get coffee.

His expression said it all. "There's a problem. We, uh, got a kind of situation."

CHAPTER THREE

The exasperating wait and the uneasy news put an edge of annoy-ance on her words. "Please tell me you ran out of coffee."

He wore that puzzled look, like when a source is caught by sur-prise and struggles to figure out what to say. Remote, a bit stand-off-ish. *All business this time.* "So what aren't you telling me?" He pushed a pair of surveillance camera images toward her. "Recognize the faces?"

"No. These look like they're from inside the precinct station. The desk?"

"Uh-huh. While we were talking before, these guys arrived. They got U.S. Marshal identification, but FISA warrants. You know, the se-cret court the feds have for surveillance of terrorists and spies?"

"Benny? A terrorist? A spy? You're joking, Phil."

"Yeah, well, I've heard of marshals doing some of the legwork for the spooks, mostly tactical ops, but FISA court warrants are usually for intelligence. These guys want us to turn you over as a material witness to some sort of federal crime. It don't add up. I know guys in the marshal's service, so I made a couple of calls. They got no ops go-ing here, no fugitive searches we don't already know about. So, Mandy, I've gotta ask: did this business with Benny involve anything in the way of a federal crime?"

"No."

"You're certain? Absolutely certain? This is not a time to get no-ble with the First Amendment."

Mandy reached into her bag. *It's also not a time to get cute with evi-dence.* "While you were out, I found this. Benny must have dropped it in my bag when he distracted me."

He examined the flash drive. "Ordinary stick you could get any—where. You've never seen it, have no idea what's on it, or where the victim got it?"

Benny. Not merely a victim. Benny. "No. I'm being straight with you, Phil. It's probably one of his silly rants about something. But right now, I'd like to get out of here."

Donatello leaned back and tapped his pen on the notepad. "Let's take a walk, next door."

"Okay, but this is starting to — never mind, sure."

At the door, he held up a hand signaling a pause while he peeked into the hall. Satisfied, he gestured to proceed a dozen feet to the un—marked door of the observation room on the back side of the mirror. Once inside, he came straight to the point. "Benny's dead. The body was found over by the Yards, a short way from the hit and run scene. We got a team on it now. No clue on the ambulance. And the guys downstairs are still working on the photos from your phone, but it doesn't look too good at the moment. You're really sure you don't know anything about this stick, maybe the vic was involved in some—thing?"

"Benny? A national security risk? It's ludicrous, Phil. I think I've done my good deed for the day, you have my number, and maybe it's time to get back to work."

Donatello shrugged. "If you want, but you won't get ten feet out the door before you're in federal custody. Alleged federal custody, anyway. They were making quite a show of bringing in a crew to search the building. Our guys are holding 'em off, but knowing our captain, he's not going to push it too hard. He should be after paper from the U.S. Attorney but what are you gonna do?"

Wait a second. This seems like... "You sure this isn't some kind of elaborate joke you guys are playing? If it is, ha-ha, well done, you've got me."

"No joke. This is real, kiddo."

Phil Donatello. Cool, calm, unflappable. Today, nervous, a little sad. "So I'm stuck here? Like an embassy refugee?"

"More like a wanted felon in a house surrounded by SWAT guys.

Only a question of time. Which is why we're in here."

Mandy slumped against the wall. "I don't believe this. Nobody hauls off a reporter to jail. I haven't done anything wrong. I told you everything I know, turned over all the evidence, been a good citizen. I'll be glad to tell them the same thing, clear all this up, and write it off to one of the more bizarre days of my life."

Movement in the interview room. Two men in light gray suits, looking around, examining the table and chairs , exchanging words she could not hear. Donatello locked the door and gestured for her to stay silent and still.

The two men left the room and seconds later the doorknob to the observation area rattled.

By the clock on the wall, Donatello remained motionless for more than a minute, before speaking in a soft voice. "I know what you're saying, but now I'm talking to you as a friend, not a detective. Some— thing's screwy. I've been a cop for a long time and carry a gold shield for a reason. I took the liberty of having the video of our interview turned off and the earlier stuff erased, so they've got nothing, like you weren't even here."

She said, "All melodrama aside, what am I supposed to do?"

"I can poke around, check these guys out, but it's gonna take a lit— tle while. Day or two, maybe. I know some people, people I trust, who can hide you. Legitimate guys from the marshal's service. Witness protection."

No, no, no. "This is way, way too strange. Are you sure this isn't some part of Benny's joke conspiracy, with you in on it, along with the Tooth Fairy and Santa Claus?" Mandy folded her arms and paced in a tight circle. "You're not kidding, are you?"

"No. I'm not." His hand smothered the doorknob. "But you can walk out, do whatever you want. Me? I'm an old city cop a couple of days away from pension, hoping this is some sort of fed bullshit, some wave-the-flag and show-some-muscle crap, and that the U.S. Attor— ney's office is going to straighten things out."

"But?"

"Like they say in the movies — "

"Yeah, yeah, bad feeling and all that." *Surreal. Absolutely surreal.*

Like maybe suddenly the door would burst open and a pack of laugh—
ing cops would pour in with booze and cupcakes. Only it didn't. *Alone.*
Alone in the dark. *Scary.* But scary like times before. The scary that
comes with a great piece, unfolding, evolving, taking form. Being ac—
tually in witness protection had the makings of an incredible story. A
once in a lifetime. A bidding war among editors. Plus, there was clear—
ly something big going on. Better to be on the inside, where the ac—
tion was, than on the outside, hearing a chorus of "no comment."

She stopped to watch her toe tap the floor. *Let go, run with it, fol—
low the trail, see what happens.*

Donatello repeated, "It's your call."

"No," she said at last. "It's yours. Contact your buddy."

* * *

There were supposed to be two, or maybe three, youngish, burly
guys with military-style haircuts. The kind of guys that maybe played
tight end or middle-linebacker for a college in Ohio or someplace,
named Chuck or Jerry or maybe Denny. They'd wear off-the-rack
suits and short-sleeved shirts from a big box in the suburbs. Sturdy
places like Islip or Massapequa or Hicksville.

They'd probably be pretty good at gin rummy, drink soda from
cans, and they would tell funny stories about their kids and the family
dog and the guy next door. There would be secret knocks on the door
for sandwich and pizza deliveries, newspapers and magazines, goodie
bags with the stuff to keep a witness happy. Or at least comfortable.
Or at least less bored.

Mandy stretched out on an enormous bed that should have come
with a ladder against a tufted brown vinyl headboard partially hidden
by more pillows than any mattress should be allowed to have. To her
right, a bay of three sealed windows were cloaked by draperies. To her
left, a desk, chair, a minimalist bathroom. Straight ahead, a giant
flatscreen television, where tasteful hotel paintings should be, the
artistic nonsense right out of Hong Kong.

Tedious. No phone. No computer. Not even notepaper, for the captured felon-turning-state's-evidence to craft a suicide note before overdosing on stale crackers and cookies at five dollars a bag.

She sighed. All the cloak-and-dagger, being hustled out a back door, an unmarked car, whisked away to Times Square — dissipated. No elaborate motorcade. Just stocky policewomen whose vests only compounded the problem, complaining about working-class spouses. Through the dim lobby, up to the seventh floor and a room a dozen paces down a silent hallway. Couldn't even see the room number, because the short-haired blonde blocked the view on the way in. Instructions, all the usual cliches. And alone, to the alternatives of pacing in speculative anxiety, hoping to live long enough to say hello to Your Honor, or the television remote and intellectual anesthesia. A talk show blending liberal politics with a presentation on cooking rutabagas won out.

A clever witness would figure out how to use the remote as a signal. Maybe they'd contact their team, have it come down from the roof, make a daring escape into New Jersey or something. *Connecticut would be better. At least I would know where things are.* Benny would probably know how to crack the secret code, but the device in Mandy's hand was not about to do anything more than change channels. On the screen, a barrage of commercials touted fabulous TV offers.

"I'm beginning to think like Benny," she told the remote. "And that's not good."

Or was it? She tapped the mute button on the remote and focused on the ceiling, where the events of the morning unfolded in slow motion, frame by frame. The flash drive was the key, but Phil had that now. Almost certain that it contained Benny's silly conspiracy ideas, this time in text documents to print out and share amid jolly laughter with friends at a cocktail party.

Such as whom? Hm. A mental file of people, come and gone. Haven't heard from since... Should have sent a card. Should have returned a call. *Yes. When you're unemployed, the camaraderie evaporates.* The last time there was a message on the phone. *Well, other than the landlord, reminding me...* College friends. Sorority sisters. Last spring they wanted to organize something. Can't remember. And all the peo—

ple in high school. *Well, maybe not.* But career moments. There were a lot of those. *Let's see. How about the time...*

The images on the real screen shifted to a new program. She clicked the remote in time to hear the end of the fanfare, the cutaway from the title screen that bragged, "Number One News Program in New York! It's Carl Jorgenson's I-Team!" The pan of the audience, applauding, cheering. And from the side, in walked Carleton T. Jorgenson. High fives, low fives, points, waves. At last on the tiny little set's centerpiece, a plastic desk in glowing fluorescent colors, and the obligatory empty chairs for as many as two exciting guests at the same time.

She said, "Oh, spare me..."

Carl rattled on with gushing appreciation for the mindless cheers of a mindless audience and vowed once again to get to the bottom of the big news issues of the day facing New York City. "My city. The one I care about. The one I investigate."

More cheers.

This is like watching a journalistic train wreck. I can't bring myself to...

Carl's obnoxiously loud voice took a serious tone as his intro sounded ominous. Soho was in danger. Resident huddled in their homes. Or they sent someone down to the deli for bread and milk be—cause...

C'mon Carl, get to it.

He leaned forward. The audience hushed. "It seems there's a pair of competing gentlemen's clubs. And you know what?"

Mandy's fingers locked onto the remote's Channel Up button. *I can't begin to imagine, Carl. Tell us.*

"They're competing for which one has the dancers who are most endowed..."

Oh, my gosh...

"Yes. It's the Battle of the Bouncing Boobies!"

The audience roared delight. Applause, big time. The stage man—ager's arms must be flailing to beat the band. Mandy's finger raced to the power button and the screen went dark. She fluffed a pillow and stretched out. *Yep. Wallowing in self-pity and mind-numbing boredom definitely has something going for it.* Self-pity. Historically impermissible. Simply not done. A family doctrine. Boredom, on the other hand, was sometimes okay. A good way to rest the mind, especially when frazzled.

Mandy rolled to her side to watch the digital clock tick away until daylight in the room slowly dimmed into semi-darkness.

A knock on the door. Lightly, tentative, probably the knuckle of a forefinger. *Not a secret knock at all. More like the kind you hear from room service.* Food, beverage, company. *That would be nice.* She rolled onto her feet, into her heels, hurrying so whoever knocked wouldn't think no one was home and go away. Or worse. The headline: Long-lost Witness Found Dead. The lead: The mummified body of a protected witness, apparently forgotten six years ago, was found yesterday in a midtown hotel...

Mandy yanked the door open.

A tall man, flanked by two others. They were pudgy, middle aged, so terribly ordinary. Definitely not Chuck, Jerry or Denny. But they had credentials. A badge. United States Marshal. I.D. card with a picture that matched.

"Miss Owens?"

Mandy looked at their hands. There was no takeout, nothing to drink. "Yes. Come in."

"I'm Bobby McKennan, with the marshal's service. Phil Donatello is a friend of mine."

At last. All I need is a notebook and pen. Got to get good notes. Bag. "Yes. Good. Let me get my — "

McKennan offered a warm and understanding smile. "Please hurry, Miss Owens. We're here to escort you to a safe location. Food, temporary place to stay, the usual comforts."

CHAPTER FOUR

613 Railroad Avenue, Jacks Ford, Pennsylvania

Charlie paced. Four steps right, four steps left. At each turn, he peeked over rimless glasses and tidied his brush mustache.

"Aw, hell." His buddy Phil needed a hand. A witness snatched, damn near in broad daylight. A bunch of favors called in. Guys who worked the street, pitching in. *My turn to do what I can.* From an open patch on his battle-scarred desk, he picked up the phone like it was a cracked egg. Following instructions, he winced and squeezed it at the same time.

He sighed and lectured all the silent objects that cluttered a tiny second-floor apartment above Frank's TV and Appliances. The rumpled bed. The nightstand lamp with the stained shade. The tattered overstuffed chair, once golden but now simply drab, facing a television that sometimes worked. Dusty venetian blinds, through which shafts of light drew prison stripes on everything. "Once upon a time there was real phones. You picked up, the local operator — mostly a nice gal named Hazel — would come on the line and fetch you the number you wanted. But no more, by god. No more. Now it's all flippin' and peckin' at a god damned tiny TV."

Taking aim, he touched the "two" button. A lot of folks snuggled up to theirs like it was a pet kitten, but they were mostly kids and he had no use for cats. *Best take it slow, careful.* He raised the object to his ear. A couple of clicks were followed by a ringing tone. *So, okay, it actually works. Don't mean I gotta love the damn thing.*

A flat voice said, "T-K-A."

"Lucy?" He tried again to conjure an image of her, but abandoned the effort as her voice brightened.

"Hey, Charlie, how's everything? I see you figured out how to use the new phone. Good for you."

His eyebrow lifted. *Caller I-D.* Couple of the guys had phones like that, the kind that told who was calling, in case it was a bad time, a bad debt or a bad deal, hawked by some sleazeball. "You don't have to get all smartassed about it. You know, down at Billy's tavern, the boys got a joke. They ask, 'If the damn phone was so smart, how come it don't work all by itself?'"

Her tone went dry as Texas dust. "Wow. That's a good one, Char—lie."

"Gets a laugh every time at Billy's," he argued.

"I'll bet it does."

"Where's Tommy?"

"Somewhere between here and the international date line."

"Dammit, young lady, cut me a little slack, hear?"

"You know I hate it when you get him involved in stuff."

"Yeah, well, I ain't excited about it neither, but it's hit the fan. So where is he?"

She paused before confessing. "He went to Uruguay — "

Charlie's right hand smacked the table. "That damn Russian again! What'd Yenchenko do this time?"

"*Ukrainian.* He's from the Ukraine. Tommy said it was some sort of misunderstanding. Apparently something to do with a local Miss Something-or-other and an incident in a bar. Details are a bit sketchy."

Charlie's fingers drummed the table. "And so Tommy went down to fix things?"

"Well, sort of. One of those buddy things you guys do. Had to spring Sergei from jail, get him out of the country. Dropped him off in southern France. Probably on the way home by now. Looks like Sergei's cattle ranching days are over."

Charlie snorted. "Yeah, ain't retirement a bitch. Prob'ly just as well anyhow. Russians don't know nothing about proper beef cows."

"I do believe they've got cattle in the *Ukraine*, Charlie. *Uruguay,* too."

"Not proper cows. Proper beef cows are *American*, Lucy. Everybody knows that."

Lucy sighed. "Just once I wish you'd speak with Tommy about getting involved in these little adventures. Especially with Sergei, who's not high on my list, either, y'know. You *do* realize I've been trying to make Tommy respectable, right? This sort of thing doesn't help."

"Tommy? Respectable? Oughta know by now that ain't ever — "

Lucy's voice soured with impatience. "I can only try, Charlie."

Charlie snorted. "Like they say, tigers never change their spots."

"Neither do leopards. But you're calling because you've got another problem. So what is it this time?"

"You got a pencil? Paper?" *Nah. Probably some sort of computer.* Charlie carried a stubby but sturdy Number Two, sharpened with a pen knife, and a used envelope in his shirt pocket. It worked fine for taking notes, making lists, adding up numbers.

"Go ahead."

Charlie unfolded an envelope. "Got a list here."

"Talk to me, Charlie. Timeline?"

"Quick turnaround."

"Got a target?"

Just above his desk, a picture frame hung crooked. He reached out and straightened it. Certificate of Appreciation. Forty-three years...dedicated service...upon retirement... signed by the head honcho himself. "Closed up rehab facility, Chatham, New Jersey. Straight-up extraction. Protected witness, kidnapped from custody. Female, if that matters."

"It doesn't."

He continued to adjust the frame on the wall. *There we go. Nice and straight.* It was too bad the director couldn't be there to present it on the day he turned in his badge and identification. Probably a busy guy, he'd thought at the time, which was why the unit secretary caught up with him in the lobby and handed him a big manila envelope that someone had nearly forgotten. Inside was the framed certificate. He had walked out with everything important in a small box un—der his left arm and the certificate in his right hand.

He scowled. "It might. The name Mandy Owens ring a bell?"

"Damn." Lucy's sigh was audible and her tone became attentive. "Okay, crew?"

Charlie smiled. *Yeah, thought so. Always nice to catch Miss Smarty Pants off guard.* His list had several numbers followed by question marks. "Seven, no six. Six oughta do."

"You sure? I can go seven if you want."

"Six is fine."

"Props?"

"I'm thinking federal, maybe Secret Service, suits, blue wind—breakers. Couple of SUVs, usual black, the big ones, with some anten—nas and stuff to look official."

"Weapons?"

"Tranks. Pistols, one each, regular loads. I'm sure Tommy don't want anyone to get carried away."

"Yeah, well, you guys keep pushing it, one of these days.... Your loads. Anesthetic or paralytic?"

"Anything quick. But nothing touchy medical-wise. And see if you can get an authentic look with the pistols. Last time, folks thought they was toys."

"Until they got shot. But I promise to mention it. Okay. Commu—nications?"

Charlie paused to think. Gear for two teams of three, check. But containment was an unknown and he'd have to admit it. "Any way we can figure out what kind of phone lines they got, block 'em, reroute maybe?"

Lucy's voice remained as calm as a diner waitress taking an order for a table of ten. "Wire work. I'll talk to my — I mean, Bug, see what he can do. What else?"

"That's it."

"Okay, got it."

"Want to read it back to me?"

"No."

"You sound sorta sure of yourself."

"I am. Anything else?"

"That's it."

"He'll be in touch. Take care, Charlie."

The connection clicked and she was gone.

Charlie lowered the phone and said to it, "And you have yourself a real fine day, too."

* * *

Tommy Kane stirred from a three-hour nap to the soft whine of the Gulfstream's engines and the caress of moving cabin air. He yawned, stretched and savored a rich blue view of the Atlantic Ocean far below, punctuated by scattered puffy clouds.

Karen appeared to collect the blanket and pillow. She wore her customary navy pant suit, open collar blouse and usual smile. Her efficient blonde hair style was still perfect.

"How we doing?"

Karen folded the blanket. "Cesar says we're at about fifty-eight fifty, forty one thousand, and making good time at four hundred fifty knots. Right on schedule. Can I get you lunch, perhaps a beverage?"

Tommy closed his eyes and stifled the temptation to yawn by inhaling a deep breath of air. He nodded. "A sandwich would be good. Did Sergei leave anything in the fridge?"

She chuckled. "I'm afraid all the vodka is gone, and some of the beer, too, but I hid the scotch."

"Good job, thank you. I'll have a beer with the sandwich."

"Right away."

"Messages?"

Karen laid the blanket aside to offer a scrap of paper. "Just another quiet day. One call, from Lucy, some sort of relayed message from Charlie." She passed the folded note to Tommy and waited while he read it.

Tommy refolded the paper and tucked it into his shirt pocket. *So much for a long, lazy vacation at the cabin.* A stack of questions for Charlie. And Lucy? *She's getting to know me too well. Nothing quite like hav-*

ing those two set up an op even before I know what it is.

He looked up at Karen. "Skip the beer. After the sandwich, bring the scotch."

"Thinking or relaxing?"

"Thinking. The eighteen-year-old Macallan will be fine."

"Sure thing. I'll be a minute or two."

Tommy nodded and looked through the window. Almost eight miles below, the ocean barely drifted past, almost like moments frozen in time. *Mandy Owens.* The party at Lyford Caye. The encounter at the bar, the teasing over a necessary double scotch. The bright eyes, the charming smile. The encounters since too fleeting, the conversa—tions too fragmented. Tommy rubbed his chin and began to organize his thoughts. *Our paths cross again.*

CHAPTER FIVE

Chatham Township, New Jersey

Light burst into the room. Mandy winced, blinked her eyes several times and shook her head. "Oh, my. Tommy Kane. Please tell me you're not on their side. I like you better as a good guy."

"I was in the neighborhood, thought I'd stop by, say hello, see if you might be interested in a jailbreak."

Mandy propped herself up on an elbow. "That's what I adore about you, Tommy. No respect for visiting hours and always some kind of mischief."

He shrugged. "Well, if it's inconvenient, I can come back later."

She brushed stray hair from her face. His tan had faded. In the dark blue windbreaker, his shoulders seemed softer than the dinner jacket at Lyford Caye. But his eyes, bright as ever, his smile equally as infectious.

She sat up. "After four days of this? Now is fine. Have a plan, do you?"

Tommy glanced at his watch. "I only heard about it thirty-two hours ago, so I'm making it up as I go."

"But of course. I should have known. And without the slightest hint of shame, apology or regret." Shoes. Dark blue. Slip-on sneakers. *Down here somewhere. Ah.* "When it comes to prison breaks, I prefer to be organized, have things well thought out."

Tommy smirked. "It's actually more of a detention center. Nice outfit you've got, by the way."

A glance in the mirror. *Oh, that is so sad.* "Penitentiary orange is *not* my color, Tommy. The fabric is too coarse and the sizing is just *wrong*."

His tone was gentle, patient. "We ought to get moving. Ten, maybe fifteen minutes tops, before reinforcements arrive and it hits the fan."

"Oh, Tommy, please. Not like this. Not like a neon tangerine. I wouldn't want to be caught dead in this... this *thing* outside."

"Dead is what we'll be if we don't hurry up." He offered a nylon sports bag. "Regular clothes. A disguise." His voice went to mock confidentiality. "It's a low budget jailbreak."

She tugged garments from the bag. "Yeah, no kidding." A jacket with block lettering on the back. "Secret Service? Are you — "

"No. But they say you need a disguise for a proper jailbreak, so... " A noise in the hallway distracted Tommy. "Time to go. You've got about a minute to change." He pulled a pistol from a shoulder holster, peeked into the corridor and made some sort of signal. The hallway went dark.

"Leave it to me to get an upscale guy but a discount rescue." She turned to lay the garments on the bed to examine them. "It'll have to do. So turn around. Or better yet, step out into the hall."

She looked up. He'd already departed. Wretched orange tumbled to the floor. Terrible disguise, a size too large, maybe more. *But still...* The first smile in days. *Tommy Kane.* Warmth. Security. *Picking up where we left off. Hurry up.*

In the gloomy hallway, she pressed her back against the wall, next to him. He held the gun close to his chest, the barrel up, toward murky ceiling tiles punctuated with a pattern of lighting fixtures, all dark. "Question?"

He glanced at her outfit and grinned, like the kid who got a new toy and was trying to find the on-switch. "Sure."

She studied the hallway. "I've always wondered if you were man— aging to stay out of trouble. I mean, sort of generally?"

His eyes twinkled like stars in the dim light. "Nah. When I see trouble coming down the road, I still like to step up and say hello."

"Most people would run the other way."

"Yeah, but I'm a friendly guy."

She struggled to pull the windbreaker sleeves up to her wrist. All at least a size or two larger and the jacket for a much taller man. She waved a finger of warning. "Not a word, Tommy. Not a single word."

He pointed toward the end of the hall and together they inched sideways. The wall, like a cliff. The long reflection on vinyl, like a chasm of certain death.

She whispered. "Where are we?"

"Abandoned drug treatment center. In New Jersey. Intelligence community crews used to use it for black ops prisoners."

"You're joking. You mean, like actual spies and stuff? And you know this because — "

"These guys aren't in the community. And they aren't federal agents. They're with something called Cinnabar Security Systems. Private contractor maybe. I have no idea why they grabbed you from the hotel."

A silhouette with a rifle popped into view. Mandy gasped, but before her eyes fully widened, Tommy turned to shield her, squared his shoulders into a shooter's stance and fired. The target crumpled to the floor.

"Oh, my.... You...you...*shot him*. You actually shot a guy...."

"Yeah. That sometimes happens in gunfights."

Mandy pressed harder into the wall and her steps became even more wary. "One minute I'm a good citizen, a witness. Next minute, I'm being hustled around to avoid, of all things, *federal* agents. I'm hauled off for days of isolation alternating with interrogation. And searched. *Completely* searched. Now — "

From somewhere in the building came the sound of two more faint pops. Tommy's posture relaxed and he moved faster on a direct path down the hall.

Mandy picked up the pace. "I don't want to be negative, but how do I know for sure if this is a rescue or another kidnapping? I've had some time to brush up on my paranoia."

Tommy paused to study the hallway. "Reasonable question." He pulled the flash drive from his pocket. "Phil Donatello sent this call—

ing card. In the trade we call it a bona fide."

"How did you get it?"

"The cop passed it to Charlie, the guy who set up this little rescue. I'm only helping out."

Charlie? Who's... Later.

Near the end of the hallway, they took several cautious steps and stopped again.

She leaned in to cling to security. "You're a good helper. I'm im—pressed."

Tommy focused on the end of the hall. "You'll meet Charlie to—morrow. He figured you'd want the stick back."

Mandy examined the device. "I honestly have no idea what's on it. Could be anything. I have to accept it as original." She began to put it in her pocket, but changed her mind and returned the stick to Tom—my. "You keep it. I suppose if this was a kidnapping, you'd toss a black bag over my head. Or at least come up with a bit more stylish disguis—es."

Tommy crept forward and grinned. "Now, now, those clothes are on loan from the costume department at the Shubert Theatre on West Forty-fourth Street in Manhattan. You're supposed to look like a Secret Service agent, like the rest of the actors we hired."

She studied the garments on her body and shook her head. "Wow. You really know how to make a girl's day, don't you?"

Tommy stopped and raised the weapon. "I'll admit I preferred that dress from the party." He held out his hand to signal they should wait. "You said it was by David Aire, a color you called raspberry."

The heat of a blush filled her cheeks and ears. "Really? You re—member the gown? That was so long ago." Mandy looked both ways, but saw nothing.

"Sixteen months. Impossible to forget."

Unexpected calm. Tranquility. A snuggly blanket of warm. *How does he...* "You know what, Tommy?"

"What?"

"It's been a really long day. I hate to be grumpy, whining during a jailbreak, but I'm really hungry, really thirsty, really cold and really tired."

"As soon as we get going, we'll pick up some food."

"And coffee. One of those nice big, gooey, fancy ones. Grande. Mocha. Mountains of cream. Caramel. The works."

Another target sprang into view. Tommy fired a second time.

Mandy gasped again. First time it was shock. This time... almost fascination. Watching the body fall. *Not the way I'm supposed to* — "Do you do this often? Kill people, I mean?"

Tommy's sigh was the familiar guy blend of patronization and as—surance. "Nobody's getting killed."

She leaned forward for a closer look. The body on the left was the guy in the ambulance. "Uh, they're on the floor, Tommy. And not moving."

He turned and displayed the pistol. "It's a tranquilizer gun, with low-dose rounds. They'll wake up in a half hour or so with a terrible headache. That's all."

She stared at him. Suspicion. Surprise. A sense of solace.

"For true, Mandy. Corpses always have consequences."

"Your gun looks real to me."

"Yep, special from a guy I know. He's got a thing for Glocks, so that's what it looks like. I'd go for a Beretta myself. Nicer grip."

While she stared at the bodies, Tommy gathered and emptied their weapons. No blood on the floor. The image of Bennie being killed by these guys formed in her imagination. Horrible. There *should* be blood on the floor. She pushed the image away. "But they had *real* guns, like, with actual bullets."

"That happens sometimes."

"And you didn't."

"That happens a lot." Tommy pointed to their destination. "We go through those glass doors, turn left. Vehicles are in the driveway, about fifty yards."

Mandy looked up. "I suppose you didn't come with a hairbrush and makeup? God, I would kill for a hairbrush."

He turned to look at her.

"Well, figuratively speaking, of course."

Tommy nodded and smiled. "Sorry."

"I know, I know. Low budget jailbreak. We're going to have a talk about how you run rescues, Tommy. Let's get out of here."

They scurried across a narrow lobby. At the glass door, Tommy paused to check again. *Look back, take it in.* Two more bodies on the far side. But not dead, so that was good. "So you really do this — how do I say? — now and then, um, sort of get involved?"

His smile was soft, patient, reassuring. "People sometimes need a little help. Kind of balancing the scale, leveling the playing field, keeping things fair."

"You mean there's still room for Robin Hood?"

He pushed the door open. "Robin Hood never went out of style."

Follow him, no questions asked. Cool night air, brisk, fresh. Actual pavement. *Yes, oh, yes. Freedom. At last.*

Shimmering shadows, slices of light from another building. Shapes. Vehicles, assorted sizes, mostly black SUVs. People standing around. Secret Service jackets, the whole crew. No. Two more, to one side. Even further, deep in a shadow, an ambulance. A New York City Fire Department ambulance. *And that sure looks like a Jersey plate.*

Tommy leaned close to whisper, "Do me one favor. Kind of look dazed, confused, quiet."

"Why?"

"The guys will feel a lot better if you evoke some sympathy. Especially if they find out they're being underpaid."

"*What?* I can't believe you said — never mind. All right, but there's one thing. Did you come across a female guard, about five-seven, kind of heavy, like she pumps iron, but doesn't diet well, has awfully bad taste in clothes and really needs a new hairdresser?"

"Yep. The woman in charge. Why?"

"I want a parting word."

"Mandy, we've only got a couple of minutes."

Give him your most serene smile. "That's all I need."

They exchanged a look. Dozens of words, in blink of an eye. Tommy's nod was faint and brief. *Wonderful. He understands where I'm going with this.*

Tommy motioned to two of the Secret Service actors and in less than a minute the sullen, handcuffed matron and defiant Mandy faced each other.

Mandy crossed her arms and shifted her weight to her left leg. *Okay. Hard glare. Mean. Nasty. Unforgiving. Now bark a command.* "Shoot her. I want her killed. Shoot her right now."

Tommy's expression went to uncertainty. "You sure about this?"

Mandy continued to stare. The matron's defiance dissolved into fear. Genuine fear. *Perfect.* "Oh, yeah. She's the one who did the cavity search. Put the bitch down."

Tommy looked at the group of agents and rubbed his chin. "We ought to go — "

Mandy stuffed her fists into her waist and stood firm. "Look. We agreed. No prisoners, right?"

Tommy's nod was stuffed with fake reluctance.

Mandy narrowed her eyes. *Look mean.* "If you won't do it..." She held out her hand and wiggled her fingers. "Gimme."

Tommy handed the gun to Mandy.

The matron blubbered an apology and begged for reprieve in a choking sob.

Mandy wrapped her hands tightly around the grip, raised the weapon and aimed. She lowered her voice to an intense growl. "I want this to be the last thing you remember."

Terror twisted the matron's face. Jaws dropped all around. Mandy pulled the trigger. A tiny tranquilizer dart shot into the matron's tor-so. She rolled her eyes and collapsed to a limp sprawl on the driveway.

Mandy returned the pistol to Tommy. "Ah, that was *so* worth it. Now we can go."

Tommy exhaled and slowly muttered, "Okay." He opened the rear door of the third SUV for her. "I kind of like the way you look dazed and confused. Not bad. You still in the news business? How's it going?"

She smiled and settled into the seat. "Yes, I am. And it definitely has its moments. How's the action-adventure business?"

Tommy glanced at the matron's body on the pavement and cocked an eyebrow. "It has its moments."

CHAPTER SIX

Near Jacks Ford, Pennsylvania

Tommy winced. Cop coffee. The bite of a cornered gator. The kick of Aunt Ernestine's mule. *Oh, yeah. That'll surely wake the dead.*

Charlie poured the brew down his throat like summer day lemon – ade. "You got a lot of qualities, Tommy, but top of the list is a first- rate cup of coffee. Don't tell Frannie at the diner, though. She always gimme extra. I don't want to mess with that. How's my witness?"

Tommy topped off mugs. "Long night. Sleeping in. She'll be okay."

"You done real good for Phil. I'm obliged. No idea how long this is gonna go, so I'll work out arrangements. Frannie's willing to put her up temporary until we sort this out."

A voice from the doorway interrupted. "Sort what out?"

One of Tommy's gray winter t-shirts hung more than halfway to Mandy's knees.

Tommy made introductions. "What happens next."

"Ah, of course. But right now, not quite me. Tommy, where's the — "

"Second door on the left."

"And there's a — "

"Yep, but watch the valve in the tub, it can be tricky."

"I don't suppose — "

Tommy gathered a worn shipping carton from the table and opened the lid.

Charlie said, "Couple of changes of clothes from the store in town. Frannie, from the diner, tossed in an extra hair dryer, cosmetic goo, that kinda stuff. It'll do 'til we figure out what's what."

She picked out the hair dryer and showered Charlie with a smile. "Oh, my. Thank you, *thank you.*"

Charlie muttered something about it being not that big a deal while Mandy accepted the package from Tommy.

Tommy asked, "Coffee?"

She had already turned and gave a little wave. "Soon, but not too strong, please."

Charlie watched. When he faced Tommy, his eyebrows were higher than usual. He tidied his brush mustache and whispered, "Damn."

"Yeah."

"So that's her, huh?

"That's her."

"Uh-huh." Charlie swirled the last of his coffee in the mug and re-treated to a scowl. "Aw, hell. Let's leave it at 'nice to see the quality of witnesses is improving.'" He nodded toward the sound of the shower in the adjacent room. "How long do you figure? Fifteen, twenty?"

"Thirty, more likely forty."

"I ever tell you about when we was working a case in Cleveland —"

"At least a hundred times. But tell it again."

Cleveland. One of Charlie's favorite war stories, longer than usual. At the sound of the hair dryer, he started a pot of French Market, on the soft side and pulled the blue enamel percolator off the heat at the moment Charlie finished.

Mandy appeared in the doorway. Her first steps tentative, soon confident. Her eyes bright, refreshed. Her smile, easy, relaxed. Sunlight streamed in across his shoulder and the kitchen basked in a honey glow.

"Now, about that coffee."

Tommy lifted the pot. "Regular?"

"Perfect."

Mandy took the chair next to Charlie and reached out to touch his arm. "Thank you *so* much for organizing my escape. The change of clothes. But *especially* the hair dryer and a brush. You can't imagine what a treat that was."

He blushes any harder, he'll look like a tomato with fur.

Charlie cleared his throat. "Weren't no...well, good...glad to help, Miss Owens."

Her dark eyes sparkled in the morning sunshine and her voice softened into assured patience. "Mandy. Call me Mandy."

Tommy filled their cups. *Don't stare. Well, not too much.* She took a tad less than a teaspoon of sugar. A splash of milk. Stirs, barely a rip—ple on the surface. Not once breaks eye contact with Charlie. *Yeah, I'd blush, too.*

Charlie found his cup and composure. "You're doing okay? Didn't hurt you any? Good. Business like that, it gets pretty scary. But you don't look none the worse for wear."

"I'm a New Yorker, Charlie. Well, that's not quite true. I'm *from* Connecticut, a transplant. But I practice a lot. And I'd love to learn how you organized my escape from whatever that was."

Charlie leaned forward to brag. Mandy echoed the gesture to lis—ten and ask. She had tossed a pebble into the story-telling pond. Charlie's tale rode the waves. At the counter, Tommy was close enough to hear but outside the conversation, where the sunshine warmed his back. He sipped coffee and watched Charlie relish the at—tention Mandy so effortlessly shared. Polite. Deferential. Respectful. *As he deserves.* Gracious, effusive, conspiratorial in a jolly way. *As she is.* At the end, Charlie expressed satisfaction the raid was routine.

Mandy laughed. "Oh, gosh, it was rather exciting, chasing down darkened hallways, watching Tommy shoot people. He even gave me a turn, which was.... You know, I've never actually had a chance to shoot anyone. But as payback for three grueling days of constant in—terrogation, it was a marvelous way to relieve stress, to unwind."

Charlie glared at Tommy. "Now, what'n hell am I supposed to do with that?"

Tommy shrugged. "Like you said, a better quality of witness."

Mandy said, "It's all right, Charlie. We're old friends."

"So how long you two actually known each other?"

Mandy briefly wore a pensive expression and looked at Tommy. "We've crossed paths a few times."

"Three," Tommy said. "Counting the Bahamas."

"And that time when — "

"Okay, four. But that was maybe ten minutes, tops, so — "

She smiled. "But it was a long ten minutes. And if you include the thing at Yankee Stadium — "

"More like a wave and a hiya. Doesn't really count."

"Fifteen, twenty hours maybe?"

"I'd say closer to ten or twelve. You slept most of the way out here."

"But we were still together. Technically."

Charlie sighed. "Okay, okay. But don't go chasing around, shooting people, okay?"

"Yessir." She sipped and beamed approval to Tommy. "Best coffee. *Ever.*"

"Breakfast?"

Indecision swept across Mandy's face. "Oh. Um, sure, whatever. Bagel, danish, yogurt, whatever's nearby."

Charlie said, "Hate to break the news, young lady, but this ain't Manhattan. We're a long ways from anywhere. Nothing out there but trees. But — lucky for us — we got us a first-rate cook."

She glanced back and forth. "Wow, is that true?"

"Yes'm. This here's the best place to eat in twenty, maybe thirty miles. Just don't tell the gals at the diner, though."

Mandy chuckled. "I bet they give you extra. Don't worry. Your secret's safe with me. What should we order?" She looked to Tommy, her eyes begging suggestion.

It was time to help out. "Omelet, maybe?"

Mandy's smile went full throttle. "Really?"

"Really."

She said to Charlie. "Let's go for an omelet, any kind. That would be wonderful. I mean, if it's not asking too much. I don't want to be any trouble."

Charlie grunted. "Food's the least of his trouble about now."

* * *

Such a contrast from the city. Slow pace, in fact, no pace at all. An unexpected nest of comfort. Calm. Pampered. As if this was normal, routine, everyday. Two good guys, good humor, good manners. And good to laugh again, too, at silly stories and terrible puns and those crazy tales that begin with, "There was this one time..." Hanging out in Tommy's cozy little kitchen somewhere, nowhere, anywhere. Such a long, long way from breakfast in a paper cup, maybe a danish on a sheet of wax paper. One day, anxiety bordering on outright fear. An impulsive, even desperate, idea, completely out of control, almost a horrible fate. Next day, serenity, security, warmth and welcome, an hour of fun and joy. And Tommy. A perfect memory realized, and now inches away. *If you ever wanted to bottle seduction, you'd start with that smile and top it off with those eyes.*

Plates were pushed to the side. Time to float down to reality. "This is really enchanting. I love this kitchen. All male, all the way."

Tommy seemed surprised, bemused. "What makes you say that?"

"There's nothing on the refrigerator door." Everyone looked. "So how does this arrangement work?"

Charlie rested his forearms on the table and with his fingertips tapped out an unheard tune to an uneven beat. "Real good question, young lady, the kind that gets us started on the right foot."

All he needs is a floppy old cowboy hat and a horse. He's buckled on his no-nonsense six-shooter and chambered an I'm-in-charge round in his trusty Winchester.

"Okay. So we got us a sort of odd situation. I used to be the go-to guy for witness protection — if I say so myself — but I'm retired, so this is unofficial, a favor. And it ain't a straight-up crime where there's indictments and subpoenas for scared witnesses or whistleblowers."

He paused. *Gathering thoughts, like rounding up stray cattle.*

"To be honest, I got no idea what sorta mess you're in. And frankly — now, don't take this personal because you seem like a nice person — I don't much care. What I do got is a phone call from an old cop buddy of mine, pretty good friend, decent fella, who's had a witness — that'd be you — on ice, only there some kinda leak, maybe a mole, and you got kidnapped."

Mandy nodded. "Phil Donatello, a good man. I was helping him. They kidnapped me outside my hotel room door. I didn't suspect any—thing until it was too late."

Tommy said. "That's because they looked like the genuine article. I saw the lobby surveillance video."

She leaned back. Questions popped up like arms at a rock concert. How, when, where? *Gently. Don't press. Take your time.*

Charlie cleared his throat. "You two can compare notes later. Let's get back to business here. With a lot of witnesses, I used to start by going over some ground rules. No need to change."

Mandy nodded. "Ground rules. Let's see if I remember them from every book and movie. No phone calls. No communication of any kind with people I know, knew or even don't know. No sneaking off alone, no taking candy from strangers, especially in the Bronx if they're wearing Red Sox jerseys."

Charlie stared. "Yeah, well, I think you got the gist of it."

"So I'm in a kind of limbo?"

"Maybe. Think of it as you got yourself a little vacation. Ain't a bad spot for that sorta thing. Lot of folks pay good money to come up here, get away. Some, anyways. Shouldn't take too long to figure out what's what, and we can all celebrate with one of them first class steaks that they got at the diner on Fridays, maybe the Fish Fry at Billy's. They got a dance hall for Saturday nights. Meantime, Tommy can get you to town for clothes and whatever do-dads you need short-term."

Seems like a plan to me. "You mentioned arrangements?"

"I'll find a place for you to stay, maybe one of the gals in town."

"Can I stay here?"

Charlie's eyebrows jumped. "With *Tommy?*"

"Is that a problem?"

Charlie looked at Tommy's shrug and sighed. "Shoulda figured." He poured the last of his coffee into his mouth, stood and hitched up his trousers. "Okay. I'll find a way to connect with Phil to see what's what." He began to leave, paused and turned to wiggle a finger at

Tommy. "You know you're in trouble, right?"

"Yep."

"She ain't a stray kitten, you know. She's a *witness*." Charlie shook his head, opened the door and mumbled something she was glad she could not hear, and was gone.

Charlie's parting words to Tommy were admonition but perhaps teasing, too, a moment for Mandy to look away in faint embarrassment and search for distraction. The cherry table, the object of Tommy's pride, invited caress. An oasis for fingertips, tracing random patterns on a soft surface. The table was not new, but not old in the sense of rickety or weary. Sturdy, solid, sensible. Warm, too. A long, easy moment, a bit tentative, a bit hopeful. "We really are in trouble, aren't we?"

Tommy shrugged. "I do believe he was talking about me."

His eyes. That endless charm. "I think he was talking about *us*." *Confession time.* "I'm afraid I've really managed to step into some sort of mess this time."

He nodded and began to collect the dishes. "How so?"

She stood to assist. "No idea. One day I'm slugging it out in a business that's going south really fast. Been downsized twice, and now I'm on my own. Now I get caught up in a fatal hit and run of a certifiable conspiracy nut. Witness protection, kidnapped, and rescued — thank you very much — by someone I've always been intrigued with. I'm a refugee with only borrowed clothes. It's been a bit hectic."

"You know you're safe here. You can take a couple of days, catch your breath, see how things play out. Charlie's growly, but first rate and dealing with folks caught in the middle, this sort of thing." The task brought them into a long moment of togetherness. He gently broke the spell. "Well, now, I really ought to get the dishes done."

"I should help. And it was a lovely breakfast, a best-ever."

"I'll wash, you dry. Best get used to eggs. A staple around here."

And he smiled. That same easy smile from Lyford Cay, when they toyed with each other at that luxurious but stuffy reception, the only genuine people in the room. A smile that somehow got whisked away in the pressing duties of a story that needed attention. A smile rediscovered washing dishes in a cabin kitchen, twenty miles from who knows where, anywhere, nowhere.

When the task was finished, he said, "Okay, grab your coffee and we'll have ourselves a kind of a tour, maybe see what we can find."

The narrow hallway divided the building into three sections — kitchen and dining on one end, bedrooms and bath in between. The functional part of the cabin, the necessaries. And an enormous den, a hundred percent all male. Wood, brass, leather. Rich plaids, subdued earthy colors. Soft easy chairs, sofa, coffee table, with a huge stone fireplace as the centerpiece. Elegant, cozy, tranquil. Space. A *lot* of space. The kind of space to put on, curl up in, snuggle down.

A pause to take it all in — and a breath, too. "Oh my, Tommy, this is amazing. I get the impression of some sort of top-end lodge, right out of the Adirondacks or maybe even Canada. The sort of place classy guys hang out."

He beamed in a bashful kind of way, with pride held in check, like art collectors when they invite a guest into the private gallery where they keep their favorites. It was time to explore, to discover, to touch, on an unhurried solo stroll around the perimeter of objects, books and furnishings. After, she turned to face him. "I love your taste. Orga—nized, uncomplicated, sturdy. It's more than a room. It's a lair, the place you go between whatever it is you do. Your private place." Their eyes met. "It's you."

Tommy shrugged it off with a chuckle. "Ah, well, a few comfort—able spots to park the fanny, kick back, unwind. Good fireplace, for when it's winter, and those big ol' windows open full in summertime. There's a decent bar, well stocked. So, yeah, I'd say it's a nice place to catch up on reading, maybe unwind with a scotch."

"Single malt?"

"Macallan."

"As old as us?"

"As *young* as us."

He motioned her toward a chair promising comfort in a field of green tartan. He went for firmer leather, opposite. Between them, a square coffee table, at first a mile wide, shrinking fast to intimacy.

No need for the reporter's interview posture here. Her legs curled under herself and she cradled the warm coffee cup close to her nose. "Just look at you. Smug as an old tomcat. A scruffy old tomcat who knows *exactly* what's going on. The baddest cat in the alley."

CHAPTER SEVEN

Five days later

Mandy held the platter high to inspect. The scent of warm blue—berries hung rich and sweet in the kitchen air. *Perfect.* Even Tommy wasn't going to have to fake applause this time. On only the third try, like the old cliché. Muffins. Warm and fresh and made from scratch by somebody whose entire experience with a kitchen was to reheat leftover takeout in a microwave.

It was the perfect afternoon for a perfect muffin. Raw and cold outside, the autumn yellows and reds and golds fading fast, the faint scent of rain, perhaps snow, in the air. Fresh pressed apple cider was yesterday. Today, big mugs of French Market coffee, made on a real stove in Tommy's ancient percolator pot.

Getting positively domesticated. Four — or was it five — days? Tommy and Charlie were correct. A little vacation *was* a good change of pace. The long walks, the long talks, idle hours on the porch, sipping mar—velous scotch, or loafing with wine in front of a real fire, catching up on reading without the temptation to edit it.

Coffee to go with the muffins for the guys, probably down by the lake, talking guy talk. As ten minutes of tranquility ticked by, she leaned against the counter to bask in the experience and savor the aro—mas of coffee and muffins. Mellow simplicity, worlds apart from the disjointed pace of an ordinary working day in the city. No need to check the time. The scent of brewing coffee had already told her it was ready to take off the heat. *Here they come. Perfect timing.* One last, long, satisfying look. Actual muffins. All by herself. *Yeah, better than a*

Pulitzer, even. And not just any old muffin. *Blueberry* muffins.

The kitchen door creaked open. Ahead of the two men, raw chill raced in like a surly dog. Conversation withered. Faces were somber. *Not a hopeful sign. Something's changed.* "I've made fresh coffee. Thought you guys might like something warm." *Say it casual, an everyday thing.* "And I made some muffins."

Tommy's eyes brightened, but only a little, a courtesy. "Definitely. Charlie?" He reached for mugs, glanced at the muffins and nodded approval.

Charlie settled into a chair next to Mandy and folded his hands on the table. "Yeah, sure."

Charlie's body language, his expression, seemed weary, drained. Not unhappy. More like embarrassed, perhaps ashamed.

Tommy delivered coffee, but did not pull the chair in tight to the table. *Almost like he's trying to distance himself. Be calm. Relax. Take the lead.*

Mandy said to Charlie. "There's a problem, isn't there? Something's come up with the case. It's stalled in the legal process, getting warrants maybe. Or the genuine marshals have decided to keep me on hold out here." The men exchanged uneasy glances. "It's okay. We're all grownups, and I'm not as fragile as you might think. C'mon. How bad can it be?"

Charlie fortified himself with a sip of coffee and a deep breath. "No sense in sugar-coating it. You're right. We got a problem, and we gotta figure out what to do. Phil Donatello's dead. Killed in a traffic accident."

A blur. Silence. All the air in her lungs, gone. A hard knot in her belly rose into her throat to suffocate her with anguish. She winced as her eyes began to sting. *Breathe. Any kind of breath. Stand.* Her own words were weak, distant, lost. "Can I have a moment? I, uh, I think... I think I need some air."

The doorknob in her hand. Gray, cold light. Icy wind, on her face, in her hair, pushing hard on her shoulders, making the forest moan. The porch railing. *Lean on it.* The raw wind, so very cold. Her father's patient smile, that silly long-ago day when it all went wrong and she was drowning in anxiety, fear, panic. His words, always calming, reas-suring, warm. *Steady. Strong. Serene. You're an Owens girl. Always show courage. Never let them see you cry.* Mandy found a tissue in her shirt pocket and wiped her eyes. At last, a breath. Another, and with it, clar-ity. The brisk air, refreshing.

Benny. Poor Benny, the nobody that no one cared about. *Not even me.* Nobody except Phil, the detective so close to retirement that ev-eryone would understand if he wrote Benny off. The grizzled, weary cop who could have looked the other way when those phony feds showed up. But he cared. *He cared enough about me to try to protect me.* The creeps at the detention center. Three days. Never once told them. Had to protect Phil. *But they knew we talked. And they killed him anyway. I just know it. Dammit, dammit, dammit.*

New memories blew by. *Tommy.* Delightful Tommy. Laughter, fun, joy. *Yes.* Pampering, coddling, the optimism of romance blurring goals. She rubbed the side of her nose with the back of her hand and brushed wrinkles from a flannel shirt she never would have worn be-fore now. *Tommy.* The temptation of walking away from it all to be with Tommy. A simple, carefree, lazy country life. No worries, no troubles, no responsibilities.

And no justice for Benny and Phil. No integrity, no honor. A long, deep gulp of air departed as a sigh. Different paths, different direc-tions, same as before. *Just not meant to be.* Like a child's kite. A sudden gust. A broken string. Fluttering away, gone on the cold wind.

She lifted her chin. *Clear your mind. Think. Party's over. Back to work.* Questions, swirling like the windswept leaves caught in the chaos of a unexpected squall. Inside, Tommy and Charlie waited, per-haps to console — but maybe, just maybe, looking for direction. Questions demanded answers. The truth needed to be in print. *It's what I do. It's who I am.*

She squared her shoulders and returned to the kitchen, to the chair between Tommy and Charlie. In Tommy's eyes she found con-cern, compassion. Sadness, too.

He asked, "You okay?"

Yes. No. Maybe. All of the above. None of the above. But I have it to—

gether. "I'll be fine. Charlie, do you have any details about what happened?"

On the counter, the muffins went cold. Forsaken. Ignored. Insignificant.

* * *

Twenty exhausting hours. Harsh words. Obstinance. Chilly silence. Emotional bruises all around. *No new identity. No relocation. No, thank you.* In the brisk morning air at a rural airport, it was time to mend a fence. Several hundred yards away, three tiny private airplanes crept about, the only sign of activity at the little airport. Tommy had gone to the Energy Aviation building, a couple of hundred feet away.

Exasperated, Charlie had stormed out yesterday. Round and round and round they'd gone. The string snapped, the guard fell. The painful memory, the awful secret, spewed like vomit. The terrible, silence of embarrassment. Tears, so many tears. Tommy's shoulders, his cradling arms, his soothing words of understanding. And support.

Charlie didn't know. Now he stood stoic, hands thrust in his pockets, looking tired and weary. Mandy turned up her collar against a wispy breeze that chilled the air coming off the longer and deserted runway. Beneath her feet, pale tarmac asphalt was criss-crossed by rivers of frozen tar to patch what she guessed were cracks of economy. It was time. But...

Okay. This is not exactly J-F-K or Newark. At either of those, there'd be lines at ticketing, baggage, security and boarding. Better coffee — maybe — and better pastry — well, maybe. But warmer. *Welcome to some little town named Montoursville, home of the sprawling Williamsport Regional Airport.* Where the only hassle is waiting for a little commuter plane to show up, standing on the tarmac, in the chilly aftermath of a gloomy day. Mandy sipped vending machine coffee that had gone cold, and dropped it into a nearby wastebasket.

It was time.

"Charlie, I'm so sorry for yesterday afternoon. I know I kind of lost it, said some hurtful things."

He surprised her with a shrug. "Happens all the time, Mandy. Witnesses get caught in a squeeze, sometimes on their own, some—times because stuff happens. But sooner or later, they think they can fix it, want to go back, take on the world or get some kinda revenge. Like I said yesterday, the smart ones, they do the right thing, suck up the loss, walk away. Nobody gets killed."

Two men in dark overalls and bright green safety vests exited En—ergy Aviation. Tommy followed, chatting like high school buddies at a reunion.

She crossed her arms and studied her shoes. "I still need to apolo—gize. I was thinking about myself when I should have been thinking about you. Phil was your friend. Were you close?"

"All cops are close."

"I'm sure you still think I should walk away. But I kind of hope that — "

"Maybe, maybe not. Worth thinking about, though. Problem is, the people lookin' for you are *organized* crime. Don't make no never—mind if they're wearing biker gang colors or thousand-dollar suits. You still get just as dead. Just sayin' s'all."

She nodded. "I've thought about it, Charlie. I really have. I've got to try. Phil Donatello was very special to me."

"And that guy, Benny, he don't count?"

That unflinching glare of disapproval. How can a guy I just met make me feel so petty? "Ouch. It's not that. I meant — "

At last he turned to face her. "Oh, I *know* what you meant, I sure do. I don't know nothing about Benny. But I do believe this is some kinda deep shit, the kind a smart fella don't step in. Tommy? He ain't never been a smart fella. He *loves* this stuff. Pretty good at it, too." He paused, like he was biting his tongue.

"And?"

"And maybe you ain't a smart fella, neither. Well, gal. I'm hoping you know when to duck. Keep all of us from getting killed."

An impulse to defend, to assert, to declare she was tough enough. *Let it go, let it go. Gently, softly.* "And you?"

"Me? Aw, hell, I'm an old beat-up deputy marshal with a pissant retirement certificate hangin' on the wall. But still vertical."

Still hard to read Charlie. The trio by the services building separat-ed and Tommy began to walk toward them. *Time to back off.* "So, Tommy's buddies, that's the entire ground crew?"

Charlie nodded. "Yeah, a marshaller and service tech. Both of them guys is new. He don't know 'em at all, leastways until now. Any-way, here comes our ride."

Mandy turned her head, then swirled completely around.

Charlie pointed southwest. "No. Out there."

A line of white, puffy clouds lounged above a low, drab ridge. Just a shimmer at first, a fuzzy gray spot with two lights underneath de-scended. Some kind of little commuter jet, taking form on the gentle descent toward the longer runway. Approaches so lightly that it almost hovers. A puff of smoke. Touchdown. Now the nose, gently, gently, down. No name or logo. Except for a thin sort-of-racing stripe, pure white.

She leaned toward Charlie. "So you've decided to join us? I mean, you were talking about feeling — "

"You're damn right I'm coming along. Someone's gotta lug the sack of common sense."

The jet. Bigger, bigger, gleaming in the sunshine, a corporate jet. Hitching a ride on somebody's — *no, he chartered it.* The aircraft thun-dered past on the runway. *Oh, my. A really gorgeous jet.* Deafening. Pri-mal.

"You know, Tommy, it's awfully nice of you to actually charter a flight. But a little excessive, maybe?"

From somewhere a pair of aviator sunglasses had found their way onto Tommy's way-too-smug face. The aircraft reappeared from the alley behind the services building and the engines screamed into the final turn. The marshaller stepped out and guided it straight toward her by extending his arms in and out.

Oh, wow, that thing is huge.

She stood her ground. When the jet was forty feet away, the mar-shaller crossed his arms above his head and the aircraft stopped like an obedient giant doing her bidding. The engines wound down to an in—

tense rush of air and the second ground guy chocked the wheels. Tommy turned to face her. Over his shoulder, the jet towered over every point of reference.

Elegance. Power. Freedom.

"Actually, it's not a charter. It's mine. Picked it up a couple of years ago. It's a Gulfstream, a four-fifty." His voice was stuffed with pride. "C'mon, I'll introduce you to everybody."

"You *own* it? An actual jet?"

"Don't get excited. I got it second-hand. It was a real steal. So do you want to go to New York or not?"

For a long moment she remained frozen in place before scamper— ing to catch up to his assured strides. "It's becoming difficult to keep up with you, Tommy Kane."

He looked over his shoulder. That disarming, boyish grin. A gust of wind ruffled his hair. *Saves me the trouble of mussing it.* "Really? And here I thought it was the other way around."

Beyond, the aircraft door opened. Steps unfurled.

A bundle of energy descended to the tarmac and conferred with the ground guys. *Lucy.* Confident. Assertive. Empathetic. *Nice suit.* Good taste, corporate colors. Some sort of notebook or planner, brown leather. Just as Tommy had described her, the all-time kid sis— ter, fearless, fun. And absolutely in charge. Now the crew. Pilot, copi— lot, flight attendant. A flurry of happy greetings, old pals reunited. *But Tommy's the big dog and they know it.*

Mandy crossed her arms and studied her shoes. Connecticut. Her first collision with authority, a high school newspaper First Amend— ment issue that really wasn't. In college, the discoveries of poverty, in— equality, injustice, the suffering that seemed so unfair. The shame of her own lofty status. The drifting away, toward disillusionment, anger, indignation. The image of poor Benny, being clobbered by an ambu— lance, all because he had some sort of whistle to blow. The image of Phil, killed because —

Connecticut. Fragments, more focused vignettes. When life was so effortless, so pampered, so comfortable. So assumed. Everything was assumed. Better schools, better transportation. Better clothes.

Better, better, better.

The voice of Tommy, calling out, so far away, so near. "C'mon, Mandy, I want you to meet — "

Meet the world I walked away from. Privilege. Prestige. Power. Tommy's world, too. They took everything from me. And, yes, now I really do want it back. Oh, yes. All of it.

Sensing their eyes upon her, she stole a glance at Charlie's calm expression that went from the usual concoction of scowl and impassive to the faintest nod of encouragement. *Thank you.* She shoved reticence, fear, anxiety into past tense. *Square your shoulders. Stand up straight. Lift your chin.* The breeze of a rural valley billowed her hair, and she raised her hand to calm it. From somewhere, long ago, Mandy found that smile of utter serenity.

Lucy dashed forward, effusive and eager. "Hello! You must be Amanda Owens. I'm Lucy Tramanian. Tommy has been absolutely raving about you."

"Mandy. Friends call me Mandy." What began as a handshake dissolved into a polite embrace. "I wanted to be sure to thank you so much for helping rescue me from those awful people in New Jersey."

Lucy chuckled. "Glad to help. You're welcome." She turned. "Hiya, Tommy. Boy, you could sure use a shave and a change of clothes."

Tommy's shoulders slumped. "Nice to be noticed."

"And you must be Charlie. So nice to meet you at last, to put a face with the voice."

"Yeah, thinkin' the same."

What? They've never met? Lucy's suit suggested she was a lot more than an aide or assistant, especially when she turned to face Mandy. *That's an in-charge kind of smile.* "I love your suit. Sebastian Elliot?"

"Why, yes, it is. A favorite. And that's, um, a nice dress."

Right. Uh-huh. Sure. "Off the rack at Polinski's Apparel in downtown Jacks Ford, I'm afraid. Not exactly David Aire. I've been roughing it. But it's a perfect disguise for the city." She struck a runway pose. "An out-of-towner."

"We can fix that. C'mon, let me introduce you to our happy little crew. Cesar is our pilot, about the best in the world. Ken is the co-pilot and good about keeping Cesar from believing what I just said."

Exuberant handshakes. Courtesy and charm. Deference.

"And Karen is our official den mother. Technically a flight attendant, but so much more than that. If you need anything — anything at all — she's the go-to person."

Karen's short blonde hair shimmered in the morning sunshine and her smile glowed a maternal welcome. "So pleased to meet you, Miss Owens. We have a change of clothes for you on board — business wear and a nice outfit that's sort of upscale casual. By David Aire. Lucy passed along your size, so I do hope we got it right."

Lovely. "Thank you. That's so kind." Mandy glanced at Lucy, chatting with Tommy and Cesar, and barely caught her attention — and a knowing grin. "I'm sure it'll be fine."

Karen elaborated in cozy confidentiality as she guided Mandy toward the jet. "With the short notice, we almost had to make do with Armani — "

"Oh, dear."

" — And I understand you're a journalist? We weren't sure about preferences, so today's *New York Times*, *Wall Street Journal* and *Washington Post* are on the credenza." She motioned with a wave of her arm toward the steps of Tommy's aircraft. "Let's get you aboard and comfortable. Have you had coffee, breakfast?"

CHAPTER EIGHT

Enroute to Teterboro, New Jersey

The engines powered up and the aircraft made the first wide turn onto the taxiway, bound for an empty spot and immediate takeoff. Tommy settled into calm. Rolling. On the move. Under way. Headed out. Back to normal.

To the left, Charlie had snagged the sports section of *The Washington Post*, did his indifferent glance at the first page and settled into standings and stats. Don't need the bozo opinion, he always said, just the numbers. To the right and opposite in block of four seats, Lucy worked her phone. One hand on the coffee cup, one hand on the phone, thumb dancing around like a clogger without a tune.

Wouldn't have a clue. Buttons I push usually end with a bang.

Quick shave, clean shirt, decent suit and favorite tie. Aroma of French Market drifting in from the aft galley. Slow turn onto oh-nine. Little pause for clearance and squawk. Throttle up. The thump-thump of the runway reflectors under the front tires, faster, faster. The landscape a flowing blur, the pavement rumble gone. Lucy tightened her grip on the coffee cup. Nose up, steady climb. Forty minutes to Teterboro.

Across the table, Lucy finished her task, looked up and gave him a once-over. "Ah, much better."

"Did you get breakfast?"

"On the flight out. Karen's got some nice fresh fruit, but you might still be in steak-and-eggs mode."

And there she was. Two carafes, and white ceramic mugs bearing the jet's registration number, *N226TK.*

Lucy slid her cup toward the aisle for a refill. "Please tell me that neither of those is decaf."

Karen nodded toward her right hand. "This is French Market." She lifted the other pot. "And this one is a lot more potent, for Charlie."

Charlie elaborated with casual authority. "Cop coffee. The good stuff."

Lucy cocked an eyebrow. "Really? Is there enough for two?"

Tommy patted his belly. *Camp lifestyle is yesterday. Ought to lose a couple of pounds.* "I'll go for the mixed fruit, Karen. Thanks."

Lucy's nostrils flared at a whiff of coffee. After a sip, a look of total satisfaction, the look she wore when all was right with the world and everything was under control. Her control. "Perfect, Charlie," she called across the aisle. "I can see we're gonna be good pals."

Charlie ruffled the newspaper. Just a little smile. His kind of compliment.

How Lucy's evolved. The day she invited him out of the rain and pointed a gun at him. From the disheveled look in an abandoned Allentown warehouse to a tailored, corporate look in Manhattan's financial district. From patched-together computer scrap to a cavern stuffed with high-end mainframe. From a legend in the world of white-hat hacking to a shrewd force to be reckoned in the big-boy world of investment banking. Sass and brass and the smartest person in the room. Any room.

When Karen delivered a bowl of cut-up fruit, Lucy gave her a plaintive look and was rewarded with a poaching fork.

Karen knows us too well. More than enough to share. "Mandy okay?"

Karen offered reassurance. "Doing fine. She should be joining you momentarily."

"Did she get something to eat?"

"Yessir, while you changed and shaved. Anything else I can get you?"

Lucy released Karen with a thank-you, leaned forward and

stabbed a strawberry. "We're going to break the law again, aren't we?"

"Probably."

She chewed the fruit. "Felony or just a routine misdemeanor?"

"Does it really make a difference?"

Lucy took aim at a slice of banana. "Felonies are more fun."

He poked around to prioritize pineapple and cantaloupe, but set—tled on a fat strawberry before Lucy got to it.

"So what's going on, Tommy?"

"Mandy wants to solve a couple of murders, try not to get killed, write some sort of article, have a regular life."

"That's it?"

"That's it."

She chuckled and went for pineapple. "You are so full of shit, Tommy."

"That obvious?"

Across the aisle, Charlie grunted. "Just figure that out, Lucy?"

Lucy slumped back, rolled her eyes and laughed. "Oh yeah. It only took about two seconds for all of us to grasp where things are. Karen's got her mother hen thing going, and I know they're back there doing the kind of magic that'll dissolve whatever common sense you have left."

"Think so?"

Charlie chuckled and turned the page of the newspaper. "Oh, yeah."

Lucy nodded. "Yep. You're doomed. Just accept it. You want that last strawberry?"

He sighed. *Grandpap said it best. You been hooked, fair and square. Give in to the plain truth that you're gonna decorate a skillet.* "Take it."

She lunged for the fruit and her laugh shifted gears from amused to lusty. "Oh, man, this is so damn cute."

Karen appeared to offer refills. She spoke not a word, but her eyes said she was in the loop, too. A rising heat filled Tommy's cheeks and ears and lingered until she retreated.

He looked at Lucy. "Okay, okay, I got it. This puppy's wagging his tail, feeling pretty fine about it, too. Can we sorta leave it there?"

"Whatever you say, big guy. So. What are we going to do?"

Tommy shrugged and gobbled up the remaining bits of fruit. "Same as usual, I guess, why?" He glanced up and responded to a scowl. "I know, I know. You've got this concept on your agenda — "

She crossed her arms and settled back. "It's not a concept, Tommy. We gotta do something soon. Too many questions. You need to get out in front."

How do you tell someone not to do a good job?

"Look, Tommy, I can't be the face of TKA. Like it or not, you're the man. If you're still worried about the new identity, don't. It's solid to the last detail. I'd never put you in harm's way."

"Understood. And I promise to give it thought. But in the meantime — "

She waved her hands, demanding elaboration. "I get where you're at. But can I try to put things into some sort of perspective?"

"Fair enough."

"For starters, we're making an awful lot of money with a new trading program I've written. The algorithm is really great. There's so much cash sloshing around that, well, you can probably afford a new wardrobe for Mandy. On the level of Bergdorf's, I think. A hundred times over."

"Let's just — "

"Okay, okay. The algorithm. Like, we shorted financials big time last week, caught the bottom within five seconds, rode 'em back up, made a killing." Her voice filled with evident pride. "The system called the right response to an unexpected negative scenario and flew on its own."

Tommy took a stab at where to go next. "What scenario?"

Lucy's story picked up steam. "Chairman of the New York Fed dropped dead. News broke fifteen minutes into trading, and of course the market freaked. We were front running by about five or six seconds at the time and the whole system kicked in on full auto."

"Ah, I see."

Lucy laughed. "No, you don't. But that's okay. My heart skipped a beat. We only had about sixteen-point-three million in play, like, because it was kinda experimental? Well, all of a sudden it's in full bore, high speed mode with our center on the west coast. Bang-bang-*bang*. I must have held my breath for damn near a minute on the swing, when the vice chairman stepped into the big seat, the guy the banks like."

"Okay...."

Lucy gulped coffee and exhaled as her words slowed and firmed. "Doesn't matter. God, Tommy, it was so...so *gorgeous*. Scalps on the hook. We cleared seventy-two-seven in thirty five minutes!"

"Seventy-two-seven what?"

"Million, Tommy. *Million*." She gave him a maternal look. "We can't stay anonymous much longer. We're trading at a level that we're beginning to move the market. All by ourselves. I'm fending off the SEC — which is certain that we're cheating — with one hand, and all the major banks — which want in on the action — with the other. We're getting into stakes in companies, and they're wondering why we don't have good ol' Tommy on the board. People are starting to speculate about TKA — whispers, but still... And I'm running out of places to hide it."

"Can you tone it down, dial it back, whatever?"

The puzzled look. *Like I said something totally incomprehensible and she doesn't know what to do with it.*

Her voice lowered to slow, firm repetition. "We are beginning... to... move... the... market. It's not a bad thing, Tommy. It's, like, well, friggin' cool."

"You know, way back when, TKA was something to stash the cash. Remember?"

Her expression went defensive. "Yeah, well, so I got a little greedy, a little carried away. It happens on Wall Street, you know. Kind of like your Mardi Gras, but with money."

A little carried away? How does anyone consider nearly a billion dollars "a little carried away?" Patience. Think this through. You knew it might come down to this.

He sighed and pushed the empty bowl to the side. "Yeah, well, we'll work something out. I'll think about it. Promise. But first things, first, okay?"

Here it comes. She's got that favorite smirk of hers, the one she uses when she's put all the pieces together and knows the answer before anyone else.

"She's gorgeous, Tommy, just gorgeous. Perfect, absolutely per‑fect."

Charlie injected a cynical sigh, shook his head and tried to con‑centrate on the newspaper.

Karen returned to clear dishes from the table. "We're in a brief hold before final. Just a lot of traffic in New York Center, but we should be landing in about ten minutes or so. I'll check on Mandy."

Forty-five minutes ago, it was Miss Owens. Now it's Mandy.

Lucy was still smirking when something caught her eye and she looked up, toward the rear of the aircraft. Softness bathed her words. "Oh, wow. Can I hate her? I mean, in a sort of friendly way?"

Tommy turned. And stood.

Lucy whispered. "Oh, Tommy, you are in such trouble..."

She chose the suit. She could walk into the bluest of blue chip board rooms and stop the conversation cold. They'd swarm around, moths to a flame, anything to be close. *Lucy's right. I'm in trouble.* Not only the clothes. Impressions of prior encounters flickered past. Al‑ways classy but... The way she carries herself, the way she marches down the aisle, the look in her eyes. *Every gawking kid knows it. Yeah. Like thirteen and stupid. The babe that takes your breath away.*

Mandy's smile was serene, her posture assured, her steps easy in the aisle of the moving jet. *Almost as though she's done this a thousand times before.* Behind her, Karen wore a relaxed smile of approval and turned away to occupy herself with the essential tasks of the descent and landing.

The way royalty moves. The titled kind. Breeding. Way beyond the high class. And way beyond an ol' bayou boy like me.

She apologized. "It's a bit cramped back there."

Say the word, we'll buy a bigger jet with a bigger can. "Quite all right. Glad you're okay. Looking fine." *Jeez. Thirteen stupid.*

He gestured to the two pairs of seats facing each other, half ex‑pecting Mandy to take the one next to Lucy and opposite him. She chose seat next to him, brushing past and rewarding him with a soft smile, a lingering glance from mischievous eyes.

Mandy said to Lucy, "Thank you again. It's perfect."

"You like it? It's okay?"

"*Perfect*," Mandy repeated. She looked at Tommy.

He stumbled into words. "Oh, yeah. For true."

Lucy rolled her eyes. "You bet it is, Tommy. It's by David Aire and it cost you a fortune."

Tommy grinned at Lucy and Mandy. "It was worth it."

"You have a wonderful sense of taste," Mandy assured Lucy. "But how did you — "

Lucy's expression could not have been more smug. "Simple, really. I tapped into Bergdorf's, which handles David Aire exclusively, found your accounts, took a peek. The rest was on the basis of past purchases."

"Seriously?"

Mandy was leaning close and when he turned to speak he caught the scent of her hair and had to find calm before he spoke. "Yeah, seriously."

Mandy sighed, and turned to Tommy and for a moment they were close. "She's that good?"

"She sure is."

Mandy laid a moment of unforgettable on Tommy and backed away. "Okay. It's time to get some work done." She pulled the flash stick from her bag. "Lucy, this seems to be at the center of it all. I have no idea what's on it."

Lucy nodded and accepted the storage device. "Tommy doesn't do computers. Just as well. Probably break them. You've got no knowledge about where it's been, so from a security standpoint you have to treat it as if it's electronic ebola. I'll have a peek back at the office in a quarantined system."

"Great. The only other real clue is 'Cinnabar'."

Lucy began to make notes on her pad. "Got it. I'll see what I can find out."

Charlie folded the newspaper. "And I'll check in with some buddies, active and retired, to do a little sniffing around myself. I want to get my hands around the turncoats."

Mandy nodded and turned to Tommy. "The next issue is my apartment, all my clothes and things."

Ordinary issues are good. I can handle ordinary. "Might be a problem. If they're still looking for you, they'll definitely have it under surveil—lance. They may have already been through it. How badly do you want your stuff?"

Mandy's shoulders drooped and her expression wilted. "I guess it's just stuff. Stuff can be replaced."

Lucy seemed shocked. "Yeah, but it's *your* stuff. I vote we get it back. I should be able to help with that. The worst they can hit us with is felony burglary, quick arraignment, low bail, and I have a pack of lawyers that can get it dismissed before close of business. C'mon, Tommy, be a sport."

Charlie sighed. "Yeah, Tommy, blow security all to hell. Give'm a juicy target. Why don't I see what I can do about your gear?"

Tommy agreed. "Okay, why not? What else?" When she cocked an eyebrow, he explained, "It's your op, Mandy. We're sort of working for you."

Lucy's firm glare was less charitable. "Definitely. I could use a break from the routine of making too much money."

Mandy looked puzzled.

Soft radio traffic from the cockpit drifted past. *"T-K-Two-two-six, cleared to land."*

Under his seat, a mechanical growl and a rush of air. *Gear down. Three green, no red.* The aircraft made a wide left turn and everyone buckled in for the final approach on a damp, cloudy afternoon. Be—yond the wingtip, the faint New York City skyline briefly edged a sprawling suburban landscape that dissipated into an endless band of dormant trees.

Tommy smiled. "C'mon, Lucy, be — what was that? — a sport."

"Ouch." She turned to Mandy. "Just a bit of an inside joke. What else can we help with?"

"Well, I hate to be a pain, but when they kidnapped me, I lost all my I.D., credit cards, everything. I feel sort of like one of those people that no country will take."

The features of Teterboro Airport zoomed up and within mo—ments the Gulfstream rumbled when its tires touched asphalt, decel—

erated and turned onto a taxiway, toward Atlantic Aviation.

Lucy tapped away as Mandy recited a shopping list of credentials and looked to Tommy.

"The Clockmaker?"

"Definitely."

Lucy scowled. "Pricey."

"Quality always is."

"Kind of old."

"I prefer 'experienced'."

"Kind of retired."

"Kind of bored."

Mandy asked, "Are you sure this isn't any trouble?"

Karen stepped past to open the door of the aircraft.

Lucy unbuckled her seat belt and stood. "Trust me. It's more like a diversion. Recreation. We've got a town car and our favorite driver waiting outside. After dropping me downtown, he'll take you to a penthouse I've organized on the Upper East Side, low-seventies, off Central Park. One of the city's best caterers is on standby for your dinner order."

Mandy looked at Tommy, her eyes begging guidance. She got a smile of reassurance and a gesture to proceed.

Lucy's phone was in her hand and her right thumb at work. She paused to take a step back and allow Tommy and Mandy to disembark first. With a gentle smile, she said to Mandy, "Welcome to the world of Tommy Kane."

CHAPTER NINE

Near Wall and William Streets, New York City

Their footsteps whispered on carpet stabbing in opposite directions from an elevator more like a service unit than a corporate invitation. With enough lighting for safety, one step above gloomy and two
steps down from cheerful, austere was an understatement to Mandy.
No reception area. No fancy logos. No wall decorations. No soothing
music from the ceiling. No people in sharp suits. No people at all.

Tommy's confident steps checked her anxiety. The creepy ten-
th-floor hallway was punctuated by plain, beige steel doors, most of
which were labelled "Private" or "No Admittance," and all probably
locked. Exceptions bore cryptic labels: Fin Svc Unit 5, Data Ops Man
NY, TJB Trading. And always underneath, a no-nonsense addendum:
Authorized Personnel Only.

Gives one pause. Not merely the belly of the beast. The bellies of all
the beasts, their shrouded lair, the side of banking empires the public
never sees, a nest of snoozing dragons.

Near the end of the hall they reached their destination: *TKA Inv –
No Admittance.* Tommy stepped up to the customary keypad and its
winking red light to methodically tap in N-2-2-6-T-K. For a moment, the light went solid red. A green light took its place and the
deadbolt lock emitted a faint click. He pushed the lever-style doorknob down and bright light poured into the corridor.

Her eyes catalogued a tiny anteroom. No windows. One so-so
knock-off painting that could have come from any two-star chain mo-
tel room. Thin counter, a beige metal credenza. Sliding door, partway

open. Couple of photos, maybe the husband and kids. Or perhaps people *supposed* to look like the husband and kids. Bag lunch, partially consumed sack of cookies. Water bottle, blue, metal, no markings. Coffee cup, from the popular chain near the building entry, probably cold by now, but too pricey to pitch. Box of facial tissues, a bunch more in the trash basket near the desk.

Maybe she's getting over a cold.

The receptionist beamed and spoke in a cheery but nasal voice. "Good morning, Mister Kane. Nice to see you again."

No, she's getting a cold.

The receptionist placed something resembling a tablet computer on the counter. "If you'd put your right hand on — "

"Thank you, Joan, I know the drill." He complied, and it beeped an apparent approval.

"Yessir." Joan picked up the phone. "I'll get Miss Tramanian for you."

A pinpoint of light next to the door beyond her switched from red to green. Another faint click.

"Thank you again, Joan. And take care of that cold, eh?" He opened the door and invited Mandy to cross the portal into an enormous space painted white with accents of taupe and pale blue. An assortment of contemporary furniture formed a square in the middle. The kind of décor chosen to fill a big, empty space. Never used, just for show.

Lucy cradled a four-inch ring binder stuffed with paper in her left arm. "Hi, guys! Welcome to our little store, Mandy. How's the apartment?"

"Very nice. Not quite as cozy as Yankee Stadium, but the view is wonderful." *This is her little store all right. She's definitely in charge.*

Lucy laughed. "Yeah, well don't get attached to it. It's a loaner, from a former trader doing five to ten for assorted errors in judgment. I think he's out on parole in a few weeks."

"Not one of yours, I trust?"

"Nah. Ours don't get caught. Wow. Did I just say that? Sure hope you're not wearing a wire. I *so* do not have time for an arraignment to—

day."

Mandy tumbled into a soft sarcasm she hadn't experienced since an internship with a pack of veterans working city hall. "I never wear a wire with casual wear. So, this is essentially a trading operation, stocks, bonds, currencies, that sort of thing?"

"Yep. We lie, cheat and steal — but legally. This is the only business where it's truly a recognized art form. Well, except for politics."

"I don't see the stereotypical trading floor, phones, chaos, that sort of thing."

"We don't need one. There's only one customer. Us. Clients, associates, partners make things complicated. The SEC is bad enough."

Mandy pointed toward a row of small offices on the perimeter in which men and women looked busy. "Who are those people?"

"They're lawyers. We keep them around to do the dirty work. All they want is an office with a window and a door and a piece of the action."

"What's their specialty?"

"Vicious. C'mon. Let's go to my office."

She seems on edge, distracted. Wonder what's going on. Ask. "Is everything okay?"

Lucy nodded. "Odd day. Market's bouncing around like a scared chipmunk and I know there's a hawk around somewhere."

"So you're worried about some sort of surprise attack, begin caught?"

"No, no, not at all. I'm after the hawk."

A voice behind them interrupted. The entourage paused for a thin, lanky man scurrying across the room. He wore a wrinkled shirt, a loosened tie and a furrowed brow, sorting a sheaf of paper as he approached.

Lucy looked up, her expression supportive, warm. "Hey, Warren. What've we got?"

Warren offered the report. "Here's a summary of their latest proposal."

Lucy scanned the first two pages and shook her head. "No way, no way. Tell those clowns we want at least an eight-point-five, no, make it *eight-point-seven*, percent stake. Ask for eight-nine, but take seven.

Or we'll let their ratty-assed retail chain get flushed with all the other bozos."

Warren nodded. "Got it."

Lucy returned the papers and offered a blend of counsel and encouragement. "We're doing those guys a favor, Warren. They get to keep on playing Wednesday afternoon golf at their club while screwing over eighteen thousand sales associates and stock clerks. Eight point seven or they go belly-up."

"Yes ma'm."

Warren looked up, briefly at Mandy before concentrating on Tommy. His jaw began to drop.

"Oh. Aren't you — ?"

Lucy crossed her arms and clutched the binder to her chest. "Yes he is, Warren. And he's not giving autographs today."

Tommy extended his arm. "Hello, Warren. I'm Tommy Kane."

So he doesn't really have an office here? Not even a regular visitor?

"The, uh, pleasure is all, um, I'm honored sir..." His voice trailed off, mired in helplessness.

Tommy said, "And may I introduce a friend and colleague, Amanda Owens?"

"Hi, Warren," Mandy said. *Little wave or handshake? Light handshake will do.*

"Very pleased..."

Tommy smiled. "Go get 'em, Warren. I hear you're doing a great job. Eight point seven, right?"

"Yessir! Absolutely, sir. Well, I'd better — "

Lucy interrupted. "Yep, Warren, you should."

Panic in his eyes. Groping for words. Tiny beads of perspiration on his forehead. As Warren fled, Mandy said, "Seems like a nice guy."

Lucy sighed. "*Very* nice guy and *very* good at what he does." She nodded toward Tommy. "But now I'm going to have to bump his bonus."

Tommy shrugged. "I think we can afford it."

I'm sure you can.

"Let's get to my office. I haven't had enough coffee today."

Corners. The boss always has a spot on the corner. But nothing seems right.

Lucy stepped toward a utility closet.

Janitorial supplies? Is this some kind of a joke?

Lucy unlocked the door with a conventional key and tapped out a keypad code on a gray locker.

No. It's not a locker. It's more like a vault door.

It swung toward the inside and Tommy followed her through a thick portal without reservation. *Like going down the rabbit hole or through the looking glass. This isn't an office. It's an enormous room, a cavern.*

The pace slowed. A chill crept up her arms to launch a shiver. A faint fluorescent glow tumbled from a buffered line around the rim of the cavern, perhaps a hundred feet square but difficult to gauge in whispered light on the canyon floor. Laid out in streets and alleys, gun-metal gray racks of electronics. A data center, mainframe, a city of relentless power, tethered by ribbons of wire, spaghetti run amok. All illuminated by tiny lights, mostly bright green stars twinkling on an overdose of amphetamines. The chatter of a thousand faint clicking sounds, creatures digesting data. In the distance, a pool of light, partially eclipsed by a wall of computer monitors.

Curious, this sensation of both awe and wary. Mandy followed Tommy to an intersection of boulevards without traffic. Like a small town, three in the morning. Sunday morning. Devoid of life.

Lucy pulled up and now held the binder in a much more casual way, no longer clutching it close but instead cradling it in folded fingers at her side. The frazzled expression of the public space dissolved into utter calm. The outer room for show. The parlor at the home of an elderly aunt. *This is the kitchen, where Lucy is most at home.*

Lucy's smile was not as polite as it was on the jet and not as patient as it was out front. It was a contented smile, like one after a bite of great chocolate. Or an incredible glass of wine. Or a great night of —

"The Gulfstream? That's Tommy's toy." She waved her arm. "This is mine."

What does one say? Amazing, astonishing, impressive, those easy clichés we reserve for monuments, for that we cannot understand? No, too easy. It's charming? Hardly. It's efficient, industrial, cold, almost scary. It's so you? That seems a bit sad. The facades we create, the facades we wear... I'm standing here with my arms wrapped around me, not sure if it's because it's so chilly in here or because I'm feeling so isolated.

Revelation. Not at all like a kitchen, where ladies gather to gossip over tea and cookies. More like a castle, a great hall. Where the queen holds court. Where even guys like Tommy cower a little. And show respect. *So smile, relax.* Mandy lowered her arms and loosely clasped her hands behind her back. "I'm not sure if I should bow or curtsey, or even how to express my admiration. But your pride in what you've built, the power you've created, is certainly justified."

During an uncertain pause, only the equipment chattered in hushed tones.

Mandy focused on Lucy while she said, "Isn't it, Tommy?"

"Oh. Yep, absolutely. Absolutely."

Lucy's gaze remained steady, but she traded a hopeful expression for a comforted smile and a soft voice. "Thank you. That's kind of you to say." She offered the notebook to Mandy.

The unexpected heft of it caught Mandy off guard. "What's this?"

Lucy's smile expanded to a grin. "It's you. Your entire history. Everything about you. *Everything.* Probably some things that you really wouldn't like people to know."

Mandy bit her lower lip and began to thumb through the pages. "That's um, well, um — "

Lucy's smile shifted again, this time to patient. "I know. Disquieting. Scary. Frightening. Terrifying, maybe. Kind of like standing naked in the middle of Times Square with your hands tied behind your back. In your world, it's all about the *public's* right to know. In this world, it's all about what *we* want to know about someone. Anyone. Anytime."

Random pages. A quick visual scan. Another page. Another scan. *She's right. I feel like all my privacy has been stripped away. No wonder Tommy is so anti-technology. No wonder Lucy built a castle, with thick walls and parapets and an army of her own.* The anger of the Cinnabar interrogation bubbled up in her mind, the humiliation of being a helpless captive, and she knew her eyes narrowed and her expression chilled in response to Lucy's demonstration. *Steady. Strong. Serene.*

"I think I understand," she told Lucy. "If you can find it, they — whoever 'They' is — have, too. And it was important for you to look, to collect all this. Because if you hadn't, couldn't, wouldn't, there's no way I'd be standing here right now."

Lucy's expression was acknowledgment and applause at once. "*Exactly.*"

Mandy began to return the binder, but Lucy waved it off.

"Keep it. It's the only copy. Maybe you'll want to write an autobiography some day."

"I think I'd rather dump it in a shredder. Got one?"

"Absolutely. How about coffee and a doughnut?"

* * *

When Lucy's cell phone chirped a series of beeps in groups of three, Tommy stepped closer to Mandy. *Awright. A little break'd be good about now.*

Lucy apologized and excused herself, turning toward a desk at the far end of the valley of server racks and the brightest spot in the cave.

He said, "No problem. Business is business." *Slow the pace, create some space. Mandy needs a moment.*

She seemed to sense the adjustment, despite focus on the fat notebook. Pages turned in thicker and thicker chunks, with reading pauses shorter and shorter. *She's got the gist of it. She's seen enough.*

Mandy closed the binder and leaned close to whisper, "Well, *that* was intensely unnerving."

Yeah. Probably so. "You okay? You appear to have taken it in stride."

"I like to think I can appear unflappable. But yes, I believe I know where she was going with it." She held the notebook aloft, beyond of his reach. "Look at this, Tommy. My entire life in a three-ring binder, outlined by age and activity. We're not talking voter registration or credit history, either. Things you tell your doctor when you know it's private. Things you did as a teenager that's best forgotten. Things you lied about on a college admission form. That kind of stuff. And no, you can't read it." She paused and her eyes narrowed as she cocked her head to the right. "Or have you?"

"No."

"You were briefed?"

"No."

"Not even a teeny little hint?"

"Nope. Couple of years ago, I'd consider what's in that binder first-rate intel, mostly boring tidbits and scraps, the kind that you'd wade through looking for the edge to take the target down. But now? It's the sort of stuff that goes into one of two bins. The stuff that never was — never will be — any of my business. Or the stuff that's fun to learn the old fashioned way, the stuff that cements friendships."

She brightened, cocked her head to the left and looked directly into his eyes. "Really? That's a hopeful sign, Tommy, a *very* hopeful sign. I'm trusting your sincerity."

"Did you notice if there is anything about, well, you know..."

For a moment, her eyes flared anger. "The incident that bonded me with Phil? Didn't notice it. Don't really want to look for it, either. Two bins, right? What about the bad guys, the people we're after?"

"There's a special bin for them. I'm curious. Something tells me you already know you cleared the hurdle with Lucy."

Mandy's smug smile. The one she saved for *you caught that, nicely done*. "Oh, I'm sure you were my ticket through the door. But I knew I was off the hook the moment she offered coffee and doughnuts. You don't share doughnuts with someone you're about to throw under the bus."

CHAPTER TEN

The coffee from an urn on a credenza led to an exchange of plain—tive expressions. *Yeah, sure, what can one cup hurt?* The doughnuts caused dismay and were quickly passed by. Behind them, Lucy cleared a stack of paper from the only extra chair in the cavern.

Mandy was smarter. She filled the mug only to the two-thirds mark and rounded out the space with cream and sugar. *Pride is pride. Go for the rim, pay the price.* And he winced when he took the first sip.

"You guys about ready?"

Mandy's smile bordered on patronizing. *Coulda told ya. You pour it, you drink it. Poor baby.* In the dozen steps to the desk, Tommy schemed to avoid the fate of his own folly.

"So. Let's start with this." Lucy hoisted the thumb drive into the air, displayed it like a magician before a trick, and offered it to Mandy. "The only file on the stick is encrypted, simple two-fifty-six byte. Any idea where it came from? Corporate, government, foreign?"

"No idea. Benny was rambling on, something about secrets, that he knew one of theirs — no, *had* one of theirs, and he slipped it into my bag, maybe for me to find later, maybe to get rid of it."

Tommy studied his coffee. *Seems odd for a conspiracy guy. They like to hang on to their trophies. The espionage crowd wants to unload as fast as they can.* "If he possessed a secret, why would he want to discard it?"

"Tommy, you don't know Benny. Kind of out there in la-la land."

Like most of the people I used to work with. Like guys who indulge in coffee like this.

Lucy gestured indifference. "File name is Mer05-7621, which I as—sume means nothing to you, right? Okay, in a nutshell, it's all financial stuff, looks sorta like transaction records, mostly Forex." She glanced at him and elaborated to what must have been puzzlement. "Foreign exchange market. Currency trading. The wild west of investing, the game played by the bigger banks. Twenty-four seven, world-wide, trillions of dollars every day. "

"The goal being...?"

"Well, on the convenience side, it sets currency conversion so companies can do import-export business a lot easier, twice a day, the fix. But on the speculation side, the big financials, mostly banks, bet on currency values, the carry trade and interest rate differences be-tween two currencies. Not for the faint of heart."

Mandy studied the storage device. "So these are records of trades?"

"Looks like, but..." Lucy's voice trailed off while she scanned sev-eral pages.

"But what?"

"Well, most of the action is through a couple of interbank plat-forms, but this is different. Structure of it seems unusual. Maybe it's a hypothetical, a college class exercise or something. Maybe a hoax set up by a bored grad student. Plus, I think the file is corrupted. There's a block of binary crap, gibberish that might be screwing up some key content that would give it context."

Mandy said, "Has to be more than a hypothetical. Nobody gets killed over a hypothetical."

"You said Benny was — "

Mandy took a breath. "You're right, Lucy. This is getting personal and it shouldn't. But — "

Tommy interrupted. "Think about it, Luce. Some poor street guy you sort of feel sorry for walks up and hands you something and — pow! — gets killed right in front of your eyes. And nobody really cares. And there's a New York City police detective."

Lucy settled into even-handed patience. "I saw the police report about the accident, Tommy."

Be firm, be clear. "I don't think it was an accident. And neither does Mandy."

"Okay, okay. That's why I asked where it came from. It would be easier to exploit the resident system."

Polite euphemism for hacking it. Kind of like releasing an asset, tossing a team member into that bucket called collateral damage.

In a glum tone, Mandy said, "And good luck with that."

Lucy appeared sympathetic. "I understand. But it's still going to be a lot easier if we — "

Mandy sat up, excited. "Follow the chain of evidence! That's the one thing Phil Donatello talked about all the time, in every interview I can remember. 'Follow the chain of evidence, solve the crime.'"

Of course she's right. Fundamental rule of tradecraft is to follow the trail of information, backtrack it to the handler. "So what about Cinnabar?"

Lucy shuffled notes. "As you probably expect, there is no such thing as Cinnabar Security Systems, no listings for it anywhere. That doesn't mean it can't exist; it's just not a corporation with filings of any kind and it's directory shy — suggesting it's a limited use entity."

Mandy said, "Strange name."

"Cinnabar? It's a mineral. Mercury sulfide. Bright red, some say blood red. It's the preferred ore from which you extract mercury. Yeah, I thought of that, too. Drove me bats all night, because you can look at mercury as the toxic metal, the ancient god, the planet, on and on. There's a zillion possibilities. I think finding the computer with your file would be easier." She paused to rip a doughnut in half and took a bite. "I even went after the chemical symbol — Hg — and all I could turn up was HG Trading. That's a dark pool outfit I sometimes bump into when we're running private. You know, instead of using high frequency trading to front-run the market. But I don't know any—thing about them. It's a market area where people don't ask a lot of questions, just ping sometimes to see what the big dogs are messing around with."

Tommy rubbed his chin. "I think that's worth a further look. Pri—vate trading, foreign exchange rates, seems like a logical place to start."

Lucy made a note and spoke to Mandy. "Okay, moving on to your stuff. There's some surveillance of your place, not too close, kind of casual, sorta half-hearted. Can't tell how much they've been inside."

Tommy said, "We need eyes of our own. I'd bet that by now

Charlie's already done a drive-by with a couple of his old police pals, but they probably won't push it without a plan."

Lucy said, "We could go electronic. Easier, less expensive, more reliable. Street work is yesterday, Tommy. Today it's tiny remote cameras you can't see, small as a speck of dust, electronic tagging, satellites that can read the labels on litter from a couple of hundred miles up. It's all changed. And while we're about it, Mandy, let's get you set up with a good phone, something really secure. Totally untraceable, totally untrackable. High speed, encrypted telemetry. A big, big step up from those toys they use to take selfies, the kind the NSA would love to have."

Tommy concurred. "And that brings us to Bug — sorry, I meant your father."

Her eyes fell away for a moment. She lifted her chin. "It's okay. I'm okay. He's okay. We're all so goddamned okay."

"Sorry. How is he?"

"Still working. Still a triple crown champion."

Mandy raised an eyebrow.

"Worst breath, worst diet, worst attitude. He holds the all-time record for worst person on the planet. I'll give my father a call. He definitely needs something to screw up his day."

"What's the working arrangement?"

Lucy fussed with a loose collection of paper on her desk. "Technically? For me. Part of that deal we worked out, to, um, settle stuff. But, dammit, Tommy, *you* more than anybody should know how it goes."

Ouch. Yeah, sure do.

Mandy leaned in. "Let me guess. You're on the front line, doing the best you can, and the boys are still — how shall I say it? — being a bit high spirited and free wheeling, a bit too independent at times?"

Lucy cocked an eyebrow and turned her attention to Tommy. "I think that about sums it up, wouldn't you say, Tommy?"

And of course, she's absolutely right. The whole pin-stripe, respectability thing again. I owe her, big time, for a whole new identity and a whole lot of money. Not a free ride anymore. No sense in being ruffled, annoyed, bothered. Until now, basking in anonymity with a wallet never empty was a dream retirement, taken for granted. Partners came with a price. *Still....* "Okay. But take this question as seriously as you can. You're sure there's no loose ends, there's no stray threads? No offense, but Mandy here — "

Lucy replied with a faint smile but a direct look into his eyes. "Yes. She might have been, but even she ran into a dead end. But now? Well, maybe she should speak for herself."

Mandy leaned back and drew a deep breath. "Lucy's correct. Under any other circumstances, I couldn't have put the pieces together. But I'm in the circle now. With all that implies. Not because I have to, but because I want to. Just like you said back at the cabin, Tommy. No second thoughts, no turning back."

Lucy's gaze was a concoction of curiosity and defiance, amusement and confrontation. Turning points whizzed past. Choices made, paths followed, some wisely, some not. If Lucy was was genuinely thorough, it might work. If she'd missed something in the Tommy Kane rebuild, it would be ultimately fatal. The last time said, it was on the way to a robbery. *If you win, you live. If you lose, you die. But if you die, the score doesn't matter much.* But combat gear and street work was not an option, not on this level, not the way this was shaping up. Lucy argued it regularly: *you don't have to do that stuff any more. You can get a zillion guys to do it for you.* She said it before the extraction that brought Mandy back into his life.

Mandy was in. Lucy was in. *Time to fish or cut bait.* Images of Jacks Ford. The guys at Billy's. The folks at the Puffin. Charlie's perpetual scowl and indignation about something or other. The kitchen table. The chairs on the cabin porch, the long hours staring mindlessly into space. The big soft sofa in the living room, the winter fire, the silky scotch. Watching the Gulfstream settle onto the runway. Feeling the Gulfstream ascend into the clouds. And Mandy. In the gown. In plaid flannel. In the suit on the plane. *Have it all. But pay the dues. Ante up.*

A dozen seconds had ticked away. Lucy's machinery chattered behind him and the hum of fluorescent lights barely covered the sound of moving air from the ventilation system.

Tommy looked down. The wretched coffee. He raised the cup.

Paused. Drank it. "Okay."

Mandy and Lucy closed their eyes and exhaled relief in unison.

"But Bug is still the best wire man in the business, and we're going to need someone to watch our back. And Charlie's loyal, dedicated and motivated, but he can't do this alone. We need to put together some sort of team on short notice."

Lucy reached for an electronic tablet. "I'll call — "

"Yenchenko."

Lucy's hand froze over the phone. "You can't be serious." Her shoulders drooped. "God, I should have guessed you'd be going there."

Sorry, but that's how I want it. Just be collaborative this time. "Besides the people in the room, name anyone you absolutely trust."

"How do you know that he'll — "

Tommy chuckled. "Sergei? He'd start a world war if he thought it would be a good way to pass some good time."

"That's what I'm afraid of. You're sure about this?"

Mandy spoke up. "Who's this guy, Yenchenk — "

Lucy turned to explain. "A pal of Tommy's. Ex-Russian spy, a Ukrainian, actually, some sort of weightlifting champion when young, now about Tommy's age. Got thrown out of the old KGB because he was a bad boy. Drinks like a fish, half in the bag most of the time. Used to start wars in Central America for kicks. Got an ego big as himself, and he is a really huge guy. Tommy recently airlifted him out of Uruguay because he couldn't stay out of trouble."

"I see..."

Tommy chimed in. "Absolutely capable, loyal, fearless. And a lot of fun, too. I bet he'd be an outstanding bodyguard."

Mandy cocked an eyebrow. "For who?"

"You, of course."

"Tommy, I don't need — "

Lucy sighed. "Sure you do. Trust me on that."

"Tommy, c'mon. I mean, really?"

He said, "If it makes you feel any better, *we're* both going to need someone to watch our back."

It was Mandy's turn to grumble. "Can I say something, sort of for the record? I'm really grateful for all your help, but I was speculating about what might have have happened if... It's not so much a guilt thing as it is a string of events that got interrupted. Bennie, the stick, the schedule I was on. Had I gone on to interview the fed chairman instead of being a witness.... I don't know. Sounds silly, I guess."

Lucy sat up. "You were supposed to meet Silverman, Martin Sil−verman?"

"Yes. I had an appointment, but he changed the time, so I thought I could get in helping Phil Donatello with his investigation."

"Did you speak to Silverman personally?"

"No, the media relations guy, Alan Rothstein, why?"

Lucy's looking at me for some kind of direction. "So she delayed the in−terview, not cancelled it? By how much?"

"Twenty minutes. What's going on, Lucy?"

"Martin Silverman died at his home early that morning."

"He's dead?"

"Yes, a stroke."

Mandy looked at Tommy. "That's *three*. Three deaths."

Lucy shrugged. "Silverman seems more coincidental. Tommy, they must have been covering, working his calendar, right around the market open. That's when it all went sideways." She turned to Mandy. "We made a killing on the market swing. I was floating on air for days. I mean, it's too bad the guy died, but these things happen."

Instinctive suspicion awakened in Tommy's mind. *Okay, but why delay the interview rather than merely cancel? Something's not right. Did they want Mandy to show up? But she said the call came before she encoun−tered Benny. Was Benny supposed to... nah, this is getting ridiculous.*

Mandy shrugged. "Probably confusion. Secretaries without direc−tion blurt out anything when they have to circle the wagons. It can take an hour or two to get the official responses together. So. What about identification, credentials, something to make me myself again?"

Let it go. No need to worry her until we have a better handle on the timing. "Okay, I.D., credentials, the Clockmaker."

Lucy scribbled a note. "Because he's old school, Mandy will have to make a personal appearance. I took the liberty of pencilling an ap—pointment for today. You're good with that?"

Mandy followed Tommy's lead and echoed a nod.

"I'll have Cesar prep the jet. You'll go directly to DPA and I'll have a car pick you up there." She glanced at her watch. "You'd better get going or you'll be late." To Mandy, she explained, "He's a punctu—al kind of guy. Hates late arrivals."

Mandy's eyes widened. "Just where do we find the Clockmaker anyway?"

Lucy was working on a text message. "Geneva."

"As in Switzerland?"

"Sorry. As in *Illinois*."

CHAPTER ELEVEN

South Third Street, Geneva, Illinois

Charming. Reserved. Elegant. Mandy's impression of forgery did a complete reversal in seconds. Modest, humble and very much out of the way, the shop seemed to be the preferred sort of place to pick up a new identity, the kind that costs, the kind that's flawless.

Karl Felchin stepped from behind the counter, eager to welcome them like old friends and dear colleagues. *But not effusive. Courtly manners. Precise demeanor, like that German diplomat, the interview last spring, whose name I can't remember now.*

Mandy sifted past voices. Foreign ministry people and business—men. That creepy guy who called the city desk to say he'd killed his mother. Those two students who were planning to hike across America. The butcher at Chelsea Market, the big, jolly guy with.... *A Westphalian* accent. But more Prussian than North Rhine, speech that could be sweetened for women and sharpened for men.

Flirtatious. In a sly and gentle way. Speaking to Tommy, but his pale blue eyes lingering on her, trying to break away but not quite making it. The ex-military guy from the embassy had muttered the same phrase: *außergewöhnlich schön.*

Today, Karl said Tommy need not be concerned. *"Ich fürchte, sie ist ein wenig zu jung für mich."*

Tommy chuckled and began to translate, but Mandy's gesture cut him off. Beer hall buddy talk. *No, thank you.*

Karl bowed. All that was missing was a click of his heels. With a wave of his arm, he directed attention to a platter of delicate pastries on a shiny antique table. "These are called *Krume-Küchen*, and they are made at a fine German bakery, which is a small distance from here, perhaps a five minute walk." He pointed. "I myself prefer the raspberry, but there is also apple and some cinnamon, too. *Bitte*. You must choose what you wish, yes?"

He offered coffee in delicate china cups, accompanied by a deferential, patient but ever so slightly uncertain smile, mustered from a lifetime of discipline and maybe introversion.

"That would be lovely." Mandy's tone seemed to fluster Karl even more as he fussed over the task of pouring. His gray head turned. "Perhaps some cream, a little sugar? Yes?"

She said, "*Bitte, danke.*" The soft and gentle old-world manners so cordial, the role of coquette so delightful to play.

Karl's cheeks went rosy. "Ah. Exactly so." He retreated to the safety of refreshments and with care loaded Mandy's choice of crumb cake onto a tiny plate, leaving Tommy to fend for himself. "Perhaps I can share with you a brief tour of my shop. It's not so much, and these days, not so many people wish to purchase a fine clock." He shrugged. "But it is for me quite comfortable."

Getting to the point was sometimes a roundabout path. "Yes. A tour would be lovely."

All antiques, elegantly restored, a collection that would be prized by museums. A gallery of Vienna Regulators by Gustav Becker and Lenzkirch, French repeaters and empires by Marti and Japy, and a smaller group of old English clocks, mostly by Elliott and Harrington. Soft questions encouraged Karl's narrative of pride, craftsmanship and admiration.

At the rear of the shop, where Seth Thomas, Ansonia and Waterbury represented the best of American heritage, Karl scratched the back of his head and with evident modesty to announce the journey's end. "And so. You have come today looking not so much for a good clock as some special work, yes?"

The clocks in Karl's shop struck the quarter hour for the second time. A gentle chorus of bells and gongs rolled front to back, some deep and reserved, some sharp and a bit brash. Wispy calls of cuckoos rounded out the melodies of neighbors along the walls. *Is it me or does he have them timed perfectly for the effect? Impossible. Nobody does that.*

A display extended almost to the opposite wall where a narrow passageway was blocked by a thin gate. *A barrier.* A barrier separating Karl from visitors. Karl can come out whenever he wishes to be perfectly charming, but The Clockmaker can retreat to a place of safety. At the front of the store, warm November sunshine poured in — but only to a point. Here, the shop was barely illuminated, save for the bright work lamp that reached like some sort of mechanical insect over a polished but worn wooden bench.

Tommy said, "Special work requiring special talent. But I'm told you've retired."

Karl laughed. "Such, eh — how does one say, *kriecherei* — oh, yes, flattery. But as you can see, this is not so true. One must never cease to work, Tommy. Work, craftsmanship, a good routine. Such things keep the hand steady, the mind, sharp, yes?"

Tommy's wry smile, the knowing smile he used when he didn't believe a word, but allowed it to pass anyway. "It's a small shop, Karl."

The Clockmaker, safe behind the counter, perched on his stool, without a back, perfect military posture, his long arms strong and agile. All the delicate tools of his trade stood at attention in neat rows on the wall to his right. The jeweler's loupes affixed to his thin-rimmed glasses, folded up. They added volume to thick, arching eyebrows at the base of a high forehead that dissipated into a shock of white hair, combed straight back except for closely trimmed sides. Below pale blue eyes, his nose took a direct line down to a thin mouth and strong jaw.

Karl glanced at Mandy, perhaps looking for empathy but hopefully getting an encouragement for candor instead. "So. You have come to disturb a fellow who enjoys his older years to dust off the cobwebs from old skills. There are many others who are capable."

"Need the best for this one, Karl. Old school."

In a glass display case that housed small and dainty clocks and pocket watches were liberally spaced. Below each timepiece, tiny cards whispered in a delicate hand that Karl was not at all modest about prices. "Oh, I don't know, Tommy. Karl probably has many, many years in a difficult and dangerous trade. Now he's looking for some — thing to, um, pass the time."

Karl's sudden glare was stern, cold, unflinching.

Yes. I know. The impertinent little child, the kid who spoke out of turn. And I don't flinch, either.

The song of the clocks began again, from front to back, in trios, duets, solo, marching from way back there to right now, the present. Revelation. *Serenity. Methodical serenity.* Karl's shop was not accidental tranquility. It was carefully orchestrated. Like the song of the clocks. He arranged them to do it. *The clocks are perfectly in time.*

Like a child in a room full of grownups, with the urge to raise her hand, the craving to interrupt, the willingness to be indicted for poor manners. Questions, so many questions. Flowers in a meadow. Fun, soft, light questions, born in fascination and grown in astonishment. The kind that build a fluffy little article for the features section in the Sunday edition and makes even the most jaded editor crack a smile. *I want to explore your old-world charm and manners. I want to know why a guy like you is content with a tiny shop in a small, out-of-the town. I want to know about the song of the clocks.* All the potential of a great article. Darn shame to have to let it go, to stand quietly off to the side, the child seen but not heard.

I know, Karl. I get it. I understand. I appreciate. The song of the clocks. Exquisite.

The frown of the harsh headmaster, dissolving into the patient smile of a charmed grandfather. Tommy, so shrewdly patient, so ut — terly calm.

"And so, *mein Fräulein* — "

"Mandy. Friends call me Mandy."

"Of course. Your friend Thomas wishes the services of a craftsman — "

"The *best*. The best ever. That's why we came to you."

Karl cocked an eyebrow and said to Tommy, "So. She seems to think... Very well. I am most certain you have some sort of list of items you require in the next days. And then?"

Tommy passed a folded sheet of paper. "Perhaps a retainer. As in times past."

Karl unfolded the list. "Yes, yes. Times past. Hm." He held it like a delicate flower in his left hand. At unpredictable intervals he made a tiny note in the margin. A stub of a pencil, well hidden in long fingers wrinkled by many years. Yet strong, like those of a pianist or surgeon, a craftsman's hands, steady, accustomed to diligence and diminutive spaces.

At last Karl again looked up. He straightened and lifted the paper. "Please — I may keep this? I am an old man, and it is for me some — times difficult to remember."

Why do I doubt that? Here's a guy who could assemble half the clocks in North America from memory alone. Maybe its's one of those spy things, where the evidence has reached a shredder and a fire.

Karl folded the paper and tucked it into his shirt pocket. "A most unusual list," he told Tommy and Mandy. "The basic items, passport, drivers license, casual documents, you can have late this afternoon. The others, they will require a bit more time, perhaps tomorrow. I need only an address for the courier. This is reasonable, yes?"

Tommy said, "More than reasonable. And your fee?"

"The usual is sufficient." Karl paused to fumble with his pockets. "Ah, yes, here it is. All has been arranged." He looked up. "Most gen — erous, Tommy. I suspect some small additional request?"

Tommy smiled.

He's shopping for more than me.

"Sergei's going to need some documents. Nothing complicated."

"Ah, so. Sufficient to enter the country or a full set of papers? You must forgive me, but my files are a small bit out of date."

Out of date? These guys had some sort of regular network? Off the books? The CIA and Russians had to provide — no, well, not quite. These guys had their own little collection of helpers.

Tommy said, "Enough to get by until — "

"Perhaps. Yes. I will use the oldest possible dating to suggest he has had these papers for a while, perhaps even give them a small amount of wear. Yes. I think this would be good."

Tommy nodded approval, but shifted his weight when Karl's weary, patient eyes zeroed in.

"You know, of course, that Yenchenko is — how does one say? — yes, unpredictable, dangerous. He is an old wolf who makes his own path, on his own terms."

"I know."

"Yes. For you, it is not so big a problem." Karl nodded toward Mandy. "But it would seem that you have complications, yes?"

"Yes."

"Aha. So this task you have taken, it is serious, serious enough to bring our old friend Sergei into the equation?"

"That's probably true."

Karl's silence suggested he was absorbing the gravity of the still-evolving investigation. "Hm. Yes. And so it must be. But first, we must assist your beautiful companion, yes?"

Okay, so now you got me to blush.

Karl turned to face her. "And now two small questions if I may be perhaps so impertinent."

"Of course."

"What name do you choose for me to use on the documents?"

"My own. Is that all right?"

Karl shrugged. "As you wish. Most people who seek out my ser—vice, well, they most often prefer..." He paused. *Almost as if on cue. As he expected to pause just then.* Another chorus of clocks, striking the three-quarter hour. The shop eased into the relative silence of tick, tocks. "Yes. It is typical for those for whom it is time to leave some uncomfortable past behind, begin anew, yes?"

"And your second question?"

"Press credentials. Most curious. I must ask why such a lovely and charming person as yourself wishes to be — forgive me — held in such low esteem."

So funny. So ironic. What can I say to that?

Tommy suddenly looked up, first into space and then toward Mandy.

He's thought of something. "What?"

"It's about time."

She shook her head. "About time for what?"

Karl's expression was puzzled, but also amused.

Tommy rubbed his forehead. "The day you encountered Benny. You said you were late. But he'd just arrived, from the subway. And the ambulance that killed him, it had to be somewhere nearby. If you had been *on time*, you wouldn't have seen him."

"So you're suggesting that he might have been meeting someone else? And I happened to be — "

"Yeah. In the wrong place at the wrong time."

They stared at each other for half a dozen ticks and tocks.

Mandy brought her hands to her face. "Oh, Tommy. It's *a matter of time*! Oh, yes!"

Like a couple of little kids in a moment of joy. The Tommy Kane grin. Boyish, mischievous, carefree. His eyes. So full of sunshine. *Karl.* She glanced at Karl. *Poor guy looks hopelessly confused.* "I'm so sorry, Karl. You must think we're crazy."

"There is no need to make an apology, Miss Owens. You are Americans, yes? Such things are to be expected. Perhaps I should go to make ready the camera — "

Mandy touched Karl's hand. "Yes, of course. And I adore all your clocks. The song of the clocks. It's perfect."

Karl grinned, broad and youthful. He quickly blushed a bit, too, while her hand lingered on his, as much a courtesy as a reward. He took a breath and retreated. "So. We must now make some photo— graphs for the documents. Not so many as I wish, of course, but the type made by poor equipment and indifferent operators when they are bored and in a rush, yes?"

Tommy rubbed his chin. "Sure thing, Karl. Take your time."

CHAPTER TWELVE

Terminal Eight, John F. Kennedy International Airport

Mandy's fingertips stroked the little screen faster, harder, and finally paused. "I don't think it's working. Maybe I broke it. I'm sure Lucy said — "

Tommy leaned in to look. *The last thing we need is a tech issue.* "Two fingers, right to left. I think she said."

"I did that. See? Something's wrong." Mandy grumbled and restarted the phone. "It's so different than my old one. I suppose you don't — "

Around them, a loose circle of padded seats tried to encourage social community in the waiting area, but impatient and bored people took sanctuary in media devices. Transient information for transient people, time killers for lives on pause, waiting for a friend, colleague, loved one. Or a soldier of fortune seeking a combat zone.

" — No, probably not," she said in a mournful tone.

Disguised in the shell of a popular cellphone brand, Bug's latest creation hadn't come with ease-of-use features for neophytes. *Time to call in the cavalry.* Tommy raised his hand to scratch his head and spoke to the cuff button of his shirt. The only reply in his ear was a faint static, like an open line with nobody on the other end.

He said, "Lucy's not there. I think the signal's okay, but — "

Movement, twelve o'clock. A figure paused. A kid, twelve, thirteen maybe. Slight, just over five feet tall, thin face, black hair, big brown eyes. Somewhere between puzzled, amused, indifferent.

Mandy looked up and leaned forward to offer an easy smile, the kind a friendly grade school teacher uses when a favorite student un—expectedly approaches. "Hi. Can I help you?"

Now a girl, several years younger, curious to see what her brother is up to. Over her shoulder, in the next circle of chairs, mom watched, her expression apologetic and anxious while another woman, friend, maybe relative, obliviously chattered away. Tommy gestured to mom that it was okay, no problem.

The boy asked, "Do you know how to work it? I can show you."

Mandy responded with an embarrassed laugh and broadened her expression to full-blown charm. "What's your name?"

"I am Izyan, and she is my sister, Eesha."

"Lovely. I'm Mandy, and this is my friend, Tommy."

Bashful smiles. Izyan took half a step forward. Eesha hung back, and their mother watched with uncertainty.

"Your phone. I know how to make them work."

"I'm sure you do. But this one is sort of, well, different, um — "

Tommy said, " — kind of a game thing, part of a puzzle — "

Mandy eagerly concurred. "That's right. We're supposed to figure it out for ourselves, kind of like, well, part of an obstacle course."

Izyan seemed confused, like he was not sure how to process it.

Mandy's words were reassuring. "But thank you so much for offer—ing to help. You're very kind."

The mom called out a sharp command to her children, who smiled for a moment at the nice lady who didn't know how to use a smartphone before they scampered away to family.

Izyan held his sister's hand and advised her, "You see? Grownups don't know everything."

Lucy's voice popped into Tommy's ear. "Hey, Tommy. Sorry, had to step away for a sec."

Tommy gestured incredulity and annoyance.

Mandy mouthed the word "bathroom."

Okay, calm, relax. "No prob. Stuck with the phone. How do you —"

Mandy said, "It's on, but the screen is blank."

Lucy chuckled. "Hold it horizontal, swish it left to right, but keep your thumb pressed on the bottom right corner of the screen."

Mandy rolled her eyes, shook her head and smiled chagrin. She followed the instructions. Enormous relief when four video images from the customs area nearby showed weary passengers trudging through the process of entering the United States. She whispered, "Oh, wow. This gives a whole new meaning to 'there's an app for that'. Thanks, Lucy. I simply forgot."

"S'okay, you're only about three light-years beyond Tommy, who still thinks you gotta put in a quarter to get a dial tone."

"Dime," he said.

Mandy's fingers caressed the phone's screen, shuffling images and zooming in and out. "Try nickel."

Lucy laughed. "We're good?"

Tommy said, "Yep, thanks." In the next circle of chairs, Izyan seemed bored with his company and continued to observe. Tommy made a gesture of success. The boy grinned and waved acknowledge—ment. *The only guy stuck in an all-female conversation. Get used to it, kid.*

Mandy said, "I suppose you didn't have these kinds of problems in the good old days."

Tommy continued to scan the disorganized parade of passers-by. "Just the opposite. Major terminals were tough. Everybody had peo—ple to watch comings and goings, so many that they'd keep bumping into each other. After a while, everybody knew everybody. Live, let live. Unwritten community rules."

She used the phone to check flight arrivals, and tucked it into her bag. "Sounds kind of cozy, actually."

Two guys in suits passed. No luggage. Earpieces. Unhurried, but purposeful. *FBI or maybe DEA?* "Sometimes. Got pretty casual in air—port bars, restaurants, rolling up big ol' expense tabs. Somebody'd get transferred out for account padding, a new hotshot would show up, upset the whole arrangement."

"Ah. They actually had to *work* as spies. Must have been tough."

He said, "Old timers say that in the fifties, at LaGuardia, the floor guys really took it seriously. Used hand signals more complicated than baseball coaches. It was a good place to break in, learn the trade. To—day, the market is simply not there."

"Kind of sad."

Tommy shrugged. "Espionage is never known for its charm. Think about it. Your whole day hanging out in an airline or railroad terminal, looking for something, anything, involving the opposition. Terrible duty. But it's all electronic now. Guys like Bug paved the way. They'd wire whole buildings with surveillance gear, always improving. Whenever a terminal was rebuilt, even upgraded, they'd have to scramble to get new tech in place before construction ended."

Right on time, Lucy's voice was in their ears. "Hate to interrupt reminiscences, but the flight's arriving. A-T-C gave it clearance to land."

Tommy yawned and stretched. "Should have got a coffee, dough—nut maybe."

Mandy shook her head and stood. "Tea, a fruit cup. Or maybe yo—gurt would be better."

Lucy chuckled. "Fruit cups and yogurt at J-F-K are terrible and overpriced. Hard to screw up a doughnut, especially one from a chain. If you want, I can have one of the courtesy people from American's Admirals Club bring you something."

Mandy drew a compact from her bag and checked her makeup. "I think we're good, Lucy. Where to?"

"Customs is on the lower level and you've got monitors to watch. Remember how to — "

Mandy finished her task. "Yes. Thumb, swish."

Lucy said, "Our guy has paper to clear immigration. I'm tapped into State to help at the checkpoint. He's a businessman making a connection en route to L-A after a sales meeting in France. You're meeting him to make sure he gets to the connecting flight. As soon as he clears, we switch it, like we discussed."

Tommy nodded.

After a moment, Lucy reiterated. "Tommy? Okay?"

She can't see me. "Oh. Yeah. Okay. Old habits. Sorry."

Lucy sighed. "Gate Twelve. I'd bet on the screen at the upper left, the cam nearest that route into C-and-I. I'll switch the cam on the lower right into the hallway at that gate."

Tommy ran interference in the pedestrian traffic to allow Mandy concentration on the phone.

A flock of uniforms scurried past. Three TSA guys, four regular cops. Another pair of feds in suits was right behind. *So far, so good may be fading fast.*

On the screen in Mandy's hand, passengers from the American flight plodded through the hallway. About twenty had passed the sur—veillance camera when a huge man, towering over all the others, stepped into the frame. *Sergei Yenchenko.*

Mandy whispered. "Oh, wow. Not exactly inconspicuous, is he?"

Tommy said, "Six-seven, maybe three-fifty, three-sixty. Did a little weightlifting when he was a kid. You there, Lucy?"

"Got him."

Mandy asked, "A *little* weightlifting?"

"Well, okay, a two-time Olympic champion. Still works out a lot, but he could probably drop a couple of pounds. Don't mention it, though. Annoys him."

Mandy cocked an eyebrow. "I'll mark that down."

Lucy's voice returned. "Okay, he should get through immigration all right. Just hope he's doesn't have anything nasty in that carry-on."

"Such as?"

Lucy's voice was off-handed casual. "Weapons. Guns, mostly. Plus currency, for that matter."

"But this is an international flight coming into — " Under the camera, Yenchenko looked up to stare at the lens. Mandy moved the phone away from her body. "That's one scary guy, Tommy. Are you sure... Well, yes, I guess that's sort of a silly question."

Tommy shrugged. "Sergei's, well, Sergei. Luce, what's with all the feds and uniforms? We saw a bunch go by just now."

Lucy spoke. "Not sure. But there's a mob of cops, uniformed and plainclothes, outside C-and-I. Looks like they're waiting for some—thing or somebody."

"Can we hear?"

"I'm on their frequency, but they've gone silent. Smart guys, know what they're doing."

Mandy and Tommy exchanged uneasy glances.

No, I don't know if it's a coincidence.

On the screen at the upper left, Yenchenko strolled directly toward the line for foreign citizens and tugged a passport from his jacket pocket.

Tommy spoke to Lucy. "I don't see an I-94."

"All electronic now for air and sea arrivals, Tommy. I took care of his in flight, so he should be okay."

Yenchenko greeted an immigration person who swiped the passport. They watched in silence. Mandy drew a breath and held it. The officer's body language suggested hesitation, uncertainty. *Stuff on the screen, can't read it.* A second look at the passport and at Yenchenko, who was placid, calm, a tired businessman working through the obstacles..

"Lucy?"

"Not sure... no, he's okay."

The officer took one last look at the screen and returned Sergei's passport. A curt nod and Yenchenko stepped past the gate, toward the luggage carousel.

Mandy exhaled at last. "You used to do this sort of stuff for a living?"

Tommy chuckled. "Much more fun at a boondocks frontier, crossing in a hail of bullets."

Her eyes widened.

"That's what Sergei says, anyway."

"I can see I'm going to have my hands full with two of you."

Tommy said, "Okay, here we go with luggage."

Lucy said, "Green bag, brown tag."

Yenchenko made his way to the moving carousel. Bags were already piling up and other passengers were impatiently seeking their possessions.

Tommy explained to Mandy. "He checked a green bag with a *red* tag in Marseilles. Our guy on the ground switched it during offload."

"Your guy on the ground? Just how... but why — "

"He's got to become an American before customs. Easiest place to change nationalities. So he needs a bag with American stuff in it."

Lucy spoke. "Okay, he's found the right bag. Checking the label. Picks it up. Good to go."

Tommy and Mandy continued to watch Sergei casually approach customs and pulled what was clearly an American passport from his jacket pocket.

He picked a young officer, female, snug uniform, hands in blue latex gloves. Friendly banter, offers a declaration form. *Dang, if he isn't staring right at her* — She ignored the checked bag but wanted a peek at the carry-on. Sergei obliges.

Lucy muttered, "God, I do hope he hasn't done anything dumb. All she needs to spot is a loaded AK-47 or something."

Tommy said, "They don't fit in carry-on any more."

Yenchenko's body blocked the view. The customs person held something aloft, checked the paperwork he offered. A nod. Object back into bag. Yenchenko zipped it and strode away, toward the exit, under a huge sign that said, "Welcome to the United States."

Tommy steered Mandy from the doorway separating arriving passengers from the arrivals waiting area, where a dozen uniformed cops formed a waiting gauntlet anchored by five guys in plain clothes. To her look of alarm, he responded with a reassuring hand gesture to signal it would be all right and they should remain unobtrusive. "Turn your back to them. Just keep an eye on the phone."

She began to protest but instead held the phone up to share the surveillance feed. Yenchenko had passed the camera and was gone.

Tommy acknowledged it. "So pretend you're making a call to a friend, a relative. Just relax, take it easy." He had eased past her and glanced across her shoulder, through the growing crowd of friends, family, limo drivers. Among them, near the wall, two women wearing hijabs. *From where we waited.* Next to them, the children. Eesha. Izyan. *Blank expressions. Bored. Sad. Just staring straight ahead.*

Lucy must have had a better view. In their ears, her voice returned. "Okay, here we go. In five...four...three..."

Movement. The door opened. Cops tensed. The plainclothes guy involuntarily put hands on hips, jacket open. Smith and Wesson M&P. FBI badge.

"Don't look, Mandy."

She ignored him and turned anyway.

Instincts. Forgivable. "Okay, so look, but casual."

Three TSA guys blocked the doorway. The other uniforms closed in tight around somebody. The FBI guys stepped in, past the two women and children. Some protest, objection, indignation from inside the swarm. Flash of handcuffs.

Tommy's words were soft but even. "Just watch. Don't react. Lucy?"

"Yeah, I'm here. Not quite sure, but it sounds like they've got one... no, *two* in custody. Lotta cops, Tommy. Okay, they're about to move."

"Yeah, we can see it from here."

"Tommy, the women, the children from the — "

The entourage of police and a guy in a suit, handcuffed, rolled past from the left, blocking the view of the family. Two uniforms pulled captured luggage.

Mandy said, "Tommy — "

"Easy, easy."

The cloud passed and the two women and children remained standing against the wall, expressionless. To the left, the TSA uni — forms opened the door. Two men in suits. Middle eastern. Suits, no ties, short beards. Closing on the women, the children. Waves, smiles, hellos. Hugs from the kids. Reunion. Together, they slipped away into the crowd.

In the doorway, the shadow of a huge man, stepping through. *Sergei.* Big grin, big wave, rolling in like running buffalo.

"We're good?" Lucy asked. "I gotta get back to the markets."

Tommy said, "Yeah, good. Nice work, well done."

"Mandy?"

"Yes, Lucy."

"Good luck with Yenchenko. You're gonna need it."

Mandy looked at Tommy and winced through a smile. "Thanks."

Sergei cranked up his exuberance another notch and bellowed. "*Koshka*! We barely make farewell and we are together again. It is most good to see you are still alive!"

Mandy cocked an eyebrow. "*Koshka?*"

Tommy sighed. "Okay, it's your turn to leave that one alone."

"Ah."

He reached for Sergei's outstretched arm to shake hands but was immediately enveloped in a bear hug. Sergei's attention turned to Mandy and his expression reminded Tommy of a starving man in an unlimited gourmet buffet, trying not to drool.

Mandy accepted the leer as a compliment and offered her hand. "Hello, I'm Mandy Owens. Nice to meet you."

He lifted her hand as though it were delicate glass and kissed it softly. "And most warm greeting to you. I am Sergei Ilyich Yenchenko and I make long journey to rescue my valued friend Tommy Kane from poor situation, *da?*"

Mandy flashed a knowing smile toward Tommy.

Sergei caught it and looked back and forth before speaking to Mandy. "You are woman from party in Nassau? *Da*, of course. All is most clear." He turned to Tommy. "So, comrade, I admit. You have most excellent taste."

Hope I'm not blushing as much as she is.

As they began to stroll toward the exit she said, "Well. I'm so glad you didn't get caught up in that bit of police business at the doorway."

"*Da, da.* Of course. They make good arrest, *Koshka?*"

"Quick and efficient, without incident."

Yenchenko grinned. "Is good. On flight I see old rival. Israeli. Mossad must pull him out of U-S some time ago for problem at UN. He try to make return, eh? Sergei knows such things," he explained to Mandy. "So I am good citizen, mention to flight attendant he is want—ed organizer of terrorists."

Hard not to smile at that one.

Mandy asked, "So you set him up?"

Yenchenko shrugged innocence. "He is poor spy, but suitable dis—traction for *Amerikanski* official, to make interest in Sergei small. At—tendant is most cooperative. Tommy, such a woman! She have such huge — "

Mandy cut him off. "I think I get the idea."

Sergei set the pace. "*Da, da.* So. You have nice car? Good accom—modation? Much food and drink? What they offer on airplane is, of course, *uzhasnyi.*"

Tommy began to translate.

Mandy raised her hand again. "Don't bother."

CHAPTER THIRTEEN

Madison Avenue at Seventy-first Street, New York City

Halfway across Madison Avenue, the traffic signal changed. On the other side of Seventy-First, a pack of cars crept forward. Esther took short but firm steps, assisted by a cane, toward St. James' Church. An impatient driver tapped his horn twice.

Mandy turned to glare and gestured to the driver with her arm. *What? What's your problem? We're crossing the street here.*

The driver shook his head and tossed his arms into the air.

"Just take your time, Mrs. Liebowitz. There's no hurry."

The driver beeped again.

Mandy glared again, ramping up ferocity in her annoyance. On the West Side, they'd be a lot more expressive. On the Upper East Side, they simply ignored it. *Slow down a little. Pick up the thread of the story. Ignore the guy in the meat truck.*

On Seventy-first, a black town car appeared. Tommy got out, his usual grin a panacea for all ills, a calming for all storms. Almost. She shot a hostile glance toward the meat truck, now twenty feet away and raised a finger of warning to the driver. *Touch the horn again, and Tommy's people will shoot your stupid truck into little pieces.* She waved to Tommy as they approached the curb and called out. "Hi, honey! Good day at the office?"

"Excellent. Everything's wrapped up. No wrinkles."

Fantastic. The raid in Chelsea done. Cops and sirens everywhere — well, fake cops and phony police cars, but still.... Hauled off her entire wardrobe. And without wrinkling anything. Maybe.

Esther stepped onto the sidewalk. Her eyes narrowed to inspect him like a slab of brisket on a sheet of brown paper in the hands of a proud butcher. "And who is this man?"

Mandy apologized. "Mrs. Liebowitz, I'd like to introduce you to my friend, Tommy Kane. Tommy, this is Esther Liebowitz, who lives with her daughter's family, two floors down from us. You remember — *the Abramsons.*"

Tommy extended his hand and offered a gracious smile. "Of course. Hello. Pleased to meet you."

He didn't make the connection, but hid it well. "Today is Mrs. Liebowitz's birthday. She's invited us to a party they're having tonight."

Tommy bowed slightly, *"Yom hu'ledet sameach. Ad me'ah ve'esrim shanah!"*

Esther beamed and thanked him in a barrage of Hebrew. Her at–tention switched to Mandy. "He is your boyfriend? You going to mar–ry this fellow? A nice-looking man. Such nice manners, and a good tailor, too. I always tell my grandchildren about manners and choos–ing a good tailor. But they don't always listen."

"I'm sure your grandchildren pay much more attention than you realize," Mandy said. "And as for.... Well, we'll see."

Esther rubbed her hands together to revive circulation. "Do not wait so long. Time so quickly flies past you. It's not good to be alone. I know this, ever since my dear Moshe passed."

Tommy appeared intrigued.

Okay, Tommy, hope you think it's the chilly air... So okay, it's a blush.

Esther sighed. "Young people these days, afraid of commitment, to have a stable life. Such a shame. So, we have said hello and you have introduced me to a nice fellow. It's a pleasant day, yes?"

"Very pleasant."

Esther spoke to Tommy. "Every day I make a little walk. I come down Seventy-first Street, two blocks, to Central Park, where I rest. In the summer, I go all the way by the statue, a famous man named Morse or something, by the Inventor's Gate, but in winter, a shorter walk, not so hard on the knees. It is important to get exercise, you know. You get exercise, Mister Kane? Yes? Good." She turned to Mandy. "He seems fit. A good match for such a lovely person as you. You bring him to my party, okay?"

Mandy glanced at Tommy with a blend of raised eyebrow and sly smile that whisked away even the slightest chance of negative. "Of course."

Tommy added, "And we are honored that you would invite us."

"You see?" Esther said to Mandy.

Like the little girl getting boy advice from a grown-up cousin. "Yes, Mrs. Liebowitz, I see."

"So. Now I must make a visit to my daughter's hairdresser. I don't wish to look so old at my party. You two, you should walk together, perhaps a coffee and danish, some *rugelach* maybe, a little time togeth‐ er, get better acquainted. I know such things."

Mandy chuckled. "I'll bet you do. Have a lovely afternoon, Mrs. Liebowitz."

For a more than a minute, they watched Mrs. Liebowitz make her way home, indifferent to the weather and whatever infirmities she car‐ ried. Mandy uncrossed her arms and warmed the entire intersection with a smile. "She's adorable, don't you think? We met in the elevator, both times by chance and today we went for a lovely walk, across Fifth Avenue, to the park. We sat on freezing benches and she told wonder‐ ful stories about her younger days in Crown Heights. Gosh, what a gorgeous human interest story that would make."

Tommy nodded. "And this birthday party?"

"Ah, yes. We may have caught a break. The party stuff sort of came up. Sidney Abramson is a major player in foreign exchange mar‐ kets. Runs the trading desk at one of the bigger investment houses. Well connected to the Fed, all the makings of a first-rate source if we play our cards right. They're having a family-and-friends kind of thing, maybe some of the neighbors, cake and cookies sort of event, gifts — oh, my gosh, we should bring something, don't you think?"

He glanced at his watch. "Kind of short on time?"

"Oh, Tommy, we can't show up empty handed. Let me think. Madison at Seventy-first. I think there's some galleries and shops south... No, north. C'mon. I've got to do my hair and figure out something to wear."

As they hurried along the east side of Madison Avenue, she said, "I didn't know you could speak Hebrew. What did you tell her?"

"Hey, I know just enough to order beer and a sandwich in an Israeli bar. And essentially it was wishing her a happy birthday and best hopes for many more. How about this shop?"

"Well, it was sweet of you." Mandy paused at a display window to scan possibilities. "Hm. Not really. A bit pricey. I know with you there's no limit but I have to respect the occasion. So where did you pick up the greeting?"

"Hung out with some guys from Mossad for a couple of years. Nice people, take it all seriously, but they were actually kind of fun between ops. Tel Aviv is a great town." He laughed. "Kind of guys who could help you buy a gift for an elderly lady that you know little about."

Mandy shrugged. "She's old-fashioned, from Crown Heights, unsure if the next generation is on board, not so much faith-wise, but tradition-wise. Ah. I think this is the shop I remember from — well, too long ago."

* * *

In a small, upscale gallery, Tommy's eyes swept through displays of handcrafted Judaic art. Wearable and hangable. Some whimsical, some somber. Some archaic-looking, rather like careful recreations of objects of thousands of years old, the icons of a religion he knew little about. Some contemporary-looking, believers pushing the limits of design.

Mandy said, "Ah, here we are. Now we have to choose. These are hamsas, an amulet kind of in the shape of a hand. See? Three fingers extended with a bent pinky finger and curved thumb on the sides. It's supposed to guard against the evil eye — yeah, yeah, I know — and bring good health, luck, abundance, goodness and help defend the owner against the forces of evil."

"Works for me," Tommy said. "Pick out which ever — "

Mandy looked up. "There's some sort of prayer that goes with it.

Let's see. How did that go? Hm. Something like *Let no sadness come to this heart. Let no trouble come to these arms.*" She paused. "Darn. Can't remember the rest. What a — "

A voice behind them spoke. "Let no conflict come to these eyes. Let my soul be filled with the blessing of joy and peace. The prayer of the hamsa. Very beautiful, don't you think?"

Tommy and Mandy turned to face an older man, dark suit, weath—ered face but bright and eager eyes. Thinning gray hair under a kip—pah. Unhurried in the way the elderly take their time to savor all the moments that remain. "I am Malakai Lipsky. Welcome. What may I show you today?"

She was being more particular than he expected, but after ten minutes settled on a choice.

Lipsky said, "A gift, yes? I'm sure it will be well received. I'll just gift wrap it for you." He stepped away.

Mandy leaned in and whispered. "You got it all, all the closets?"

"Yes, no trouble. Well, not too much trouble."

"Did you get your hands dirty?"

"No. Bug and I ran the op from his van. Charlie looked good, es—pecially when actual cops dropped by."

"And Sergei?"

"Everyone survived, just a few bruises. He had fun."

"I'm trying to picture Sergei carefully packing lingerie. *My lin—gerie.* Not quite sure I want to go there."

Lipsky returned with a package wrapped in silver with a delicate white bow. Tommy dug into his pocket for three hundred dollars and declined the change.

Lipsky asked, "Is there anything else I can do for you today?"

Tommy locked onto an idea. "Maybe. If I wanted the best *rugelach* in Crown Heights, where would I go?"

Lipsky called a young sales associate to assist. After conferring, he said there were several fine bakeries on Kingston Avenue. The young man cited his grandmother's personal preference, the place they went for special. Chocolate, cinnamon, vanilla were her favorites, and Lip—sky suggested an assortment.

On Madison Avenue, he tugged the special phone from his pocket.

Mandy waved a hand of warning. "Lucy said it was only for emer−gencies."

He pressed the number two icon. "This is."

Lucy's voice was immediate and tinged with anxiety. "What's wrong?"

"We need some *rugelach*."

"What?"

"*Rugelach*. Can someone run over to Crown Heights for maybe a couple of dozen, assorted and deliver them to the apartment?"

"Hold on a sec while I mop up the spilled coffee. Jeez, Tommy, you scared the crap out of me."

Tommy winced. Mandy's expression said, *told ya*. "No big deal. Just the routine little stuff that goes with the quiet social life on the Upper East Side. A birthday party for an elderly neighbor."

* * *

On the periphery of celebration, Tommy stood with Mandy and glasses of good scotch, immersed in the icons of professional success. But family values had not been left behind. Sidney and Barbara Abramson and a bubbly daughter formed the core of applause and ad−miration for Esther, around a table rich with tradition and ritual.

The extended family numbered fifteen. *Nothing phony or artificial here. Even in unguarded moments, the group is tight and friendly.* Not like the hard times of life on The Teche, and not at all with the preten−tiousness of teen years in St. Tammany Parish with an aunt and uncle addicted to social climbing. *Yeah. Feeling a little envy.*

Beyond the cozy circle of humanity, Barbara's taste in décor ran to high key and understated elegance. Not surprising. While they pre−pared for the party, Mandy had explained Barbara's status in the fine art scene, most notably her connections with Lincoln Center and the Museum of Modern Art. *No idea what I'm looking at, but it's got to be special considering the way it's displayed.* Judging from her expressions as she surveyed the collection, Mandy almost certainly knew. But it did not compete with the reality of good people at the peak in New York City.

Mandy seemed much more at ease in the social bleachers, happy her gift was well-received, confident in a simple black dress that ran well into four figures at Bergdorf's, reunited with her mother's pearls, rescued that afternoon by the guys from her apartment across town, the pearls she wore at Lyford Caye. *Calm, comfortable, gorgeous.* They probably did this sort of thing all the time in Connecticut.

Before they arrived, it had likely been a family dinner rich with expressions of faith. Now, with dessert and gifts, it was all laughter, teasing, social. Later it would be business in the inner circle, and a chance for Mandy to work her journalistic magic.

A knock on the door. Polite at first, then more urgency. *A late arrival. A cousin caught in traffic.*

Barbara looked toward Mandy, her eyes plaintive. Mandy nodded. The scene slowing, slowing to a crawl. The party behind. Mandy reaching for the knob. Door opens, partway. Her expression somber, bites her lower lip. Gestures to beckon, uses her body to block the view into the hallway.

But the shadow beyond her said it all.

Yenchenko.

Sergei was indifferent and not at all apologetic. "A small inconvenience. We must make rapid exit from building."

One minute, the stuff of ordinary people. Next minute, the stuff that always seems to tag along. "What happened?"

"We have stirred nest, anger wasp when we make raid. Now, they come to us."

Mandy said, "I knew it sounded way too easy."

Sergei wore an expression halfway between puzzled and astonished. "*Nyet.* Is good. Clumsy trap, but we draw enemy from hiding place, to make battle on our ground. But it is not so good to return to apartment. Too many bodies in hall. *Tovarich* Charlie and I return from meal at restaurant nearby, discover team working on lock to door."

Tommy's eyebrow lifted. "And — ?"

Sergei shrugged. "No more working on lock. *Koshka*, you fail to inform me Charlie is fisherman, like myself. Our pleasant conversation becomes spoiled when we must defend apartment."

Mandy shook her head and whispered. "I don't believe this..."

Sergei pulled a Beretta nine mil from his waistband. "We make sweep of apartment, remove all clothes and other object into truck. Charlie is friend of police, so he informs them of bodies upstairs. Now we must go." He offered the pistol grip first to Tommy. "Koshka, you must concur completely. This is no time for weapon that shoot tranquilizer. These are dangerous enemy. We are, of course, superior. But we must prepare, eh?"

Tommy accepted the weapon. He tugged the emergency phone from his pocket to have Lucy help manage the escape and get the jet prepped in Teterboro. "Mandy, you'll need to make our apologies, okay?"

She sighed and rehearsed. "It's been a lovely party, thanks for inviting us, but I'm sorry, we now have to run for our lives from a contingent of professional killers. Yes. That works."

Sergei thrust his hands into his pockets and tried to peek into the apartment as Mandy stepped back through the door. "Is good party? Much food, vodka? Attractive women?"

"It *was* a good party, Serge. *Was.*"

Sergei ran point to the street, where he stepped outside and pretended to smoke a cigarette. After a few pantomimed drags, he extinguished the invisible smoke with the toe of his shoe and returned to the lobby. "Light gray vehicle, two o'clock, perhaps fifty meters."

Mandy took possession of the phone and tucked in an earbud. "She's been in touch with Cesar, but wants to know whether you're routing for speed or distance. She can have a regular town car and driver here in two minutes."

This is not the time for high style. Or a civilian in the mix. Need a better plan... "Let's go for intercepts. If we take these guys out — well, who knows how many more? Serge, remember that breadcrumb thing in Buenos Aires? With the rental car?"

Yenchenko said, "Charlie is eighty, eighty-five meters perhaps, to left, but with truck. But Buenos Aires opponent are professional. These seem amateur. Clumsy, careless, no challenge."

CHAPTER FOURTEEN

Mandy crossed her arms, leaned against a block of mailboxes, and focused on the delicate mosaic of a ceramic lobby floor, sorting out disconnect between minutes before and right now.

A dozen floors above, Esther Liebowitz was the center of attention of a warm and gracious and loving family. In the tiny lobby next to her, Tommy waited with all the anxiety of a brick. With a gun. Across the narrow space, Sergei kept watch. With a gun. Just outside, some sort of exotic scheme was playing out to induce Cinnabar's people to plant a tracking device on the car they'd use to try to escape. A forty-mile escapade described as drawing the enemy out and then ... whatever.

A dozen floors above, a good, solid, unexpected lead on a story oozing with possibilities. A guy who might know the players, fill in the blanks, provide direction. Just outside the lobby door, the seedy world of espionage, the games Tommy and Sergei so loved to play. *Upstairs, what I do, what I am. Out there, what they do, what they are.*

Not much of a choice. Kick the hornets' nest, expect the hornets to swarm. Maybe it was better this way, to confront, to send a message to their people. *We're not to be trifled with.* It sounded brave. It sounded ridiculous.

"Tommy?"

Whatever thought in which he was lost abruptly floated away.

"Hm?"

"You should know that I'm not experienced at this sort of thing. I mean, the most running I do is late, with a coffee, for a subway. You guys, well, you're old hands at skulking about, igniting chaos, high oc—

tane chases, running gun battles."

"We'll be okay. Trust me. The waiting, that's the hard part."

"Charlie was right, you know. You *love* this stuff."

He shrugged. "A whole lot easier than starting with a shift key, ending with a period, and making sense in between."

You're sure about that?

Sergei's gesture beat her for attention. "Is good. These *vanka*, they are slow-witted."

Tommy asked, "Ready?"

Mandy took a breath. The rental car, bait for whoever was trailing. Cinnabar, planting a tracking device. Bug, tracking the trackers from a van nearby. Lucy... *Oh, gosh. Forgot the ear bud.* The phone had come to life without sound. She tucked it into her right ear and apologized. Tommy smirked. "Okay, let's leave that one alone. Yes. I'm ready."

Straight to the car. Sergei strolling away, to slip into Charlie's truck. The Cinnabar guys, alert. *And I'm working the phone with Lucy and am not off to a good start.* "Lucy says any time you want to quit goofing around, you can head west on Seventy-first, make a left at Fifth Avenue. She's got the lights. So how does this work, Tommy?"

"Serge and I once partnered on a job in Buenos Aires. We use two vehicles, a car and light truck as a blocker, enough to keep 'em from calling in reinforcements. We'll try to open up a little space and send 'em off on a wild goose chase. Works best in traffic, at high-speed in—terchanges. Lucy feeds information, you relay it while I drive."

Slow and easy at first to let everyone get settled in. Across the park, left onto Central Park West. Fourth right. "Bear to the right for Sixty-second." Car, honking protest after Tommy's abrupt swerve. "Lucy says there's another tracking signal, coming up fast, from the south, toward us." She pointed. "There. That's the turn... Lucy says to cross Broadway and make a left onto Columbus Avenue. And that sec—ond signal is gaining. Tommy, she can't get control of the traffic lights..."

"We're gonna get stuck at that red. Maybe run it?"

"*Broadway?* I'd rethink that..."

The light remained red. The tracking car, a blue sedan, slowed, drifted left. Sneaking in for the kill. Lucy muttering she was working on it. Light's still red. The blue car pulls alongside. Younger guys, cold eyes, a question of time, unless —

On the sidewalk, pedestrians scattered in all directions. Charlie's truck rumbled around the blue sedan, scraping the side of it. Into the intersection, blocking the bad guys. Cars swerving. Honking. Chaos. The light changes. *Hit it.* Rear view mirror. The huge body of Yenchenko, bailing out of the truck. *Shotgun, a pump, short barrel.* Chambering a round. Methodically marching around the front of the car, blasting tires, engine, windshield. Pieces of car flying in all directions.

"Oh, Tommy. He's *murdering* a car. Oh, my..."

Tommy applied pressure to the accelerator. "And people want to know why I asked Yenchenko to give us a hand...."

The southbound lanes of Broadway whisked past. In the rear view mirror, Sergei climbed back into the truck and it began to follow again. "Yes, Lucy, we're fine. Just the one now. Sergei murdered their car. Left on Columbus, got it."

"Zig-zagging?"

"Yes, I think so. Lucy says your original tail is across Broadway and a short distance behind the truck. Wait. The truck with all my things. Oh, gosh, Tommy, you don't suppose..."

The convoy slid into the left turn lane and this time the light was friendly.

"Lincoln Tunnel. Of course. I bet we'll turn at Fifty-seventh and..." Lucy, safe and comfy in her command center, coffee, doughnut, the commander of a video game. "Exactly, left onto Eleventh Avenue. There's some sort of a car dealership... um, make that *was.*"

Surprisingly calm, relaxed. She said to Tommy, "See those two really tall buildings? When we pass them, you're going to want to get into the left lane. The tunnel is a couple of blocks."

"Gotcha, no problem," Tommy said. He thrust his arm out the window and pointed. Charlie changed lanes and the box truck fell back.

Not too shabby, Owens. Tommy, calm, relaxed, even, toodling along like a good ol' Southern boy drag racing on a country road. In a pick—up truck. *Yeah, he loves it.* "Okay, you're looking for West Fortieth, just up there, at that bus parking lot. Left, then right onto the ramp. Lucy says Cesar is getting the jet prepped and a flight plan filed. And she'll be right back." The phone was temporarily quiet after a discon—nect. "Very cool. Almost fun. Now that we're out of the city, the rest looks easy."

Tommy grunted. "Don't get too cocky. We still have a tail."

The phone vibrated in Mandy's hand and she hoisted it to her ear. "Hey, Lucy."

Lucy's voice remained calm, assured. "Doing okay?"

"Absolutely."

"With Tommy, I meant."

To her left, Tommy's face seemed serene. More than okay. I could actually get used to this. "It's an interesting experience. Nothing quite like a nice, cozy tunnel to calm the spirit. What's next?"

Lucy said, "After the tunnel, you're on Four-ninety-five west. You'll have three lanes with traffic at about fifty, a bit on the heavyish side, running through a bunch of overpasses and stone cuts. Your tail is half a mile behind, but not pushing it."

As the pavement began to climb, the handful of lights gave way to spots of mercury vapor and neon glow around cars going with the flow. Overpass. Stone gully. Overpass. Again and again, flowing past entry ramps, westbound.

Lucy's voice returned, more tense. "Okay, we got two more tracks, coming in from behind, total of three on your tail."

Mandy relayed the message.

Tommy said, "We'll have to figure something out. How far to switch?"

"Lucy says about six miles."

In Mandy's ear, Lucy's tone seemed tighter, terse. "Those cuts you're in flatten out around the Kennedy Boulevard exit. Keep it steady."

Tommy continually drifted across lanes as the dark landscape of suburban New Jersey floated past in a dreamy state.

Mandy said, "Coming up on One and Nine. Lucy, do we stay on

Four-ninety-five or do we go onto Three?"

Lucy said, "Shit. Two more tracks. They're at six, no, five miles and closing. Okay, bear right onto Route Three toward Secaucus. When you cross Paterson Plank Road, stay to the right, toward Secaucus, and stay on Three west. Gotta figure out what to do here."

Not good.

Tommy said, "Have the truck back off a bit and let Sergei take 'em. Nothing fancy. It'll be messy, but maybe we can shut down the road."

"You're joking."

"Not a bit. Do it."

She began to relay the message, but Lucy already acknowledged she'd heard it. *If they start shooting up cars on an interstate highway, it's going to be a really bad thing for a lot of people.*

"Tommy — "

"Okay, do it *surgically.*"

"He says *surgically*, Lucy." She chuckled. "Apparently Charlie's already got some sort of plan. You're now up two, two-and-a-half-miles. Cesar's set, keeping ETA and wheels-up open with the tower. Lucy says he'll need three and a half minutes, but would really like to have closer to five."

"Tommy's nodding. What about my stuff in the truck?"

Lucy said, "Let me ask."

The silence on the phone seemed eternal. Finally Mandy could contain herself no longer. "Lucy?"

"Yup, still here. Sorry, they were shooting the tires out of two of the tails. Ran them up onto exit ramps and rolled 'em. Musta been *really* cool."

More like scary beyond belief.

"Charlie says the stuff from your Chelsea apartment is going west by motor freight. The stuff in the box truck are your *new* outfits, in some big green contractor trash bags — six or seven he can't remember which — so it shouldn't take long to load. Exit onto the ramp at Harmon Meadow, a shopping center."

I'm trying to concentrate on instructions, but all I can picture are

thirty-five-hundred-dollar suits and eight-hundred-dollar dresses
stuffed in a trash bag. Some of which haven't yet been worn. David
Aire, weeping. Focus. A rendezvous with Dunk's rig from D&D Tow-
ing, like the night in Chatham. "There. See it? Coming down the
ramp?"

"Yep, got it." He braked harder than he should have and the
sound of squealing tires pushed by, followed by honking horns. In the
side view mirror, unfriendly hand gestures. But nobody was about to
argue with a big flatbed truck. Within seconds, his turn signal came
on. Tommy followed the truck up a ramp into a shopping center
stuffed with big-box chain stores and asked about time.

"Lucy says five, six minutes, tops." Mandy held a finger aloft.
"Wait. She has an idea and wants us and Dunk to find an out-of-the-
way spot, preferably in shadows." *Now it's a matter of trust.*

Tommy guided the tow truck behind a row of dumpsters at the
rear of a furniture outlet, got out and chatted with Dunk. The headlights went out and the air became still when Tommy returned.

Two black sport utility vehicles. Creeping. Stopping. Some conversation. Creeping again. *Searching for the signal on the bumper of our
car.*

Mandy froze. *Hard to breathe.* Tommy with a gun in his hand,
working the slide, chambering a round. The passenger in the first
SUV probing corners with a flashlight. Closer, closer, methodically
closer. *Another foot and...*

Light. Searing, bright white light. Now blue and red, too, flashing
in stabbing pulses, all from a pair of police cars at the ramp. State police troopers soon homed in on the two SUVs.

"Lucy?"

"Cavalry arrive yet?"

"Definitely. What's — "

Her tone was matter-of-fact, garnished with pride. "I patched into
their system and put out a BOLO for two suspect SUVs involved in a
string of burglaries."

Troopers, out of their cars, guns drawn, starting the procedure of
apprehending probably armed felons. Four guys in dark jumpsuits,

hands up, on the ground, face down, handcuffs. More squad cars sweeping in, a nice clean bust with no resistance, no shots fired, nice and neat, the stuff that looks good on a report to the troop commander.

Mandy whispered to Tommy. "They're taking forever, looking at the weapons, searching the cars, standing around."

"For cops, the best part of the hunt. Everyone's okay, suspects secure, and you get to tell the tale."

"What about Charlie and Sergei?"

Lucy answered. "Waiting near a diner a mile behind you."

"Very slick," Tommy said. "Tell Lucy — "

Mandy looked at Tommy's grin. "She heard. And she said — "

He sighed. "I know."

Another wait. Easier this time. When the troopers departed, Tommy and Mandy left a plush Audi to cross the lot. A second tow truck pulled in and offloaded a scruffy compact desperately needing a wax, no, a paint job — but only after a major visit to an auto body shop.

"Kind of a letdown. What about our heroic luxury ride?"

He said, "Off to Jersey City. With the tracking device beeping away. For a little while, anyway, before Bug turns it off."

"And this?"

The skinny driver smiled. A wicked grin. A mouth full of bad teeth. "Just some ratty-assed repo I picked up an hour ago. Ain't even done paper onto it. Probably want to keep the windows down. I think the guy musta had a sick dog or some kinda shit."

Tommy shrugged and waved her aboard. "It's innocuous transportation, the next leg of our trip. There's still at least one guy out there and it's always been my luck that they saved the best for last."

Mandy complied and winced. "Innocuous, Tommy? Just getting in is an act of courage. The smell. The stench. It's awful." She looked around to see what might have died a week or more ago. "This car is just... just — "

"Yeah," Tommy said as the car windows stuttered, shuddered and stalled partway open.

Lucy's voice in her ear. "Sorry, pot luck. Just a couple of miles to go. Well, maybe five."

Tommy started the car. It vibrated and rumbled and filled the air around them with the scent of acrid exhaust. "Brakes are really soft, and the transmission is sticky. Not exactly the sort of thing we need for a high-speed chase."

We've come this far and now this. Mandy said, "Lucy? Please tell me — "

"Checking. Yeah, this is probably that abandoned junker Dunk pulled out of a lot in Clifton half hour ago. Sorry, no time for a re-placement. You guys doing okay?"

Mandy sighed. "Marginally." The car struggled with acceleration in the slow lane. Traffic flowed effortlessly around and past in a steady and indifferent stream, and the unheated air from outside helped Mandy suppress the urge to gag.

"That's the spirit," Lucy said. "Okay. Let's try a couple of moves just in case." Right onto One-twenty, past the the Meadowlands com-plex, on and off and on again. Charlie's truck, boxed in on the center lane, missing an exit, headed off into the night. Lucy excused herself to reroute them while Tommy turned into an industrial park to wait. The car began to sputter and stall at the curb. Tommy kept it run-ning, but it made a grinding sound.

Mandy slumped in her seat, then lunged forward. "I felt some-thing go crunch behind me. But I think the smell is gone."

Lucy returned. Charlie and Sergei were a bit growly, but okay, and she guided Tommy through deserted, silent streets of a brick and con-crete maze. At a tee intersection, the promised metal fence guarding an immense white or light gray structure. The car sputtered and near-ly died at the stop sign. Make a left. Big sign on the building, Jet Avia-tion. Next right into the airport. *Almost there.*

Tommy asked, "Charlie and Serge?"

"Lucy says they're moving, but to go ahead. They'll make their way on their own." Mandy sought Tommy's reaction and spoke to the phone. "No. We'll wait for them. Is there some place we can — "

"Bunch of mobile homes on the left," Tommy said.

Mandy pointed. "And some sort of deli, just ahead, across from the entrance."

He pulled into the parking area, backed into a space and switched off the ignition. The car wheezed and quit.

Yes. Now we wait. Again. Deep breath. Relax. Ignore the crunch in the seat. She brushed off a six-hundred dollar party dress. "Well, I wanted to thank you for a lovely evening. Going on a date with you is always such an experience."

The truck appeared from the right and slowed before the airport entry.

"They're here," Mandy told Lucy. "But — "

"Yeah, I know, it's gated. Employee entrance. Hold on a sec."

The gate began to rise.

Mandy said, "She's really that good, isn't she?"

"Yeah, that good."

"Think this old clunker will start?"

Tommy opened the door. "Not even going to try. I think it's a nice night for a walk, don't you?"

Mandy repeated Lucy's reply. "About a quarter mile, up the entry road and bear left, toward Landmark Aviation." She glanced at Tommy's nod of understanding. "Yeah, we got it."

They crossed the street. Again, the gate opened. In brisk, fresh air they passed darkened buildings, made the turn. And there it was, shimmering on the runway. Dark green bags being tossed into the cargo hold.

"Tommy?"

"Hmm?"

"Do they have a really good dry cleaner in Jacks Ford?"

Moments after Karen secured the door, the faint, rising whine of the auxiliary power unit, spooling up. Then the left engine, as she buckled her seat belt in a cabin full of smiles and laughter. A glass of really nice scotch, the sound of the second engine starting, almost drowned out by the impromptu party.

And Karen's cheery voice. "Lucy messengered a package for you, a few minutes ago. It looks like one of those computer tablet things."

The promised subway videos. Hours and hours of them. It'll wait until tomorrow. "Thank you, Karen."

Yenchenko and Charlie toasted each other. Vodka, bourbon. Ce—

sar advanced the throttles and the jet began to roll, three and a half minutes after she crossed the tarmac. Across from her, Tommy's contented smile. She closed her eyes and imagined the tower saying, *two-two-six, cleared for takeoff.*

CHAPTER FIFTEEN

Billy's Tavern, Jacks Ford, Pennsylvania

Tommy stepped through a battered gray-green door. *Attaboy. Just drop them shades a couple of times.* A few blinks and the dim, hazy light of the bar came up to full on. Like stepping into old man Babineaux's grocery, back in the time when the boys on the porch'd call him T-Tommy, mostly on account he was a scrawny kid, still itching for his first icy bottle of Jax, but nearly two years after his first smoke. In to fetch an orange drink, slip back out front and look tough, leaning on a post, taking in the tales.

The men talked soft and sipped shine from Gator Thibodeaux's still, ten miles out in the swamp. A good notch above a Jax beer, but way beyond a kid who still had to refer to the grocer as *Mister* Babineaux, at least to his face. Fifty yards down the road, everybody called him Greasy, same as the men on the crowded porch.

Had to stand on that porch, too. It had a bunch of rockers and old kitchen chairs, one of which was always occupied by one of Greasy's two raggedy old hounds, Booray and Podna. One day, T-Tommy craved a regular chair because his butt was sore from falling off a tree. The old timers chuckled. *You want yo'self a spot, you move the dawg.*

Now Tommy stared into another bar. Billy's. Not quite as good as Greasy's, but for a Yankee bar, it'd do. A tartan den, muted by a per—petual nicotine fog. One of the last places in the state that didn't care squat about smoking laws. A workingman's refuge. A sportsman's den. Kind of like stepping into a duck blind with a twenty-two and a prayer. Beer and bourbon. The fancy city drinks? They were for Sat—

urday nights, when the place welcomed the ladies for a night on the town.

He hung his jacket on a rack already stuffed with the favorites of a dozen regulars, cuffs frayed, big patches of laborer's stains providing a camo effect without the dye.

It was oddly quiet. An antique Wurlitzer jukebox was pulled away from the wall and the legs of Andy Karr, twisted into a contorted line, extended from the opening.

Half a dozen of the gaunt and whiskered guys guarded cigarettes tucked into ashtrays and rationed shots of cheap bourbon. In their day, they were hard men, wiry and mean, loggers and miners and rail—road guys. Now the pensioners stared into distant memories of better times. As shadows, they arrived early and left early to fill empty days with a routine as steady as the hum of dirtied gears in a plastic Bud—weiser clock that dangled like a gaudy spider over the cash register.

Andy was twenty, maybe twenty-one, out of a tech school some—where near Scranton and had come back to town to snag a repair job at Frank's Appliances on Railroad Avenue. Lately, he spent more time on the plank floor behind the jukebox than the old ones, the boys de—voted to killing time at the bar before drifting to sad little houses scat—tered along the graveled path and rusting rails of a more prosperous era.

Toward the back, a loose ring of chairs had formed around one of the tables, in the center of which Charlie and Sergei held court. Yenchenko was the new guy, the one with fresh perspectives on one of the three golden topics in the tavern: football, hunting and fishing. Eight or nine of the Legion boys listened with occasional solemn nods and periodic mumbled questions, broad bellies oozing over hidden belt buckles. And, as usual, strangling Marlboros between thick fin—gers or chewing cigars into shaggy blends of tobacco and spittle. The law said it was a public place and nobody was supposed to smoke, but the law was fifteen or twenty miles down the road and Billy's lived by its own code, rules known only to those who gathered to escape a po—litically-correct world. One of those rules was good country music, the old and favorite tunes, played over and over for quarters on a bust—ed Wurlitzer jukebox.

Andy Karr came up for air, fear and anxiety in his eyes. "Oh. Hi, Mister Kane."

"Tommy. Everybody calls me Tommy. Still no luck with the juke— box?"

Andy's eyes fell. "No, sir. I'm kind of thinking it's hopeless. They don't make parts for this model any more, I can't patch the stuff that's in there, and Billy's gonna be really pissed about it."

Tommy glanced toward the bar and followed the line to the bar- tender, wiping and stacking glasses, trying to hear the fishing talk. "Maybe so, but he'll have to accept that it's time for a replacement. They still make those things?"

"Yessir. Now they're all digital, the music even. Still have the same look, but, um, you know how it is."

Yeah. Technology. New-fangled. Pricey. Probably made in China and'll fall apart next week. "I can break the news for you if you'd like."

Andy went pensive and pulled himself to his feet and dusted off his hands. He was slight and thin in the way a lot of young guys are be- fore too many burgers, too many beers, too many miles. "Thanks, Mister Kane — "

"Tommy."

" — Yessir, but Frank says I've got to learn to, well, you know..."

Yeah. Stand up for yourself. Like the day I was hired out to clean Gator's ol' fourteen gauge side-by-side and the damn thing went off, blowing out a window at Greasy's store. Scared right down to my socks. But Babineaux said the scattergun shouldn't have been left loaded and was right behind me when I stood up to old man Gator Thibodeaux, went from boy to bro'. The day they first called me podna.

Andy gathered up an assortment of tools and dropped them into a canvas kit bag.

Tommy said, "C'mon. I'll buy you a beer. Billy's always in a better mood when there's cash money on the bar."

Andy glanced at his watch and looked at Tommy. "It's a little ear— ly."

"Bar's open for a reason, Andy. Grab your gear, take a break."

With trepidation at first, but with growing confidence, Andy gave Billy the sad news, taking punctuating sips from a glass of Yuengling draft. The bartender's eyes narrowed for a moment but saddened at realizing change in a world where there was too much change.

At last Billy turned to Tommy. "Jesus, this ain't good."

Tommy lowered his voice into gentle sympathy. "I know. It happens. But what can a guy do, right?"

"Whatcha think?"

"I'm thinking Andy here's probably got a point. I mean, the guy's been bustin' ass trying to get that machine back up, but it's starting to look like trying to patch up a bum boat."

"You think so?"

"Yeah, Billy, I think."

"Can't do without a jukebox, Tommy." He sighed and turned to Andy. "So, what's the damage gonna be? And how long?"

Andy seemed caught off guard for a moment, but pulled out a cell phone and called his boss. Billy mopped the already spotless bar with a towel and briefly looked up at Tommy.

Yeah, it's okay, don't worry about it. I got it.

Andy finished his call and put the phone away. "Wally says he can get a reconditioned unit for twenty-four-hundred or a brand new one for eighty-nine, depending on how much power you want in the speakers."

"Wurlitzer? Ain't much of a fan of them. They don't last."

Tommy laughed. "Yeah, not more than thirty or forty years, running all day long."

Andy said, "Um, it would be a Rock-Ola. You can get American Beauties, Jack Daniels, or Bubbling. All digital, holds thousands and thousands of songs. Takes dollar bills — "

"So no making change all the time?"

Tommy said, "Latest thing. Very tech." And he nodded in a faint gesture of approval.

Billy scratched his jaw. "Maybe you could get it down to eighty-three, eighty-four?"

Andy's eyes were firmer now and his posture more erect. "I can see what we could do..."

Billy asked, "You get a commission on that?"

"I, uh, I guess so."

Billy crossed his arms and nodded. "Okay, Andy, order the damn thing. Gimme a bubbler."

"Great! Yessir, right away." Andy thrust out an eager hand to shake on the deal.

Billy reciprocated. "Yeah, yeah. Now get the hell back to your shop and order my box. Losin' my ass with no sound in the bar." While Andy zoomed off, he tugged another round for Tommy and set it on a coaster. "Kids."

"Yeah."

"We was young once."

Tommy hoisted the glass and tipped a salute. "Yeah. We was."

Billy leaned back against a display of hard liquor and stuck a toothpick into his mouth. "So what's this about you running for may—or?"

"Not running for mayor. Not running for nothing."

"Talk around town about it."

"Not gonna happen. No way, no how."

"Folks is gettin' tired of Bob Ferguson anymore."

"Yeah, well, they can yawn some more." Tommy reached into his jeans and tugged out paper money, peeled off a few twenties and ordered a batch of sandwiches for the guys surrounding Charlie and Sergei.

Billy scooped up the twenties and dropped them into a cash register drawer that was never fully closed during the daytime hours to help reduce his sales tax burden. "Also heard you got some kinda girlfriend, a real looker. City girl. Staying up to your place."

Tommy sipped his beer and settled on a stool. "Lotta talk in a small town. How about those sandwiches, some chips maybe?"

Billy grunted. "Yeah, comin' right up."

Tommy lounged on the periphery of an earnest discussion of ferrules, tip action and cigar versus half wells grips. Charlie and Sergei had bonded over Winston flyrods in a good-hearted defense against the Orvis crowd and graphite enthusiasts generally. As a native of Montana, it was no surprise that Charlie leaned toward Winston gear, but the Ukrainian's fondness for the same brand brought them together in a standoff with all comers in the circle.

Cast-length bragging in the four and five-weight group alternated with admissions of backcasting hangups and broken tips, which seemed to especially plague Yenchenko. Besides recommending three section rods to rotate the tip sections, Charlie's counsel was to slow down and smooth out the stroke to avoid tailing loops, techniques that were generally lost on Tommy, waiting patiently for the bait of a platter of sandwiches and a free round of draft beer to dissolve the conversation.

Billy's presentation had the desired effect. The topic faded fast and the program adjourned to the bar and a free lunch. Tommy joined Sergei and Charlie, a pitcher of beer and a plate of half-slice sand—wiches in hand.

"Tommy don't fish worth a shit," Charlie said.

"You have lake, and yet... *Da, da.* Of course, Koshka. You are man with no patience. And *zhmot*. Stingy person who is too cheap to ap—preciate good equipment, eh?"

And utterly no interest in fishing, period. "Upkeep on the jet is ex—pensive. Especially the liquor supply when certain people are aboard."

Yenchenko broke out into unabashed laughter and even Charlie managed to chuckle.

The teasing turned to the absence of Mandy, but to Tommy's sat—isfaction lingered on the topic only briefly. "She's going through all that surveillance video from Lucy, frame by frame. Two trains, bunch of stops, three cameras at each, twenty-four frames a second."

"Damn," Charlie told his beer. "Better her'n me."

Yenchenko nodded, his expression one of somber appreciation. "Most tedious. So — "

Tommy took a bite of a smoked turkey with mayo, tomato and lettuce on a slice of rye. " — she wanted some concentration time and here I am."

Sergei shook his head. "Tossed out of own lair. Such a sad little wolf you are, *Koshka.*"

Tommy turned to Charlie. "Any news yet?"

The old marshal nodded. "Couple of cop buddies think a deputy named McKennan, Bobby McKennan, might be the inside guy on

Mandy's kidnapping. They say he was a pal of Phil Donatello, but they haven't seen him around lately. I got a call into some people I know at the service but ain't heard yet. Yeah, yeah, I know. This crap sometimes moves real slow, Tommy."

Tommy pulled the cell phone from his pocket. Charlie leaned back and looked around, anxious. Yenchenko caught it and hoisted an eyebrow.

Charlie said, "You're gonna start some talk showing you actually use that thing — "

Tommy shrugged as he pressed a spot on the phone. "Already got talk going. May as well make the six o'clock news. Lucy? Yeah, it's me. Can you check on a deputy U.S. marshal name of McKennan? Bobby, uh, probably Robert?"

Charlie nodded.

"Yeah, Robert McKennan, out of New York City." He pulled the phone away from his ear and took a sip of beer. "She's checking." Yenchenko reached for another sandwich. Tommy spoke to the phone. "Yeah, that's probably him. Really? Great, thanks. No, we're good. She's working on it. Yup, talk to you later. Bye." Charlie leaned forward to hear the report. "Your buddies haven't seen McKennan around because he retired, short notice, the day before Donatello was killed. Dropped out of sight."

Yenchenko sighed. "So. Traitor make escape, perhaps anywhere in America, maybe world. We reach poor conclusion, uh — how you say, *mertvii kinets'?*

"Dead end."

"*Da,* of course. End of useful trail. Dead end."

Charlie swallowed a hunk of sandwich with some sort of spicy sausage. He put a fist to the center of his chest, belched, and said to Tommy, "Serge might know a lot about flyrods, and he might be really good in a firefight, but he don't know shit about Lucy Tramanian."

Maybe not this time. It's a big world and this has got all the marks of a serious-money show. McKennan could be anywhere.

Yenchenko looked puzzled. Tommy explained. "Lucy Tramanian. Just about the last person you want hunting you."

CHAPTER SIXTEEN

Jacks Ford, Pennsylvania

Tommy's red pickup paused at the intersection of Oak Street and Railroad Avenue. And there it was, dangling from a cable that extend—ed from Ferguson's Hardware diagonally to a power pole. The blinker light. Or as folks at the diner called it, The Winking Lemon.

Mandy said, "It was a wonderful idea, getting out, into town, tak—ing a break. Thank you."

"The chamber of commerce says it's the right thing, show visitors a nice time."

"This is the second time in two days for you. Must be some sort of record. You're becoming a regular cosmopolitan, Tommy. A genuine man about town."

He grunted. "Aw, shucks, now you're gonna have folks talkin'. Reputation going down the tubes."

"*Viral.* Shared everywhere on social media."

He made a left onto Railroad Avenue and into downtown Jacks Ford. "Like a nasty case of stomach flu, which is sort of what social media is, eh? Charlie says it's where minds go to pass gas. And worse. But technically, Billy's is outside of town, so it doesn't exactly count."

Mandy took in the view. Railroad Avenue. Named for a short line logging railroad, the story went. And once upon a time a locomotive set the town on fire, burning most of it to the ground. After the tim—ber company vanished, the rails were alleged to be buried right in the asphalt. *The sort of legend and lore that gives a town character. Love it. I could so get used to this.* Like a snuggly pair of fuzzy slippers. *Kind of like coming home.* "So. Getting back to the blinker light..."

"Still a hot topic. Got an earful at Billy's yesterday. Right after mourning the dead jukebox and the fishing workshop hosted by Charlie and Sergei."

Twenty-one miles north and west, there was the tedium of the cabin chore from Lucy, leaning much too close to study images of New Yorkers. Sometimes blurry, unclear, bodies jammed together on platforms, looking for a little guy who walked like a duck. Moving from spot to spot in the cabin, never quite finding a point to settle, going bleary-eyed until this morning, after breakfast, the moment when she had enough and cried out "Argh!" in the most frustrated tone she could muster.

In her bag on the truck floor mat, the tablet, the only precious evidence she had on a trail of multiple murders and dark high-tech conspiracies. In Jacks Ford, it was all about a blinker light. Not that it was trivial. It was about threshold, and on Railroad Avenue it was a big deal.

Past Polinski's Apparel, where she bought her first pair of Carhartts and a dress that must have been a joke to Lucy. "They're getting along?"

Tommy sighed. "They're *fishermen.* The second they discovered they used the same brand of gear, the cold war evaporated, peace broke out all over the world."

Past the drugstore, the only place in town to buy cosmetics and even then it was a sampling of an ordinary brand. "That's nice."

Past Frank's TV and Appliances, where Charlie lived on the second floor, now with a giant Ukrainian who was very good at murdering cars.

And it *was* nice. Good to feel the warmth of town again, but from a more settled perspective. Instead of dazed disorientation in borrowed clothes and temporary outfits very off-the-rack, her own things now filling rods in ordered rows, the options familiar, the routine taking form. His place, so gently shared.

Cruising down Railroad Avenue. Tommy doing little waves with his hand off the steering wheel, people turning to look, wave back.

And, as before, into an open parking space, without a meter, in the middle of the day.

The Puffin Diner. A classic small-town grill meant to look like a railroad car but never ran the rails. Stainless steel, born in the late for— ties, early fifties maybe, but no one really knew for sure. An off-the-shelf neon sign proclaimed "Diner – Good Food." A reliable mooring in a sheltered cove. The social hub of a community of seventeen hun— dred. *Open a menu a couple days in a row, you're a regular.*

"So why do they call it the Puffin?" she had asked him the first time in town. "There's no sign — "

"No idea. Just is, always has been. Lexicon of locals. Some truths you accept for what they are."

After the hum of breakfast, before the buzz of lunch. After the merchants and professionals had gathered for ritual conversation be— fore fanning out along Railroad Avenue for another ordinary day. The lingering scent of kitchen grease. The soft clatter of diner china being washed, stacked and organized for burgers and subs and clubs. The gentle time when gray-haired patrons trickled in, assured of favorite spots and an affordable meal, what Frannie called her middle shift, not much in the way of tips but steady work for the guys in the kitchen.

Louie Rissland's broad body oozed well past the third stool and the greeting came from between hefty bites of a gooey-looking dan— ish. "Hey, Tommy," he said after gulping it down. "We gotta talk about that thing, right?"

"Right. One of these days."

Always the mysterious thing.

"Yeah. Good t'see ya."

"Have a good one."

"Yeah."

From the second booth, the eyes of Peter Lempka narrowed into his usual concern. "Tommy. Haven't seen you around the last few days."

"Out of town. Business trip."

Peter nodded toward Mandy.

"Hi, Mister Lempka," Mandy said with a wave and leaned past the side of the booth to pat Mrs. Lempka on the shoulder. "Hi, Miriam.

How's the historical society doing?"

Peter looked like he wanted to stand to greet her, but was trapped with a fork full of hash browns and his hand was balancing too much jam on a slice of rye toast. He gave up when Mandy gestured him to remain seated.

A slight woman with a grandmotherly smile, Miriam said, "Why, fine, Mandy. We're going to have a meeting next week, a social thing of sorts, at the library. You'd be most welcome."

Peter scowled. "Welcome to sell some raffle tickets. Always trying to raise money for some rusty artifact."

Miriam waggled a finger. "Shush, Peter. Mind your manners. You maybe the retired banker, but your political activism is not any less ridiculous."

Peter sighed impatience and turned his attention to Tommy. "Look, son, you sure can't run much of a campaign if you're always out of town."

Mandy cocked her head and looked at Tommy. "Campaign?"

"Well, for mayor, of course," Peter said.

Tommy chuckled through embarrassment. "Not running for may—or. Or anything else."

Peter stabbed at the air with his fork. "Lot of talk, Tommy. You'd be a fine mayor."

Miriam rolled her eyes and sighed. "I don't believe Tommy's in—terested in your pet topic, Peter."

Tommy said, "Thank you. Besides, the town's already got a may—or."

"Aw, hell. Bob Ferguson's time is done. Time for new blood, new direction. Folks are saying you ought to make a run."

"No thanks."

Miriam looked to Mandy and with an expression that showed a confidence being shared said, "It's about the blinker light. Again."

Peter snorted. "Damn right. The Winking Lemon. Again. Look, Tommy, first it's this newfangled blinker light we don't need. Next thing, they'll be putting in municipal sewers and water, raising taxes, pulling in a bunch of tourists and traffic and all. Getting to a point that a fellow can't retire in peace — "

Tommy sighed. "You *are* retired, Peter. Remember?"

Peter shook his head and the fluorescent light shimmered across his balding skull. "Retirement comes when a man sells out, moves to Florida for his golden years."

Tommy asked, "So why not sell and move?"

"Can't. Property values are going all to hell because of that damn blinker light. Real estate is an investment, Tommy. You should under—stand that. Young people, these days? Well, I don't know."

Miriam looked up, an expression of helplessness on her face.

"I'll give it some thought," Tommy promised.

"Selling out or running for mayor?"

Tommy raised his hands in resignation. "Both."

Peter glared for a moment and turned his attention back to his meal. "You do that, son. You do that."

"Well, I'm sure you young people are busy and we won't keep you any longer," Miriam said to Mandy. "Have a lovely day."

"Pleasure was all mine," Mandy replied and followed Tommy down the aisle.

More handshakes, more pauses, more snippets of conversation, a couple of offers to share a quarter of venison in exchange for permis—sion to hunt on Tommy's land, plus the news that Charlie and Sergei were off to a sporting goods store near State College, looking for reels.

At the second to last booth, Tommy paused and gestured an invi—tation to sit.

"I understand why you go this far down," she said while sliding onto the tufted red vinyl. "Nobody walks past to socialize while you're eating. Do you think we can find a place in town where I can pick up a proper notepad and pen? I've got to start taking notes."

Tommy settled into the opposite seat. "Drug store, probably. There used to be a little office supply place, but it closed last fall."

"Done in by the big chains?"

"Done in by death."

Frannie appeared with two mugs, a carafe of coffee and a smile. Her uniform was stained, already broken in for the day during the breakfast rush and her blonde hair in a messy bun tending more to—

ward messy than bun. "How's the town's most talked about couple do—ing today?"

Tommy sighed and reached for a menu.

"You've really got to bring her into town more often, Tommy."

So funny. But that's Frannie. "I'll never forget the day we met, when I was wearing an outfit you loaned Charlie so I'd have a change of clothes."

Frannie chuckled. "And I said 'you must be the new girl because I recognize my clothes' and you stood up..."

"And you said nobody stands up for a waitress..."

"And you said, 'I do.'"

Chuckles grew into giggles and were approaching laughter as Tommy rolled his eyes and struggled to concentrate on a menu.

Frannie took half a step back and studied Mandy. "But wow, look at you now. Those are some really fancy duds, girl. Tommy, you abso—lutely gotta get her into town more often, hear?"

Mandy said, "Actually, it's my fault. I've been holed up with this." She held the tablet aloft.

"Well, this is the right place. Look around. Used to be that folks would come in, talk about operations, funerals, politics and the price of gas, but now it's all poke and tap, trying to keep up with family by computer. Texts and tweets and social channels and whatnot." Fran—nie pulled an order pad from her apron pocket. "Enough. So. Tommy, how's life treating you? Or is that a real stupid question today?"

Tommy cracked open a pair of tiny creamer cups and chased it with three paper packets of sugar, all to take the edge off the Puffin's legendary coffee. "Doing fine, Frannie, just fine. Yourself?"

"One day at a time, better and better. You guys need a minute?"

Mandy opened her menu and her eyes raced through all the usual options. "Oh, gosh... Tommy, have you decided?"

Tommy spoke to Frannie. "Ernie got any of that waffle batter left?"

"The Puffin Special? For you, Tommy, absolutely."

He explained to Mandy. "They make these incredible waffles here. Waffles like nowhere else."

Frannie lowered her voice to share a confidence. "Ernie loads them up with rum. It's sort of a secret that everybody knows, except maybe Pastor Ed from the Community Church down the street, who wouldn't approve." She glanced at Tommy. "Although I sometimes think he does know, but doesn't want to admit it."

Tommy nodded. Mandy promised to keep it confidential.

"Two Puffin Specials? Comes with two eggs, bacon or sausage."

Mandy closed the menu. "Bacon. And if it's okay, scrambled eggs."

Frannie repeated the order. "And Tommy? Eggs up, sausage as usual?"

"No, not today. I'll go with the scrambled and the bacon."

Frannie cocked an eyebrow and, as she wrote, murmured, "Okay..."

When they were alone, Mandy stirred cream into her coffee. "Thank you."

"For...?"

"Bringing me into town for a second breakfast. I really needed a break. Don't get me wrong, it's a wonderful cabin, but..."

"Yeah, it's good to get into town for a change of scene. At least be−fore winter digs in hard. Okay. Florida. Sergei and I will run down to deal with McKennan. I know, I know. You want in." For several min−utes they parried, but it was a losing cause. The guys had made up their mind. "Trust me, this is not a time for us to worry about extra hands. Besides, you've got all that video on your plate."

Frannie arrived with platters of waffles, eggs and bacon.

Mandy brightened. "Oh, wow, this looks wonderful. Thank you."

"So can I ask what kind of work thing you're doing? I've been thinking about getting one of those tablet things for here, but I'm not sure. The new guy at Frank's TV has been suggesting it."

Tommy looked up. "Andy Karr?"

Frannie took a half step to the side. "Yep, over there at the counter, third from — "

"I know him. Nice guy."

Frannie nodded and refilled coffee cups, leaned in and spoke in a confidential tone. "Word is that he sold a really expensive new juke−box to Billy down to the tavern yesterday. Can you imagine? Billy?"

Tommy smiled and seemed astonished. "Amazing."

Mandy looked at him and cocked her head. "Yes. Isn't it?" She turned to Frannie. "Anyway. To give you an idea of how dull my work is, I've got tons of surveillance videos from the city that I have to slog through, one frame at a time, looking for a guy getting onto a sub—way."

"Really?"

It's an incredibly miserable task. "Yes. Really."

"You ought to get some extra sets of eyes, make it quicker."

Were it so simple. "I'm afraid it's just me."

Frannie shrugged and gestured toward the people in the booths and at the counter. "How about all these folks?"

"Uh, well, I, um, couldn't — "

"Trust me, Mandy, they're all killing time, looking for anything in the way of excitement. You'd be doing everyone a huge favor, some—thing to make their day special."

Tommy seemed intrigued. "Why not? I mean, you describe what Bennie looked like, make it kind of a game."

Frannie brightened. "Like bingo!"

"Winner gets a big prize," Tommy said. "Maybe a trip to visit family or whatever, all expenses. You know, *fly* anywhere."

Mandy drummed her fingertips on the table. "You're both joking, right?"

Tommy and Frannie exchanged glances of incredulity.

Okay, they are serious. Still, to share the files with everyone... "But how — "

Frannie grinned. "Andy will know." She turned and called out, "Hey, Andy! Got a sec?"

CHAPTER SEVENTEEN

Bay Street, Panama City Beach, Florida

Lousy coffee. Cold, in a paper cup. In a deserted parking lot. In the faint blue light, before dawn. Deserted streets, silent sidewalks. And the ghostly masts of sailboats, stabbing at the sky, as still as Yenchenko, dozing in the passenger seat. *Yeah. This line of work is a whole lotta fun.*

Tommy began to take another sip through the plastic lid. *Enough.* He dropped the container into a cup holder and planned to deposit it in a nearby trash bin when he could stand the stiffness in his legs no longer.

As night eased into day, Tommy's attention floated through the masts, mostly singles, but occasionally paired on a ketch. Barely visible and partly hidden by a bushy palm tree, two thin vertical lines sug—gested a yawl. *The Alden I never found. The dream that started all of this.* His eyelids drooped and images of Sandy and Doc and Duffy drifted through his mind. Doc, somewhere in Mexico. Duffy, back in Ireland, the bar gone, not long after the day Yenchenko rolled in and made the case to rob a couple of million dollars from Cuban army officers deal—ing narcotics. And Sandy, the kid with the forty-two foot Morgan. Who knows where, but on a boat, and free. He revived the half-baked scheme to buy an Alden and go roaming. *A fifty footer. A totally idiotic idea because Aldens are hard to find, even harder with the empty wallet I had back then.*

But now.... The hum of Bug's special phone kicked him out of a yawn and he blinked to focus on the shimmering name on the screen.

Mandy.

Hard not to smile, eager to touch the phone and make the connection.

"Hey," she said, her voice soft and husky and soothing all at once, a voice that conjured the sensation of her fingers in his hair, on his cheek.

"Hey. What a really great way to start the day."

"Aw, sweet. You guys doing okay?"

Sergei yawned and stretched.

"Yep, kind of hanging out in a dinky little parking lot at the marina, waiting for our guy to actually show. Looks like you made a really good call, putting McKennan with Donatello's mention of partnering up with a buddy."

"Thanks. And I wasn't even paying half attention. More reporter in me than I thought."

Probably first rate intelligence potential. Analyst material. "So everything all right? You're okay?"

"I *am*. Well, I think. Charlie's here, and he decided to take pity on the coffee-and-danish city girl and make some sort of proper breakfast. I'm kind of staying out of the way. Armed with a fire extinguisher."

Tommy chuckled. "Another good call."

"Just remember, McKennan is about six-two, two-thirty, maybe two thirty-five, military-type haircut. Charlie says to be careful. But you have Sergei."

"Exactly. And no offense to Charlie, but a deputy marshal against Yenchenko is no contest."

"Just take care, okay? I want you back in one piece."

Tommy sighed. "It's only an interview. Not exactly World War Three. I think I see our guy coming."

Mandy said, "Charlie's getting breakfast onto plates and it actually looks pretty decent."

"From Charlie?"

"Yup. You've got competition, pal. Hurry home to defend your honor."

"Sure thing."

Sergei was alert and checking the clip in a military-issue nine mil‐
limeter automatic. He chambered a round and slipped it back into a
shoulder holster.

"And, uh, Tommy? Is it okay to say I, um, well, miss you?"

Nice. Really nice. "You just made my whole day. Okay, gotta go,
get to work."

Sergei flexed his fingers and with light field glasses tracked Bobby
McKennan as he strolled along Bayview on the sidewalk closest to the
marina. "What is plan, Koshka?"

"Let's let him get out onto the pier where he keeps his boat. I'll
have a talk with him. You hang back, keep civilians off the pier. We're
only interested in who hired him to set up Mandy's kidnapping, that's
it."

"Da, of course, if this is all you wish." He tapped the side of his
forehead. "But inside voice says this seems much too easy. We must
be cautious."

McKennan drew closer and for a minute was hidden from view by
a red SUV that had driven slowly along the road and pulled over near
the lone pedestrian. Directions, maybe. Warning, maybe. But proba‐
bly directions, someone lost or looking for a charter they'd hired.

"Let's follow him out into that parking area, keep the distances
short."

Yenchenko nodded.

McKennan passed a little zig-zag in the plank sidewalk and
reached a stop sign. He looked across the street, to the building next
to the parking area where Tommy and Yenchenko froze.

He's either sensed something and is stalling for a look-around or
he's thinking about coffee, maybe breakfast.

McKennan peeked at his watch, lingered for a moment, turned
onto the parking area sidewalk, past a pipe railing.

Too early for the restaurant. Tommy started the car, backed out
of the space and crept onto Bayview, turned left and right into the
long parking lot that sheltered the marina from the bay beyond.

"Slowly, Koshka, slowly."

At about a hundred and fifty feet, McKennan paused to talk to a
guy coiling rope on the second pier, close to the breakwater. Tommy

pulled into one of the parking spaces to wait until the target resumed his walk. The rental car backed up and rolled forward at a couple of miles per hour.

Second pier. Smaller boats, including the one that looked like the Alden in daybreak light but turned out to be a pair of sailboats in slips that lined up perfectly to create the illusion for a memory.

McKennan stepped out onto the pier.

Tommy parked and together they got out of the car. Yenchenko hung back, taking the role of the guy watching the gear while his part—ner looked for the day charter they'd hired.

McKennon slowed up at a slip two thirds of the way down the pier.

Tommy called out. "Mister McKennan?"

McKennan turned. "What can I do for ya?"

"Interested in a charter."

McKennan shrugged. "You found one. How many in the party?"

"Just two of us." Tommy strode forward, the sun behind him, low in the sky.

McKennan held a hand above his brow. "Yeah, sure, no problem."

"That your boat?"

He reflexively turned to look, checking in case it wasn't. When he turned back, Tommy stood close. "Yeah, sure. That's mine. So what are you and your buddy after today? They're running pretty good just offshore."

Tommy focused on the boat and stepped past McKennan. "Wow. Nice boat. What is it, thirty, thirty-two feet?"

His eyes narrowed. "Thirty-six."

"A Bayliner, twin inboard diesels, about 18 knots, right?"

"You know your boats, my friend."

"Looks nearly new. Bet it cost a bundle. Been chartering for long?"

"You ask a lot of questions, buddy."

Nice, easy, relaxed grin. The sensation of the Beretta in the small of his back was firm against his body, hidden by a light nylon wind—breaker. "Yep. Yep, that's for true. Everybody says that."

"You some kinda cop? If you are, you oughta know I'm — "

Now a nice, wry, smile. " — No longer on the job, Bobby. You were a deputy marshal, but now you're only an ex-cop with a boat, am I right?"

McKennan eased into a tense posture, his legs slightly apart, his arms up, the muscles in his neck tightening. "You're messing with the wrong guy, pal."

Tommy nodded and sighed. "Yeah, probably so. That's why I brought a little help."

McKennan's tall body whirled and looked into, then up at, Sergei Yenchenko. He began to reach into his jacket but froze when Tommy pressed the barrel of the Beretta between his shoulder blades.

"Don't."

McKennan's hands slowly rose into the air and Yenchenko collect—ed the hardware, a Smith and Wesson forty-caliber, and cleared the chamber.

"So what the hell do you guys want, anyway? If this is some kinda roust, you're making a big mistake. And I sure's shit don't got nothing of value aboard."

Tommy nodded and he and Yenchenko each took a step back.

Easy smile, confident, comforting. "No big deal, Bobby. We heard you were planning on partnering up with a guy in New York — a cop, Phil Donatello, a cop who was going to retire, set up a little charter op down here, cruise into the sunset."

McKennan glanced both ways.

Don't even think about running.

McKennan folded. "Yeah, well, it didn't work out."

Tommy nodded. "It didn't, mostly because Phil Donatello got killed."

"Didn't have nothin' to do with that."

"Something about a witness?"

"Maybe."

Tommy sighed impatience and spoke to Yenchenko. "He's not be—ing helpful. You were right, Serge, that he'd be a problem and you'd have to break a couple of bones." Returning attention to McKennan, he continued. "Sorry, Bobby. I guess it's just not gonna be your day."

McKennan held a hand up higher. "Just hold it, now. So okay, we were doing a witness, some broad Phil was handling, and some guys come to me and said it's worth a hundred — a hundred grand — for each of us if we look the other way this one time."

"So Donatello was in on the deal?"

McKennan's eyes fell. "Nah. I didn't find out until after they croaked him, some kinda accident. He was an old juicer and they made it look like he was saucing again."

Yenchenko rubbed his chin.

Sergei's about a half a second from taking McKennan apart for turn-coating a partner. Make it work for me. "You ought to know that my partner here is a special ops guy, right out of Russian military in–telligence, working with us in D-I-A, and nobody gives a rat's ass whether you leave this pier alive. And worse for you, Sergei hates guys who screw over their partners."

McKennan used the back of his hand to rub his nose. "Look, it's not like you think. The people running the op were some government alphabet agency, some kind of contractor field crew on a case, and they had Phil down as some kind of mole. When they handed me a bag with the money, they said it included his share, not to say a word, get the hell out."

"And the witness?"

A bend of fear and sadness filled his eyes. "They snatched her on a shift change and re-lo, after we left the hotel. I don't know what hap–pened to her."

Tommy paused with an exchange of facial gestures involving Yenchenko, designed to convey a growing sense of trust. He said, "Yeah, well, we got her back okay, and now we're running down ev–eryone involved. That includes you, Bobby."

McKennan stepped back, his eyes showing panic. "Hey, c'mon." He bumped into Yenchenko, who unceremoniously shoved him for–ward again, toward the gun in Tommy's hand leveled at Bobby's belly.

"I need names, Bobby."

"Jesus Christ, I'm tellin' you, I don't know. I saw some ID, some badge, but, shit, it didn't register. I got twenty years in, man. I got an ex-wife and alimony and shit and now all I got is this boat and I gotta live with the fact that I fucked up and a good friend of mine is fucking dead." He began to blubber, a wilting shell of a cop who'd screwed up big time and was jammed up on a long and lonely pier at an insignificant marina in a tacky town in Florida. *And he's more scared than tough.*

Yenchenko shrugged.

Yeah. Dead end. This guy's got nothing.

Tommy scratched his ear and rubbed his jaw. "Okay, Bobby, this is how it's gonna be. We're gonna check out what you said, and if you've been straight with us, fine, you go your way and you live with it. But, man, if you're not being straight, the guys you did business with'll be the last of your problem. I hope you have dental records on file somewhere."

McKennan's nod was meek, subdued, totally beaten down.

Tommy stuck his piece back into his belt and put his hands on his hips, took a deep breath an exhaled. "Yeah, yeah, okay." He gestured toward the boat to direct McKennan to go aboard. "Have a nice day, Bobby."

Yenchenko shook his head.

Tommy nodded and looked up and away, across Sergei's shoulder, toward a tall building. On Bay Street. Just outside the marina.

Something metallic, catching the light. On a balcony. Sixth floor.

McKennan, disappearing into the boat. Sergei, puzzled look.

A flash.

Smoke. Streaming light.

Tommy yelled, "Water!"

Sergei, turning.

Incoming. Screaming. Grenade.

Falling, tumbling, off the pier.

Fireball.

CHAPTER EIGHTEEN

Williamsport Regional Airport, Montoursville, Pennsylvania

The marshaller brought his arms together above his head. On a tarmac darkened to near black from an icy drizzle whispering through a gray, sad, winter sky, the aircraft halted.

Charlie and Mandy stood in somber silence as the engines wound down to a mournful whine and, like her, wore a long, dark coat, no umbrella. The steps unfurled.

Oh, Tommy. Tommy...Tommy.

At the first sight of Karen in the doorway, Mandy burst forward, brushing past the ground guys, racing for any sense of hope, fleeing choking uncertainty and the fear of loss.

Oh, Tommy. Please.

He appeared in the doorway. A gasp of relief. A gasp of shock. Tired, beat up, worn out. A giant bandage across his forehead. Such a brave little wave. Her body, up and down, quivering with excitement and joy, her hands to her lips, palms together.

Oh, Tommy. A deep, full, exhilarating breath. *Tommy.*

He was barely off the last step when she was in his arms, clinging to delight, her face pressed tight against the security of his chest, tears on her cheeks. The bandage. Ominous. But up close, not so terrifying.

He said, "Wow. Nice to see you, too."

She gasped a laugh and lightly pounded a fist on his shoulder. "Oh, you. I was so scared... we heard all about it from Lucy, who by the way is really unhappy with you putting yourself on the line like that, but there were no details. All we heard was you were both hurt,

hurt bad."

"Karen did a good job patching us up."

Sergei. "And Sergei? Is he — " She leaned left to see.

Yenchenko stepped onto the tarmac and raised his arm to display a bandaged fist. He grinned. "So, no hug for poor Sergei?"

Mandy laughed. She clung to Tommy's hand, but did her best to reward Yenchenko with a one-armed embrace while Charlie stepped toward the huddle.

"*Da, da.* Is most suitable."

Charlie snorted. "Don't even think about gettin' one outa me."

Yenchenko straightened as if startled by the implausibility of the remark. "Of course. We are comrades, eh? We must find good food, much drink, warm place to tell story of hunt."

Karen lingered near the steps, her perpetual smile still functioning even as the weather deteriorated. "So," she said at the first convenient moment, "is everyone okay?"

Mandy stepped closer. "Thank you *so* much. For everything."

"My pleasure."

"Say, why don't you join us? I mean, if you're free and have no plans..."

Karen's smile expanded. "That's very kind. But actually I have a cousin outside of Williamsport. He and Cesar are good friends. He flies thirty-sevens, usually out of Newark, and he's got a rare layover. So we'll do a full shutdown here and — "

Mandy asked, "You're sure?"

Karen nodded and patted Mandy's arm. "Have a wonderful evening."

Mandy grinned. "Oh, yes. I'm sure we will."

* * *

Tommy's den had never been warmer. A stack of logs crackled and sizzled, ablaze in the massive stone fireplace, warming bones and cheeks and spirits, too, filling the room with golden security and set-ting the stage for the tale of adventure.

On the big, fluffy sofa, she curled up close to Tommy. Under her cheek, fuzzy green flannel, barely muting the pulsing, strong, steady heartbeat from his chest. He'd stretched out, one arm around her shoulder, the other across the back of the sofa, his feet resting on the coffee table.

They'd cracked open a bottle of very old Gran Duque d'Alba and filled crystal brandy snifters without restraint to banish the chill and lingering anxiety. To the left, Charlie, the sportsman's bar bourbon man, now sipped with a gentleman's class. To the right, Sergei the vodka inhaler, his huge hand smothering the snifter, but even he was being well-mannered in the presence of brandy that probably ran a few hundred dollars a bottle. Empty plates and a platter, the fin—ger-food gone amid an exchange of stories traded by Charlie and Sergei, littered the tables. An old cop, an old soldier, years of adven—ture and harrowing legacies, back and forth, fireside entertainment as it was always supposed to be.

A couple of weeks ago, I would have thought this display of affection em—barrassing. But now? Natural, routine, ordinary. And everyone seemed to understand, no teasing, no smirks, no ho-ho-ho. The sensation of security — a curious blend of soothing and exhilarating and it was im—possible to imagine when she hadn't felt this way.

Charlie asked some sort of question and Sergei leaned forward, the brandy sloshing almost to the rim when he waved his arm to make a point. "So this small *svoloch*, this bastard, he prefer not to be helpful and *tovarich* Tommy — "

Tommy grinned and interrupted. "Who has always been called *Koshka* — "

" — *Da, da,* it is so."

Charlie swallowed a sip of brandy. "And what'n hell does that mean?"

Mandy chuckled. "Little kitten." She patted Tommy on the chest. "And not because he's so cute and adorable, but because — " She ges—tured to Sergei to elaborate.

Yenchenko sat up, his chest fluffed out with pride and his finger—tips upon it. " — Because Tommy is not so superior as myself, Sergei

Ilyich Yenchenko, who is always one small pace of boot ahead of sad, little *Amerikanski. Da,* comrade Charlie."

Charlie grunted and glanced at Tommy. "Find that a bit of a stretch." The snifter came to his lips and he drank again.

Tommy gestured indifference with his free hand.

"But now Sergei becomes like old wolf, not so cautious. He stands with back to only place of ambush like old *vanka* — idiot person of village — when entire situation goes all to shit."

Charlie cocked an eyebrow.

Yes. I really want to know exactly what happened.

With all the mastery of a champion story-teller, Sergei gave his re—port, how Tommy had called the correct warning, how they'd tum—bled into the water on the opposite side of the pier. The blast went over their heads. "So. We are in such hurry to get into water, there is no time for good breath. In few moment, we must surface, eh? But too early. Pieces of boat come down like hard summer rain." He smacked his injured hand on his thigh several times for effect. "Small piece land on Tommy's head, make cut."

Charlie asked, "And your hand?"

Sergei grunted. "Tommy of course is not so fast to duck. Sergei sees large piece of boat and try to catch it, but light is poor and I make small error." He studied the bandaged paw he'd used to pound on this thigh. "Some bruise, but it does not seem to be broken."

Mandy looked up at Tommy. "How big was the chunk that hit you?"

A shrug rippled through his shoulders. "No idea. I didn't have a ruler handy."

Yenchenko sighed disdain. "Most unfortunate. Perhaps you are still *Koshka,* eh?" He roared with laughter at his own joke, and when he calmed, he held his glass aloft toward Tommy. "To my good friend and comrade Tommy Kane. To you, I owe my life."

Glasses went up.

Tommy said, "Any time, buddy."

"Hear, hear," Charlie said.

Mandy studied Tommy's profile. *Yes, the bashful look. Aw shucks, no big deal, nothing that anyone else wouldn't have done.* A sensation of pride flooded through her and the heat in the room seemed to rise several degrees. "Nicely done, Tommy. Elegant, even. So, um, after you got blown up....?"

Yenchenko shrugged and spoke in a voice suggesting it was an-other routine day in the produce department at the local supermarket. "Most simple. We make swim to end of pier, get from water, prepare field dressing and drive to airport."

Charlie's tone was quiet admiration. "Damn. Busted up hand and all that."

"Flight attendant is good nurse, make good repair."

"Maybe you oughta get the local doc to have a look at it."

Mandy whispered to Tommy. "Same goes for your head."

She and Charlie finished a long pause by looking at each other.

He said, "Don't reckon that's gonna happen."

Mandy sighed. "You might be right."

Charlie swirled the last of the brandy in his glass and tossed it into his throat. "Fire's gettin' down. And we oughta hit the road, Sergei. Long drive to town."

Yenchenko finished his drink and stood. "*Da, da.* It is so. I fix fire."

Charlie was on his feet. "Naw, I'll get it. You got a bum hand."

Yenchenko protested and within seconds they were at the hearth and began to compete for the honor. Sergei had the tools, but Charlie held the logs.

"Nah, nah, now you're doin' it all wrong. You gotta get deeper in there and — "

Sergei stabbed at the bed coals with ferocity. "I am expert at such things. You need two more log to make good fire."

"This here's more'n enough, dammit."

"Two more."

Charlie reached toward the cache of firewood and muttered, "Damn Russian."

In unison, three voices called out. "Ukrainian!"

"Yeah, yeah, whatever."

Mandy chuckled and turned to Tommy. "Are they always like

this?"

"*Always.*"

The entire room shimmered, a charming dream, wrapping around like a comfy old blanket. "Ah. Kind of cute, actually."

Tommy grunted so softly that she felt it more than heard it. "G'night guys."

Yenchenko snatched logs from Charlie's arm and tossed them into the fireplace. As they ignited, he stood back in satisfaction. "Is good. Now you have nice fire for most romantic evening, eh?"

Charlie rolled his eyes and shook his head at Yenchenko's audacity. "Let's get the hell outa here."

The farewells, the fading good-natured bickering, the flare of the fire when the kitchen door opened and the chill of passing outside air. And quiet. An amazing, peaceful silence. The tick of the clock in the kitchen. The crackle of the fire. *Rest.*

A dozen drowsy minutes drifted past before she said, "We should tidy up, wash the dishes and things."

"Later."

"Okay."

Drowsy, dreamy, soft. Another couple of minutes disappeared.

"Tommy?"

"Hm?"

"You *do* realize that we're sticking together from here on out, right?"

He took a breath. "Like I said. It's dangerous. People, good peo‒ ple, can get killed doing this kind of stuff. We nearly proved that."

"I know. But being separated, not knowing? Much worse. Trust me. I'd rather take my chances."

"Can't talk you out of it?"

"No. Sorry, but I don't quit. *Not ever.* So, too bad, I'm afraid you're stuck with me. In fact, we have to go back to New York. I know where Benny got on the subway, and we need to find out from Alan Rothstein at the Fed exactly what was going on before ‒ "

He was more alert, interested,. The time of proximity evaporated.

"You had a winner?"

"I did. Martha Wescott — you remember, the lady who always comes in with a couple of the most outrageous friends — "

"Three booths from the cash register. Short kind of reddish hair, a little on the — "

Mandy sat up and swirled the last of her brandy in her glass. "Yes. It was so funny. I had half the diner working the M trains and other half the F. She literally called out 'Bingo!' and she was so proud when she pointed to her phone. There he was, getting on the F train at Prospect Park, near the traffic circle at Fifteenth Street. Time stamped and everything. It makes sense because he was headed toward the northbound and I think he lives way uptown. So the question is, what's so special about Prospect Park?"

Tommy began to stack plates. "Sounds like we're going to have to find out. Where does Martha want to go?"

Mandy joined the task of cleaning up. "She wants to take her friends to one of those movie theme parks in Florida. She's a widow and the other two are divorcees, family scattered and evidently not close. I guess it's a bucket list kind of thing."

Tommy grinned. "Absolutely. First class, all expenses, the time of their lives, whenever they want."

"Thank you. It'll mean a lot to her."

"What about this guy at the Fed?"

"Media guy. He was the one who kept shifting the appointment I had with the late chairman, who apparently was already dead. I need to see if there's some sort of connection between Benny and Martin Silverman."

Tommy nodded. "Long shot."

"I know. Maybe Silverman's stroke was, like Lucy said, a coincidence. The chances of those two knowing each other? I can't get there. Something doesn't feel right." She took a sip and looked deep into Tommy's eyes. "You know what it's like. An itch you can't quite scratch."

"We can't risk another apartment in New York. And I don't want Lucy anywhere near the action."

She took a sip of brandy. *Off the wall, but try.* "Maybe we could commute?"

He studied the fireplace for several seconds and turned back, with a reassuring, casual, confident smile. "That's what jets are for, isn't it?"

CHAPTER NINETEEN

Prospect Park, Brooklyn, New York

On a park bench in the eye of a traffic circle, Mandy leaned forward, her head tilted slightly left, right, left again. On her lap, one hand lay atop the other and periodically her index finger tapped impatience, pointed in imagined directions, oblivious to the chill and the song of passing traffic.

She's thinking, sifting ideas, hunting possibilities. Staring in the direction of Prospect Park West, but her mind probably retracing steps in the park. Her brow furrowed, relaxed and furrowed again as she glanced toward Fifteenth Street and back to the front. Her right hand rose and her fingertip lightly tapped her lip. *Yeah. Just about time to discuss the situation.* Compare notes. Brainstorm if she wants.

She sighed. "Okay, it was a long shot, a dumb idea."

"Not at all. When it's the only solid lead you have, that's where you start."

"We've been all over this park and there's nothing. *Nothing.*" Her eyes tracked several passing cars. "This couldn't be more appropriate. Cars going in circles, the way we seem to be."

She fluffed out her hair and stretched. The chirp of the secure cell phone interrupted. "Hi, Lucy. Anything? I understand. No, I don't want to see it. Please thank Charlie for me. No, we're stalled, sitting on park benches near some sort of war memorial like a couple of lost tourists. Yep. Okay, bye."

Doesn't sound optimistic. First stop had been the Federal Reserve Bank, barely into business hours, on familiar turf to her. Straight to

the executive offices on the upper floor, into a posh, conservative re—
ception area. Fairly firm confrontation with the receptionist, half
school marm, half bureaucrat, still on the job, guardian of the gate —
despite the change in occupancy of the big dog on the other side of an
office door most working stiffs'd like to have. The curt response, the
call for help. He'd half expected a couple of security guards when she
pressed hard, more from exasperation than annoyance. Instead, a
smiling guy in a crisp suit, a nameless guy from public relations, had
ushered them to a quiet corner to defuse a showdown with a no-non—
sense media gal, forged credentials dangling from her neck. *The Clockmaker did nice work. Would have fooled even me.*

The media guy's face went mournful, the news sad. Poor Mister
Rothstein had passed away, injuries from some sort of terrible mug—
ging in Soho, the details a bit sketchy, but it was a police matter, there
was nothing more to say, and was there anything else he could help
with. *The guy was good. Put us in a corner and herded us right out the door.
Probably a future in politics. Poor Alan.*

In the traffic circle, Tommy crossed his arms. *Looking weary, worn
down.* He hung a question mark on a cocked eyebrow.

Mandy hung up and shook her head. "Alan was indeed killed day
before yesterday, in an alley near a gay bar in Soho. Charlie got some
details from a couple of homicide detectives working the case, no sus—
pects yet other than it was three men. Lucy tracked down a copy of
surveillance video and wanted to know if I was interested in seeing it."
She looked away and sighed. "And I said no. Just can't bear to even
think about it, Tommy."

"I understand."

She turned back. "That's five. It's getting to be more than coinci—
dence. What in the world is going on?"

"No idea. My experience with conspiracy theorists is that when
they've got nothing but speculation, they huddle up with others on
the same wavelength. But when they get an actual scrap of evidence,
no matter what shape or form, they start tugging on shirtsleeves to
share the news."

"With the media?"

"Yep. Or assets they perceive as a handler or potential handler. It's all a matter of justifying whatever notion they think is true. If they're into cloak and dagger, they'll try to play the espionage strategy, but it usually turns out to be a kind of silly cold approach that screams 'amateur.' Trust me, it can get pretty embarrassing when you're out in the field and some clown comes rushing up with a secret map to a cache of nuclear weapons. Or the king's stash of Twinkies."

That brought a smile, a tension relaxer, a friendly roll of the eyes.

"Okay, Mister Big Time Spy, this experienced investigative journalist has been combing an enormous city park for anything that Benny might have been involved with, but whoever or whatever it was, it's gone now. Just a bunch of people walking dogs, riding bikes, jogging, normal stuff. I'm cold and tired and really hungry, so if you have any thoughts — "

Not as gone as she thinks. Some habits never go away. He leaned into the conversation, resting his forearms on his thighs and gestured with his hands. "Maybe."

"You're going to show me up, aren't you?"

"Not at all. It's your op, but I'm your partner, okay?"

"Okay. Sorry, it's been — "

"Frustrating, I know. I was thinking back about people we saw, people we asked if they knew anything. And there were those five guys, the ones hanging around that area where the big mob of joggers came through."

She turned to look. "Exactly. They didn't fit the pattern of the park users. But when we started to get closer to them, they left."

"Opposite directions. At the time I thought maybe another drug deal, kind of a group discount thing. But..." He paused.

"But what?"

"The pair of guys is on the sidewalk, your ten o'clock, headed toward the street you were staring at."

Mandy began to track them as they scurried along. One glanced in their direction, furtive but obvious, and picked up pace.

Time to take charge for a moment. Low, steady, serious tone. "Okay, look at me, smile, like I told a funny joke and you don't care who they are. I'll keep an eye on them. Yeah, like that. Terrific smile, always—"

"I feel silly. You're not paying attention to me."

"Just stay with the game. Okay they're going down the street right in front of us."

"Should we follow them?"

"Yeah, but loose. Okay, let's go. Our little encounter is winding down and now we're thinking maybe a coffee or something."

She stood and played the role of the adoring girlfriend. "I know I'm supposed to look all kinds of goo-goo romantic, but a coffee doesn't cut it. I need some serious lunch."

Broad smile, light laughter. "Sit-down with a waitress but no reservation or some sort of a deli thing on the fly?"

"Doesn't matter. Are we good to go yet? I feel like an actress stuck in a bad commercial shoot."

Quick hug, light kiss, just for show, but still... "Yep, we're good. Let's go for the west side of the street. They've skipped some sort of a nice looking little place, maybe going for something in the next block."

Mandy laughed, genuine this time. "Organizing lunch is a ball with you, Tommy. You know what? I'd love to ask for the Espionage Special with the Black Ops salad."

* * *

A genuine Brooklyn deli came complete with a flirtatious counter guy, fifty maybe, thinning black hair combed straight back, tall, food-stained whites, the name Big Tony embroidered on the chef's jacket.

She's got three ways to deal with this. Be totally annoyed, chilly, offend-ed. Be totally complimented, the way models and acting wannabes crave to stroke an ego, make the clown's day. Or have a little fun and work him like a puppy on a leash.

The counter guy beamed with the same lecherous smile pudgy middle-aged guys save up for moments like this, and for a while she teased back with the sort of warm and sassy smile she saved up for pudgy middle-aged guys like him. A casual sort of fun, lasting long enough to order hot capicola and prosciutto heros, two egg creams.

A thirty-dollar tip helped fill in the blanks about regulars, the conspiracy guys, who congregated at the park and drifted in for loosies and lunch. Two of whom were huddled at a postage-stamp table in the rear, huddled over maybe a phone, tablet, paper notes.

Mandy whispered. "Any suggestions on how we drop in on their conversation and win their hearts and minds?"

They took seats at the front, near the door, unwrapped and sampled the sandwiches. Big Tony arrived with beverages and for ten dollars said the rear exit was beyond restrooms and unlocked on the interior side.

It was a good hoagie, not a best ever, but solid, welcome, satisfying. "In the trade, it's called a cold approach. Just walk up and say hello. If the asset is anything above stupid, they walk away before you even arrive. If you get there first, block the escape, you use whatever you have to squeeze them, put some pressure on, frighten them."

"Ah, I see. In my field, we call it an ambush interview, which works best if you've got a microphone and a video guy, but if you're on your own they brush past you and ignore the public's right to know. Whistleblowers sometimes get edgy at the moment of truth, like when you click on a recorder or open a notepad. Of course, we could never do money, but, yes, charm works. And no, I never did more than that, but I know some political writers who..." She peeked past his shoulder. "You know, I don't think they'll run. They have that gentle nerdy look, something I can work with."

An unexpectedly big chunk of sandwich and a race through chewing it. Hard swallow, almost a gulp. "So I'll get a demo of what probably makes you great intelligence material?"

"You don't mind terribly, do you, Tommy?"

"Still your op. I can be a tag-along?"

She rummaged through her bag for one of the Clockmaker's better examples of working press identification. "My name, but no photo."

He pulled one of his own from his jacket pocket. *Special Assistant, White House Chief of Staff.* "It's an old favorite."

Her eyebrows fluttered. "Do they even have such a person?"

"No clue. You're the first who asked. Good sandwich. But I have this compelling desire to visit the men's room, wash my hands."

"Such a good concept. Who knows who you'll bump into on the

way to the toilet."

Tommy led the way. Just before the target table, he snagged two chairs and planted them in the aisle. *Unless they go over me, no way in or out.*

Mandy slid into a booth seat with a bit of a wriggle. Just the faintest physical touch with the thigh of the man the chair. And a warm, knowing smile, like an effervescent assistant district attorney with an air tight indictment. "Hi, guys. Heard any good conspiracy theories lately?"

Tommy put on a pleasant expression blending sympathy with ar-rogance. *Never met a Columbia grad school dropout, but this is what they probably look like.*

Hint of panic, touch of apprehension in their eyes. "Y-y-you're with them, aren't you?"

Reassuring smile. "Nah. I'm with her, and what you didn't know until just now is that she's a friend of yours." He extended a hand. "Hi. I'm Tommy Kane. And she's Mandy Owens."

The guy meekly took Tommy's hand in a grip about as firm as a stick of overcooked fettuccine. "Delphy."

You've got to be joking. "Got a last name?"

"Not that I share with anybody." He nodded toward the guy op-posite, but his eyes flitted like a crazy moth, in all directions. "Every-one calls him Pootis."

Every floater I ever knew in the trade came up with better code names. Sounds more like one of those oddball names the internet crowd and the elec-tronic gamers would go for.

Mandy's smile was warm, maternal. "Some sort of secret code?"

"Just, um, a meme," Pootis said. "And, sorry, but I don't know who you are. You can't be my friend because — "

You don't have any.

Pootis grabbed at a scrap of courage floating by. "Um, maybe you have some sort of identification?"

Mandy hoisted the press credentials on the lanyard around her neck to allow Delphy a close, almost intimate, look. He was unim-pressed, crossed his arms and slumped in his seat. *He's been a butt of jokes on live TV* before. Late twenties, soft in the belly and arms and probably head, too, his mind fried by talk radio. The guy who called himself Pootis appeared more attentive and less suspicious, examining the forged credentials with great care. *That's right, pal. Karl's a master and no way are you gonna find flaws in his work.*

Mandy went to work on the weaker link, building rapport with all the charm of the girl next door in every guy's dreams, the sweetheart every guy wished he had. *Like Belle and me. When I was thirteen stupid. Smile like that and the toughest field agent would hand over secrets without shame.*

Delphy sat forward, his arms on the table. Pootis shifted his weight so he was very close, almost — well, *probably* — touching, his elbow on the table, his cheekbone in the palm of his right hand, mes—merized. Mandy. Lover, sister, mommy, all rolled into one, uncorking candor, relentlessly and painlessly working a source, learning every—thing she wanted to know about the private life of a guy named Benny. *Dang if she isn't that good.*

It all came down a single morning a couple of weeks ago when a suit from the enforcement end of the Department of the Treasury, scared witless about being sucked into being a whistleblower, got the dust off from a local television news hotshot in Prospect Park.

Delphy was eager, assured, helpful. "He had some sort of top se—cret file on a flash drive. Supposed to be the evidence that something really terrible could happen to economies on a global scale, and the stupid TV guy, Carl Jorgenson, never showed."

Pootis said, "As usual. When citizens like us get hard evidence, they always think it's a joke or something, make fun of us. You ought to see the camera guys laughing their asses off."

Probably with good cause.

Neither of the tipsters could remember the name of the guy Ben—ny spoke with that day, but they had all trooped in for coffee, a bagel, enlightenment.

Pootis said, "We were sitting right over there, near the door. The guy was really upset."

Delphy nodded. "Unhinged. But a big mistake, that close to the door. They've got special devices, you know, to see through walls that close."

Pootis jumped in. "He was, well, kind of half a step away from crying, like he was doomed. So Benny said he knew a reporter, somebody who would listen, get to the bottom of it, make an article out of it."

With all the aplomb of a confessor, she said, "That would be me. And I am definitely looking into it."

They exchanged excited looks. "No kidding? Really?"

Mandy had closed the distance to them even more and softened her voice into a tone of confidence. "I had a trusted expert, the best in the business, examine the contents, but it raised more questions than it answered. Did Benny's source by any chance have anything more?"

Pootis shrugged. "You'd have to ask Benny. We haven't seen him around for a while, so maybe he's working on something."

Mandy's face went somber, serious. "Benny's dead. He was killed."

A pall of shock and horror hovered over table.

"He was probably killed by the same people who gave this contact the drive in the first place. And trust me, they could be anywhere, looking for anyone connected to him."

Tommy said, "Look fellows, this is much larger than your friend. It's a matter of national security, at the highest level. Is there anything else you can remember?"

Pootis did his best to describe the overwrought man and apologized for not knowing any more.

Mandy leaned slightly away and reviewed the notes she had been taking. "No need. You've been most helpful. But do be careful who you share this with. There's some really bad people involved and I wouldn't want to see decent guys like you get hurt."

Nice. Push their panic button. Interview's over and she's shoving them out the door.

"Okay," she said, playing the con right to the end. "I won't take any more of your time. Mister Kane, do you think your people can offer them some sort of protective custody, keep them out of harm's way?

Nicely done. Leave them paranoid.

Delphy looked shaken. "No, no, that's all right. We, uh, have heard about..."

Mandy stood. "Fair enough. Thanks again, guys. I'm sure Benny would appreciate it."

CHAPTER TWENTY

234 Prospect Park West, Brooklyn, N.Y.

On the street, they waited for Charlie, circling the block in the town car.

Mandy sighed. *Carl Jorgenson. Why did it have to be Carl Jorgenson?*

Tommy asked, "You okay?"

"Yes, why?"

He stirred incredulity, sympathy and disbelief into an cocktail of empathy.

"So, okay, I'm not okay, but I'll be okay."

He chuckled and waved toward the car, gliding along in heavy traffic. "Oh, okay."

"That sounds so patronizing." *Gosh, he can read me like a book.*

A knowing smile shifted gears into a smirk as they stepped between a pair of parked cars and settled into the town car. "It was meant to be. Care to fill in the blanks or are you flying solo on this one?"

Charlie asked for the next destination.

She said, "West Fifty-Seventh and Eighth Avenue, near Columbus Circle. It's a terrible time of day. But there's a parking garage right around the corner, I think."

"Uh-huh. Well, first off, I sure'n hell ain't about to pay for no goddamn parking garage. And second off, if you two are having some sorta spat, I can swing up to that park so's you can settle it."

That obvious? Jorgenson's miles away and he's still causing... The town car, double parked, idling. Impatient honks from behind. Charlie tap—

ping his fingers on the wheel. Tommy staring straight ahead, like some sort of serene Zen monk contemplating a patch of gravel. *Yes. That obvious. Candor. Can't be a team without candor.* "Sounds like a good idea, Charlie."

Charlie drove into Prospect Park, wound around a lake, found a deserted parking area and excused himself. "Okay. I got my usual kit in the truck. Magnetic plates, stickers, what-not. What do you think, Tommy? Local, state, diplomatic, federal?"

Amazing. New Yorkers make an art of beating parking fees. These guys take it to a new level.

Tommy took a moment. "Federal, I think. Nobody argues with a limo and fed plates."

Charlie reached down to pop the trunk lid. "I'll give you folks a minute to either patch things up or kill each other, okay?"

I swear I'll never say okay again. She bit her lip, looked out the window, took a breath. "Okay..." A wince. *Darn it! So much for vows...* "Have you ever had someone who really got under your skin?"

Tommy turned to look longingly at her. *But with a smirk.* "Uh, well, yeah..."

She punched his shoulder. "No, not *that* way. I mean, someone who always managed to find a way to pull your chain, to get to you, mess with your head? Hm. No. In your case, probably not. But in my case, Carlton T. Jorgenson is the guy."

Tommy cocked an eyebrow and his expression settled into the patient comfort of a best friend, a person who understands, a confidante. Outside, Charlie stood with his hands in his pockets, looking at nothing in particular. She caught his eye and motioned for him to return.

Okay, organize thoughts. Try not to be emotional or, worse, silly. Steady, strong, serene. An Owens girl, right? "It's probably going to sound rather pathetic. First of all, you have to understand that Carlton T. Jorgenson sees himself as God's gift to women. And he seems to take particular delight in sharing that concept with anyone he's drooling over at the moment. But he's also incredibly arrogant and obnoxious, the product of a pampered, unfettered upbringing."

"Sounds like the kind of person you'd ignore."

So funny. "Avoid is the operative word. It's like this. Carl and I both went to Medill, at Northwestern, at the same time. He was head—ed for broadcast, and I was doing print. But when I set my heart on being the editor of *The Daily Northwestern*, he pulled some strings and got the chair. I got the second seat."

Tommy nodded. "No, you got the shaft. Let me guess. Family comes with some donor history, maybe alumni types plugged into the trustees — "

Very good, right on the mark. "Yep. Big money in the D-C area, Virginia I think, own a string of independent stations, a lot of pull in—side the Beltway. Which is how Carl got into Northwestern. Sure wasn't because of brains or talent."

Charlie got into the car and reached for the ignition key. "We good?"

She said, "Almost. But we're also a team."

He let go of the key to wait. "Okay."

Tommy said, "But there's more to it than a raw deal in college."

Oh, yes, there truly is. But I can't bring myself to be a whiner.

His eyes went soft and reassuring. "Nothing but good friends here. You can complain all you want about it."

Really? I shouldn't. But... "Back then, I was pushing him off on the one hand but trying to play the long-term game of resume building, so I was making the best of it for over a year. He continually remind—ed me that I was his 'gal Friday' — you know, Rosalind Russell as Hildy Johnson?"

"But he was no Cary Grant."

"Not by a long shot. He used to call me '*B-B,*' his 'Boston babe' even though I was from Connecticut. But to rich boys in Virginia, anything north of New York is Boston."

"And I take it that he hasn't, well, improved?"

"No, afraid not. I bump into him occasionally and the first thing he does... Well, anyway, bottom line is that I don't think we'll get much out of him unless I play along or he's in a very good mood or there's something in it for him. Look, Tommy, I've run the gauntlet before. I can run it again. It's a woman-thing. Guys are usually out of their depth. It's a scrap of information. You can wait in the car. I'll do my best."

He's got that mischievous look again, when he's scheming.

Tommy said, "Nah, that's no fun. Charlie, can you pull in a few favors from your old cop buddies — especially the marshals?"

"Yeah, sure."

"And Mandy, can you let me use the magic phone? I've got a little chore for Lucy."

She passed it to him. "You've got a plan, haven't you?"

"Yep."

"Why do I get this feeling..."

CHAPTER TWENTY-ONE

West Fifty-seventh Street and Eighth Avenue, New York City

And it was *such* a good plan. In the lobby restroom, she practiced a polite but serious expression in the mirror. *Just can't do it.* The wacky grin was too much to contain. She cleared her throat and forced her cheeks into a somber slump. The grin popped back out. *This is taking way too long. Again. Again. Keep practicing.*

Another woman entered. Tall. Severe, almost haughty. Into the bag for all the stuff to freshen up.

Mandy cleared her throat, more forcefully this time, and struggled for a whisper of a smile, something a bit more serene than smug, but not a full blown smile. Laughter. The same idiotic grin. *Like a kid who's heard the funniest joke ever. Stop.*

The other woman stole a glance. Confused. Compassion, with a hint of disdain.

"It's all right," Mandy said. "I'm struggling not to smile."

"That seems a bit odd."

"I'm on my way up to the television studios upstairs and I'm hop–ing not to look, well, goofy."

"Ah, yes. The weather girl look. Popular in smaller markets on in–dependents, but definitely not here." She stepped closer and extended a hand. "Hello, I'm Marsha Collingsworth."

"Mandy — er, *Amanda* — Owens. How do you do?"

Marsha said, "Here for an audition?"

"Well — what makes you ask?"

"That's what lobby restrooms are for. Let's have a look at you."

Marsha stepped right, left, and back to face Mandy head on. "Hair could use some work, makeup work is so-so, but the camera will be kind to you. And yes, you have to lose that silly smile. Just keep your shoulders square and maybe sit ever so slightly left, but stay on the front edge of the chair. Tell the cameraman to shoot a little higher than usual, maybe two or three inches will be fine. That'll let you look up a bit, help your chin."

Mandy said, "That's kind advice. You must be auditioning for a prime-time anchor spot."

"Oh, good lord, no. I'm here about an E-P — um, *executive producer* position — they're trying to fill. They're in ratings trouble and they need someone to clean house." She glanced at her hair, somewhat askew from the breeze on the street. Her shoulders drooped to suggest disappointment and she sighed. "You know, I may be a senior producer with a major network, but I still have to park in a garage around the corner and hoof it. Not like the person that came in the limo out front with the tag-along security detail. Four big good-looking guys standing around, armed to the teeth. Wonder who's upstairs..." She paused, as if embarrassed to be rattling on in a peevish sort of way. "But no matter. You'll do fine, dear."

Be honest. "I'm not really here to apply for a job. I'm trying to run down some information for an investigative piece. The printed kind."

Marsha cocked an eyebrow and continued to examine Mandy's features. "Pity. You've got marvelous presence. I'd much rather have someone like you in the first chair than the one they have now. You've got a fresh, honest look about you. Well. I've got an appointment in — " She looked at her watch " — about two minutes ago."

Mandy apologized.

"No apology needed. My plan was to arrive about ten minutes late. The news director knows I have a reputation to uphold." She gathered her bag, checked the mirror for a moment and turned to leave. "Give me a call if you're ever interested in air work. And keep that smile. It makes all the rest of us jealous."

Alone again, Mandy turned to face the mirror. *Oh, my gosh. The funniest thing.* And the unabashed grin revived. And laughter. *Stop.*

Compose yourself. Well, a little, anyway.

Mandy tilted her head to tuck the tiny receiver into her ear and smoothed her jacket. "Lucy? Bug? Can you hear me all right?"

Lucy was warm, calm. "Hey. So where are you?"

"Restroom in the lobby. Sorry for the delay but — "

Bug interrupted. "Yeah, yeah, I heard. Friggin' party in the can. So okay, solid signal, but your voice is muffled. The mic's maybe a little too far under your collar."

Mandy made an adjustment and asked, "Is that better?"

"Good enough. Okay. I'm outa here. Tell Tommy it's goodwill discount day, five hundred off the usual. But if you damage the goods, it'll cost four grand."

Mandy said, "Thanks, Bug. I really app — "

"Yeah, yeah, no prob. See ya's."

More like 'hear ya's.' She sighed and took one last look at the mirror. The grin calmed into a pleasant, efficient smile, with a hint of patronization in it. *Perfect.*

* * *

A reception area with the station's enormous call-letters and affiliation sprawled across the wall behind a pecan-colored counter. *Oh, yeah. Long way from the shack outside of town with a radio tower in the back. All Cajun, all the time. Fat, sweaty guy behind the mike, blabbering away.* A matched pair of twenty-something receptionists, red blazers, blonde and cheerleader-cute with a lot of teeth, handled telephone traffic like a sorority chapter organizing the big spring social. The receptionist on the right finished with the phone first and poured an eager-to-please smile all over him. "Can I help you?"

Mandy rolled her eyes. "Hello. Amanda Owens to see Carl Jorgenson."

She reached for a computer screen of some sort and tapped it. "Do you have an appointment?"

The other receptionist glanced toward Tommy and he rewarded her with a grin that caused her cheeks to redden.

"Well — "

The receptionist focused on the screen. "Oh, yes. Here you are. If you'd care to take a seat, I'll contact his assistant."

Bravo, Lucy. Nice touch.

Lucy sighed in his earpiece. "Don't say it, Tommy."

My turn to have some fun. "She's really that good, Mandy."

Lucy groaned. "Argh! Okay. Jorgenson's assistant is a former intern, Adrian Willis, about five-six, thinnish, glasses, light brown hair which she wears back, in a bun. Single. Columbia, a bachelors in broadcast, three, no, four years ago."

They thumbed through brochures on upcoming new series and news specials. Mandy's elbow tapped him into attention and he caught her nod toward a young woman approaching from a hallway, a clipboard cradled in her arm.

Tommy stood and Mandy leaned forward.

He extended a hand and said, "Miss Willis?"

She seemed surprised and said, "Hello. I'm Adrian, Mister Jorgenson's assistant." She studied her clipboard. "I'm afraid I'm a bit confused — "

Now Mandy stood, a patient expression on her face. "It's quite all right. Carl and I are old acquaintances. I'm in town for the day and thought I'd drop by to say hello."

She looked relieved. "Ah, okay. Carl sometimes juggles his own calendar. If you'd follow me — his offices are this way."

They strolled past production offices. A control room darkened except for the tiny screens and winking panel lights. A open area in which shirt-sleeved writers labored at grouped desks. An office door with Adrian's name. To the far end of the hall, where they kept the windows.

Adrian tapped on the open door, said something in a soft voice, looked at her clipboard and said something more. Meek. Submissive. She stepped aside, her head slightly bowed and waved Mandy and Tommy into the lair of Carlton T. Jorgenson.

Carl was on his feet, rolling down shirtsleeves and adjusting his tie. "Well, well, sweet little Friday's come to visit Big Carl. Looking gorgeous as usual, Owens." He turned to Adrian. "Fetch us some coffee, couple of sweet rolls, will ya, honey?"

Tommy spoke to Adrian. "I think Miss Owens and I are good, thank you."

Carl laughed. "*Miss* Owens, eh? Adrian here's my newest Friday." To Adrian, he said. "And this one here, she was my first one. Used to call her B-B, for — "

Mandy's expression cooled. "I'm sure Miss Willis isn't interested."

Carl's eyes swept through the expressions of everyone in the tense room. "Yeah, probably so. Grab a seat," he said while he plopped back into his chair, leaned forward and balled his hands on the desk. "So to what do I owe this, uh, unexpected pleasure?"

Mandy took a chair and a posture of command, flanked by the standing Tommy and Adrian. "I'm working a piece, Carl, trying to run down a couple of leads. You had an appointment the other day at Prospect Park with a whistleblower, a conspiracy guy. But you stood him up. Who was it? How come he was blown off? I'd like your help."

"My help?" His eyes narrowed and he leaned back, his hands clasped behind his head. "What makes you think... Say, you really get bounced from that newspaper?"

"Yes."

"That's right. I heard you got canned. Some kind of newsroom cutback. It's a dying business, you know." He leaned forward again. "But they always let the problem people go first, don't they?"

Steady. Now, a patronizing smile. Yeah, like that.

"I'm still pretty good at it, Carl."

"Yeah, sure. Probably still get your information from handouts."

"Think so?" Mandy plucked a pen from a pot on his desk and a scrap of paper from a notepad, scribbled something and passed it to his waiting hand.

"What's this?"

"Your social security number. And your bank account number. And current balance."

His expression soured. "So you're one of those goddamn hackers."

Mandy sighed. "In a manner of speaking. What would you like me to talk about next? The amount you overpaid for your co-op in the Village? The relationship your family has with the station owner here? Say, how about the details of the settlement with that girl's family in Roanoke, you know, the one involved in that statutory rape mess you were involved with when you were pulling my chain at North-western?"

"Jesus, that was — "

"Sealed, I know."

Tommy shrugged. "She's that good, Carl."

Jorgenson tossed the paper and pulled back from the desk. He pointed a thumb at Tommy. "So you got this weenie to try to put the squeeze on me, eh? Do whatever but I'm never giving up a source, especially to you, *honey*."

"Never?"

He stood and put his hands on his hips, his face red with anger. "Never. Now get out."

Okay, Mandy, now wilt a bit. Perfect.

"Look, Carl, I'm trying..."

"Shit. You're always gonna be a Friday, B-B. *Always*. Take a hike. No room in the bigs for you, never was."

Now a helpless glance at Adrian. Look humiliated. Adrian was somewhere between numb and astonished.

Mandy stood and in an anguished tone said to Tommy, "Darn it, I told you — "

Knock on the door. *Oops. What now?*

A bald, chubby guy peeked in. "Can we have a moment?"

Carl waved him in. "Yeah, Jerry, of course. Our meeting was breaking up."

Jerry wore a jolly smile and a light gray suit with a silly tie and his eyes toured the room. "Jeez! Mandy! What a terrific surprise. How's it going for you?"

She brightened and produced one of those polite laughs. "Great, Jerry, just great. Wow, that's another award-winning tie. Tommy, this is Jerry Ulbrecht, the news director of the station."

After quick exchange of handshakes and pleasantries, Jerry retreated to apologies for interrupting and ebulliently ushered a tall woman forward. "Carl, I'd like you to meet Marsha Collingsworth, our new executive producer. Just joined us today."

Marsha ignored Carl and gave Mandy her full attention. "Mandy, so nice to see you again."

Carl looked confused.

Mandy said, "Congratulations, I'm sure you're going to be successful here."

Jerry seemed surprised. "You two know each other?"

Marsha's eyes stayed on Mandy. "Yes, we've met. You know, Jerry, if you ever want to hire a real natural — "

He sighed. "Already tried. A dozen times. She's not interested in television work."

Marsha nodded. "She could be a real star, you know."

"Yeah, I know."

Mandy's million-dollar smile, the room glowing.

"You're both so kind. Oh, I'm sorry, I'd like to introduce my friend and colleague, Tommy Kane."

Marsha's eyebrows rose. "*The* Tommy Kane?"

"Hello. And yes, the only one I know. Very pleased to meet you." Polite laughter. Carl looking out of the loop. Adrian anxious, uncertain.

Marsha said, "Now I know what the limo and security detail are all about. It's quite an honor to meet you Mister Kane. If there's anything, anything at all I can do for you..."

"Very kind of you. Well, we're finishing up, so why don't we let you folks have your meeting."

Marsha took command of the room. "Thank you, Mister Kane. And my best to you Miss Owens — if you need any help at all, please don't hesitate. Adrian, perhaps you could escort our guests? Thank you. And close the door on your way out, please."

Halfway down the hallway, Adrian paused. She looked around, fidgeted with her clipboard, and said to Mandy, "Henry Hirschfield."

"The person who Carl was — "

"Yes. We were going to do one of our regular pieces on the conspiracy nuts that gathered in Prospect Park. They're usually good for something crazy about the United Nations, but he was involved with some sort of banking thing."

"What happened?"

"We got called to another story, some sort of investigative slant on the usual corruption in City Hall. So we had to skip it, but there was no way to get in touch with the source, reschedule. Carl's call."

Tommy asked, "Know who might have made the change?"

"No idea. Sorry, but that's all I know. Really."

Mandy said, "Thanks so much. Don't worry, I won't let Carl know."

Adrian shrugged. "I don't think it'll make any difference. There's been talk all over the station that they were going to bring a new E-P to clean house. Ratings are down, heads are going to roll. Like he said, the problem people go first. What do you know about Marsha Collingsworth?"

Shifting allegiances, shifting alliances. The working stiffs trying to hold on.

Mandy reached out and patted Adrian's arm. "Be your best. I don't think she believes in Fridays."

Adrian nodded. "It was nice meeting you Mister Kane — I'm sorry I didn't recognize — "

"Quite all right. Not many people do." The encounter was dissipating. Adrian was itching to share gossip. "Have a great day."

A little soft wave as Adrian turned and walked back down the hallway.

He said, "Helpful person. At least we caught a lucky — "

Mandy cocked her head and her smile was one of satisfaction. "Lucky? I rather thought it was elegant."

Put it together. She wasn't working Carl after all. "An audible. You called an audible."

She pressed the elevator call button. "First and ten, Tommy. I've been in the business long enough. I know how to work a source."

CHAPTER TWENTY-TWO

Second Avenue and Crain Highway, Glen Burnie, Maryland

Mandy counted fourteen concrete steps, with the church's arched wooden door at the top. They were going to have to do for a spot to sit and rest, but at least the top step offered a good view of the area. "I'm sorry, Tommy, but I've got to stop, sit, think. We've been up and down these two streets a dozen times and we've knocked on virtually every door."

Tommy leaned against the thick red brick edge of the steps, his hand gripping a metal railing. "It's suburbia. Nobody ever sees any—thing, nobody really knows anyone, especially neighbors."

Mandy sighed at the sight of the street, left and right. Three lanes, one shared for left turns. Hardly any traffic at all. Hidden from view, Second Street, where Henry Hirschfield had lived in a now-locked up house. Making wider circles, Charlie in his clunky green SUV. *We could have flown, got a nice rental.* Instead they bounced through Penn—sylvania's notorious roads all because Tommy had brought Charlie further into the game after Lucy came through with an address for Hirschfield.

"He was going nuts with Yenchenko," Tommy had explained to her after a suitable bribe of marvelous scotch. "Busted hand, living on a shooting range to learn left handed, shamelessly mooching off the sympathetic waitresses at the Puffin, small space for two guys that need a lot of room. Besides, he gave me the mournful look, last hur—rah, maybe the last time at bat."

And so I said, sure, why not. And went for a six hour drive in that mangy truck. It seemed like old times.

Tommy grinned, trying to be positive. "Charlie should be along any minute. You can warm up, we can go find a coffee, maybe a sweet roll or something."

"No. It's okay. I can recognize a dead end when I see one, Tommy. Maybe we should think about heading back home. It's a long drive. I mean, a *really* long drive."

"Charlie's been cruising the neighborhood, but maybe we can make one more pass door-to-door."

A click. Behind. A door, being unlocked.

"Hello?" a man said. "Can I be of any help to you?"

A man in a suit, slight build, maybe five-ten or five-eleven, with thinning gray hair, close cropped on the sides and nearly gone on top. His rimless glasses were a little out of fashion. An optimistic smile, a blend of compassion and eager. *Eight to five it's a —*

"I'm Pastor John. Would you like to come in?"

— A minister, the guy's whose church steps I'm using to give my ankles a break.

Mandy stood and brushed any possibility of dust from her coat. "That's all right. I needed to get off my feet for a moment."

"Oh, I see. Well, if you'd like to wait in the vestibule, I can get you some coffee or something. You're sure everything's all right?"

Mandy exchanged a look and shrug with Tommy. "Well, actually, we're trying to find anyone who might have known a fellow who recently passed away. He lived about a block from here, on Second — "

Pastor John nodded and began to walk down the stairs. "You must be referring to the late Mister Hirschfield."

Mandy asked, "Was he a member of your congregation?"

"Regretfully, no. I don't believe he belonged to any parish. But we did have a service for him. Simple, but members thought it the decent thing to do. For his friend, too."

Tommy cocked an eyebrow. "Friend?"

"Yes, so it would seem. Are you related, members of his or her families?"

Mandy took a step closer and became more cordial. "No, afraid not. I'm a reporter and we were trying to gain some insight into what happened."

"Oh, dear. I hope he wasn't involved with — "

"No, no. Nothing wrong. In fact, he was trying to do the right thing."

Pastor John crossed his arms and bowed his head. "I gather it didn't work out. The poor man must have been very distraught."

Tommy asked, "Why do you say that?"

Pastor Bob looked up, puzzled. "People who take their own lives are usually distraught about something."

Mandy stepped closer. "You mentioned a friend."

"Yes. Miss Panko. Audrey Panko. It was so unfortunate?"

"She committed suicide, also?"

"Yes. In our parking lot, as a matter of fact, down there." He pointed to a lot toward the end of the block. "Shot herself."

Tommy's voice was gentle, patient. "Mister Hirschfield and Miss Panko. Were they, well, involved?"

"Oh, I doubt it. I'm given to understand they were, um, gay, shar—ing a house. I think they both worked at the same place, some sort of government job. A lot of those around here. Some people said they often gave the impression of dating when they had to make social ap—pearances. You see, Mister Kane, we try not to judge, but rather serve when needed. There were evidently no family members in the area, so we made arrangements for them."

"With whom?"

"There's a funeral home and crematory a block that way, and we were able organize a modest but appropriate resting place for them."

Mandy said, "You asked if we were family — "

"Oh, yes. It seems that when Miss Panko, well, *died*, she was clutching a laptop computer. It may have been damaged when she fell, but I have it in my office, in case."

Tommy asked, "You didn't give it to the police?"

Pastor Bob flushed with embarrassment. "Well, no. Given their lifestyle, I thought perhaps that there might be some materials on the computer that would not reflect well on either of them. Sometimes ethical decisions are a bit difficult, but frankly I didn't see the need to, well, you know."

"I see."

"Tommy, I know we can find next of kin. Didn't Charlie and Lucy have some information about relatives?"

"Oh, yes. The people up in New York."

He lies better than I do.

Pastor John nodded. "Someone did say he had been to New York not long ago."

"I'm with a newspaper in New York City," Mandy said. "It would be most helpful — "

Pastor John pursed his lips and looked down. *He's stuck with it, doesn't want it, and at this point doesn't want to admit he withheld evidence.* "Very well. I'll get it for you — unless you'd like to come into my office and have a coffee. It's really quite chilly out here."

Mandy looked past Tommy's shoulder at an approaching sedan. "That's all right. Our friend is pulling up now."

Pastor John smiled. "I'll be a moment."

Charlie's dark green SUV swept to the curb, the spatters of Pennsylvania mud clinging to the aft end of wheel wells and the mid-day sunshine unable to bounce off the weathered paint. He leaned toward the passenger side and motioned. *C'mon, c'mon, drop what you're doing and let's get going. Now.*

Mandy looked around. *Nothing.* "Go ahead. See what he wants. I'll wait for Pastor John."

Charlie motioned a second time. More urgency this time.

Tommy raised his hand and unfurled a forefinger. *Just a minute.*

A gray sedan whispered past from the opposite direction, the driver a woman oblivious to everything but her cell phone. Quiet. Peaceful. Empty. Just an ordinary suburban street on a day when all the traffic was somewhere else. *Still...*

And there it was. Two blocks south, a dark car turns right, pauses. Waiting. A second car comes up from behind, pulls into the middle lane, passes. Charlie, waving for them to get into his vehicle. Second car turns left, onto a side street. First car, still there.

But closer.

Tommy's voice lowered to a whisper. "What do you think? Find the minister? Let it go and get out? You wait inside while we — "

She shook her head. "Can't let it go. This has got to be what Lucy's looking for. And it might be a church, but — "

He nodded. "We're not sure Pastor John is the genuine..."

The door next to them opened. Pleasant smile, kindly eyes, a man who looked relieved that an indiscretion no longer haunted him. A large, padded manila envelope settled into Mandy's hand and the un-expected weight of it caused her arm to sink.

"There is is. I hope the family will find some comfort in it."

An outstretched hand. An exchange of glances all around. The handshake neither soft nor firm, but cordial. The car down the street was still parked by the curb, and two others went around it.

Mandy said, "I'm sure. Thank you *so* much for your help."

They scampered down the steps toward the waiting vehicle. Mandy clutched the envelope close and reached for the passenger side rear door. Tommy took the front seat and explained the delay to Charlie.

The other car was now parked beyond the church lot where Au-drey chose to die. Mandy squinted into the sunlight to try, without luck, for a headcount.

Cinnabar.

They'd laid a trap. *And we walked right into it.*

CHAPTER TWENTY-THREE

Charlie looked into the rear view mirror and sighed. "Aw, hell, my own damn fault. I picked up our friend, yonder, on my third run down Second Avenue. Come out of a driveway, been on my ass ever since."

Tommy turned to look. "It's okay. We should have guessed they'd have a team in the area. Stuff happens. Still sitting. Loose tail? Waiting for instructions?"

"No idea. Like god damn fleas on a field dog, though. Annoying as hell. So, you two come up with something?"

Mandy nodded. "The minister of this church might have had the laptop Lucy was looking for." She turned the envelope over in her hand. "Looks like a return address of a religious book publisher. Yep. Book rate. Maybe a sample. An optimistic sign, anyway." She peeked in. "And, sure enough, there's a laptop inside. Dented, scratched."

Charlie said, "Ain't sitting no more. Looks like our fleas are inching closer. Shaking 'em in a town like this is going to be tough to do. Want to drive, Tommy?"

"No. You know what you're doing. Let's see if we can't box them up somewhere."

Charlie grunted. "Yeah, bust-and-cuff'd be good, but I... Hey, maybe I got us a plan. Mandy, reach under the driver's seat, oughta be one of them little sport bags down there."

Mandy gasped. "Guns, some — looks like I.D. holders — and oh, wow. Are these badges real?"

"Yeah, yeah. Always had spares, never could tell when... Okay, you grab yourself a set, pass the others up here."

Tommy extended an arm and for several seconds it hung in the air.

Mandy said, "You mean, take an actual gun? Badge?"

"Yeah, I figured you secretly always wanted to be a cop or some—thing. Today's your chance."

Mandy studied the holster as if it were infected.

Tommy said, "Goes on your hip, usually right, halfway back. Clip the badge to the right front."

"But, Tommy — "

"What's the problem?"

Her shoulders slumped. "My belt? It's my favorite. A Prada saffi—ano. It's *Italian*. I don't want to — "

Tommy and Charlie exchanged glances of exasperation.

Mandy shifted her body in the seat. "Oh, all right. But if I ruin this with a silly holster clip..."

Charlie said, "Ain't never seen a cop making a fashion statement."

Tommy chambered a round and clipped the equipment to a belt he couldn't remember where he bought or when. "What can I say, buddy? Better quality of witness and all that."

"We still gotta have us a plan, Tommy."

"Let's get rolling, figure out something."

Mandy leaned forward. "I hate to be a spoil sport, but how do we plan to make an arrest on a public street without a warrant or any—thing? The first regular policeman who comes along will take us down, too."

Charlie guided the SUV away from the curb and northbound. "She's got a point, Tommy. Ain't nothing useful up that way," he said. "I think we gotta go south. Look, I got an old pal in the local FBI field office — "

Tommy watched the sedan in the rear view mirror. Keeping a dis—tance. Not in a hurry. But not a lot of time if it's surveillance and they saw Mandy with the envelope. "Cavalry. Always a good plan."

"But without any reason to make an arrest — wait, I think I have an idea." She settled back in the seat and pulled the phone from her bag.

Lucy. In the system, making people feel wanted. Awright. Good think—ing. Buy a little time. He directed Charlie to make a left toward a low brick building with reddish-brown trim designed to look like a cross between a lodge and a fast-food restaurant. "Pull into that bank, the drive-up window. I feel a sudden urge to make a deposit to my non-existent account, only I forgot the check or money or whatever."

"They got cameras."

"Yeah, but we got Lucy, and she's got an eraser."

"Okay, pal, here we go."

The trailing car followed and backed into an open space in the lot. Two guys, medium height, build. One wears glasses. *Looks like short hair, maybe.*

Charlie studied the rear view mirror. "Maryland plates. Want the number?"

"Lucy says absolutely. I'll repeat it. And she wonders why you guys are taking up the whole screen on the surveillance monitor so she can't see it for herself."

Charlie called it out and told the teller's image on the tiny screen his passenger was looking for something.

The teller said, "No problem. I'll wait."

Tommy pretended to fumble with imaginary paper in his empty hands and muttered some frustration.

"Yeah, sorry," Charlie said to the screen. "The dummy left the check at home. Gotta come back."

The teller assured them it was all right, happens all the time, and have a nice day.

Mandy said, "Okay, Lucy's patching something together. She says she's going to need at least ten minutes to get it into the federal sys—tem but promises to make it good enough to justify the FBI being on scene. Tommy, uh, no, never — "

"What's wrong?"

"Lucy's voice. It sounded... well, kind of strained."

"She's got a lot of irons in the fire, probably overloaded on dough—nuts and coffee."

"I don't know... oh, it's probably my imagination. Never mind. Charlie, do you want me to call your friend?"

Charlie started to ease the vehicle toward the exit. "Right?"

Tommy said, "Yes. Take your time."

Charlie recited a phone number from memory. "Ask for... Aw, hell, gimme the damn phone. Gotta pull off somewhere's. Not right to use a damn phone while driving. This'll do. A goddamn funeral home. Perfect."

Eight minutes later they stayed well under the speed limit, their tail having no trouble keeping pace, in light traffic.

Tommy said, "Need a good sized lot, with cars in it."

"Got ya. These are all... maybe... naw, too small. A traffic light would be nice to slow things down. Just when you could use a delay..."

Mandy spoke up. "Lucy says there's nothing, but a few hundred yards on the right, some sort of a taxi place... and she says she's going live, to plug in."

Tommy stuffed an earbud into his left ear, heard Lucy, and point—ed. *Her tone, kind of clipped, jagged.* "Just up there — "

Charlie pressed the accelerator hard. "Yeah, yeah, I see it. Okay, we'll roll in, turn, face 'em. Mandy? Gun drawn as soon as you get out. Be sure your badge is showing. Feel free to tug it loose with your left hand and show it if you want to be cowboy, otherwise, let your piece do the talking, both hands. Name of the game is shock and awe, okay?" *Anxiety in her eyes.* "Don't worry. You don't have to shoot any—one." He grunted as the vehicle swerved into the lot, made a wide loop and cut off the surveillance car as it followed them in. "Hopeful—ly."

She exhaled and reached for the door handle. "Yes. Hopefully."

The surveillance car lurched to a stop. Tommy and Charlie fanned out left and right and Mandy took the center, all three yelling commands from behind aimed weapons. Hands went up.

Mandy snarled and hollered. "Driver! Show your hands! Show your hands *now!*"

Charlie and Tommy glanced at each other. *Yep, she's impressive.*

Amid barked commands, suspects exited the car, one at a time. Weapons checks. Both armed. Sullen, silent, legs spread, hands on the trunk of their car. Charlie retreated to his SUV and the sport bag.

He forgot the doggone handcuffs. "Okay, the one on the left, two steps back, hands behind your head. Two more steps. Attaboy. Okay, on your knees. Let's go, let's go!"

Charlie stepped forward with handcuffs and rolled his eyes.

It's okay. No sweat.

Second suspect secured.

Tommy leaned in close and put a smooth and mellow edge on his drawl. "You gonna help us out here, tell us who you're working for?"

The driver shook his head.

"Nah? I didn't think so. That's okay, pal. The warrant they're busting you on is an espionage charge, so you're jammed up really bad, probably off for a chat with the dark side of the CIA. More than likely be on your way out of the country tonight. My guess? There's a great little castle in Romania, just an outstanding dungeon. Or, maybe an old warehouse in Turkey."

The driver's partner answered. "Up yours, asshole."

"Yeah, the warehouse outside Ankara. It's so isolated you can't even hear the screams for miles. Aw, man, they are gonna do such things to your body... But, hey, my partner's gathering up your com gear, and by tonight, we'll know who you belong to. Just be glad of one thing, pal."

"Yeah, what's that?"

"We coulda put you down for kiddie porn. In the Baltimore city jail."

The driver spat an epithet.

From the street, the whoop-whoop of a police car.

"Lucy's tracking a cop. Ann Arundel unit, five-five-seven. Corpo—ral, uh, Daniel, no, *Darius* Johnson."

While Tommy acknowledged the report, Charlie checked to see if the prisoners were secure and spoke to his partners, "Okay, holster the weapons, badges in your left hand, high."

The county officer turned his vehicle to act as a shield and drew his pistol as he exited the dark blue car.

The dispatcher caused him to pause. "Five-five-seven, be advised a federal arrest in progress at your location. Stand by." Tommy, Charlie and Mandy hoisted badges and identification. "Five-five-seven, assist three agents, two male, one female, as needed, FBI is enroute."

Five-five-seven acknowledged and returned his weapon to his hol—
ster.

Charlie exchanged introductions and handshakes with Corporal
Darius Johnson. "Couple of escapees on federal warrants. It's an un—
dercover operation."

Johnson nodded and said to his radio, "Dispatch, advise on nature
of arrest."

"Five-five-seven, wants and warrants on two suspects, escape from
a federal detention facility."

Corporal Johnson relaxed even more.

Whew.

Corporal Johnson grinned and shook hands all around. He chuck—
led while Mandy struggled to secured the badge to her belt. "Wow.
Guess you guys have got the life, eh?" He glanced at Charlie's SUV.
"Well, maybe not, huh?"

Lights flashing, a pair of black SUVs pulled in and FBI agents
swarmed the lot.

Corporal Johnson lingered to help secure the scene, spoke to his
dispatcher and waved goodbye. His cruiser crept out of the lot and
rolled northbound. The surveillance guys were loaded into one of the
FBI vehicles and Charlie spoke privately to the lead agent. Several
minutes later, they were alone except for a dozen or so curious on—
lookers who lingered far out of earshot, sharing with their cellphones
what they had witnessed. The soft hum of traffic resumed, and from
the repair bay in the taxi building, the clatter of tools and impact
wrenches spilled out onto the asphalt. Charlie and Tommy cleared
the chambers of their weapons and they began the process of gather—
ing equipment.

Charlie approached Mandy. She seemed almost reluctant to part
with the holster, but tugged it from her belt and gently handed it over.
For a longer moment, she held the badge and caressed it with her
thumb.

He nodded. "You done good, young lady. Lotta style. Got to ad—
mit, I had my doubts at first. Today, you was the real thing, the gen—
uine. Sure'n hell had me fooled. Well 'cept for the high fashion and
what not. But, yeah, you done pretty fair work."

"Thank you, Charlie." She placed the badge in his hand. "I believe this is yours."

He studied it for a moment and turned it over twice and gave it back. "Aw, hell, you keep it. Ain't hardly right you goin' home without some kind of souvenir, is it now?"

Mandy listened to the earpiece, grinned and said, "Yes, Lucy, everybody's okay. No, we don't need a lawyer or bail bonds. Yes, the laptop is secure." She disconnected the earpiece and handed the phone to Tommy.

Lucy voice asked, "So how soon can I get it? Disregard that. Tommy, if you guys can manage to stay out trouble and get it over to Signature at BWI, I can have Karen and Cesar round it up in, let's see, an hour, hour-fifteen."

"You okay, Luce?"

"Yeah, yeah, fine. Just need a pot of coffee, no sweat. So, to Signature?"

Tommy studied Mandy's face and said, "Sounds good to me."

Lucy said, "You'll gotta wait for a bit. Go in from Route One-Sixty... Sixty... Sixty Two. You're only a couple of miles. Should be there in ten minutes or so. Grab a coffee or lunch or something. Or lunch. Or coffee. Whatever. I'm good. Just need that laptop. Anyone need a lift back up here?"

Mandy leaned close to the phone, "No, thanks. After the airport, we'll drive back. We owe Charlie a first class steak dinner." She turned toward Charlie and smiled. "C'mon, guys. Let's go home."

CHAPTER TWENTY-FOUR

Near Wall and Williams Streets, New York City

The dark castle was in disarray. The gloomy great hall, littered with the aftermath of combat. The queen, not at all regal, cackling and swearing, muttering and growling. Her fingers, scampering around a keyboard under a solitary desk lamp. Like evil had come and gone, leaving an awful spell in its wake.

Tommy looked shocked, stunned.

An understatement. I'm flat-out horrified. "Oh, my God... Lucy? What's — "

She looked up. Haggard. Frazzled. A wispy smile that would frighten the most jaded child. "Watch your step. I've got everything organized."

Organized? This is a disaster. Gently. "Tommy, maybe you should have Sergei run out, get us some decent food while I — "

Lucy cackled again. Her eyes, so red. The bags under her eyes, so heavy. "No, no, we're good. I got coffee. I got doughnuts." She lifted the lid on a box near her desk. "Hm. Well, maybe not. Pink ones, all gone. Lost twenty-two million on a bad call in futures, but got it back, banging the close. Bergdorf's called. Uh, they... Can't remember why. Coffee, though."

"Oh, Lucy...."

"Yeah, yeah, I remember. We got friggin' *Armageddon,* guys. Hm. Need another coffee."

Tommy grasped her wrist to block the path to a half-full cup and lowered his voice to gentle, soothing. "Maybe we ought to give it a rest. Maybe you need — "

Lucy's voice took a mournful tone. "Yeah, country's going all to hell."

Mandy said, "Okay, let's just — "

Her voice brightened. "Yeah, yeah. All to hell. The ultimate al— gor... al... uh, *algorithm.*"

She looked down at his hand, holding her wrist and he let go. Tommy and Mandy exchanged glances of uncertainty.

Lucy laughed. "The ultimate trading program. The Doomsday App. They call it Mercury-five, but I think it should be... No. What difference would it make, the day after. But they probably would want to have a name, to put in the archive. If they have one." She shook her head and laughed with greater ease. "Yeah, guys, I thought I was pretty good, but this? Wow. Unlock the box, open lid. Look right into Hell."

Mandy drew Lucy into a consoling hug. "It's okay. It's okay. Take a breath. How long have you been..."

Tommy looked around. "All day, all night, non-stop." He pointed to a crumpled stack of doughnut boxes in a heap beyond the desk. "Running on caffeine, sugar. Probably ought to get her out of here, let her sleep."

Lucy waved him off. "No. No. Not yet."

Mandy squatted down and took Lucy's hands. "You need a break, Luce."

Lucy closed her eyes for a moment. Drawing strength. Composure. "Tommy, we've got to.... Okay, okay, gimme a sec to focus."

In the pause, the sound of the mainframe, chittering away, sparkling green lights in the gloom.

Lucy said, "Okay. Got it together." She rummaged through piles of loose paper on her desk. "First. Ah, here we go. Your magic list. This is HG Trading."

She handed the paper to Tommy. *David R. Morris. Andrew T. Chamberlain. Michael B. Eaton. Joshua J. Gibbons. Susan M. Halsey.*

"People who could buy this entire room and everyone in it with an hour's profit. Fattest of the fat cats." She gave Tommy a direct, seri—

ous look. "People with ten zeros."

Huh? What does that —

Tommy's smile was wry. "People with a personal wealth of more than ten billion dollars."

Lucy pointed to what was once a laptop computer. A strand of wires poured off the table, onto the floor, and into one of the racked devices near the temporary workbench. "Everything was all right except the case and the screen. The on-off functions were dead, which is why the good folks at the church couldn't make it go."

"Yup." Lucy picked up a yellow pencil and used it as a pointer, ticking off the names of sections like a dissection in a biology class. Her voice picked up tempo. "It's a pretty basic model, the kind you could get off-the-shelf at any big box appliance or office supply place, online even, a personal unit and not part of a larger contract purchase. Pretty basic model. Was. Yeah."

Mandy kept a distance from the electronic corpse. "So this was not used in a government office."

"Well, it could have been. It's a laptop after all. You know, a basic model, and way too many government employees lug storage devices back and forth, or transfer files by email, to work at home, which is how stuff like this gets leaked." She picked up the stick that came from Benny. "But I can say with reasonable certainty that the file on here, um, yeah, here, the... The file came from this computer — it's a fluke that it was corrupted on the transfer. Pretty basic model."

Benny. Henry Hirschfield. Audrey Panko. And people whose path it might have crossed along the way. Martin Silverman. Alan Rothstein. Phil Donatello. Bobby McKennan. All killed because of one corrupted file on a stick making the rounds. Now here was the whole thing. Crossing more paths. *Me. And Tommy. And now Lucy.* "Please tell me that whatever's here really matters. I'd hate think life is so cheap."

Lucy took a gulp of coffee. "As a matter of fact, it is. These are trading results. Theoreticals. But before you get upset, they're the result of test runs of a really scary trading application. You know. Theoreticals. I'll try to keep it simple, um, like, simple. In high-speed securities or commodities trading, the algorithms you write into your program are everything. The systems run so fast, so fast, so incredibly fast. And fast. And in so many places, that any unaccounted-for situation usually causes the program to stop and wait for instructions. Theoreticals even. Very fast. Want coffee?"

She spoke even faster, as if hurrying to the next point of her presentation. Tommy and Mandy exchanged glances. He shrugged and rubbed his chin, anxiety in his eyes. "Okay, that makes sense. And I guess once the operator tells it what to do, it kind of remembers and takes off again. Luce, don't you think you should— "

She waved him off, tapped a key and a stream of data began to flow across a screen, columns of green and red on a flat black canvas. "Exactly. In this kind of trading, interruptions of a few seconds can cost a company tens of thousands of dollars, thousands and thousands. Tens. But, um, but you have to write it off to a bad day or unexpected surprise, adjust, do better next time. It's a pretty basic model. I mean, theoreticals."

Which is what she's done on Tommy's behalf. And made a fortune. She's exhausted, completely overloaded. "But I sense there's something more to this?"

Lucy nodded, finished her coffee in one gulp and took command of the keyboard. "So I spent most of the night working back through the algorithm and discovered they have a problem. Right... right... Where the hell... Oh, here." She pressed a key and the flow paused.

Tommy cocked an eyebrow. "Are you okay?"

"Yeah, yeah, no troubles. Anyway... Where was I?"

Mandy asked, "You mimicked what they're up to?"

She replied with a weary look of impatience. "I recreated it. Worked out their app. Pretty basic model for theoretical. Very fast. At first, I thought I'd screwed up, because — well, watch." She pressed the return key. The numbers lost whatever progression they had. *It's spinning out of control.*

Tommy said, "In plain old English for me, this means — "

Lucy grunted and tapped keys for several seconds. "It means it doesn't stop. It has a life of its own. Unless I force it." She held a combination of keys down and the screen fluttered for a moment before going dark. "It means a trading program is out of control, which in a lab setting is harmless, but on the trading floors would be disaster. I mean, a disaster."

She's had way too much of that potent coffee. How far do we push this?

Tommy scowled. "But there are safeguards."

"Circuit breakers. Trading halts in a market when something whacks out, like this. In regulated markets. Tens of thousands. Millions. Billions. Basic model. Theoretical. Fast, so very fast. Um, what was I gonna say? Oh, yeah, but in dark pool, where there are no rules, regulations or speed limits — "

Mandy said, "Panic. Chaos." *A little chuckle to be polite.* "Sort of like your voice now."

"Just excited." Lucy smiled reassurance. "On a worldwide scale, and in seconds."

Tommy nodded. "Which is what caused Audrey Panko to become anxious, and she shared it with Hirschfield, who was going to the media with it..."

Oh, wow. "And the Federal Reserve Bank."

Lucy pulled some notes from a stack of disorganized paper. "So here's the scorecard. Hirschfield and Panko work at FinCEN. Different departments, but they were sharing a house, you said. You did say that, right?"

Tommy cocked an eyebrow. "FinCEN?"

"Financial Crimes Enforcement Network. The Treasury Department, Tommy boy. He's very fast, Mandy. Investigates mostly money laundering stuff but, anyway, so they were sharing a house."

"Yes. The one in Glen Burnie. The minister said they were —"

Lucy walked over to the coffee pot for a refill. "Exactly. And I think, based on some of the email and images on the computer... pretty basic model for theoreticals, you know. Very fast. But she was like, um, was involved with her supervisor, Francine Huttenback, the director at FinCEN."

I don't even want to guess. But will. "And I'll bet we can't talk with Huttenback because — "

Lucy shrugged. "Died. Day before yesterday. Suicide. No question about that one. Pow. Very fast, tens of thousands."

Tommy exhaled a sigh. "So a director at FinCEN is involved in a relationship with a subordinate — "

Lucy checked her notes. "Let me... no, here. Um. Yeah. Administrative assistant."

Mandy said " — and there's a falling out and for whatever reason the subordinate gathers, or possesses, incriminating information and wants to make it public..."

"And a bunch of people die."

Mandy turned to Tommy. "Specifically, eight."

"That we know of. Lucy, how does this connect to those five people from HG Trading?"

"Just a pretty good guess. When I was rummaging around in HG, the structure of the system had a distinct style, like this one. Um..." Her brow furrowed in concentration. "Yeah, yeah, I'm okay. Um. It's kind of like a painter or musician or writer. Read enough of it and you can kind of see the style of the code, the syntax, the way it's put together. No, I don't know the author's name. Writes code like a guy, though, but really well disciplined, like maybe ex-military or more likely former intelligence work. Theoreticals. Hypo-whatever. Very, very fast."

She is so wired...

Tommy scratched an ear. "So what are people in the Treasury Department doing with code from a private trading firm? And aside from the obvious whistleblowing — "

Lucy shrugged. "That's a question. Yes. A question. Thousands of questions. For... for... for Halsey, Morris, Chamberlain, Eaton and Gibbons. Damn, sounds almost like a law firm. I can poke around. Really, I can. I'm okay. Just... But, anyway. But these people strike me as the kind that don't have their hands right on the throttle. The kind that know where to hire good henchmen, and I don't mean the ones you find on Google."

Mandy sighed. *Not merely too much coffee and sugar. Overload. The trading, the investigating, the helping us on the fly.*

Behind Lucy's desk, a light began to blink, a throbbing pulse of bright red that reflected off everything metal it touched.

Her expression tumbled from anxiety into fear. "Shit.

Just...just...*shit*. 'Scuse me, but I've gotta — "

Tommy tensed. "What?" He followed her toward her desk, the pace quickening as they went.

Something seems terribly wrong.

Lucy called out over her shoulder. "We've got a breach. That's Joan. She's got someone in the front office who... there's a code she enters when she calls me, touches off an alarm... people who shouldn't be... shit, shit, shit."

Lucy plopped into her chair and grabbed a keyboard. A brief command. The screen went from a silent line of flowing data to an image of three men. Medium build, short gray hair on one, a bit longer on the other two, more salt-and-pepper. Just the backs of heads. Lucy cursed and typed. The image flickered and switched to the opposite side.

Three men. Forty-ish. One in glasses. All looking grim.

Joan was doing a good job. Calm, efficient, pleasant. Firm. On the phone, talking to somebody. *Can't quite hear.* She hung up.

Lucy slumped back, a closed fist on her lips, her stare at the screen intense. "I'm afraid Miss Tramanian is out of the building at the moment," Joan lied in the most casual, almost sympathetic way. "But I'm sure our Mister Clayborne will be able to assist you."

Lucy whispered. "Oh, god, be good, Warren." She steepled her hands and covered her mouth.

Warren. Anxious and uncertain Warren, the young lawyer who stammered his way through introductions the last time.

Lucy's voice was barely audible. "SEC. God damn SEC. I just know it."

Warren stepped into the anteroom, more firm than before. "Gentlemen?"

Paper from an overcoat jacket pocket, a legal document. A declaration about a reliable source and a referral from a federal agency.

Lucy gasped. "Not just a subpoena. A friggin' Wells. A goddamn friggin' Wells. Shit, shit, shit."

Tommy asked, "What's a — "

Lucy closed her eyes and tilted her head toward the ceiling. Some—

thing glistened on her cheek and when she turned to face them, her eyes were more red. "A Wells Notice. The god damn Securities and Exchange Commission delivers them when they want to run your ass through the wringer, and I mean wringer. Pretty basic model, too, for thousands of hypothet... No, okay. So. When they have enough on you to haul you in violating federal law. Even if you didn't, they get into all your paper. All of it. This is serious shit, Tommy. A mess. Big time."

"Take it easy," he said.

"Easy?" Her voice choked. "Tommy, I screwed us something ter-rible."

He softened his voice further. "One step at a time. Who are the other guys?"

Lucy shook her head and she seemed to struggle to contain pain. "They don't look like SEC, but they could be the devil's own and it doesn't even begin to rank with the friggin' SEC." Her voice withered to whisper. "I got bagged, Tommy. Those bastards from HG Trading caught me in with a honey trap, probably logged it, turned me in. I am so, so very..." Her voice trailed off.

Steady, strong, serene. Mandy stepped to embrace Lucy, to share the mantra, to absorb the growing despondency. Cradling Lucy in her arms, she pleaded with her eyes. "We have to do *something*, Tommy."

The two men produced identification, but the angle was poor and their voices muffled. They pressed Warren into retreat. *They're trying to get into the trading area.*

Light from the open doorway darkened.

Sergei.

Tommy muttered. "Just don't pull a piece, Serge."

Yenchenko's bulk pushed Warren into a tight sandwich. Voices rose, everyone arguing at once. More paper went onto Warren, more argument.

Lucy murmured incoherent apologies, indifferent, utterly crushed. Revelation. Clarity. *Until this very moment, Lucy had been undefeated, the queen, the legend. But now...* Mandy held Lucy even closer, having been in the same cold, dark, lonely abyss. *They want to get into the cas—*

tle. They're on the drawbridge. We're locked in, no way out. A siege. We're trapped. "Tommy?"

"Patience."

Mandy's voice went to a whisper at the screen. "Please, Sergei, don't..." *Take a breath. Shelter Lucy.*

Yenchenko grinned, like he knew he had the upper hand. One of the guys pushed back, hard. Yenchenko's huge left hand shot forward. The guy crumpled and crashed into a table lamp. A meager effort at a scuffle. The two visitors still standing barked unpleasantries, collected their partner and left the office.

Poor Warren. Shocked, amazed, stunned. She looked down at Lucy, all her energy drained, her bright eyes closed, her usual smile gone. "Tommy? I think we're going to need a new plan."

CHAPTER TWENTY-FIVE

449 North Franklin Street, Allentown, Pennsylvania

Mandy held sample swatches at arm's length, blocking a portion of a concrete block wall that was more yellowed with age than painted color. "So, Tommy, which do you think? Polar Bear or Moon Rise?"

There's no real difference. But she was doing what she could, trying to spruce things up in Lucy's old office, focusing on something other than the uncertainty of the moment. "Whatever happened to regular old white?"

Mandy rummaged through slips of paper. "Well, they have that, too...." In a moment, she gave up. "But it's boring."

"And these aren't?"

"No. I think the Moon Rise is a bit greenish and maybe the Polar Bear is too tan."

Be patient. "What about that one?"

"Snow Fall? Too gray. A guy color."

Sergei strode in with an immense cardboard box. The container said "Net 45 pounds" but he handled it as if it were empty.

Tommy said, "We could ask Serge — "

"*Nyet.* To Sergei, color is not important. Perhaps in camouflage, but in office of someone else?" He shrugged.

Mandy sighed. "Maybe I should go back to the store. Get more samples, see if I can find the right shade. I want her office to be nice."

Tommy leaned back in a gray metal chair. Long days, long nights. An endless parade of boxes, packing anything, everything. Guys with clipboards, scribbling notes, draining pens, trying to keep some sense of order in a flood of chaos. A dozen guys with tool bags, shutting down, unplugging, disconnecting. A long weekend, gone in a blur, thieves in the night. The screaming beeps of trucks in reverse gear, the spits of air brakes, the lumbering sound of rollup doors opening, closing.

Yeah. Some plan. Grab the gear, run like hell. And now his eyes burned and every muscle from neck to ankle ached and demanded rest. In a metal chair. In a warehouse office. In Allentown. He laced his fingers behind his head. "Polar Bear."

"You're sure? You don't think it's too tannish?" She thought for a moment while she compared paint samples. "No. You don't care at all. You're being expedient."

"Polar Bear is fine. I like polar bears. Polar Bear gets my vote. C'mon, Serge, a little help."

Sergei pulled a combat knife from a sheath on his belt and with a delicate flourish slit the tape across the seam on the top of the box. "*Da, da.* Bear color is good choice."

Mandy's shoulders drooped. "You're not even looking, Sergei."

"*Nyet,* of course not. But it is of no matter. Koshka and Sergei are comrades, eh?" He paused in his labor and rested an arm on the box. "Perhaps Lucy should make choice for her office."

A groggy voice from the doorway said, "What choice?"

"Hey, Lucy." Mandy flashed a welcoming smile, a blend of relief that her patient was still alive and her friend was back in the land of coherent. Groggy-looking, not quite up to speed, but better. They embraced, Mandy in the upscale casual wear of the outer rings of the city, Lucy in baggy green pajamas under an oversized, faded pink bathrobe.

Mandy said, "The guys and I were... Not important. How are you feeling?"

"Like I woke up after drinking two boxes of really bad wine. What's going on? I thought I had this weird dream I was back in the warehouse in Allentown and came to, only to discover I really was."

Sergei nodded and showed a toothy grin. "You make good sleep. Very long time. Get rest, relax, we make new office for you to work."

Lucy shook her head, winced and waved. "How long?"

Tommy said, "A few days."

"Well more like four, Tommy. Okay, three and not quite a — "

Lucy waved again. "Never mind. And I don't care about color. What I need is coffee. Jeez, I feel like I was drugged or something."

Charlie entered the room with an armload and an excuse-me. "You was. Our Ukrainian buddy put you under."

Lucy rubbed her temples. "No shit. With what?"

Yenchenko shrugged. "Native medicine from tribal doctor in jungle. Most useful to — "

"I don't really want to know. *Four days?*"

Tommy said, "You really needed it, Luce."

Mandy nodded, a maternal smile of concern on her face. "We were pushing too hard. I think the stress got to you."

True enough. The dark side of the old days. When assets were pushed too fast, too hard, without one bit of regard for their humanity. He poured a coffee.

Lucy, in a subdued voice said, "Yeah. I guess so. Tommy, I am so, so sorry..."

And she's feeling guilty? She'd signed on at the chance to go legitimate, to use her mind to run a business, to make a fortune, a favor for a favor. *But she stepped up and gave it her best.* Like when he was a kid, shucking oysters with his grandpap, racing to keep up with a pro, warned to be careful. *You go too quick with that blade, boy, you for sho' gonna bleed.*

He shrugged. The words of the Obi-Man, old Joseph, on Cat Island whispered in his mind. *What is money but paper and metal?* Now Lucy's eyes sought forgiveness, but he had no difficulty in responding with apology. "It's okay. Mandy's right, though. We were being much too demanding, and you were doing a first-class job. Just too much to juggle. No one thinks badly of you. For true, Luce. For true."

"Yeah, but — what, um, where, how?"

Mandy leaned against Lucy's old desk and patted the surface. "We found this in the back, cleaned it up. Your old chair, too. We, well, sort of took it upon ourselves to clean out this room, which Tommy says was once your office?"

Lucy took a sip. "And all the TKA equipment?"

Charlie put his hands on his hips. "Crated, loaded, delivered, stacked in the warehouse yonder."

"Oh, please tell me..."

Sergei chuckled. "We have good help from expert."

Bug entered the office, dusting off his hands. "Jeez, kiddo, you think you're the only person what knows how to handle mainframe shit? No time for the racks, though. Typical freakin' Tommy, a hurry-up, which is gonna cost him a friggin' fortune. And them bozos Tommy and Charlie rounded up? They worked like they was packin' poultry at a meat locker. Christ, it was... But mostly, you doin' okay?"

Lucy fell silent and she stood with her head bowed in the center of the room.

Tommy gestured it was time for Charlie and Sergei to step out, give a little privacy.

Charlie said, "I'm thinkin' enough's enough."

Bug glared defiance. "Damn right, Tommy."

Yenchenko nodded and cocked an eyebrow.

Charlie said, "Yeah, well, we gotta get our asses back to the truck. Let's go, Sergei."

For a moment, Mandy looked like she wanted to stay close to Lucy, but instead drifted over to Tommy's right.

Bug took a tentative step forward. Inch by inch, his left arm rose, starting, stopping, starting again. Bug. The crudest, coldest, toughest of the tough guys who took no crap from anybody. Uncertain, nervous. *Scared, maybe.* At last the side of his forefinger reached Lucy's chin and guided her head up so he could look into her eyes.

She wants to turn away, run, fly off like a little frightened bird.

But she didn't.

"I blew it, dad. I got sloppy, left a footprint. I know it. I spent too much time, stayed too long, went one directory too far. I got lost in the code, trying to figure out — "

Bug's voice was raspy but soft, more patient than Tommy had ever heard it. "It happens. We learn. We fix it. It's part of the business, what we do."

"But... but... *but not to me.* I mean, the SEC is — "

He grunted. "Buncha Twinkies, what don't know nothin'. And they got nothin' neither. All they got is an empty office suite."

She bit her lower lip. "And what about all the staff?"

Tommy said, "Two million each. Except for Warren and Joan, who got four."

Bug and Lucy continued to stare at each other, and he said, "So they got out okay. And so did you, kiddo. Maybe you got banged up a little, but nothin' that won't heal. Give yourself a coupla days, maybe a few of them crappy doughnuts, get back in the saddle, kick some ass."

Her voice dropped to a whisper. "But... oh, I don't know."

"I got ya a present, to do a restart. A nice little T-1 line, for all that stuff we got boxed up."

She gasped. "A T-1? How did you..."

He shrugged. "Hey, what Verizon don't know won't hurt 'em. All that excess cable and shit. This ain't the city. It's freakin' Allentown. And you know how it goes."

Her head began to lower. "I'm not sure I earned it, dad."

Bug's finger lifted her chin again, a rare smile on his face. "You're still number one, the best there is, the best there ever was. A mile bet—ter'n me, that's for damn sure. Yeah, Luce. Better than your old man."

Tears streamed down her cheeks. She sniffed and began to wipe them away but in a choking voice said, "Daddy?"

Bug opened his arms. "Yeah, kiddo. I'm here."

Mandy leaned close to Tommy and whispered, "Let's go get some doughnuts or something."

From her father's chest, Lucy's face beamed, safe and happy. And home. "Oh, gosh, please. Pink frosting. With sprinkles. And coffee. Lots and lots of coffee. And Tommy, Mandy? Thank you. Thank you so very much..."

CHAPTER TWENTY-SIX

Enroute to Nassau, The Bahamas

A cocoon of comfort. An oasis of calm, security. Floating through time and space, a feather on a summer breeze. A few days ago, mar—veling at how easily she could reconnect. Today, a routine as settled as...

As what? Bagel and coffee on the run? A day planner of chaotic scribbles? The constant flutter of anxiety when the phone rang? The right dress, the right sweater, the right suit for the endless parade of meetings, interviews, events? Parties not for fun and pleasure, but for working a story? The last managing editor. *Jeez, Owens, you gotta get more juice in this piece, up high, first coupla 'graphs. Readers don't wanna think. They wanna drool.*

The hard, cold, grinding industrial noise of the business, hundreds of miles behind, seven miles below. *Going to where they keep the sun. And guys like Walter Campos.*

The faint sound of the engines to the rear, the whisper of circulat—ing air, so soft that to breathe felt like an interruption. On the table, a perfectly-brewed cup of French Market coffee. And in her hands, the business section of *The Washington Post*. Buried below the fold on the second page, an amusing speculative piece by an eager, probably young, reporter about the sudden silence from the powerhouse invest—ment firm, TKA Associates, and its legendary reclusive leader, wheel—er-dealer Tommy Kane.

Charmingly inaccurate. Almost kind of fun.

She peeked beyond the edge of the curtain of newsprint. Tommy, stretched out in a reclining pond of gentle beige leather, sound asleep. Utterly calm. *The only guy I've ever met who could lose a hundred million dollars and not flinch. Not even flutter. Not even blink.*

Just yesterday, he stood in a half-painted room with second-hand furniture all around, draped in plastic, paint spatters on his arms, his hands, his nose and forehead, ratty clothes and a phone in his hand. And he told Warren that it was a good deal, he'd settle with the SEC, no harm done, no blame, no fault, no guilt, no hassle.

A hundred million dollars. After, we ordered out for pizza.

Mandy took a sip of coffee and ventured back into the article in *The Post.*

Lucy had spoken about a handful of energetic business writers, but this name was new and his sources only so-so. Familiar people, those of whom were listed as "unnamed" or "in a position to know" fairly easy to guess on the syntax of their comments. Yet another piece about the murky guys in the dark pools of trading. Whatever they were doing, it was okay. It was where the school of sharks were going next that counted. Sharks like Walter Campos. What to buy, what to sell. When. For how much. Anything good that came out of it was in—cidental. Social justice? A thread spun in the public relations office.

The article author was new and unaware of Tommy's bargain with the SEC. Not that Tommy would have cared. *Lucy might have. Knowing what was going on was her stock and trade.* So much so that it over—loaded her mind. Crashed. Froze. The only thing to do is to shut it down and restart. *Maybe better this time.* Whatever was between Lucy and Bug, simmering as some kind of truce, was hopefully settled at last. *The two of them together? What a scary thought that is.*

Mandy waded through another eight or nine paragraphs of stuff straight out of the newspaper's morgue, fragments of trading floor gossip from a year, eighteen, twenty months ago, and turned her at—tention to news from the fashion industry.

Karen appeared and the handouts from the fashion houses became unimportant. "More coffee? Fruit?"

"Yes, by all means, thank you."

"It's a shame Lucy couldn't make the trip," Karen said while she ladled a refill of cheerful colors of tropical fruit into the bowl. "I'm sure she'd love a break in her hectic routine."

A lot less hectic now. Rebounding fast, probably going crazy with two dads and a big brother to enforce Tommy's mandate to slow down, relax, no more all-nighters and a sharp cutback in coffee. "Well, you know Lucy. Her electronic gadgets would get sunburned. How's our flight time?"

Karen filled the aircraft's signature mug. "About two and a half hours. We're passing Washington. Have you been to Nassau before?"

Oh yes. The party at Lyford Caye. Tommy Kane. Walter Campos. The dirty guys from the CIA. And a good source who got murdered because she was helping me. "Just once. It was most interesting. Memorable, in fact."

Karen's smile widened to absolute delight. "I adore the little duty-free shops, and of course, this time of year, the beaches. One of the perks of the job." She glanced over her shoulder. "I don't think Tommy will be looking for coffee anytime soon."

"No, probably not."

She chuckled. "You'll get used to it. Most flights, it's like having no one aboard at all. There's something about the jet, the sound, the altitude, something. He sleeps like a baby."

Mandy took another peek. *So cute.* "More like a cat." She looked up at Karen and said, "Say, would you care to join me? I'd love to hear about all the best places to visit in Nassau. And all the stories about traveling with Tommy, too."

* * *

With a long, easy approach into Pindling International, Cesar's touchdown could not have been more gentle. A blur of low trees swept past, coming into focus as the jet slowed into a respectful crawl along a taxiway.

Tommy unclipped his seatbelt, yawned and stretched. "Ah, I sure could use a few days to relax, unwind."

"Not fair. You got a head start, three hours ago. We were hardly wheels-up in Allentown and you were totally gone. Like a baby, Karen said."

He chuckled at the concept. "Aw, that's nice." He lifted his two-two-six mug in salute to Karen and tossed what little coffee was left into his mouth.

"I rather thought more like a cat. You know, the kind you shouldn't have let into the house, the kind that *looks* cuddly but is really after your sympathy and good will — and all the comfort it can get away with."

Tommy winced and handed the cup to Karen. "Ouch. Such cruelty so early in the day."

Karen displayed a knowing smile while she collected Tommy's empty bowl from the table.

Mandy laughed. "But it's so true. I honestly don't understand how you do it. I've read an entire *Washington Post*, drank all your coffee, had a wonderful conversation with Karen about some of your more legendary flights, ate way too much and now I'm going to have to make major repairs as soon as we get to the hotel."

He nodded, but goaded her with the twinkle in his eyes, bluer and brighter in the sunshine streaming through the window as the jet slowed to a crawl and stopped. Karen's knowing smile seemed to border on a smirk.

"You, on the other hand, look completely rested, refreshed. Maybe a little scruffy around the edges. Still a couple of flecks of paint in your hair, too. You grab one cup of coffee, a teeny bowl of papaya and mango and pineapple and you're good to go. All you need is a pair of shorts, sandals and one of those silly shirts with flowers on it and you're set. Gosh, Tommy, you'll take one step outside and probably pick up a gorgeous tan, too."

He nodded and stood. "It's the leg room. You're probably not used to it yet. Shall we?"

Karen opened the aircraft door and the steps unfurled to the tarmac.

"Yes, you charming rascal. I hope Walter's booked us into a nice hotel."

Tommy grinned and motioned her forward. "For you, first class.

All the way."

"Ah. Now *that* is hopeful."

They followed Karen to the tarmac and the bawdy warmth of a Caribbean breeze that ruffled hair and painted smiles on faces all around. Sea air. Calm. Luxury. Pampering. She glanced at Tommy. *Yes. Someone's let the cat back in, and he knows he's about to get away with it. Whatever it is.*

Ground guys scampered about with wheel chocks. High above, Cesar and Ken were going through shutdown. The marshaller waved permission to a guy in a sort of glorified golf cart and the little vehicle pulled in tight.

There's no way that guy could not smile wider.

"Hallo, mistah and missus. Please get in. I'll go, bring your lug-gage."

On the bench seat for passengers, she leaned in close to Tommy. "We could actually walk to the terminal, you know."

"We're not going to the terminal." He pointed to the right front. A snow-white helicopter swooped in from the southeast, hovered for a moment and plopped to the pavement about seventy or eighty yards away.

"I see what you mean about Walter's hospitality, hiring a chopper to ferry is to the hotel."

Tommy laughed while the driver hopped in behind the steering wheel and put the cart into motion. "He didn't *hire* it, Mandy. It came with the yacht."

"Of course. How silly of me not to think of — well, the most in-congruous possibility imaginable."

Tommy folded his hands on his lap, tinged his voice with phony sympathy. "Yeah. I know. It's what happens when you take pity on some ratty ol' tomcat."

The main rotor had slowed to a slow whoosh-whoosh. The mar-shaller opened the aircraft door and gestured instructions. Seat belts. Headsets danging from hooks above. He held Mandy's hand as she climbed aboard and waved a greeting to the pilot. Tommy followed plus the bags. The door rolled closed and the ground guy motioned to the pilot.

Tommy pointed to the headsets and she followed his pantomimed direction. The sounds of air traffic control crackled in her ears.

And the voice of the pilot. "Morning, folks. Everybody buckled in?" He was deeply tanned in a cowboy sort of way, his eyes hidden behind aviator glasses and his short blond hair thinning a bit from front to back. The earphones barely muffled the rising howl of the jet engine throttling up. The rotor soon followed into a rhythm of stac‐cato thutter-thutter that shuddered throughout the chopper. A lurch. A wiggle. And a lift, mostly up, a little forward, a slight floating turn to the left. And the chopper picked up pace and made a straight run for the coastline of New Providence Island.

"Just a short hop." The pilot spoke in a casual tone perhaps de‐signed to ally anxieties about zipping across green tufts of trees and hot-color houses and crawling traffic in an aircraft that seemed like it was trying to rip itself apart. "Your first visit to the island, Mister Kane?"

Tommy said, "No. Been here a couple of times before."

"How about you, Miss?"

"Just once."

"Great. Welcome back. Hope you enjoy your stay. Weather's go‐ing to be fabulous for the next couple of weeks. Sunny, upper seven‐ties. That four-fifty your Gulfstream, Mister Kane?"

"It is."

"She's a beauty."

Tommy looked at Mandy. "Oh, yeah. They *both* are."

Heat filled Mandy's cheeks and ears and this time instead of look‐ing away in embarrassment, she turned toward his easy grin and eyes, sparkling like sunshine on the water, and rewarded him with her most open smile.

The pilot interrupted. "Just to the left, that's Lyford Caye. Great golf course down there, Mister Kane. One of Walter's favorites. Do you play, sir?"

Tommy smiled. "Once in a while."

Lyford Caye. The reception. All cheery yellow, very black tie. Walter needling Carter Blackmann. Tommy, at the bar, squeezing a drop of water from an ice cube into twenty-five-year old Macallan.

She glanced at him. That storied golf match when, on the run from professional killers, he walked right up to one of the greens and dropped a fifty-thousand-dollar putt. Just to say hello. *How legends are born.*

In her ears, the pilot said, "We'll hang a right at Love Beach, fol-low the coast over to Nassau."

The ocean, a mosaic of random blues and greens, revealing depth and the coral floor. The beaches, white as new snow, shimmering in the midday sunshine. The impression that the pilot was showing off a favorite jewel, a good place to hang out. Forever. He called out land-marks. Cable Beach hotels and casinos. Dead ahead, Arawak Cay.

Near Colonial Beach, the chopper went into a wide banking turn around a pair of cruise ships in Nassau's main harbor. Aligned with the channel that separated New Providence from Paradise Island, the pilot guided the aircraft into a gentle descent. The fading white wakes of larger craft scarred the shades of turquoise below, punctuated with sailboats and cruisers.

One spot grew larger and larger as the helicopter floated to earth, to the right of the pink towers of the Atlantis Resort. Two, no, three decks. Smaller boats moored next to the yacht, like pilot fish clinging to the protection of a great white shark.

Rushing in. *Too fast, too fast.* Mandy fingers tightened on the tufted vinyl edge of the seat and her lungs clung to a breath that didn't want to leave. About to crash into an upper deck or at least the radar and navigation equipment that towered high into the air.

Easy. He knows what he's doing. Her fingers relaxed but she tapped the tips on the seat edge.

The little pilot fish boat wasn't in the water at all. It was a kind of skiff, perhaps twenty or twenty five feet long, suspended from a pair of starboard hoists on one of two platforms that extended from the hull, above the waterline.

She shifted her hands to her lap. "Oh, wow. How big is that boat, anyway?"

The pilot chuckled. "A hundred and ninety feet."

Mandy curbed an another urge to ask the pilot to slow down, but tapped her fingertips together. Closer, closer. A flat square at the rear with a circle in the center, a target. *He's going right into the upper decks.* A glance at Tommy. *Totally indifferent. He's done this before. Take a breath. Be calm.*

Rotor shadows spun right to left against the white of the yacht. Just in the nick of time, the aircraft hung still in a hover that seemed like the chopper really didn't want to stop having fun. To the right, two guys in bright green vests cringed against the draft of the rotor. *At airports, they have ground guys. What do they have on boats?*

The helicopter settled with a soft plop. Directly ahead, above them on the second deck, a tall, lean man in khaki stepped forward and thrust his fists into his waist. He wore a long-billed cap and, from a chin thrust forward, grinned like a pirate that had recently sacked an entire town.

Ten zeroes. Master and commander. A guy who makes his own adventure. A rascal with a capital R. And Tommy's pal.

Walter Campos.

CHAPTER TWENTY-SEVEN

Aboard the Sassy Jane, Nassau, The Bahamas

He stood with his legs apart, his hands stuffed into his waist, chin up and grinned from ear to ear. As they climbed the stairs, Walter's greeting boomed across the harbor and ricocheted around Paradise Island. "By damn, Tommy, welcome aboard!"

Tommy looked up. *Still in khaki, still lean, still the big dog, towering above everyone else.* "Hey, Walter. You're looking good, really good."

Walter roared unabashed laughter. "Still vertical, son, still vertical. That's all that counts, eh? So, what do you think about my little tub?"

And still a bone-crushing handshake. "Just what I'd expect, buddy."

Walter's grin somehow managed to go wider and his tone shifted to lecherous confidentiality. "A fella's got to pamper himself with a little luxury sometimes. Yessir, as much as he can grab." His eyes turned to Mandy, who took a posture of courtesy without the slightest hint of intimidation. "But I see you already know that. My apologies for the failing manners of an old man, young lady." He closed the distance between them in one bold step and extended a hand. "You must be Amanda Owens. Mandy, I hear they call you. May I as well?"

She took his hand, politician-style, the right making a handshake, the left lingering atop his to enforce warmth. "You certainly may. It's a lovely yacht, Mister Campos, just gorgeous. Thank you for having us aboard."

"Around here, I'm just Walter." He shot a glance at Tommy. "I like the cut of her jib, son. I really do." He turned his attention back to her easy smile and unflinching eyes. "O'course, what I said didn't have any of that sexual innuendo business so popular these days. It's a nautical expression, you see."

She might be gorgeous, but Walter's not paying attention to her looks. He's measuring her character.

Mandy didn't miss a beat. "None taken, Walter. I grew up in Connecticut. That's an expression usually attributed to seventeenth century pirates. Because the course and speed of a ship is determined by the cut of the ship's jib, you're saying you like the way I'm heading. But that's what some say about the phrase."

Walter beamed again, his defiant chin leaning into the conversation and his eyes bright and steady to measure response. "Hah. And so it is. You tell that to Sir Walter Scott, who most folks say coined the saying."

Mandy's eyes twinkled, too. "I'd love to, but he's been dead since 1832. So I'll go with the pirate legend. Are you a pirate, Walter?"

Campos took half a step back and planted his hands on his hips. "Well, Mandy, I'd wager that we all are. Wouldn't you agree, Tommy? Sure you would. Everybody agrees with the guy who's picking up the tab. So, young lady, can I offer you some lunch? Tommy, here, he's probably missed the good food of the Caribbean. Eats like a wolf, too. But he's got damn good taste in companionship and I'd welcome some first-rate conversation. Yes indeed. First-rate."

Mandy blushed and chuckled. "It would be my pleasure. And I'm famished."

Walter beckoned a steward and pointed to their luggage. He turned to Tommy and Mandy. "Say, you kids haven't gone off and gotten hitched or anything, have you?"

"No, afraid not," Tommy said.

Mandy cocked an eyebrow.

"You probably ought to give it some thought, Tommy. Settle down, have some stability your life. I'm an old man, you see, and I miss that sort of thing. I surely do. But..." He brightened. "No matter. Jimmy, be a good lad and take their gear to the guest staterooms. Give Miss Owens the bigger one. Tommy can rough it." Again he turned to the couple. "Got rules, you see. I might be an old pirate, lie, cheat, steal, have the ethics of a stray dog, but I do have a sense of morality, okay?"

Mandy chuckled. "Perfectly fine with me."

Tommy said, "I'm good. Your boat, your rules."

Walter clapped his hands together and rubbed them with vigor. "Good. Now let's go get some grub. We've got a first-rate cook aboard, keeps me fat and sassy, but in good shape for an old rogue. Yessir, good shape."

They took the long route to a sheltered area on an upper deck where four chairs circled a round table under fine linen, sturdy china, sterling silverware and cut glass stemware. Walter invited them to choose seats. Mandy picked one facing away from Atlantis, while his looked out straight east across harbor and the bridge Yenchenko used when they shook a tail of Cuban intelligence. Now it was populated by tourists oblivious to the hidden side of Nassau, presumably as busy as ever.

Another steward arrived to take beverage orders. Mandy opted for a French chardonnay. If it bothered Walter, a guy who drifted be—tween lusty bourbons and the local beers, he didn't show it. *An ice-cold Kalik would be great. But Sands is lighter, probably a better choice. For lat—er.*

"We have an excellent Chateau Genot-Boulanger, an oh-nine," the steward said.

Walter leaned back and motioned a circle with his hand. "That's grand, just grand. All around, then. What's for lunch today, Freddie?"

Freddie's nod bordered on a bow. "For today, chef has prepared a very nice conch salad with a sour orange dressing, white crab soup with rice and a hint of bacon fat, and Abaco baked grouper, Caicos style with tomato, onion and green pepper."

Walter extended his hands to grant permission for dissent.

Mandy smiled. "It all sounds marvelous. Only not too much hot pepper on the salad, if I may." When Freddie nodded, she replied with a thousand-dollar smile and a million-dollar attitude, settling back in her deck chair with all the aplomb of someone who'd done this many times before. "Thank you."

Just no way all the money around the table could begin to buy that kind of class. Born and bred, polished to hundreds of sparkling facets. Just no way a kid out of the Teche can begin to match that.

Freddie returned with a bottle sheltered in a white towel, un—corked and poured. And the view on both sides began to drift by.

Mandy asked, "Is the yacht moving?"

Walter nodded. "It usually does when the boys cut loose the mooring, weigh anchor and start up the engines."

"Ah. For a moment, Walter, I was beginning to wonder about the wine."

He laughed. "Much too early in the day. And I hate being boxed up in a harbor, especially Nassau. More of an open sea kind of fellow. Isn't that right, Tommy?"

"Absolutely."

Freddie delivered enormous conch salads and Walter dismissed polite protests about size. "Eat up. We're going to be awful busy next couple of days. Yessir, awful busy." He stabbed at his plate and came up with a big prize. "So Tommy, how's that jet working out for you? Gulfstream, wasn't it?"

"Yes. A four-fifty."

"Pretty aircraft, those. Halfway around the world on a tank of gas, they say. Just the thing for a guy in a hurry."

"It gets me from here to there."

Walter chuckled and nodded toward Mandy. "She know?"

Tommy nodded. No big deal.

Mandy leaned forward and gave Walter the look, the one she saved up to encourage a source eager to unmask a tale. Charm and ex—citement and fascination, all rolled into one, her big brown eyes mas—saging every confidence a guy ever held close to his chest. And while Walter might be a shrewd old fox, he sauntered right into the trap she laid.

"Well, Mandy, it was a helluva thing. Just a helluva thing. I hear they still talk about it around here. They way Tommy's mob busted into a hanger and stole a forty-million dollar jet from the Cuban gov—ernment, changed the registration, flew the hell out of here like they were a bunch of good time boys packing up a little vacation."

"Amazing," Mandy said. "And Tommy used to say he got it sec—

ond hand, a real steal."

Except she knows the story and she could twist a true statement into feigned ignorance.

Walter rolled right along. "It was an inside job, you see. He had a gal real handy with computers working the magic. Had the Cubans, the CIA, the FAA, not to mention Homeland Security running in such tight circles that they never noticed ol' Tommy slip through the back door, more than likely laughing all the way."

By the time the soup bowls were cleared, Walter had made his point. The table was indeed populated with pirates. *He's got to be comfortable. We're about to ask him for six hundred and fifty million dollars.*

Beyond the harbor limit, the yacht picked up speed, its bow slicing through crystal water, making a wide turn to the right with New Providence in its wake. They dined at a leisurely pace, teasing, tattling, testing the boundaries of a partnership being forged bite by bite.

She asked, "So why is it — *she* — named *Sassy Jane*?"

Walter smiled. "Gal I new once, a long time ago. Pretty gal, a lot like you. And she was a sassy one, too. One thing or another kept getting in the way, mostly business, deals, a lot of travel. Finally got so frustrated about it that I dropped a three-million-dollar deal that took months, right at closing, went home, found she'd got sick, some kind of cancer, died."

Mandy's expression softened and she reached out to place her hand on his. "I'm so sorry, I didn't mean to — "

Walter shrugged. "It's all right. It was a long time ago, a long time. And a smart-thinking man knows sickness is sickness and in the end it wouldn't have mattered. But time is time, and there never seems to be enough of it. Since then? Well, it's so much stuff, stuff that don't really matter." After a respectful moment of silence, Walter looked up again and laughed. "Now, let me tell you about the time when Tommy..."

Oh, man, not that one again. Tommy sat back and concentrated on his meal in the hope that he wouldn't look too embarrassed while Mandy and Walter gossiped.

When she dabbed her lips with the napkin, she passed her compliments to the chef for the best grouper she'd ever enjoyed.

Go ahead. Say it.

She beamed and looked at Walter and Freddie. "A best ever. Ab—solutely. Please tell him."

Walter mopped up his chin with less gentility. "Any dessert, Fred—die?"

"Yessir. A lovely coconut duff, with a butter-rum sauce."

"Splendid. And bring some coffee, too."

The open sea. Limitless. Free. Adventure on every horizon.

Walter said, "Ever find that Alden, Tommy?"

"No, never did. Haven't given up though."

"A yawl, wasn't it?"

"Yes. Fifty feet or so, a wooden one."

"Hell, you oughta make do with a ketch. Better under sail, they say. Say, whatever happened to that crazy gal with the — what was it, a Morgan?"

Tommy said, "Last seen going through the Panama Canal, headed west."

Mandy seemed to be doing her best not to intrude.

Tommy lifted his coffee cup to sip. "Times change. Everyone charts their own course." He looked at Mandy. "She was a good friend, Walter, a free spirit. Asked me to crew when she wanted to come up to the Virgin Islands, when I was flat broke and kicking around. Yeah, she argued for a ketch, but I always dreamt of an Alden yawl." He tugged the folded list of names given by Lucy, sheltered in his pocket ever since and passed it to Walter.

"Playing in the big leagues now, I see. You *do* understand, son, there's a difference between a baby barracuda and a full-grown great white."

"Yeah, Walter, I do."

"Personal, is it?"

"Some. But there's more to it. It's Mandy's inquiry, so it's her story to tell."

Walter listened to Mandy summarize events, the trading applica—tion and flaw in the most layman's terms Lucy could muster, the plan to confront the conspiracy players to pry loose where the application was housed, the goal to replace it with a benign dummy, the notion of faking a meltdown to nail whoever was ultimately responsible.

"Ambitious, young lady. God damn ambitious. How do you know it's going to work?"

Tommy said, "We don't."

"And what's it going to take to light the fuse?"

"A billion. To bang the close."

Mandy said, "Well, Lucy said seven or eight hundred million might work."

"Yeah, but a billion is better."

Walter chuckled. "And what's your end? I heard some chatter that had a little trouble with the SEC and — "

" — It took a hundred million to make it go away, Walter. I pressed too hard, got pinched, okay? We're trying to get assets off—shore, but you know how that goes. Best I can do right now is three-fifty."

Mandy shrugged. "So we're sort of looking at six-fifty." She re—turned her cup to the saucer with all the aplomb of someone borrow—ing twenty bucks because they were momentarily short of tip cash.

When she finished, he chuckled. "Now, don't take this the wrong way, Mandy. I'm sure you're probably correct about some sort of global meltdown. Serious business. Six-fifty on a handshake is also se—rious business."

"You'll consider our business proposition?"

"Like I said, I like the cut of your jib. Business is *always* personal. And personal's the course I'd prefer to set."

"Thank you, Walter. It's kind of you to hear us out. Speaking of courses, where are we headed?"

"Why, out for a cruise, that's all. You folks are down here to bring this old — yeah, this old pirate into your scheme. But that doesn't mean you can't see some of the sights. When was the last time you were the Exumas, Tommy?"

"Been a while."

Walter turned to Mandy. "Hundreds of islands in the Bahamas, Mandy. Tourist folks, they say seven hundred, but nobody really knows for sure. Now, up at the top of the chain, you've got your Grand Bahama and New Providence, the big tourist magnet. Way down south, by Haiti, you've got the Turks and Caicos. And right in between, the Exumas. That's where they keep half the islands. Including the one I want you to see."

CHAPTER TWENTY-EIGHT

Off Halsey Island, The Exumas

She found him toward the bow, his forearms resting on the gun—wale. The moment of sunrise. Blue becomes gold. The air stirs. The sea awakens. Shafts of light skewered the island, scattering all its mys—tery. To port, a swirl of sandbars wriggled toward a distant line of low trees.

Mandy held a pair of mugs. "I've raided the galley for coffee, but I'm afraid Freddie wasn't much opposition. He said they just made it."

Tommy took a sip. "Terrific."

"Do you miss it? Being at sea, away from it all?"

"The lifestyle has its moments. Simplicity. Clarity. For almost all the time, an enormous sense of tranquility. Just mindlessly floating through space and time."

Another dazzling day in the Caribbean, puffy clouds, terns, fish jumping here and there to avoid predators from below, not even thinking about the brown pelicans dive bombing from above. "You said 'almost'."

"I did. Because that other fraction of one percent, it's scary beyond belief. A squall is one thing. You batten down, puke a lot, ride it out. But when you get caught in a big one, you're riding a thin line be—tween life and death. There's no do-overs, no second chances. You can do everything right and in moments be lost, vanish, never heard from again. If you're lucky, pieces of the boat might wash up some—where and they'll figure out what happened."

She nodded. "And there are those who thrive on the edge, taking a certain sort of pride in staring certain death right in the face, not even thinking it could be their last moment."

"For true. The crews that like to take a forty-footer around Cape Horn, through the Magellan Straight, when the williwaws are running high. They say — always after — that it heightens the sense of being alive. Mostly in seedy out-of-the-way ports in smoky little bars with cheap rum and a lot of lies."

She took a sip of coffee that had gone cold. "I'm not so sure I could. Go roaming, I mean. Alone. I need people, Tommy. I especial-ly need to reconnect, get involved again. So, are you still looking for that yawl, the Alden?"

"Priorities change."

"So, the cabin, way out of town, a small country town."

He swirled the remaining coffee in his cup. "And the Gulfstream, and Lucy's enterprise."

"And a billion dollars."

He smiled, a rueful smile, his face basking in the warming sun-shine, and collected the cup. "A real smart guy, an Obi-Man — that's sort of Bahamian witchcraft, big time — once reminded me that mon-ey means nothing. It's just paper and metal. And usually responsible for a lot of stuff that isn't anywhere near as nice as that sun, coming up in the morning."

"Sort of a romantic set of values."

He shrugged. "Think about it. The billion, or whatever it is, comes from Lucy's efforts doing what she loves best. And all it really means to her is a means of keeping score."

"So what do we do?"

Tommy looked past her shoulder. He grinned and gestured with the arm holding the cup. "We say good morning to Walter, who's probably got a full schedule for us today."

She turned and waved. "G'morning, Walter."

Walter grinned and spread his arms high and wide. "You kids up for breakfast? We've got stew fish and johnnycake for the seafarers, eggs and bacon for the landlubbers, and the best damn coffee this side of Jamaica. Which, I see, you've already found. That's all right. We'll get a second round, talk a little business, lay out our plans."

He motioned toward the captain's table on the upper deck and marched away.

Tommy shrugged. "Oh, well. Another routine day of fun, adven—ture, kicking a little ass." He sighed. "Will it ever end?"

She punched him lightly on the shoulder. "With you? I tend to doubt it."

"You ready?"

He's asking if I'm all right. "Yes. Not sure about stew fish, though. It seems, well, kind of..."

His smile of utter confidence was back. "Try it. You'll like it." He produced a sly grin. "Trust me."

Mandy said, "You're a complicated man, Tommy Kane. Rather comforting, though."

"I'll take that as a compliment."

Nice to laugh again, a laugh from the innocence and simplicity of so long ago. "You should. It's the best you're going to get this time of day."

* * *

A lazy and lighthearted ninety minutes later, the *Sassy Jane's* skiff wove through slithering sandbars, endless random patterns of pure white and shades of pale blue, ripples sparking in balmy tropical sun—shine.

Walter seemed to relish the role of tour guide. He pointed left to right, his extended fingers tracing a line along a thin, dark green line of trees. Armed with a net full of statistics, numbers rolled off his tongue. *Way too fast for even my note-taking skills. At a press conference, I'd have my hand in the air begging repetition. Today I don't care.*

The rushing wind fluttered their shirts and hair, but Walter's eyes and grin were steady. "They made a bunch of those old pirate movies over there, all because they've got three things down here. No people, hanging around, watching. No aircraft or boats to screw up the long shots. And an endless supply of perfect weather, like this. Some folks'd call it seven hundred acres of paradise."

She turned for a look at *Sassy Jane*, anchored outside the reef line.

All it needed was a couple of tall masts and a jolly roger. Ahead, half a dozen vacant beaches, each a quarter to a third of a mile long, hugging a long, thin stretch of the island.

"And the best part, Tommy, is that tucked in there, in that line of trees, is an actual airstrip, a runway over a mile long and room for more."

The skiff picked up speed, more brazen in deeper water that looked like it was only a few inches but was more likely six or seven feet deep. A wide turn to port, around a point. The beach became irrelevant. Perched atop a low hill, shimmering white and pale green, sprawling out in three directions, wrapped in a second story deck. The house. Huge. Gorgeous.

Walter directed the helmsman to put in at a narrow dock. "We've paid the caretaker to take the day off, run some errands, have a little fun, over in Georgetown. So we've got the place to ourselves." He chuckled and his grin went sly. "Hard to say if it's trespassing if nobody's home. One of those 'if a tree falls in a forest does it make a sound' sort of things."

What's the penalty for breaking and entering an island?

Walter's step was spry, assured, confident, as he stepped from the skiff onto the dock and turned to offer Mandy a courtly gentleman's hand. His tour mode resumed. "So here it is, folks. Halsey Island. This is Susan Halsey's place. Been in the family six or seven generations."

Mandy crossed her arms and paused. "I feel like we're intruding, that we shouldn't — "

"Nonsense. Let's have a look around."

Tommy's eyes narrowed and he cocked his head. "*Our* Susan Halsey?"

"The same."

Tommy shrugged. "I'm guessing that Walter's brought us here to make a point. We ought to hear him out."

Mandy stepped forward. "You're right, Tommy. We should." Like the long-ago time in Quebec. The scary barn down the road. When we were six or seven. There were supposed to be ghosts and monsters in there, and the others were certain that if they snuck in when the moon was full... And so they crept through the little field, across the stone wall fence, their hands chilled and their summer shoes soaked from the dew. They giggled and snickered and taunted one another. Hardly a surprise attack. In a swirl of whispers, they circled the barn, looking for the creaky door — all spooky doors are creaky — through which they could enter. A clatter, a yell. A snarling curse in French. The old guy that owned the place, Marcel something. And the squeals and screams as they fled, oblivious to the darkness, to the safety of home. Adventure. The stuff of secret stories and charming memories. No Marcel here today. Still —

They climbed ten white steps to a landing, turned and silently counted off several more until they reached a spotless deck and the main floor of the house. Ahead, a screened veranda with tables and chairs. To the right, a causeway to an observation tower. Beyond and below, a swimming pool guarded by half a dozen chaise lounges, up—holstered in red. To the left, the inevitable sliding doors that could open an entire building to the gentle weather and fair winds of the southern Bahamas.

Tommy said, "Very impressive. An amazing getaway."

Walter reached for the door and laughed. "Only she never gets away, Tommy. She never comes here. The caretaker is the second generation to keep this place picture perfect and he says his father re—membered an occasion when she came by."

Mandy said, "You're joking."

Tommy took a long look. "It's got to be worth a fortune."

Walter chuckled and opened the door. "Down here? Fifty, sixty million at least." Tommy followed, but Mandy took more tentative steps, her senses tingling like when she was a little girl and the only one brave enough to reach for the latch of the creepy barn door. While the room was light, airy, spacious, plush with soft pastel furni—ture, it felt hollow and empty, even a little sad.

"Six bedrooms, the guy said. All with their own can." Walter waved a hand. "Kitchen, lot of places to entertain. Maybe five or six thousand square feet, good views all around, high enough to ride out any storm."

Mandy reached out to touch, but pulled her hand back. "I don't understand. I mean, why keep something like, well, *all* of this and never — "

"Why, pride o'course, Mandy. Place has been in the family for generations. No golf course on the island, though, but she could put in her own if she wanted. I know of half a dozen blue chippers and movie stars who would pay anything to own this place. Hell, even our president made a pitch, but no luck."

She asked, "Your company president?"

Walter laughed. "No, Mandy. *The* president. The one in the White House. We go back a ways. Tossed him a few million to get him over a campaign hump. Nice fellow, a little stubborn on some half-baked ideas, but overall a nice fellow. Wanted a spot to retire, do a little fishing, write memoirs, that sort of thing. Asked me to put in a word, a bid, for him. But she won't sell. No, Mandy, she keeps it because she *can*."

Tommy nodded. "Ten zeroes."

Walter beamed at Tommy's grasp of the situation. "You got it, son. You got it. C'mon. Let's go get some fresh air."

They strolled across the deck and causeway to an observation tower with a couple of chairs and a table. The breeze was stronger here, unfettered by the trees below. The *Sassy Jane* was a distant speck, a dot on the horizon.

Walter plopped into one chair and motioned to Mandy to take the second. Tommy leaned against a thick railing, a little lower than his waist.

"There's a couple of other houses on the island. The caretaker's o'course and a place for guests — "

Tommy smiled. " — Who never come. And the caretaker?"

Walter shrugged. "Getting on in years. Bored as hell. Thinking about buying himself a charter or something out of Georgetown, maybe do something else with his life. Halsey won't care. She'll find someone else. Actually, her personnel people will handle it."

Mandy leaned forward and folded her hands together. "But there's a point to all of this, Walter. Isn't there?"

"You're a smart gal, Mandy. A damn good reporter, I'm told. Run with the best of 'em."

Don't flinch. "I try."

"I wanted you kids to get a sense of who you're dealing with, that's for sure." His voice lowered into dead serious. "You're trying to con—vict people who will never go to jail. They don't have to merely kill you — they've got plenty of people who'd do that in an instant. No. They'll take you apart right to the bones and toss you overboard like chum to feed the sharks. And not even give it a second thought."

Despite the balmy sunshine, a chill slithered down Mandy's spine.

Tommy seemed unperturbed, even a little defiant. "Maybe so, Walter. But I — we — believe it's worth a shot."

Walter glanced at Mandy and focused on Tommy. "You certain about that 'we'?"

I'm with Tommy. "Walter, I'm so weary about being pushed and shoved and dragged by situations and circumstances and things I can't control. I'm so frustrated about being dragged into some global eco—nomic power play that I could frankly care less about anymore. But most of all, I'm really furious that some sad, paranoid, little, lonely, miserable, man who stepped up to do the right thing doesn't matter. Just collateral damage. Just the first guy to get squashed by the Susan Halseys of the world. I care deeply about a city detective who cared about me when it counted. But mostly, I care about a guy named Ben—ny."

For once, neither of the men had anything to say. The silence hung long in the sheltered tower before it whisked away on the eter—nal wind of the sea.

Mandy drew a breath and stared at Walter. "On your big, luxuri—ous, beautiful yacht, Tommy and I laid out our plan. It's complicated, it's scary, it's expensive and the odds are really long that it's going to work. We need your help. Are you in or out?"

Walter leaned back in his seat, a contemplative expression on his face. He said, "She's got an awful lot of brass, Tommy. A lot of brass. Helluva woman. The kind that comes along maybe once in a life—time."

Tommy smiled. "Yes, Walter. I already know that."

Walter looked back and forth several times before settling on

Mandy. "Just give an old man a moment of patience, young lady. Okay?"

She nodded.

"Twenty-five, twenty-six years ago, we were all young hotshots. Me and Halsey. Eaton, Chamberlain, Morris and Gibbons, too. Wheeling, dealing, making a god damn fortune. Hell, we *ran* the equity markets, buying, selling, taking companies apart, putting the pieces back together the way we wanted. Our private little game. Enormous profits. Couldn't spend it fast enough."

Don't ask. Don't interrupt.

Walter's expression was distant, rueful. "But Halsey? She wanted to control the whole show, be the alpha bitch. The men? No balls at all. They were fat and content, so they fell into line. Still do. Me? Well, that isn't the cut of *my* jib. So things got a little tense. And like the runt of the litter, I got kicked out. But not just kicked out, Mandy. She clipped me for millions — *millions* — as a way of putting her boot on my ass."

Oh, gosh. It's about revenge.

Walter's eyes narrowed and he leaned in to face Mandy, but spoke to Tommy.

"A point is a difficult coastline to defend, Tommy. Every green naval cadet and every experienced pirate knows it. Susan Halsey's point is *pride*. And this, right here, is it. An island she keeps but never visits. I'll give you the six hundred million. Hell, I'll give you a billion if you need it."

Mandy remained focused on Walter and spoke in a soft, encouraging voice.

"But there's a price, a condition."

A smile of determination spread across Walter's jaw. "Yes, Mandy, there is. I want her god damn island."

CHAPTER TWENTY-NINE

Near Jack's Ford, Pennsylvania

Fresh snow deflected lights from Tommy's truck into his burning eyes. Shapes were different. Unfamiliar. Maybe a wrong turn. Onto the wrong road altogether. Impossible. At last. The huge boulder, the three big trees.

Mandy asked, "Are you all right?"

"Yeah, beat. Long day, long flight, long drive. The snow hasn't made it any easier." He slowed to a crawl and made the turn onto a narrow unpaved lane that, especially in the dark, looked like an ominous logging road. *Quarter mile to home.*

Her tone was sympathetic, comforting, warm. "You are *so* right about that. The Bahamas were great, the support from Walter wonderful, our plan is right on track, the flight was a delight. But right now, I want to get out of these shoes, put my feet up and unwind. I've been thinking about that big, soft sofa and a really mellow scotch for the past twenty miles."

Clumps of snow tumbled from the trees above, distracting blobs in the blackness, and he eased off the accelerator even more. That narrow turn, around a bank of rock, an easy place to slip off into the downslope even in the best of conditions. But treacherous when the lane was blanketed with snow.

Focus. Take it easy. Just an eighth of a mile. "I must be getting really old. Hot cocoa and a cookie would work for me."

She chuckled. "We're out of cookies, and I don't plan to bake... Say, you *must* be getting old. You left the lights on."

Huh?

Tommy looked out ahead. A glow. From the kitchen window. And beyond, from the den, backlighting the roof.

Watch it!

He shoved the brake pedal, too hard. The truck wiggled, waggled, slid forward toward the edge of the roadway. Stop.

Whew.

Tommy stared ahead at the cabin, hands gripping the steering wheel, tension gripping his jaw. *Think.* "No. I didn't."

Her stare was one of puzzlement. "Hey, Tommy, no big deal. It's okay. Only for a couple of days and it's not like you can't afford — "

"I didn't leave the lights on."

He doused the headlights and a black silence filled the cab of the truck. Rubbed the back of his hand across his nose, he stared at the glowing silhouette of the cabin, more washed out by the kitchen win—dow, lighting up the porch like a bunch of candles.

Mandy bit her lower lip. "I can't imagine... oh, gosh, Tommy, this is too much... What can we — "

"Reach into the glovebox. Yeah, it's a gun and be careful, it's load—ed."

She pulled the weapon out into the faint light of the instrument panel. She held the grip with her fingertips, the barrel pointing straight down, passing it to him like it was a dead animal.

"Maybe we could back out, go to town, get somebody? I could di—rect you, maybe." She turned her attention back to the cabin. "This is not good, Tommy. We ought to get out of — "

Tommy chambered a round and released the safety. "Let's go ahead, see who's come to visit. It's the hospitable thing to do."

"There are *never* visitors. Except for... Maybe it's Charlie."

"He's in Allentown."

"Or Sergei?"

"Definitely Allentown. And besides, he wouldn't be able to find this place."

She sighed and slumped in her seat. "Just like you said. Some peo—ple see trouble coming and run. But you? You have to walk right up and say hello. Okay. Let's go get killed or something. But you're going to make my scotch a double, all right?"

Tommy eased the truck into low gear and released the brake. The light coating of snow muffled the gravel and the truck lurched forward. "With any luck, we've got the element of surprise."

"With any luck, they haven't consumed all the scotch."

Just a couple of hundred feet to go. Slight grade, all down hill. Go to neutral, kill the engine, coast to a stop. Between the truck and the porch steps, a dark green, mid-sized SUV. Jersey plates. Next to the door, kitchen lights on. No attempt to hide. Nobody watching.

Tommy eased the door open with his left hand and gripped the pistol with his right. "Wait here."

"Not on your life. We're together on this."

He slid out and lowered his voice to a whisper. "Okay, but stay behind me."

"Gladly. I draw the line at being a human shield, Tommy."

Slow, measured steps past the SUV. A peek inside. Might be a rental. Just too clean to be... Tommy signaled a pause and focused on the cabin window and door.

Just ten feet to go.

He pointed to the stairs and motioned a reminder that they might creak when stepped on. She nodded. He placed a shoe on the first tread. Up they crept, one stair at a time. *Just a couple of feet.* Tommy gestured for Mandy to hug the wall and he took a position next to the door, the gun aimed down and gripped with two hands. He leaned in to listen.

Voices. Not loud, not soft, talking at the same time. Four or more. Living room. A shadow in the kitchen, moving around. A warning to Mandy, then wait. The light shifted again, and stabilized. Coast's clear.

Tommy's fingers gripped the knob. *Turn, turn, slowly, gently, easy.* The latch released. *Now push.* The kitchen door swung open and Tommy poured himself into the kitchen, froze, took a breath. Mandy slid in behind. The voices, familiar.

Relief.

Mandy savored a breath and rolled her eyes. Tommy put the weapon on safety and tucked it under his jacket.

Lucy appeared in the hallway, holding an empty plate. She called out toward the living room. "Hey guys, they're here!" Her gaze returned to Tommy and Mandy. "Where've you guys been? We've been worried sick."

Mandy said, "We tried to call, but there was no answer — so we thought you might be really busy."

Lucy laughed. "Probably because this place is so isolated. Tommy, I didn't know they still made parts of the country where you couldn't make a phone call. Cell hell, they call it."

On the counter, a platter of crackers, breads, cheese, lunch meats. Two six packs of beer, half empty. Tommy said, "Long flight, traffic, the weather. So why is everyone here?"

She shrugged. "We had to beat feet out of Allentown. After the gun battle, we had no place to go, so Charlie brought us here."

Mandy's eyes widened. "What gun battle?"

"The Cinnabar people. *Again*. Shot up the building something terrible. Automatic weapons, couple of flash grenades. Sergei and Charlie dished it right back, though. Even my father was blasting away. Kinda cool. I've never been in the middle of a firefight before."

Tommy drew his weapon and cleared the chamber. "Anyone hurt?"

"Dad got a little cut by flying glass, but otherwise we're okay." She gestured to the counter. "We've got snacks, goodies."

Mandy hung her coat on the hook by the door. "Thanks, Lucy. But I'm already committed to scotch." She glanced at Tommy. "A *lot* of scotch. Which is where I'm headed right now."

Lucy turned to Tommy as Mandy breezed past. "Oops. One of *those* situations, huh?"

She's back to normal. Just the way she was. "You know how it is, Luce. I sometimes get a little too cautious, see the boogeyman in every shadow."

Lucy laughed. "That'll always screw up a perfectly nice date." Her expression went solemn. "But this time, maybe you should be. C'mon.

We'll fill you in. Grab a beer. Sorry, no crab cakes. Just too far from Harrisburg."

A post-mortem with an icy edge to it was still under way when Tommy entered his own den. The leak that gave them away. Who screwed up. When. Where. All the security of a shopping mall on a Saturday night. Disgraceful. *Hang back. You'll only pour gas on the fire, have to referee, take a side, annoy somebody. She's better at this.* Mandy had wasted little time, making the rounds of three growling men, flooding the room with charm, melting the argument with the sheer warmth of her personality.

Lucy stopped at Tommy's side, leaned close and whispered. "She's really that good, isn't she?"

"Oh, yeah."

"How long, do you think?"

"Give her another twenty seconds or so."

A gentle calm took root and blossomed. Good friends, having a nice time. Cozy fire. Everyone in fine spirits. Mandy found her cus—tomary spot on the big soft sofa, turned to look for Tommy, and urged him to join her with that look in her eyes.

He accepted the invitation with two glasses of scotch. Doubles.

"Ah," she said. "That's better. We could about break out a round of hot chocolate and toast marshmallows and sing those old campfire songs, couldn't we?"

The men chuckled.

"But scotch is better."

Yenchenko beamed and hoisted his drink in salute. The others fol—lowed.

"So," Tommy said at last. "What's new?"

Lucy took the lead. "We were getting the system back up on line with one of the system modules, managed to get the liquid three hun—dred million stashed offshore. Then all the accounts got frozen by the SEC again. Someone's really pulling the chain, Tommy."

"So the bulk of the assets are stuck?"

"Afraid so. Dad busted his ass looking for a route to let me in, but the more we pressed, the more footprints we left. I'm — well, *we* —

are really sorry about that."

Mandy said, "It's okay. It was a tough spot to start with, I'm sure."

"Okay, so we're banging around the networks when the building gets surrounded by the guys from Cinnabar, posing as feds. All the black vehicles swooping in, lights, bullhorns, the pseudo-military gear."

Charlie elaborated. "They was tryin' to come off as FBI, but they don't know crap about how a good raid works. Too many red flags for me, so I figured maybe we could see if it actually was for real."

Bug's turn. "So I took the only free line I had, traced it back to the local FBI field office, the local cops, the other services. Nothing. No-body had people on an op, leastwise there was no traffic. You know and I know that sometimes they go silent, but that's only until the shit hits the fan."

Tommy nodded.

Yenchenko spoke, "*Da, da, koshka*, it is so. And it is of course not so good a plan to surround the den of old wolf such as myself. Wolf is always prepared for such situation."

Charlie said, "So Sergei pulls out a couple of AR-15s and an AK-47 on full goddamn auto, boxes of ammo, and says 'let's shoot them all into little pieces'. I used to think that damn Russian — er, *Ukrainian* — was too goddamn dangerous, but it sure'n hell was good this time around. All I had on me was a standard-issue and one clip."

Mandy shook her head. "So, Sergei where did you — "

Yenchenko shrugged. "We make turn as guard. I use my brief time away off duty to make small walk and find pleasant gun show. Make good bargain, obtain weapons. In America, you can buy loaf of bread or machine gun, just the same." He lifted his bottle. "But beer? Is shit."

Mandy pointed to a collection of liquor on a table near the door. "If you'd like, help yourself to the vodka. I'm sure you've earned it."

Yenchenko spoke to Tommy. "It is permitted?"

"Absolutely, *tovarich*."

Charlie continued the story of how the firefight erupted, how Sergei led the defense of the building, how Bug tipped local police, how they slipped away during a snow squall.

Lucy said, "The upside is that I snagged the files and apps on the way out. But the downside is that all the gear is — or was — still in the warehouse. I can't see a simple way to get it back. We've already attracted way too much attention."

Tommy shrugged. "So we rebuild."

Lucy laughed. "Tommy, each one of those racks goes for about a million-three and there were thirty-two of them. That's close to forty-two *million* dollars. And you don't waltz into your neighborhood big-box appliance store and drop a few into your shopping cart."

She's right, of course. But indecision and uncertainty aren't options right now. They're looking for a plan.

Mandy had kicked off her shoes and parked her feet on the coffee table, legs crossed at the ankles, a glass of favorite scotch under her nose. Her eyes were on Tommy. "You know, we've all had a long, hectic day. Why don't we all get some rest, look at it tomorrow with fresh minds?"

Thank you.

Nods of approval came fast, without a hint of reservation. Lucy seemed to be caught off-guard.

Mandy smiled and sat up. "I'm sure that Charlie can find a spot for the guys. Lucy, would you like to stay with us tonight?"

"Uh, well, if it's no trouble — "

Tommy said, "No trouble at all. We'd love to have you."

"I don't want to sound ungrateful, Tommy, but you've got no computers, no phone lines, no TV, not even an electric clock."

Mandy grinned. "That's right. Isn't it wonderful?"

CHAPTER THIRTY

The Puffin Diner, Jack's Ford, Pennsylvania

Indecision. The turkey club was nice, the BLTs a bit too lettucey, the burgers greasy enough for Charlie. It was possible to get lucky with a platter, depending on tolerance for the bloated feeling that would tag along for the rest of the day. *A small salad will have to do.*

Tommy adored the baskets, chicken or shrimp, but lately had leaned toward immense salads drenched in dressings. *He'll do a salad. Probably ranch dressing. He seems in a ranch kind of mood.*

Across the table, Lucy opened the menu, but didn't really look. "I'd kill for a really good crab cake. You know, Tommy, like the ones at our favorite little rendezvous in Harrisburg, that upscale place near the capitol."

Mandy said, "They have them, but..."

Directly opposite, Lucy scanned the room to gather the flavor of the diner. "Got it. I'll do whatever you guys have. This is nice. Tommy's mentioned it, but..."

"You've never been here before?"

Lucy grinned. That semi-bashful, semi-embarrassed expression she used so often. "No. Tommy's had this security thing like forever so I'd stay out of his space and he'd stay out of mine. It worked out pretty well. For a while."

"Which was, I gather, humming along nicely until I had a bad morning in Chelsea."

Lucy shrugged. "It's okay. We really needed a change of pace. Tommy's been trying to put the brakes on my messing around with

money and markets, one of those things it's so easy to become ob—
sessed with. And I was trying to bundle him up in pinstripe, make him
into something he really isn't. Armageddon is a lovely distraction."

Frannie returned and asked if they were ready to order.

Mandy said, "How are the crab cakes today?"

Frannie sighed. "I'd try something else, Mandy. Ernie keeps try—
ing, he really does, but if you want a first-class crab cake, you'd have
to go all the way to a place in Harrisburg. People say they have some
sort of a secret recipe or something, but it's about ten miles better
than my little ol' diner."

For just a moment, Lucy seemed puzzled. But there was that look
in her eye and the little smirk that grew into a sly smile as she reached
into her bag and found her phone. "Let's see…" Her fingers tapped,
flicked, paused, flicked again. "Ah. Here we are. They think it's secret,
but they're lax with security." She held the phone out for Frannie to
see. "Try that."

Frannie's eyes narrowed as she scribbled on her pad. "You're
telling me that this is the actual recipe for that restaurant's crab
cakes?"

"Yep."

Oh, gosh. She really is that good.

When Lucy withdrew the phone and dropped it back into her bag,
her expression was one of serene satisfaction. "So. I'd really love to
have a nice order of crab cakes, maybe a little corn chowder on the
side. You know, the way they make it around Lancaster."

"Make that two."

Tommy chuckled. "Three."

Frannie's grin was wall to wall. When she walked away, her step
had never been lighter.

Lucy tucked the menu back behind the sugar, salt and pepper,
folded her hands on the table and smiled as sweetly as an eager kid sis—
ter. "So," she said, "what was all this talk I heard when we came in
about Tommy running for mayor?"

Tommy winced. "It's nothing. Just small town — "

Mandy explained. "Some people are trying to organize a kind of a
write-in campaign. They're unhappy about the blinker light by the

hardware store. The hardware guy is the current mayor."

"Oh, that blinker light, the one you asked me about the other day."

Tommy nodded while he fiddled with the flatware wrapped in the customary napkin. "You got it. Bob Ferguson's stuck with a bunch of angry voters over what he thought was a chunk of pork from the local assemblyman."

Mandy said, "So, the write-in campaign got started..."

Lucy reached for her bag again. "About this election. Do you want to win? By how much?"

Mandy and Tommy spoke at once. "No."

Lucy's expression softened and her hand retreated. "Oh. Okay."

Whew. Rigging an election. Maybe they do it all the time, but still... "I wonder what's going on with the blinker light, anyway?"

Lucy said, "Well, it's the highway department. They like to use years of studies to dodge coming out and cutting a wire. I put in a work order for you. But I can follow up."

Tommy voted encouragement. "Anything to help Bob win, keep Charlie from growling, stop the speculation at Billy's."

Lucy laughed. "Exactly. We don't need a stupid blinker light in—terfering with the end of civilization as we know it."

Tommy cocked an eyebrow. "So it really is as dangerous as you first thought?"

"Yep. While you two were catching some sun in the Bahamas, dad and I went over Mercury Five again and again. Same conclusion. Just a demo would bring a fence-sitting government to its knees. Kinda like pointing a loaded gun at someone's head."

Tommy said, "Tipping the balance of power. Kind of like one side having all the nuclear weapons."

Lucy sighed. "Yeah, but this time they're steering an asteroid in from outer space, big enough to cause mass extinction. And they don't know it. Ever hear the story about the sorcerer's apprentice? The little guy gets magic brooms to lug the water, but things get out of hand and it compounds and compounds until there's a complete mess?"

Mandy nodded.

Lucy said, "One of the really dangerous things in code are subrou—

tines that point to themselves. They've got one in this program that would cause it to escalate, compounding, going faster and faster until the whole system crashes. Even overrides all the triggers the markets have in place. For a mistake in programming, this one gets a gold star. We're not talking about a few million dollars going to people who game the system. Even the HG Trading people would be dumpster diving for food scraps."

"You're really certain?"

Lucy sighed. "C'mon, Tommy, give me a little credit." She pulled a pair of flash drives from her bag and placed them on the table. "It's all we got left from when Allentown went ballistic. While they were shooting away, I was shutting down the store."

Mandy looked at the pair of innocuous storage devices. "Is that — "

"Yep. A genuine ticking bomb. Only this happens to be ther—monuclear. It's like the time the Air Force dropped a live hundred megaton hydrogen bomb on a runway in Texas. Only, this one sorta rolled our way. Kinda cute, isn't it?"

Frannie reappeared with platters of crab cakes and a happy smile. "There's extra for everybody, compliments of Ernie, whose day you just made."

Lucy's eyes tracked the steaming platter to the table. "Ah. These look fantastic."

"Mind the plates, hon. They're hot. Oh, aren't those flash drives so handy for storing snapshots and music? Those are so cute. Can I get you all anything else?"

Tommy said. "No, thanks. We're good."

"Great," Frannie said. "Enjoy."

"Do you think they know? Maybe it's a prototype, untested. Maybe they're still working on it. I mean, if they had actually used it... Oh, wow. No wonder they're so desperate to get it back. If it fell into the wrong hands — I mean, if some foreign power got ahold of it... I can't even begin to think of a scenario where this is a good thing."

On the other side of the window, cars and trucks silently floated past. People said hello, chatted, moved along. Lunch customers all around enjoyed, maybe tolerated, a midday meal on an ordinary day in an ordinary town. Everyone trusting in the order of things, in rhythms secure and safe and predictable. Tommy and I, enjoying a meal. "So what do we do next with our lovely little Pandora's box?"

Lucy revived her suggestion from Allentown, of working through the code on a quarantined machine, creating two altered versions. One, she said, would be a sterilized edition of the original, the difference being that if it was ever launched, it would fizzle, crash and devour itself. The second would be a simulation that isolated itself from the actual markets and spun hopelessly out of control to give the illusion of financial panic.

Like me, he probably doesn't understand any of the lingo.

Mandy said, "That's why you need the billion dollars. It primes the pump, begins the sequence, which immediately disconnects and runs harmlessly on the side?"

"Yep, leaving the original billion intact, maybe up or down a few million, but okay. The idea is that we concurrently snag the sell order from HG Trading, bag their assets, slip out the back door. Last I looked, it was a little over one-point-two, one-point-three, give or take. Their trading system should dump right away. If we time it right, we can get it all for pennies on the dollar."

Tommy asked, "And if it doesn't work?"

Lucy shrugged. "Best case scenario, you lose it all. Remember, we've got three fifty liquid and on the line. The rest is frozen because of SEC. I mean, I can try to uncork it, but no guarantees."

Mandy asked, "And Walter's six-fifty?"

"The all-time I-O-U. But worst case scenario is that it doesn't switch on time and the global economy goes all to hell. In which case, your three-fifty and his six-fifty aren't going to matter."

He asked, "What's the probability of success? Is there any way to test it?"

Lucy shrugged. "Unknown and no. I mean, if I still had my gear, I could give you a better answer. But all I've got is a pad with no USB ports and a couple of sticks that would probably be a big hit on the other side of the world."

Frannie arrived to refresh coffees and inquire about dessert.

Lucy's mood shifted from grim to pleasant. "You know, maybe I will. How's the pies here?"

Tommy said, "I lean toward cherry, but Mandy, you've had the apple..."

Mandy brightened. "It's good. They warm it a little and put a scoop of vanilla ice cream on the side. Go for a second scoop. I have a feeling that Tommy's about to drag us into something."

Tommy sighed. "Okay, Lucy. So we need some sort of computer."

Lucy laughed. "I love you guys. We need really good hardware, and we're going to have to piggy back into a system. Remember, ours is dismantled, HG is definitely onto us, and TKA's connections with the banks are frozen."

Mandy said, "Hm. One step at a time. What else, Tommy?"

Frannie delivered warmed plates of pie and put the check face down on the table next to him. Lucy reached for it, muttering that lunch was on her, but his hand got there first.

He said, "Seems to me that one of two things is true. If the HG people believe we've got a live bomb and are willing to use it, they'll have to communicate, figure out what to do. If they don't know they're holding a lit stick of dynamite, they still have to consider the possibility of deterrence, that they're just as threatened. Again, they're going to have to figure out what to do."

Mandy said, "But they still have the weapon, Tommy."

Lucy nibbled on ice cream, looking intrigued. "Not likely. These are money people, not tech people. I'd bet it's somewhere else, in the possession of people who could run it. Even if their people have it... Well, let's put it this way. If I can disarm it, I can also sterilize it, set it up so it merely fizzles and crashes, maybe even self-destructs. I'm sure that once we find out where it's residing, we could sub malware. Dad's certainly good enough to work on delivery."

Tommy attacked his pie and crust shattered under his fork. "Meanwhile, Mandy, you're going to have to hit that collection of designer clothes, try to play the role of a really polished socialite."

Lucy chuckled. "Lucky you."

He continued. "We're going to need a little help with paper from Karl, a couple of bodyguards — Charlie and Serge — someone to work phones."

"My father. Nobody better. And if I could get a brand new unit, I could modify the operating system to work the way we need *before* we start poking around. A desktop, lot of juice. Where's the nearest big box?"

Tommy's attention raced up the aisle of the diner to a new arrival. He half-stood and motioned for Andy Karr to join them.

"Hi, Andy. How's that jukebox working out?"

"Getting there. Having some trouble with the electronics on the unit they sent. Billy's getting impatient, my boss is getting nervous, and I'm hoping I don't lose my commission."

Mandy said, "Hi, Andy. Would you mind terribly saying how much was the commission?"

"Oh gosh, Miss Owens, it was six hundred and sixty-four dollars and thirty-five cents. A lot of money. But I'd feel terrible if I let you folks down, after Mister Kane helped me make the sale."

Mandy said, "Wow, that is a lot at stake. Say, I'd like you to meet a good friend of ours, Lucy Tramanian."

After they exchanged greetings, Lucy asked, "So what's this about a jukebox?"

Andy related his situation in talk that tumbled into technical and left everyone else at the table outside the conversation.

At the first lull, Tommy said to Lucy, "Among other things over at the appliance store, Andy sells a few computers, I think."

Andy's voice blossomed with excitement and began to list a limited inventory. He took a breath when he reached the apex of prices and named a popular brand. "Our most powerful. Great for gaming. Use one myself. Best that you can buy."

Lucy said, "Well, that's not quite true but... hm. Might work."

Andy pressed on. "And it's got the latest firewall and virus protec‐ tion. That's really important. Gotta prevent those hackers from get‐ ting in, you know."

CHAPTER THIRTY-ONE

Atlantic Aviation, Philadelphia International Airport

They stood in front of a high, two-tiered wooden service counter, directly under a soft gray canopy. The familiar *Atlantic* name and logo echoing the sweeping curve of a dark marble convenience surface. An antique wooden propeller adorned the wall to the right and light streamed through double doors on the left.

Next to Tommy, Mandy worked to project an image of patience. *These things happen.* Atlantic was Cesar's favorite fixed base operator for a reason. Smoothing little bumps on the runway of their kind of travelers topped the list.

An attendant waited on the other side, a phone to her ear, probably on hold. Tommy seemed placid, his left hand in his pocket, looking every bit the role of a VIP who managed serenity despite an embarrassing glitch. Placid, but not quite calm.

He's anxious about that tie. Karen noticed it first, a tiny spot dead center in the middle of his favorite, the red and blue stripe, and agreed with Mandy that it could not be made presentable in time. So he wore the darker blue, which was perfectly okay. But it was a backup tie and so...

The attendant spoke in such a soft voice that her words were inaudible. But she smiled when she hung up and gave her full attention to Mandy and Tommy. "I'm so sorry about the inconvenience. Your driver has been delayed, some sort of a minor accident on the entry ramp."

"Oh, dear," Mandy said. "I do hope everyone is all right."

"I'm sure. Minor, but it created a bit of a traffic jam. Your driver should be here in a few minutes. Can we get you anything, Mister Kane? Coffee, a newspaper, perhaps?"

Tommy smiled. "No, thank you. We'll be fine."

The attendant's phone chirped again. "There's a lounge over there if you'd care to — "

Mandy said, "Thank you. We'll be fine. You've been most help—ful."

The relieved attendant took her next call, and shifted her focus to another bump in the runway of life, something about treats for a dog on an inbound flight.

The entry area of the building was vacant except for a flight crew relaxing at the far end of the lounge. She picked up a copy of *The Inquirer*, glanced at the headlines and whispered. "It's fine. Goes well with the shirt and suit. Matches the color of your eyes perfectly."

"Think so? The other one, it was — "

"I know, I know, a favorite. Here. Let me adjust the knot a bit. Good. Perfect. Very classy."

He wore an expression of resignation. She sighed and resumed a scan of the newspaper. "And they talk about how women..." *Wait. It's not vanity.* "But it has nothing to do with the color of the tie at all. It's superstition, like those little rituals athletes have, to concentrate, get in the zone, up their game."

He scowled. "It's only a tie."

Mandy chuckled and allowed the newspaper to open to full height. "Yes, Tommy. It's only a tie. Oh, wow. Look at this." She folded the paper to its original shape, but this time held the bottom half of the page up for view. "We've made the news, even all the way down here."

Together they skimmed an article spread over several columns at the bottom of the page. *Allentown. A bizarre shootout... still under investigation... federal authorities involved... a burglary gone bad... four men in custody... gun battle with apparent burglars... abandoned warehouse... thirty crates of high technology computer equipment... being shipped to China.*

Mandy looked up. "China?"

He nodded. "One of the moving guys got creative, I guess. Proba—

bly how Cinnabar or HG or whatever managed to find it. Manifests that didn't seem right."

"Oh. But *China?*"

"Red flag for the feds. Instant custody for their assault team, lot of explaining to do. Myself, I would have gone with Iran or — no, North Korea would have been a bit much. Still, a domestic address would have been better."

"But how...?"

He turned his attention to the door. "Between Sergei, Charlie and Bug? Anything's possible. But if I had to guess, I'd vote for Sergei lay— ing the evidence on the way out the back door. He's innovative that way. Ah, here's our ride."

"It's a nice tie. What a lovely day to sort of break it in."

They stepped toward bright light. The attendant smiled and wished them a pleasant day. Tommy waved back. Mandy said, "Oh, I'm sure. Thank you very much."

Tommy winced at the sight of the limo. "A little stretchy, don't you think?"

The driver scampered around to open the door. "It'll be fine. You're supposed be a fat cat."

"This is more rock star than ordinary multi-millionaire business— man. Best Lucy could do on short notice, I guess."

After Mandy exchanged hellos with the driver, she said, "Buck up, pal. We're just on a routine little mission to scare the daylights out of two nasty billionaires. I haven't been to one of these things in a while, but I'm comfortable. I've got our invitations, we're fashionably late and looking good. Well, even if you are wearing that blue tie."

* * *

She was amused. The Merion Fields Hunt Club wasn't quite up to the standards of Greenwich, Back Bay or North Shore, but was all right for a Main Line attempt at old-guard understated dignity. The deferential but chilly cloakroom staff seemed to take invasion of hal— lowed ground in stride. Only a cursory glance at The Clockmaker's simple forged invitation. The doormen at the interior castle gate, handsomely paid and liveried. A soft, dim, almost cozy reception room with dark sage-green carpet with a lighter four-pointed star pattern, deep mahogany and black marble, black leather furnishings, perhaps in the fashion of the more traditional clubs in England, maybe Wales but not likely Scotland. From somewhere, a piano and old jazz standards. From everywhere, the hum of subdued conversations, the occasional tinkle of ice cubes against glass. Conservative suits, classic daytime dresses, the sort of thing expected when the well-to-do chase lunch with charity.

An all-male waitstaff, one of whom appeared with a tray of crystal glasses and soft, white wine, whispering that more potent beverages could be found at the round, paneled bar over there.

Tommy opted for the wine. *I could use a scotch. Hope it's a decent chardonnay.* It was. Calm for the palate, balm for the nerves. *The net worth in this room is probably pushing forty or fifty billion dollars.* More sips wine while Tommy's more experienced eyes roamed the room for his targets.

A twinkle in his eye. The faint recognition, not of the target, but the way he smirks when he knows he's about to win a round. *Take a breath. Just like old times.*

Drifting left while he went right, a flanking maneuver. *Smiles, smiles, smiles.* An entire room full of practiced smiles, smiles that looked so authentic. Within moments, the sly smiles of guys ranging from late thirties into seventies, their glasses gripped firmly in their left hands and therefore ready to shake with their right, teasing a maiden as if she were a princess. And the pleasant smiles of women with a bit too much makeup, holding glasses higher in their right hand, glowering eyes evaluating an interloper at court.

Tommy. The good ol' boy, whose plantation family once owned all the cotton fields and most of the oil. Smooth, rascally glamor, certainly more counterfeit than confederate, but they didn't catch on. The guys were instant barbeque buddies, pals since they caddied together as teenagers at the country club. More like grins than smiles. The women, all under forty or forty-five, drooling. More like leers than smiles. Eat your hearts out, ladies.

Something tells me that blue tie's going to move to the front of the rack. Pay attention. Smile. Yes, it's such a pleasure to meet you. I've heard so much about you. No, not originally from Philadelphia, but it's so charming. Yes, Connecticut, how did you ever guess? Such a delight. Yes, the Greenwich Owens'. We might have mutual friends. Isn't he related to... No, sadly, I haven't been in years. Oh, yes, she is so lovely, isn't she? I'm visiting with my friend, Tommy Kane. Yes, *that* Tommy Kane.

The call to attention. A pudgy guy with glasses and a balding head moist with perspiration, on a makeshift dais. The inevitable tap-tap-tap on the microphone, the perennial questions, "Hello? Is this working? Can everyone hear me? Good. Thank you all, for coming."

And the predictable pitch, as Bug had forecast the night before, when he tapped their phones and took good notes of their conversation.

The key players at the chummy little get-together were dedicated alums, passionate about the stature of The Wharton School at Penn, how the education they'd received paved the way to astonishing success in business. And the speaker ticked off a list of names present — wave of a hand, polite applause — and past, solemnly remembered names of people who ran the region's most blue chip enterprises.

An appeal for donations, an admonition to not be shy, make a pledge, write a check. At least one that didn't bounce, right? The usual light laughter and conviviality. Snacks coming soon on silver trays, thanks for coming, enjoy some time together. *I could practically recite it from memory. I ought to get a more comfortable pair of shoes, a thicker heel.*

A circle of navy suits, tailored, Armani or better. Wives a few feet away, blonde updos and dresses from better designers at Niemann-Marcus, a little sad, maybe a little intoxicated. Andrew Chamberlain, tallish, tanned, relaxed. The kind of guy who'd coach the kids. Soccer, lacrosse, softball. *Hard to imagine him as a murderer.* Closer to Tommy, Michael Eaton, squat, forty pounds overweight, jowly, loose skin under his eyes, brooding, intent, a guy more at home holding court in his box at Eagles games with ordinary beer, but in better glasses, and pizza, but not pâté. The kind of guy who'd like to own a piece of the team but never will.

Released to mingle by the alumni guy, Tommy said, "Hey, Mandy, having a nice time?"

Gushing smile. "Oh, absolutely. It's such a delight."

"Allow me to make introductions," Tommy said and launched an exchange of names and handshakes and how-do-you-do. Chamberlain was an Andrew, but Eaton preferred Mike. "These guys are the principles of Chamberlain, Eaton, the brokerage outfit. They really know what they're doing. Made a fortune calling the market about dead-on for a long time."

Andrew beamed, a proud smile. "We've had some good luck, haven't we, Mike?"

Eaton shrugged. "Lot of time, lot of hard work, and we've attracted a lot of talent. I hear you've done quite well yourself, Mister Kane. Bit of chatter about some trouble with the SEC, though."

Tommy said, "No trouble, just a little misunderstanding. All smoothed out."

Andrew continued to smile, but now rather smug. "I'm glad to hear that Mister Kane. All the rules, the laws, the procedures — it can get overwhelming sometimes, especially for rogue outfits, unless of course you've got great staff."

Maybe he's on a second marriage, got a kid in a cub scout program or something. All-American dad.

Tommy pantomimed currency between thumb and forefinger. "Or if you know your way around, eh?"

Eaton seemed intrigued at the potential for Tommy to blurt out an indiscreet confession. "There's also talk around the street that you've closed up shop, absconded with funds, perhaps moved capital offshore. Serious penalties for laundering, they say."

Tommy nodded. "Nah, nothing like that. Just rearranging."

Andrew asked, "Buying or selling? Perhaps we can do some business, turn a profit."

"Selling. Nice little asset."

"Oh?"

"Yessir. Technology, actually."

Eaton sipped his drink. "Risky business, technology. Lot of play—

ers, very fluid, hot today but down in flames tomorrow."

Tommy chuckled. "This is revolutionary stuff, guys. Forex trading. Professional grade.

Mandy said, "Amazing concept. Tommy and I are going all in. There's a lot of room on the ground floor if you're interested."

Andrew and Eaton seemed amused but disinterested. "We don't do much in currency, Miss Owens. Much too volatile for our clients."

Tommy said, "What about the folks over at HG Trading? I hear they run a solid shop, dark pool. Maybe you could set up a meeting with Sue Halsey, talk things over."

Eaton was unfazed. "Never heard of HG Trading."

Andrew looked utterly calm, politely puzzled. "What's this technology called, Mister Kane?"

He asked Mandy, "Mercury Five, wasn't it?"

"Yes, that's what the tech guy said."

Andrew looked into his glass. Like he's pretending to sift through recollections of gossip and whispers from the trade's private newsletters and doing a decent job of faking it. "Nope, sorry, never heard of that either. Might be one of those scams. Lot of that going around. I'd advise caution, folks."

Mandy sighed. "See, I told you. Tommy. But now we're totally committed."

Eaton swirled the last of his beverage and poured it into his mouth. "Your lady friend has a good head on her shoulders, Mister Kane. Probably a good idea to pay more heed to her warnings."

Andrew's expression was warm with sympathy and his soft words coated with compassion. A wicked smile. "There's a expression on the trading floors, missy, that goes, 'Be careful. Or you'll get your tits caught in a wringer."

Tommy's eyes widened. "Hey, hey..."

She raised her hand to quiet him. *Steady, strong, serene. Look him right in the eye and smile, just a bit.* "Thank you *so* much for your concern, Mister Chamberlain. But I wear a cast-iron bra."

CHAPTER THIRTY-TWO

Columbia Metropolitan Convention Center, Columbia, South Carolina

Tommy gripped an inexpensive blue vinyl ring binder in his left hand and fiddled with three badges dangling from his collar. Another first-rate forgery from the grand master himself.

On the opposite side of a narrow corridor formed by towers of black drapery, chairs, an idle flock of microphone stands and six portable off-duty lecterns. And Mandy, watching her shoe rock up and down, side to side. A little further away, a young guy with a crewcut and a headset commanded a panel of lighted buttons knobs and sliding controls for the audio.

The waiting. Looking casual, a tad to the polite side of disinterested. The practiced art of blending. Like reading, but not really, a paper at a sidewalk cafe. Tropical chaise lounges, trying not to doze off. Leaning against stucco walls that eventually hurt. Jungles in the pouring rain, wishing for chaise lounges to doze off in. Standing offstage in a convention center's main hall, shifting weight from left foot to right and back again.

Beyond the control panel guy, a cavern of a room, dimly lit, tables for eight, dozens and dozens, in precise rank and file, each one big ol' patch of white linen. Decorated with fancy place settings. Skirted by armless red upholstered stackable chairs on spindly black legs. Nearly all occupied by people in suits. Food was probably so-so, lukewarm, half-eaten except for the desserts, maybe chicken or overcooked beef on the chewy side.

Waiting. Looking like the nearly invisible convention hall staff, the good folks nobody pays attention to, pulling the extra shift, making a couple of dollars to pay the bills. Mandy. Looking good, hanging out and waiting, too, a notebook and pen in her hand, that big ol' bag hanging from her shoulder. Tough load compared to the ring binder. *Gals get used to it, I suppose.* And the press. They learn to wait, too, lurking in the hallways outside the back rooms where the action takes place. Like jungle cats, ready to pounce when the door opens and their prey tumbles out in a race to the exit. *You see it all the time on the news. Lights, mikes, cameras, recorders, all that stuff, shoved in some guy's wincing face.* Sometimes the big dog stops, everyone makes a little respectful circle, gets a crumb or two. Sometimes, the poor ol' bunny makes a run for it, and the pack hangs tight, noisy, yappy. Today, Mandy. Looking cool, calm, casual.

The master of ceremonies trotted up half a dozen steps onto the little stage. The giant screen on the other wall came alive. Lights in the room dimmed more, and the control panel guy brought the spotlight up to mid-day sunshine.

Mandy shifted her weight. She knew.

The emcee called the session to order, did the usual little banter and a joke or two, got some chuckles, tugged out a round of applause for the committee that organized a great dinner. A warm welcome to the Chamber of Commerce's southern executive leadership conference. Out in the hall, chairs facing the wrong way were probably being turned around, a few peeling nametags were being slapped back into place and the working stiffs in black pants, white shirts and vests making a sweep through the hall to harvest plates and flatware.

Mandy looked up. A faint nod. *She's ready to go. Cue the bastard.*

The master of ceremonies gently turned his chatter into the introduction of the conference keynote speaker, a nationally-recognized executive who'd built an empire in commercial properties, coast to coast, the king of skyscrapers.

A door opened on the right. *David Morris.* Genteel in a sort of grandfatherly way. Corporate, conservative, rather handsome with a squarish face, strong jaw, steady eyes, blue even in the subdued light of backstage. Hundred-dollar haircut, five hundred dollar tie. Some—

where in the mid-teens as billionaires go, Lucy said. Had a nice place in Lake Forest, Illinois, the usual apartments abroad and in major cities where MorCor Holdings had stakes. Big player in the world of real estate investment trusts, close pal of midwestern governors and senators, both parties, a regular at the White House when Republicans were in vogue and on a first-name basis with Treasury, Commerce, and the Federal Reserve board.

Aw, he don't look so tough. That's what a juvenile Tommy Kane would have said, back in Tammany Parish, but probably would have meant it more on the Teche. And the wiser heads would always reply, "They never do, Tommy. You take care, you hear?"

David Morris, the tipsters said, was the epitome of cool, confident, detached. Even the family dog had to make an appointment with a senior aide to get within five feet of the guy. Get an inch too deep in his space, he'll have his body guys push you down the nearest flight of stairs.

But today, Morris was alone, his thugs out in the hall where Sergei Yenchenko lurked. Nah. He don't look so tough. All he carried was an inexpensive blue vinyl three-ring binder, the kind you could get anywhere. The binder that held his keynote speech to the chamber guests. The kind Tommy held at his side.

Tommy and Mandy turned at once, closing the gate to the stage. Morris pulled up several feet away, unperturbed. "You're in my way."

Tommy introduced himself and extended a hand that Morris ignored. "We wanted a brief word to discuss a little business matter."

Morris was unfazed. "You call my office, talk to my people, Mister Crane. Now, step aside."

Tommy exchanged a puzzled, astonished glance with Mandy. "I'm sorry. My name is Kane, Tommy Kane."

Morris hinted impatience. Behind them, the emcee was extolling the achievements of the featured speaker for the evening. "Yes, yes. Kane it is. Now, I'm being introduced and it's a bit tiresome, you two standing in my way."

The control panel guy turned to look. Mandy gestured that everything was fine, but the guy didn't look convinced.

She said, "Mister Morris, I'm Amanda Owens, a reporter, and

we're looking into any relationship MorCor might have with an in—
vestment firm called H and G Partnership..."

Hesitation. The instinct to correct her. And thinking better of it.

His voice tensed, his patience going fast. "I don't have any idea
what you're talking about. You'll have to contact our media people in
the morning — "

Tommy took a step closer. Morris took half a step back. "Just a
moment of your time for the lady, sir. I'm sure you can clarify about
— what was it? — oh, yes, HG Trading."

Morris lowered his voice to an intense growl and he spat each
word. "For the last time, Crane, get out of my way."

Tommy said, "I don't — "

Mandy showed an expression of astonishment and dismay. "Oh,
gosh, Mister Morris, your tie!"

He started to look down. She stepped in, close, and reached out to
touch him. "You've got a terrible spot on your tie. Here. Let me — "
A handkerchief appeared in her hand and she began to scrub a point
on the tie an inch below the knot.

Morris tried to twist away. "Dammit — "

Mandy's left hand tightened to a firm grip.

He started to raise his hands to push hers away. "Just... get off,
dammit!"

The notebook. Pure instinct for a guy like Morris. Hands it to
Tommy, the aide, the body guy, the assistant, the butler. Sputters of
profanity and protest. Mandy's earnest efforts withdrawn, apologetic
but mentally wounded, into retreat, two steps back, eyes down.

Morris adjusted his tie. Extended his hand. Tommy put a note—
book into it. They stepped aside and allowed David Morris to huff
and puff and stride out into the bright spotlight. Applause from the
emcee. Applause from the audience. Tommy stepped forward, leaning
as far as he dared to see.

Yeah. Standing ovation. Lot of respect for those billionaire guys,
the words of wisdom they're about to share.

He retreated and joined Mandy offstage, hidden from the audi—
ence that gradually quieted, settled into their seats.

David Morris managed a grin, a wave of appreciation, a gesture to be seated, relax. He opened the notebook on the lectern and began to speak. "Thank you, ladies and gentlemen. It's always such an honor to be with the backbone of American business. I wanted to start tonight — "

A glance at the script. Oh, yeah. The guy's reading it cold, like Bug said.

" — By telling you all about a trading program called Mercury Five, but first a little bit about — " He slowed and began to stammer and looked again at the script. "Peter... Pan... and, um... Tinkerbell..."

Morris turned to glare at Tommy, who shrugged, held the note-book aloft and wiggled it. Mandy's smile was sympathetic. Under-standing. And she gave him a little wave.

The lighting guy's jaw hung open and he stared. Tommy handed him David's ring binder and joined Mandy on the walk toward the exit.

She said, "Beautiful. You know, Tommy, you're really that good. Where to next?"

"Ever been to Texas?"

"No, never."

"Aw, you'll love it. They got scumbags out there the size of barns. It's amazing."

CHAPTER THIRTY-THREE

Near Weatherford, Texas

Mandy studied the foam dinner plate in her hand and continued to gauge the weight of it. *It's lunch for ten, maybe twelve.* Blackened meat, in stages of disintegration, shrinking away from stubs of bone. Ribs. Pungently sharp, the nip of crushed red or cayenne lurking in the rising scent of barbeque. Something suggesting sausage. A bowl of beans, possibly chili. A mound of potato salad.

Wispy smoke curled through the air, some sort of hardwood, sharp, the kind that really shouldn't take refuge in the fiber of clothes, even if they were upscale causal. Beyond, a swing band in matching dark yellow western-cut jackets and trousers, brilliant white shirts and string ties. Everyone under the mandatory and only faintly gray wide-brimmed cowboy hats. The song ended and the singer, a young and strong tenor voice, accepted applause from fifty or sixty people. When it faded, "Okay, here we go with everybody's favorite *Turnin' the Corn.*" A drummer got things started, a guy seated at a slide guitar chimed in, and the man with the bass fiddle began to smack out an en—ergetic tempo.

Oh, please. After Tommy's preference for cajun and zydeco, and Billy's fondness for bluegrass, a gentle lounge piano trio would be... Yep, the corn is getting turned, the sound of it rippling like the conse—quences of a rock in a still pond. Across board-flat brown fields in all directions. Punctuated by fenceposts from old logs. The occasional tree adjacent to the edge of road, strings of barbed wire, maybe one of the boxy spots that were, in fact, huge hay barns.

She looked down again. The five pounds of meat hadn't diminished. To her left, local folks were making their way along a cafeteria line that she'd inadvertently gotten into and handed an immense platter of food.

The wiry man with gray hair and blue eyes next to her organized a bashful smile and spoke in a gentle voice. "Looks like they loaded you up pretty good."

He had a matching platter and seemed to be okay with it.

"I'm afraid so. I really hate to be inhospitable, but — "

The man, in a denim shirt, brown canvas pants and a light field jacket, chuckled. In a corral full of fancy stiff cowboy hats, his was rumpled and sweat stained. "Best thing's probably to settle somewhere near one of the dogs hanging around, set your plate within reach, quietly move on. But it's pretty good beef. Maybe you oughta give it a try. Mind the beans, though. Lot of zippity for your do-dah."

"You're right, of course. I should at least make the effort."

He nodded. "Pretty fair band, there. But I'm guessing it's not your kind of music."

"You might be right."

"City gal?" They had moved several steps out and away from the line, and he used a plastic fork to peel off strings of brisket.

"New York. New England, actually. Connecticut. I'm a reporter."

"Uh-huh. Thought for a second you might be with the *Democrat* — that's the local paper — or maybe out of Austin, Dallas, Fort Worth. That your friend over there, doing the deep cutting?"

"Sorry?"

"Local expression. This area's known for training cutting horses, what riders use to manage a herd of cattle. When you deep cut, you're picking a cow from pretty well into the herd, rather than from along the edges. Say, I'm sorry. Left my manners down by the gate. I'm Henry MacAllister. Most folks say Henry Mac and that's good enough for me."

Mandy struggled to shift the weight of the platter into her left hand but abandoned a handshake attempt when he smiled and waved it off. "Mandy Owens. And yes, I'm very much a guest out of her element."

He motioned her toward a picnic table blanketed with red and white gingham. "Maybe we oughta get you a spot where you can try some of JJ's beef."

Mandy took the side of the table that gave her the best view of Tommy working through the tiers of hangers on. In the center of it, Joshua J. Gibbons held court. She took a small bite. *Don't wince.*

Henry Mac said, "It's the rub. Authentic central Texas barbeque. Takes some getting used to. They're cooking it over pecan wood. Gives it a distinct flavor."

"Pecan? That sounds fancy."

"Nothing but the best for ol' JJ when he's tossing himself a party, reminding the governor who's in charge." He pointed toward the cen‐ter of the action. "Looks like your friend is working the crowd pretty smooth. Banker maybe?"

"In a manner of speaking."

"Money guys are money guys. Titles don't mean much."

"So he's deep cutting."

Henry Mac worked on the platter from left to right, adroit with a clear plastic fork and knife. "Yep. Now, you're cutting for shape, working the outside edges instead of going right into the herd to drive a cow out."

"You seem to know a lot about horses and cattle. Do you work on the Gibbons Ranch?"

Henry Mac laughed. "No ma'm. I'm decoration like most every‐one else here. Mister Gibbons puts on a nice affair when he wants folks around, and we kind of oblige. Lunch, maybe coffee or a little bit o'bourbon, help fluff up the crowd. JJ's got the governor coming in to press the flesh a little, round himself up a little campaign cash, keep everybody happy in Austin. Myself, I've got a little spread down the road. Came by for barbeque, the trimmings."

The musicians shifted into the next tune, keeping the event festive and the crowd smiling.

Henry Mac said, "Band's chomping at the bit to light up *Eyes of Texas.* They're a local group, Parker County's own Chuck Wagoneers. Play the fairs, the peach festival, some dances." For a few moments,

they watched couples two-stepping to the music of the Chuck Wag—
oneers. He looked back at her, the faintest hope in his eyes. "You ever
do much dancing?"

In any other situation, I'd oblige. Just as a courtesy to a decent gen—
tlemanly fellow more than old enough to be her father. *Like the cour—
tesy I should have extended to Benny.* But not today. Tommy's patience
was working. He'd advanced several layers through the onion of influ—
encers — buyers and sellers — surrounding Gibbons. "It's been a long
time."

He nodded, having taken the rejection reasonably well. "To be
honest, I'm not much good at it. Haven't stepped onto a dance floor
in a lot of years."

The chili had a kick but not as bad as expected. *Change the subject.*
"So I'd bet you have a lot of experience with horses and cattle."

Henry Mac concentrated on his platter, stabbing beef with effi—
ciency. "All my life, until recent."

Mandy took more aggressive bites into the portions on the plate.
"What happened?"

The gentle, soft smile under his thin, handlebar mustache never
wavered. "Well, livestock's a lot of work and I'm pretty much by my—
self. Got a steady hired man, pay the local kids a good wage to pick.
Peaches are a whole lot easier and it's a good crop around these parts.
Lot of folks like to call this area the cutting horse capital of the world,
but the local chamber of commerce touts the peaches."

"And you and Gibbons. Been neighbors for a lot of years."

Henry Mac chuckled. "I said I lived down the road a bit. I didn't
say we were neighbors."

"Oh, sorry. I guess with all his oil wells and — " *Wait. Not a sign of
an oil or gas well anywhere in the area.* From the time they turned off
the two-lane asphalt highway, crossed a culvert and entered through
the automatic gate there were simple fences, horses here, cattle there.
But no evidence of drilling.

"No, no, that's not the issue. Not much oil and gas in these parts
anyway. Some, of course, but this is the Fort Worth Basin, kind of
lean. The big fields are more to the southwest. Midlands, West Texas

Crude. JJ's got a big piece of the action out there, but he lives over in Southlake, near Fort Worth. He's got this place for show. Don't often get out here unless he's showing off."

Fort Worth. The home offices of Gibbons Petroleum Partners. Lucy's briefing notes. Started out with oil, expanded into distribution, field equipment, leasing, offshore lease speculation. Well connected in the Middle East, owns most of the politicians in Alaska. "So what's this song called?" she asked.

"Miles and Miles of Texas. Looks like your friend's passed the muster. Got himself into the inner circle. Must be a special guy."

"He is. But how can you — "

Henry Mac pointed. "Them three, over by the bar there, that's JJ's crew in Austin, the fellas that do the day-to-day. Used to be county, state electeds, but he bought 'em up when they got tired of the public job. I call 'em Baldy, Frosted and Brindle, on account that they're the best cows in JJ's corral."

Mandy studied the plate. About halfway. But it would have to do.

"So's your friend buying or selling?"

Tommy began to speak directly to JJ Gibbons.

"A little both. It's a business proposition. Frankly, I don't — "

Henry Mac tilted his head and watched with evident interest. Gib— bons seemed puzzled. Exasperated. Tommy pressed. JJ growing an— noyed. Tommy chattering away, easy smile, making some kind of point. Gibbons getting angry, red faced. Baldy, Frosted and Brindle moved in close. Gibbons really furious, pointing. Tommy being led away. Mandy sighed.

"Don't look like things worked out too well for your friend. Don't fret on it. Hardly anybody makes a dent in JJ, especially talking busi— ness when he's picking up the strings to make his governor dance."

Actually, it was rather nice that Tommy didn't get killed. But, how do you kill a guy in the middle of your own political rally?

Baldy, Frosted and Brindle glared at Tommy's back, but on Mandy's side he showed a wicked little grin and gave a thumbs up sign.

Mandy said, "I'd guess he did fine, Henry. Sort of a plan to put the squeeze on Gibbons a little, try to prod him into doing something."

Henry Mac nodded in a thoughtful way. "A blow up. When a horse — or a cow — panics and does something kind of stupid."

Tommy strolled into proximity. "I think we've worn out our wel-come."

"Tommy, I'd like you to meet Henry Mac, who's an expert on cows and horses and peaches and these little shindigs."

Henry stood to shake hands. "Well, I reckon I'll leave you folks to talk. Been a pleasure sharing a meal with you Miss Owens. Helped me work up the nerve to do something that's been on my mind for a few years now."

Tommy cocked an eyebrow.

"See that handsome woman sitting over there? She's from town, works at the city library. I've been getting books, regular, not reading most, but getting 'em anyway, to say hello." He pulled his hat back from his head to rub his neck. "Yeah. I'm kind of sweet on her, just... "

Mandy said, "You should, Henry. Walk right up and ask her to dance. She'd be a very fortunate woman. I don't think she'll mind a bit if you're a little out of practice."

He nodded. "I believe I will. Nice meeting you, sir. You and the lady have yourself a nice day." He paused and shared a moment with Mandy. "And you two should do the same. Dance. Before you get too far out of practice."

Tommy watched Henry Mac approach the librarian. "What's that all about?"

"Oh, nothing. How did things go with Gibbons?"

"Just as well that you got waylaid by that fellow. Gibbons is a nasty guy."

"I didn't get waylaid, Tommy. There was no sense in cutting for shape when you were so good at cutting deep."

He chuckled. "Okay, whatever. Anyway he gave me a lashing up and down, stuff you wouldn't want to hear, and said, 'You know what a flare is, Kane? That's where we burn off crap gas, and that's where you're headed, boy.' And I said, 'And do you know what a blowout is, Mister Gibbons? That's a well gone out of control. Could take a whole field up in flames.'

"Nicely done, Tommy. But you probably mean *blow up*."

CHAPTER THIRTY-FOUR

809 Railroad Avenue, Jacks Ford, Pennsylvania

Tommy twisted an industrial handle, gave it a tentative tug to see if it was locked, and pulled a steel door, once painted dark grey, open. Gloomy light from dense November clouds scampered across the concrete floor, eager to escape the raw drizzle.

He confessed. "Never even knew it was here."

Mandy prodded him forward. "We really have to get you into town more often, Tommy. Learn the lay of the land. All the creepy little corners of Jacks Ford. Frannie says — "

" — I know, I know. What's an appliance store without a loading dock? I haven't had cause to break in before. Most folks go through the front door."

She brushed extra raindrops from her coat sleeve. With caution they stepped through a cardboard cavern of immense cartons of re— frigerators and pallets of plastic-wrapped microwaves, toaster ovens, televisions. They made a left onto a boulevard of washers and dryers, footsteps gaining confidence near a pool of warm light oozing from the bottom of an office door.

Mandy whispered. "Should we knock? Or walk in? What's the po— lite thing to — "

Tommy turned away to give her a view of a scrap of cardboard, about eight inches square, thumb-tacked to the door at eye level. A scribble from the tip of a felt marking pen said, "TKA Associates."

Lesson in humility, for sure. Tommy turned the knob. "At least she hasn't lost her sense of humor."

Mandy chuckled. "It would be nice if there was a secret knock. Like they have in those old gangster movies."

"Shave and a haircut."

Lucy looked up from a monitor. "Two bits. Hey, welcome home."

Mandy sighed. "Oh, wow. You really are spending too much time underground." She surveyed the scene. "I'm half tempted to get back on the plane."

Three filing cabinets, two of which had drawers that didn't close. Stacks of paper, probably shipping and receiving documents, invoices, manuals and catalogs. A makeshift desk created by clearing off a folding table by moving even more paper into a heap along the bottom of an unpainted cinder block wall. A lone lightbulb struggling to brighten the room from a dangling, caged industrial fixture that went out of style forty years ago. And failing.

Lucy wore a dark blue Penn State hoodie a size too large, a firm smile and a hairstyle this side of utter disregard. She spoke in an assured, commanding but cheery voice. "Grab a couple of chairs. We've got a lot of ground to cover."

Tommy and Mandy traded shrugs. The room couldn't have been more than twelve feet square and the ground to be covered was little more than pathways through the clutter. Two folding chairs leaned against one of the drooping file cabinets, away from the inevitable makeshift home for a coffee pot and open box of doughnuts. *Pink frosting. Sprinkles. Nice to see everything's back to normal.*

He said, "So what happened to Franks's Appliances, the blinker light, the — "

Lucy waved him off while Mandy opened a folding chair with a clear sense of foreboding and a weak smile of disappointment. "It's now Karr TV and Appliances. I know, I know. Not terribly original. I needed a spot to set up shop and Frank Feldman kept muttering about retiring to Florida or someplace warm. We bought him out."

So that's Frank's last name. "Just out of curiosity, how much?"

"Four-fifty. I would have preferred about three seventy-five, but it came with the apartments upstairs and Andy needed the inventory for startup."

"No problem."

"The blinker light came down a couple of days ago. Dad and I took a peek at PennDOT work orders and they hadn't even scheduled it. I was really pissed. I mean, when I put in an order, I sort of expect action. So Sergei and Dad rounded up a crew from the district garage — they swear not at gunpoint — and that was that."

Mandy said, "Charlie should be pleased."

"Yep. They had a big turnout for the removal. Including Bob Fer—guson, grinning from ear to ear, making a little speech about how the state had forced it on the town in the first place, but he managed to pull some strings in Harrisburg."

Tommy shrugged and picked up a mug adorned with cute little flowers. "Coffee?"

"Oh, yeah, help yourself, guys."

Mandy winced. "Sure. I think."

He chose a second one, with a cartoon fox on it, for himself.

"And there's still some doughnuts."

Tommy said, "I think we're good."

Mandy nodded and sipped with a faint roll of her eyes.

"Anyway, Bob took the credit and, um, well, you kind of, uh, didn't quite make it in the election. Total wipeout. I heard you got four votes."

Mandy patted Tommy's arm, her eyes sympathetic but her lips a smirk. "I'm so sorry, Tommy. I know it meant a lot to you. And not even here to make a stirring concession speech, all those usual clichés."

Tommy said, "Whew. Just another one of them little ol' close calls. The thought of being mayor? Now *that* is scary."

Lucy grinned. "For you? Or Jack's Ford?"

Time for a consolation prize. A doughnut from the box would do. *Okay, long on consolation, short on prize.*

Mandy shook her head in dismay. "So this is Andy's store now?"

"Yep. We kind of gave incorporation papers a little help in Harris—burg. I was thinking we could have gone somewhere else, Delaware, offshore even, but I guessed you wouldn't want me to cause any rip—ples. You know, like that old *Star Trek* mandate to not screw with the

local state of affairs. Hope Andy does okay. Taxes in this state are terrible. Pass me another doughnut."

Mandy used a napkin to comply. "Speaking of Andy, where is,
well, everybody?"

"Over at that bar south of town — "

"Billy's."

"Yeah. Talk about local wildlife... Anyway, they're out installing
that new jukebox. Sergei's doing the heavy lifting and Charlie's sort of
directing."

Tommy said, "That's probably worth seeing. And Bug?"

"Dad's still the man. Got himself hired on to help install some new
switching equipment at the local telephone facility. Met a guy at that
bar yesterday, and a couple of beers later, dad's off in a borrowed van
with all his tools."

Mandy seemed stunned. "Oh, wow. Talk about the proverbial fox
in the henhouse... I can't begin to imagine — "

Lucy shrugged. "Yeah, well, normally I'd agree. Keep a low profile and all that. But we kinda needed to get some long-line help, some
solid fiber-optic. I've been trying to find a back door into a mainframe
somewhere and dad convinced me that twisted pair isn't going to cut
it for speed."

The doughnut was terrible and the wastebasket was out of discre-
tion range. "You've lost me."

Lucy passed her empty cup to Tommy for a refill. *Logical. Not
enough space to get out of her way.* "Okay, I've got our little Mercury
Five quarantined, and managed to get an impotent version together,
plus a trainer that we an use for a demo. But we need a lot of network
power to make this convincing. It's gotta run at extremely high
speed."

Mandy cocked an eyebrow. "So...?"

Lucy went for patience. "So I need to exploit at least one, but
preferably more, systems and tie them together. Like hitching up a
team of six or eight big horses that know how to run instead of one
sad little mule, plodding along." She gestured toward a desktop computer that Andy said was state-of-the-art.

Tommy asked, "Any luck?"

She nodded. "Took a while. I was going for commercial systems head on — major banks and stuff — but they're getting harder to crack. I guess they don't want organized criminals rummaging around in customer accounts any more. Anyway, the sweatshirt I got at Polinski's — you're right, Mandy, it's not exactly David Aire — gave me an idea. Spent most of yesterday morning in Penn State's system. On the public side. Finally found a couple of administrators doing a lunch meeting, faked an email with an attachment from a participant and, bam, like that. I can't believe they still fall for that old phishing scam."

Tommy said, "Nicely done. And...?"

Lucy explained to Mandy. "Once you get into the password database, it's zip-zip-zip. I started to go for a nice quiet out of the way corner, but happened to notice connects to, of all things, the Federal Reserve. Some sort of a joint economics project. So I did a piggyback and we're good."

Mandy's eyes widened. "You're into the secure areas of the Federal Reserve in New York?"

Lucy displayed a sly grin. "No. The *entire* system."

"Oh, wow..."

After swallowing a chunk of doughnut, Lucy waved her hands. "But this can only be temporary. Right now, we're not on the radar. Just a stray ping, won't be noticeable on the daily logs. But when we run this thing, we're going to have a tight time window. Twenty, thirty minutes tops. The admins'll be all over it and shut us down."

Tommy sipped his coffee. Cold, but not worth replacement, and there was no way out of the second half of the doughnut. "How reliable is this?"

Lucy fell silent for several seconds, before taking a deep breath. "Frankly, I don't know. I *think* I have a good command and control on it, but you never really know."

Mandy leaned forward. "What are the alternatives?"

"Same as before."

Mandy turned to face him. "Tommy, this is so risky — "

He nodded. "This is what's going to happen anyway if whoever has this thing tries it without knowing what kind of a bomb they have. We've got to keep that in mind. We've got to have confidence in

Lucy."

Lucy bit her lower lip. "Look, Tommy, I appreciate the vote of confidence, but..."

Mandy said, "But what?"

"I'd, well, I'd rather prefer knowing if whoever has the original has either snuffed it or fixed it. We still need to identify the resident system." She gently rubbed her chin with the tips of her fingers. "And exploit it."

Mandy very slowly shook her head. "Oh, gosh. We are *so* playing with fire. I sure don't mind saying how apprehensive I'm starting to feel."

Lucy lowered her voice. "You're not alone. I'm the one who's got a finger on the trigger. This is really one of those moments that I'd prefer a nice quiet little beach house, a stack of books ten feet high, and not a keyboard in sight."

Tommy said, "But we can't walk away. Not knowing what we do." The others slumped back in their chairs. "We've got to play it out to the end. Lucy, how about the HG people? Any hints at all?"

She leaned into her computer and pressed some keys. "Got some transcripts here. Yeah. Dad's been plugged in. They're getting nervous. Gibbons and Chamberlain especially. They've been debating whether to simply have you guys killed and take their chances or see if they can bag you with the missing app. *Then* kill you. So far, they're tied two-two."

Mandy gasped. "I'm so relieved. Tommy, this a really good time for a plan."

He rubbed the back of his neck. "I'm thinking, I'm thinking. Wait. Let me... Okay. First, how are we doing on TKA assets?"

"Divesting as fast as I can. We got into the SEC and DOJ systems and thawed a lot of the frozen stuff. Wasn't easy. I mean, I've never been locked out before. Unloading in dark pool, away from prying eyes, going offshore. Bought a little bank down in the Caymans, but you can only transfer so much at a time. Plus, we've been busy with building our scam."

"How much?"

"Five hundred, five-fifty maybe. I was planning on shifting anoth–

er seventy million in a couple of hours."

"Is that plus the three-fifty?"

"The old liquid stuff you're using with Walter Campos?"

"Yup."

"That brings you up to about eight-fifty at least."

"Okay. That's enough. Let's shift our attention to Susan Halsey. She's the deciding vote."

Mandy said, "And I'm certain that she really is the key. If the others knew or had access to the source, they would have said or done something by now. But there's been nothing from her?"

Lucy shook her head. "No. My father has tapped in, but the only chatter has to do with some sort of big party she's planning on the West Coast. That and her regular golfing get together with the power crowd is screwed up."

"How so?"

Lucy skimmed through an electronic file. "She had originally scheduled a round with some people from Treasury... Yep, including the secretary himself. But he's got some sort of conference in Geneva."

Mandy smiled at the reminiscence. "As in Illinois?"

"Sorry, as in Switzerland."

Tommy said, "Speaking of Geneva, we're going to need some first class paper from Karl. It's the only way a team is going to get into the same room with a member of the cabinet, alone."

Lucy scribbled a note. "Done."

"And the party?"

"Not much intel, Tommy. Caterer is one of the more upscale outfits. She doesn't use a conventional party planner. Some guy name of... let's see... ah, here we are. Scapini."

Mandy perked up. "*Freddie Scapini?*"

"Maybe. I only have 'F. Scapini' from her calendar."

Mandy chuckled. "Freddie Scapini is an Italian designer. More known for notoriety on the Hollywood celebrity circuit than the runways and garment district in New York. He has an ego as big as California, but unfortunately not a collection to match."

Tommy asked, "How does he stack up against your favorite,

David Aire?"

Mandy tugged a phone from her bag. "Not anywhere near David's level. But David really hates the way Freddie gets attention on all those insider-type television shows and in the trade press."

Lucy interrupted. "Use this one. We've got to have dad outfit you with new equipment. With these people, I don't want to take any chances."

Mandy nodded and tapped in a telephone number.

Wow. How many women know the phone number of a big league fashion designer right off the top of their heads? He looked at Lucy and shared expressions of astonishment. I am so out of my depth...

"David? Hi. Mandy Owens. Yes, it's been much too long. Oh, yes, I adore your new line. Oh, absolutely! Still a perfect six. I know, I know. Watch what I eat, get lots of exercise. Aw, that's so thoughtful. Say, David, I was wondering if I could trouble you for a little advice..."

CHAPTER THIRTY-FIVE

Cinco Reyes Country Club, Los Altos Hills, California

Just about the cutest little pot of raspberry jam he ever saw. Gor—geous as ever. As memorable as the night they met over glasses of twenty-five-year-old Macallan single malt.

"They say the color is raspberry, but I never thought of myself destined for a pot of jam," she had told him at Lyford Caye. Sleeveless, to the floor, impossible to wear without heels high enough to bring her eyes level to his own. And now he was grinning and knew it and didn't care, a sense of pride and admiration nearly popping the studs from the silk shirt, bow tie to cummerbund.

Raspberry. The color that became David Aire's trademark, a brand that anyone with a sense of fashion recognized right away. *Excluding me. I only remember the dress when she walked, no marched, right into my life and said hello.*

Twenty feet away, she sponged up all the limelight and wrapped it around herself, about as stunning an entrance as any major star could have made. They were the last to present their invitation in the coun—try club lobby, a good dozen minutes after Susan Halsey, the reigning and upstaged monarch, clearly already stewing. Tommy broke away to greet the loose circle on the right. *Just like the politicians do. Double hand shakes, lots of teeth, warm hello and how do you do.* All he needed were campaign buttons to distribute — no, a starry-eyed intern tag—ging along behind, passing out election materials. *Yeah, that would have been better. Write my name in for mayor. Vote early, vote often, vote for me.*

Mandy had, by luck of the draw, won the longer route on the left. Her mother's pearls caught every eye and led them to an effervescent smile and those sparkling eyes. Bashful. Girl next door. Elegant. Regal. Belle of the ball. Somehow she'd tossed it all into her pot of raspberry jam and in a matter of seconds took command of the room. Soft shakes of hands, warm and fuzzy moments of introduction, leaning in, connecting. A joy to watch, even if she wasn't wearing a tiara. An artist at work.

She's that good. Maybe she actually does have a tiara.

Susan Halsey, wearing a shiny green long dress with a more matronly cut, had reached the end of the line, near the entry to the ballroom. She and her entourage turned to see the genteel commotion coming up from behind. Her smile was weak, forced. Ice cold.

The entire scene had played out in an entry hall with a medieval feel to it. Twenty-foot vaulted ceilings and a network of nearly black woodwork gave the ancient mansion a Tudor atmosphere. Hard to tell whether the furnishings around the edges were legitimate antiques or good reproductions, but no one used them.

Several guys in black tie coalesced around Tommy, beverages already in hand, all focused on Mandy instead of Susan Halsey, speculating who she was, who she was with, where she was from. Tommy listened and when time and distance seemed right, excused himself. "Sorry. Time for me to get back to my date."

Yeah. Suck it up, guys.

He organized a smile of assurance and cruised across the open floor to offer Mandy his arm. At the moment she'd finished greeting the last guests, she turned and reeled him in. Together they stepped up to Susan Halsey. Mandy's smile shifted to faintly embarrassed, slightly bashful, lightly apologetic.

"Hello. I'm Tommy Kane. You must be Susan Halsey."

She shook his hand. "Nice of you to join us — at last — Mister Kane. I've heard so much about you." She turned her attention to Mandy. "And you're Amanda Owens."

Mandy nearly curtsied. "Mandy. All my friends call me Mandy."

Susan's expression looked like the smug smile of the baddest gator in the bayou. "But of course they do. We'll have to see about that,

won't we? And I'd like to introduce my good friend and favorite designer, Freddie Scapini. He's managed to organize our little Thanksgiving ball for us."

After a round of polite compliments and welcomes to the club, Susan took half a step back to study Mandy's gown. She gestured a command for a twirl and Mandy complied. "That's a lovely gown. You
clearly know the better shops in San Francisco."

Mandy smiled. "Actually, it's an original."

Susan reacted with pseudo-astonishment. "Really? Isn't that lovely."

Freddie leaned in. "It's a David Aire. He's — "

Susan's eyes narrowed and her smile evaporated when she turned
to Freddie and spoke in a growl. "I know god damn well who he is,
Freddie." Returning to Tommy and Mandy, she mustered a revived
smile. "You must excuse Freddie. Freddie always tries to be helpful.
Don't you Freddie? Now be a good boy and fetch me something to
drink."

Stay steady. She's got nothin' but money. "So, it was kind of you to invite us to your annual event, ma'am. New York gets a bit chilly this
time of year."

"Absolutely," Mandy said. "They're already talking about stormy
weather on the horizon and it's not even Thanksgiving."

"Well, I'll be pleased to pass along your compliments to my social
secretary. I give her a great deal of latitude when it comes to inviting
all the *right* people. Sometimes too much, perhaps, but we must always forgive overly eager staff. Tell me, Mister Kane, do you play
golf?"

Tommy said, "Why, yes, as does Mandy. Perhaps we'll find somewhere to get in a round before we head back east."

"We have an excellent course right here, Mister Kane."

"Is that right?"

She sweetened her smile. "One of the best in the bay area, if I do
say so myself. Quite private, but we occasionally welcome guests interested in a challenging course, well kept, but also to enjoy quiet moments of conversation."

Mandy said, "I'll wager that some interesting business has been done on the greens and fairways."

Susan brightened a bit more. "Oh, yes, my dear. I'm sure. Of course, one of the qualities of our little course is the opportunity to chat with an expected level of confidentiality."

Tommy said, "Nice to find places where the traditional values are honored. You don't see much of that anymore."

Susan opted to take the high road. If her feathers were ruffled, she was holding it close to her chest. She said, "Well. I think all our members, friends and guest are fairly chomping at the bit to get out into the ballroom, do a little dancing, a little mingling and hopefully not too much drinking."

Behind her, an aide stepped halfway through the door and gave a wave of his arm. The orchestra struck up a bright two-step, *Just in Time*.

Susan continued to smile and she gestured toward the doorway. "Ah. I see the festivities have begun. Let's go have a look, shall we?"

They walked side by side into an expansive ballroom. The orchestra on the far end continued, shifting to a fresh segment of a medley.

Mandy beamed. "Oh, how lovely. That's *Moderate Society*, isn't it? Look, Tommy, isn't the late Tudor décor charming? Late sixteenth, early seventeenth century, perhaps Elizabethan. Just on the cusp of Stuart. Of course, I'm sure it's a restoration, but rather faithful all the same."

"How good of you to notice," Susan said. "Enjoy your evening. Tee time is ten o'clock."

Tommy asked, "You've already made a reservation."

"As a matter of fact, Mister Kane, I have a standard tee time. I usually play with Brendan Kenwood and his guests."

Brendan Kenwood. The Secretary of the Treasury.

"...But unfortunately, he's out of town. Some sort of an economic conference. Geneva, I believe."

Mandy said, "I'm sorry that your usual foursome won't work out. But it's nice that they kept the tee time for you, anyway."

Susan's smile went to patronizing. "That, my dear, is because I *own* the club."

Tommy nodded. "But of course. May we bring a guest to round out the foursome?"

Susan studied the river of formal wear drifting past into the ball-room. "Certainly. Once again, Mister Kane, enjoy your evening. Now I really must — "

"Of course. Nice to meet you, Susan."

"I'm sure. Good night, *Mister Kane.*"

* * *

Mandy took an easier backswing, as her mentor suggested. *Yes. That should... no, it's too soft.* The ball sputtered to rest four inches from the cup. Her shoulders drooped.

Walter leaned down and gently placed another ball at her feet. "It's all right, Mandy. Perfectly all right. Course is a tad dry. Greens running a tad fast. Californians don't have any sense about water man-agement, so their golf courses go all to hell."

Mandy tapped the head of her putter on the grass and looked up at the placid grin of Walter Campos. A half-dozen charmed men watched from a respectful distance. "I haven't played in a long time, Walter. They don't have many courses in Manhattan." *Speak up a bit, so all the others can hear.*

Walter chuckled. "You should get out of the city more often. Do something more worthwhile."

"Like golf?"

His perpetual grin went wide. "Oh, absolutely. That, or fish, deep sea, for the really big ones, the trophies. 'Course, lot of folks like to dabble with bonefish, light tackle, all that, but for my money, it's go-ing man-a-mano with the heavyweights, five hundred pounders and up. Way out in the Gulf, Cuba, the big islands."

She focused on the ball and tested the weight of the putter in her hand. "Sergei's quite a fisherman. Or so he says."

"He is. We've been out a couple of times."

"And Charlie, too. They're both into fly fishing, talk about it all the time."

Walter nodded in a thoughtful way and promised to invite them when the project was done. *Always a "project." Life in the land of eu-phemisms. Okay. The ball is staring at me, annoying me. Ought to just...*

Settle. Dummy swing. Feel the flow of it. Look. Picture the putt. Now step up. Settle. Breath. *Step back, step back. Make it look good.* "This is not going to work, Walter. My arms are killing me from an hour on the driving range, I'm hopelessly out of touch with the mini-mal game I used to have way back when. I mean, I was in college the last time I played, Walter."

"Like a bicycle. It's like — "

She shook her head. "No. Don't even... You know what? I don't see Tommy out here. He's buddied up with half a dozen guys at the starter's shack, only took a couple of practice shots on the range, looks like he's about to go messing around, just for funsies."

Walter's smile switched gears into patience. "Tommy? Hell of a golfer. Technically, sort of so-so. Weekend kind of duffer, the kind of player that just loves the game and doesn't give a crap about the score. But a hell of a golfer. Drives with *ferocity*, absolute ferocity. Approach shots get a little mushy, but that's to be expected with a style of play like that. But he putts like a god damn pro. No fear, none at all. Reads a green like a woman's — "

Mandy waved him off and laughed. "I get the picture, Walter."

Walter's eyes sparkled and his expression went to smug satisfac-tion as he leaned back and stepped away. "So what are you waiting for? Pat that little puppy, take it home."

Mandy cocked her head and glanced at the ball. *Steady, strong, serene.* A gentle and confident tap, a nice steady run. *Perfect. Piece of cake. Hope I didn't make it look too easy.*

Walter nodded. "Damn nice putt, Mandy. Just in nick o'time, too. Here comes Halsey, just twelve minutes late. Starter won't mind — "

"I know. It's her little sandbox."

CHAPTER THIRTY-SIX

A hook. A slice that reddened her face and raised eyebrows from the others. A clean drive, not terribly long, but thankfully on a par three, and a moment to collect while the others waited on the green. A little chip, like she'd done so many times with giggling girlfriends on lazy summer afternoons when tennis was boring and the pool boys annoying. *How we teenagers so annoyed the serious guys, filling retirement with stock trading talk and testosterone.*

A nine iron, tarnished, worn, familiar in her hand. The dawn briefing over hotel toast and orange juice and what they called scram—bled eggs. Lucy in fine form with another of her incredible dossiers, the facts and foibles and whispers, the hints of soft spots in suits of ar—mor. Susan Halsey. Very driven, very smart, very resilient, very fo—cused. *Very, very, very. How do you quantify "very"?* Tommy had coun—seled caution. Caution causes trepidation, and trepidation, tentative.

Mandy addressed the ball. Quick look for the pin. Even from a distance, the conversation looked forced, like predators testing one another. With Halsey, tentative could be fatal. The shower of details. Pushing it away, because it really didn't matter. *I'm supposed to be a duf—fer, but this is trying my patience.* Loosen up. Relax. Head still, very still. *Focus. Focus...*

Swing.

The ball got up nicely, good backspin, floating, floating. Good drop, hardly any roll. A bogie at best. *But that's okay. This is for fun. Yeah, right, uh-huh.*

Just a pleasant day, everyone playing their own game, almost cor—dial. Tommy and Walter were having a good round, but Susan's fa—

miliarity with the course and frequency of play gave her an early edge. A couple of par fours, a long five with a nasty dogleg, and into the long haul, trying to keep pace but pretending to regret the lack of practice.

They made the turn and gave Mandy the honors in the tee box at ten. Not that it mattered. Cards were being filled more out of habit than any sense of competitiveness. *I'm almost certain that Tommy isn't marking a score at all.*

The old adage. *It's a game of inches. The six or seven between your ears.* Settled into the routine of the round, it was all about the ears of Susan Halsey. Millimeter by millimeter.

Walter babbling on, an old man, struggling with the infirmities of age, the difficult vision fouling his short game. Tommy, whacking the ball with abandon, probably not the best of form but with a great deal of power. Susan, experience, assured, in command, lurking like a barracuda on the fringes of a reef.

Walter, chattering observations, commentary and suggestions that at first were gregarious but now grinding the nerves. *Even mine. Wonder how many rounds he's won by annoying the others.*

Tommy, loaded up with southern charm and courtly manners, working Walter but in fact egging him on, his own *joie de vivre* so methodically and gently getting under Susan's skin that her putting game was beginning to suffer.

And me. The tagalong girlfriend. Yuck. Having confessed distance from the game, the obvious option at breakfast. Just a little helpless. Just a little dumb. Just a little inept. Anything for the cause. Tommy had said there would be a point, he didn't know when, that the time would be right. Meanwhile, park the ego and any serious talent that might unexpectedly pop out of a locker with a sticky door.

Little hints on the back nine. Testing, probing, getting around to deal-making. Susan blew a trap shot and the ball bounded across the fifteenth green and down an embankment into the tall grass. Ouch. I remember guys who'd put the club twenty feet into the air, into a tree.

Tommy shook his head. His voice cooed in sympathy. "Oh, my. Bad luck."

Walter did a couple of tsk-tsks and said, "Looks like you're away, Susan."

Tense jaw. Clenched fist. Eyes narrow and ice cold. "I can see that perfectly well, Walter."

"It's only a game."

She marched past and growled. "You know perfectly well what this is. Kane and Owens have been messing around in places they shouldn't go. I think it's about time that we think about settling the matter. That way, everyone walks away."

Tommy said, "Walking's good."

Susan paused and glared. "Better than being carried in body bag, Mister Kane. You think about that while I find my god damn ball."

Numbers began to float on seventeen. Susan thought twenty-five thousand, apiece, might be fair for a single data file that probably wasn't all that helpful.

"What about the entire application, all the data sets, a working copy? It would be a shame to see that turn up in the hands of, say, the Chinese. Russians. Iranians. Oh, man, the auction would be — "

Halsey smiled, the first time in a dozen holes. " — Fatal, Mister Kane. Fatal."

He opened his arms in an expansive gesture. "Tommy. Friends call me Tommy. I believe it's your honor, Susan."

Amid an escalating round of banter, tension rose in the eighteenth fairway and the quality of golf collapsed. Par five, nearly six hundred yards. Just can't tell if the guys are tanking shots. But darn it, Tommy, you're cutting it awfully close. Mandy pulled a three iron from her bag and paused. Her hand was shaking. Just a tremor. But...can't...quite...grip. She leaned the club against her thigh and rubbed her hands together, flexed her fingers. Breathe. Deep, deep breath.

Tommy called out from twenty-five feet away. "You okay?"

Mandy nodded.

Susan was watching. Intent. *The way a cat does, before it...*

"I'll be fine, Tommy. Just a little out of shape."

Step up. Practice swing. Got to pull it right. Okay. Here we go. Stance. Focus. Swing.

What an incredibly awful shot.

Susan followed the flight of the ball, looked back at Mandy and lingered long enough. Curious. Intrigued. She's thinking. We are so screwed...

In methodical silence, the foursome worked their way toward the green, guarded by a massive swirling bunker that caught the mid-day sunshine and shot it straight back into Mandy's eyes. Two terrible shots later, she was on, but lying seven, maybe eight, thinking about the long drive back to San Francisco and the longer flight home.

Susan's fortunes were only slightly better. A wicked green, looking quite fast and she had an uphill lie. Tommy had laid up, and the chip took a friendly hop. He'll two-putt and be one over. Walter circled his ball beyond the trap and chose a wedge. His strange, sloppy swing. Too much. The ball hopped twice and rolled steadily to a spot three inches away from Susan.

Thirty five, forty feet. And we're all going to walk away in a foul mood.

Walter marched onto the green. "Tommy, you go ahead and putt out. I'm an old man, you see, can't see so well any more, got to spend a little time thinking about what to do. I assume that's all right with you, Susan?"

Her impatience, frazzled to the point of indifference. "Whatever makes you happy, Walter."

"O'course. It always seems to come down to that. No sense in marking your ball. You'd just be in my way. Tell you what. Why don't you go ahead?"

So he can read the green.

Tommy fluffed his first putt and eventually tugged the ball from the cup and strolled closer. Walter began to verbalize his opinion of the lie, speculating on which way the ball would break. Tommy began to comment, but Susan cut them off.

"Goddammit," she said. "I'm starting to... Never mind. I'll make my shot and we'll call this one rotten round and let it go."

Tommy and Walter exchanged guy glances and patronizing shrugs. Susan took a long look at the shot and stepped up to her ball. Her practice swing stopped halfway back.

A flash drive tumbled to the turf, beyond her ball.

Susan spoke in a soft, controlled tone. "You've dropped some—thing, Mister Kane."

"Fifty million."

"A lot of money."

"Not negotiable. But worth every penny if you want it back."

"And if I say no?"

"Who knows where it might go next. But I tell you what. You make that putt, and it's yours. Free."

Susan looked up and offered the faintest of smiles. She returned her attention to the ball at her feet and took her stroke. It bobbled, hopped, sputtered, rolled. And went six inches left and ten inches long.

Walter said, "Oh, bad luck. But I knew it'd break. Easy putt, too. Anybody could make it."

Susan stepped back. "Care to show us, Walter?"

Tommy said, "Hey, Walter, even Mandy could make that putt."

"Naw, no way."

"Sure she could."

Susan sighed exasperation and turned to Mandy. "Go ahead, my dear. Show me."

"Oh, no. I agree with Walter — "

Susan stepped closer, her eyes ice cold and her voice a growl. "For once, dear, why don't you *just try*?"

"Oughta to be some sort of wager on this, Tommy. Yessir, a fine little wager. Now, you've got that computer gizmo. What'd you say? Fifty?"

Mandy's voice was edged with panic. "Tommy, I couldn't. We'd be risking everything..."

Walter rubbed his chin. "That's true enough, Tommy. True enough. How about it, Susan? What've you got to make this sporting? Tommy, here, he's willing to bet fifty million on this gal."

Susan's jaw tightened even more and her voice lowered to an eerie growl. "All right, Walter, how about — "

Walter's expression went serious. " — how about that island of yours, in the Exumas?"

She began to laugh, like it was the most ludicrous thing she'd heard all day. She paused and looked at Mandy. "Sure. Why not?" She stepped aside and gestured toward the hole.

Mandy cried out in protest. "Tommy!"

Tommy grinned. "Let me see if I've got this right. Mandy makes the putt, Walter gets the island. She misses, I'll give you the stick."

Mandy shook her head. "No, no, no. You people can't be serious. A fifty million dollar wager on me making an impossible shot? This is so — "

Walter chuckled. "Interesting, Mandy. Interesting."

"I can't do this. Tommy, please..."

Tommy stepped around the ball to study the lie. "Sure you can."

She held her shaking hands aloft. "No. I can't."

Walter crossed his arms. "What are you waiting for, Mandy? Pat that little puppy, take it home."

Oh my gosh... Tommy. Smiling. The kind of smile when he knows. Steady, strong, serene. She flexed her fingers and tested her grip on the putter. About as firm as... never mind. Just a routine, every day, fifty million dollar golf shot. Steady. Calm. Focus. Focus. Easy swing.

The ball was away, echoing the path of Susan's a couple of minutes earlier. Running a little right. Curling back, back, on line. Go, go, go. Slowing down. Slower. Slower. On the edge...

Aw, man...

Susan's instant fist in the air, a pump. "Yes! Yes!" A stamp of her foot, too quick, too soon.

The vibration, racing across the green. The last blade of grass shuddering.

And the ball dropped.

A rush of air, in and out of Mandy's lungs. "Oh, my... Tommy, it... Oh, Tommy..."

Tommy and Walter, smiling, grinning, stepping forward to share the joy.

Susan's fist, opening into a limp hand dangling from a weak wrist. Dropping to her knees. Her head bowed. Her fancy putter laying on the grass.

Tommy picked up Susan's club and offered his hand to help her to her feet. She looked stunned, beaten, the gravity of her impulsive de‑cision sinking in hard. Tommy lifted her hand and dropped the flash drive into it. "Sorry it had to go against you. Consider this a consola‑tion prize. It's not just a file. It's Mercury Five, and it's all yours. I think we're square."

He turned to Mandy and Walter. "Well, I think it's time to get some lunch or something. Maybe a nice glass of scotch. Unless you want to play out your own putt, Mandy."

She shook her head. "No, that's okay. I've had enough golf for one day." *Play it out, right to the end. Gosh, I love being a low-handicap golfer.*

Together, they gathered their bags and walked off toward the clubhouse, leaving Susan to the events unfolded.

Tommy said, "Walter, that was one amazing golf shot. Not one guy in a thousand could have parked a chip so close to another ball." He chuckled. "Bad eyes and all."

"Grand fun, Tommy. Just grand. And it works every time. Learned that from a touring pro many years ago. They didn't have all the money from endorsements in those days, so they had to hustle some on the side. Most guys go right for the pin if they've got half a chance. Fellows I knew, they'd go for the money. But you folks ran the game pretty fair, I believe."

Tommy stole a glance at Mandy. "Couldn't have been sweeter."

She took his hand. "Tommy, I want to say you scared me half to death back there. I mean, you pushed it right to the limit. I'd have died if she hadn't have stamped her foot."

He chuckled. "You couldn't possibly lose. I mean, the island was a plus, but you know and I know that the file on the stick is a dud. Not only a dud, but Lucy says it'll eat the system alive."

She punched his shoulder. "She *thinks*, Tommy. She doesn't *know*. And what's this 'we're square' business?"

He sighed. "Details, details... And of course, I was lying through my teeth. Trust me on that."

CHAPTER THIRTY-SEVEN

Enroute to Geneva, Switzerland

Mandy shuffled through a stack of paper from the briefing book assembled by Lucy. "Tommy, this is so complicated, I'm not sure I can memorize it. Couldn't we be disguised as FBI or Secret Service or something simple, IRS maybe?"

She's right about complicated. "Sorry, but if you want to bring down a member of the Cabinet, you don't send law enforcement types. Special counsel to the president looks better."

"Well, I didn't think I was going to have to memorize the entire West Wing on six-hour flight to Europe. I think Lucy gets carried away with creativity sometimes, and Karl is much too willing to oblige." She held an identification badge up. "Look at this. It's a terrible picture. I look like one of those wanted posters you see in the post offices, not a legal eagle from the White House."

"I heard that," a voice from the phone said.

Tommy chuckled. "Between Bug and Lucy, you have to assume someone's listening, Mandy."

She rolled her eyes and stuck out her tongue.

"It's a good thing. We'd better have it together this time if we're going to persuade a very smart guy that his world is going up in flames. Timing is going to be everything and there are an awful lot of variables."

"Starting with Sergei's accent," Lucy said.

A few feet aft, Charlie and Yenchenko cleaned and prepped weapons while they debated the relative merits of fly versus nymph fishing on opposite sides of the world.

Mandy said, "I hope I don't have to pack one of those pistols. This suit isn't tailored for it. Do you think the women packing weapons have jackets modified, or do they allow themselves to be Calamity Jane? Guys have it easy, trust me."

Lucy chimed in. "Secret Service guys have to lug around those H&Ks. Talk about bulk...."

Tommy said, "Mac-Tens and Uzis are my preference, but that's personal taste. H&K is good. A sniper friend of mine loves them. But we're supposed to be lawyers, so all we get is a stack of intel."

Mandy scowled. "That we have to memorize. In my business, we call them backgrounders. I am never going to learn this stuff. Lucy, are you sure we can't crash in, bop the guy over the head, call the local cops?"

Lucy laughed. "Definitely not very elegant. Tommy likes a little more class. Don't you, Tommy?"

"Absolutely. Bopping guys isn't done. Well, maybe in alleys out-side biker bars or strip joints, but the Swiss take a dim view. Poor for tourist trade. How are we doing with all our variants of Mercury Five?"

Lucy said, "As ready as we'll ever be. Dad's a little anxious about long lines and distance delays, but we've done front-running for so long that I can wing it in my sleep. Speaking of elegant, that round of golf was super. Halsey was so pissed that she grabbed the first unse-cure line she could find and called her guy at DNI to ream his ass. Should have sent more thugs to smish the two of you. Let me see if I can remember. Oh, yeah, she wanted you guys like bugs on wind-shield, a patch of goo."

Mandy turned a briefing page and kept reading. "Not very nice. I mean, some people are poor losers, I guess. Tommy was so consoling when he handed her the booby prize. You should have seen the look in Walter's eyes when that putt dropped and he won the island. Like a kid with a new toy."

Lucy said, "It's a guy thing. Not happy unless they're planting their flag on some island somewhere."

Tommy grunted. "Hey, hey."

"Okay, Mister Fifteen Hundred Acres in Pennsylvania..."

"She's got you there, Tommy."

"Yeah, afraid so." Last page. One more time, turn it over and start again. So what happened with our Trojan horse that we so casually turned over to Halsey?"

Mandy continued to scan paper. "More like Trojan pony. Can't believe something so small — "

"It was an eight-gig stick, mostly because of all the frigging data. The app itself is not too big. Anyway, Tommy, the damn thing got a private flight back to Washington. Our guys at Reagan did a good track to the private little store of the director of national intelligence in rural Maryland. I tuned in in time for the load — can you believe they didn't even quarantine it? — and it's sitting there, ready to run. You do know that once I pull the trigger, I've got to get out."

Mandy finished her briefing packet and started again. "No foot-print, right?"

"Exactly. So we'll be flying blind. Who knows what's going to hit the fan."

Tommy sipped coffee. "You're okay with that?"

"Yep. What the hell. Sooner or later you gotta stand on the edge of the cliff and see if the wind picks up."

"Anything on the target?"

"Dad's got a rope on the suite your guy's using. They've got some gear from the home office set up for a data feed, the usual. If it works, he'll probably crap in his drawers or keel over in cardiac arrest."

Mandy asked, "And if it doesn't?"

"Leavenworth has great accommodations for people who enjoy the peace and comforts of solitary confinement for the next fifty or sixty years. Beats Gitmo, though, right, Tommy?"

Tommy leaned back and rubbed his eyes. This is getting to be overload. Time to stretch. "Absolutely. Cuban jail food is terrible."

Mandy said, "What about Susan's guy — the director of national intelligence?"

"Martin Gillborn? I so prefer to call him Marty. He looks like a Marty."

"Whatever."

"Seems like Tommy's old buddy, Walter Campos, is a pal of the president. Not real close, but close enough to get on the calendar for the Oval Office. Ran a political action committee for the prez when he was in the Senate. *Ahem.* It would have been nice if Tommy had mentioned it."

Tommy arched his back and motioned to Karen for a fresh round of snacks and beverages. "Sorry about that."

Lucy laughed. "I'll let it go, this once."

He said, "Walter's pleased with the outcome of the golf match and promised to get a word with the president when you let him know it's time. Marty's toast."

Lucy said, "Works for me. Okay, I guess we're good."

Mandy slumped in her seat. "Tommy's taking a stretch and I should, too. How long to — "

"You should be wheels down in a little under two hours. Half hour to the hotel, do your thing, get the hell out. Yeah, yeah, I promise to join you for a little R-n-R on Walter's boat. Want to drop in on my little bank in Grand Cayman, say hello. Anyway, have fun. I gotta step out and reload on doughnuts before we destroy the world."

Mandy chuckled. "Pink frosting with sprinkles."

"Oh, absolutely! Nothing better for armageddon. Except maybe popcorn."

CHAPTER THIRTY-EIGHT

Hotel Schweizerhof, Bahnhofplatz 11, Bern, Switzerland

Gray. Staid. Old Guard. *Old guard luxury, as a matter of fact.* But gloomy, a little sad. Probably the dense cloud cover, the hint of drizzle in the air.

Mandy turned up the collar of her coat and winced through the thick plastic frame of phony glasses, craving a moment to console her hair, tied back tight into a bureaucrat's bun by Karen before they got off the plane.

Behind, a red city bus whisked past, silent under the electric over—head wires except for the sound of its fat tires on wet pavement. The doors of the black SUV smacking shut. The temptation to look around and take in the rest of the sights. *Don't. Look official.*

Uneasy, a little nervous, and, yes, a little frightened. *They've done this cloak-and-dagger stuff a thousand times.* Except for the occasional but necessary ambush interview on the run in a hallway, it had been press conferences, cordial interviews, small-group briefings, back—grounders.

This is so different. The stuff from espionage movies and spy nov—els, the precision timing, the elaborate plans. Sergei, ordering the seating arrangement in the car at the airport, all of it silly until the ve—hicle glided to a stop in front of the hotel and a lanky old man, wispy white hair, dark blazer, white piping etching the lapel edges, stepped out to open the car door. Karl. A faint salute, the twinkle in his eyes, the cordial, bemused smile.

"Bitte, mein Fraulein. A package for you." He offered a thick enve—

lope to Yenchenko.

Conference credentials. A set for everybody. Struggling journalist to deputy White House counsel and now a ticket to the inner sanctum, just like that. No time to admire the handiwork of The Clockmaker. Just get it on, take a breath, roll out of the car and look like you mean business.

Halfway out, Tommy's said, "Sorry about the glasses. You've got to match the I-D photos."

A numb nod, a scramble through a cheap and tacky bag, much too small. Ah. Better. Stupid, but better. Falling into a pack to swarm the door under the centermost of a line of arches, under the big hotel sign, into the opulence of the lobby. The first layer of the onion. Security everywhere. Lots of guys with crewcuts who talk to their shirt cuffs and maybe actually believed no one noticed the transparent wires coming up from their collars and into their ears. Of course. Economic ministers from half of Europe and all their attendants are in the building. The barbarians lurked on the perimeter. And some of us were actually inside.

Tommy, Sergei, Charlie, marching forward like they owned the place. Hard to keep pace in these shoes. Hard to keep a straight face. Look determined, relentless, official, they had told her. Well, pardon me while I adjust my makeup — it's a bit too K Street and not quite enough West Wing.

Hotel security, dressed like the courier outside, folding in near the front desk, looking darker against the high, white marble facade with the tops of computer monitors sticking up like ears. Beyond, a raised lounge with club chairs and cozy comfort for fleeting meetings. The entire area in shades of dark brown to near white, mostly standard hotel beige. Tommy and Sergei, calm, relaxed, like the kind of guys who rob banks every other day except for weekends. Charlie, growly more than usual, lugging a battered brown leather briefcase. Like the guy who'd busted the bank robbers and was escorting them into a courtroom. *No. Like the lawyer who's going to get them out on bail after the arraignment.*

The hotel staff forming a weak barrier. Crisp, efficient, haughty in the way that arrogant guardians of the gate always seem to be.

"Guten Tag, Mein Herr. Wie kann ich Ihnen behilflich sein?"

Even before Tommy hoisted the badges hanging from the noose around his neck, the other guy spoke. A blond guy who hikes and skis and swims a lot, a nice little sneer, the kind everyone would like to smack, and not at all intimidated by Sergei. *"Es tut mir leid, aber das Hotel ausgebucht ist."*

The first guard, after a close but brief look, relented. *"Ah. Entschuldigen Sie.* My apologies. You are, of course, Americans. With *Herr* Kenwood's delegation."

No, actually the White House. The president's staff. Kind of. Let it go.

The security people stepped aside and gestured toward toward the elevators.

Tommy's advice, the final words before the operation began. Just don't get cocky. Expect a lot of checkpoints, tougher as we get closer. But don't look nervous, either. Like the first interview, just fourteen, the school newspaper a journalistic joke, but the headmistress had such a mean assistant that merely going through the portal was enough to make knees flutter and sweat to form on the back of the neck. She turned out to be a nice and gracious lady, helpful and en—couraging, and the snotty gate guard was forever after relegated to the status of annoying jerk.

Elevators. And another layer of security, these a mixed lot, scruti—nizing everyone entering the area, eyes first, then badges. Two of them stepped forward and introduced themselves as Secret Service, bulges under their left arms obvious to make a point.

Remember the headmistress. Steady, strong, serene.

Tommy stepped forward to respond, identifying his team.

They'll check.

They did. Efficient, inaudible exchanges of information. Bug on the intercept, Lucy on the audio. For a moment, the Secret Service guy seemed to pause to consider something, took one last look at Tommy's credentials, paused a second time, listened to instructions, and hurried through the other three. Without any reaction, he pressed the call button for the elevator.

He held the door while Mandy followed the others into the car. Don't look, don't respond, don't do anything but move forward. Tommy's instructions didn't feel right. She slowed and looked up at the Secret Service guy. Smile. He's just doing his job. "Thank you. Have a nice day."

He relaxed, nodded and seemed to savor the view. "Yes ma'am. You do the same."

The door closed and two seconds later the car began to move.

"Whew," she said.

Tommy pointed up and around and whispered assurance. "Doing fine. Steady as she goes."

The elevator slowed and lurched as it stopped. A tiny bell rang and the door whooshed open to the third floor and directional signs for ranges of room numbers.

Another layer of the onion. A more cursory glance at Tommy's credentials and a deferential pointing to the left, into a section of suites. Secret Service guys, lounging at the last portal, coming to at—tention, talking to someone, maybe the people in the lobby. A raised hand, the eternal gesture of the traffic cop, apologies for the inconve—nience, but everyone understands and a call into a colleague in the room.

Another delay. Yes, I know. We're not expected.

Tommy and Charlie filled the void with small talk, while Sergei devoted his attention to Mandy, whispering nonsensical Russian proverbs to give the illusion of conversation and avoid Secret Service people who'd probably find it odd that a United States deputy marshal could only muster fractured English.

Someone inside unlocked the door. The Secret Service guy smiled and opened it. "Step right in, folks."

Here we go. The end of the trail.

Aides, assistants. Younger than expected, looking frazzled, tense, somewhere around the edge of panic. The higher the rank, the more eager and willing volunteers, craving the periphery of power, making their mark, upward bound. Bickering, positioning, forever sorting out the pecking order, vying for dominance, to be the chosen one who has the ear of the big dog. The one currently in favor over there, twenty

feet away, briefing the boss from a binder while the boss listens as at—
tentively as he can while taking off his jacket.

Lucy's timing, exquisite. A meeting downstairs completed, the
usual cordiality finally faded, the return to the inner sanctum to prep
for the next round, probably over dinner. That would mean a shirt
change, a fresh tie, maybe a little rest. On a credenza past the desk, a
computer monitor ran a ticker of the market summary.

The aide a rung lower confronted Tommy but almost immediate—
ly tumbled into submission and retreat.

If he's any good, he hasn't folded. Yeah. Cell phone. He doesn't
recognize us.

Charlie and Yenchenko pushed into the center of an area that had
been converted into a makeshift conference center.

Charlie said, "Okay, folks. I'd like all of you to step out, give us the
room."

Heads turned. An uneasy silence.

"Don't think I made myself clear. I need the room, and I need it
now."

A voice from the pack demanded justification.

Charlie sighed, stepped to a chair and dropped his briefcase onto
it. "Okay. Now here's how it is. My name is Charlie Burke, and I'm
the United States marshal for the District of Columbia. I've got my—
self a sack full of subpoenas in here, mostly having to do with obstruc—
tion of justice, but other stuff, too. Conspiracy always sounds good.
Might even have some from them people on Capitol Hill, banking
committees and such. Now, I can pull 'em out, start calling roll, hand
'em out, and come tomorrow morning we can have ourselves a real in—
teresting meeting with a federal judge."

Jaws went slack.

"Or you folks can do what I asked in the first place, which is to
give us the god damn room and do it now. These people are senior
White House legal staff and they got themselves a whole lot more pull
than you want to tangle with. Do I make myself clear?"

The guy on the phone hung up and nodded toward the others.
Lucy and Bug had done it again, the classic reroute of a phone line,
the routing to someone filling in for a known name.

Brendan Kenwood put his jacket back on and fluffed the lapels to get it to park right on his shoulders. "Just what the hell is going on here?"

Tommy presented his credentials. "Good afternoon, Mister Sec—retary. I'll be glad to explain as soon as we have the room."

Any other time, I'd challenge why the guy is the alpha and the girl is the assistant. But not today. I'm out of my depth.

Kenwood sputtered. "These are my staff, my aides."

Tommy nodded. "It's about a matter called Mercury Five, sir."

Kenwood's breathing stalled for a moment and went shallow. His voice was weak. "I see. Uh, well, okay everyone. Let's take a break from matters at hand. POTUS always, uh, takes priority, I'm afraid."

You should be. You're the reason Benny and Phil were killed.

Tommy leaned in and whispered. "Easy, Mandy. Just relax."

"Is it that obvious?"

His nod was faint but clear. *Ouch.*

With Sergei's silent assistance, Charlie herded the flock of aides out the door and into the hallway. "Now, that's better. Me and my deputy here will secure the room for a few minutes, then you can get on with your day. Won't be long."

Yenchenko and Charlie followed and with the click of the door latch the room fell into an uneasy silence. Tommy turned to Mandy. The look. *He's set it up, he's handing it off to me. Oh, no, no.*

CHAPTER THIRTY-NINE

Brendan Kenwood put his hands on his hips, his arms pulling his jacket away. "All right, what's this all about?"

C'mon, Tommy. I'd screw it up. Yes. I would. I can't. I... The sunny spring day. Going out to ride my bike. *Four or five, can't remember.* Dad in the driveway, outside the garage, his hands smudged with grease, a look of triumph on his face. A pair of wrenches in one hand. The training wheels in the other. And right in front, my first bike, leaning on the kickstand. *I can't. I can't. Daddy, please.* "*You're an Owens girl. Yes, you can. Here, get on. I'll get you started.*"

Mandy took a step forward, another, then a third. "Please, Mister Secretary, take a seat. We need to have a rather frank conversation."

"I'll stand, dammit."

"As you wish." She settled into a chair, staying close to the front edge to sit up straight, unafraid, unintimidated, and leaned a little forward. "Mister Secretary, there's been a bit of an issue involving Director Gibbons at National Intelligence. It concerns an unauthorized project called Mercury Five and its potential impact on foreign exchange markets, worldwide."

"And how does this concern me?"

"I'm sorry, but others involved in the conspiracy have implicated you. Director Gillborn has already been indicted and is prepared to testify against you. Mister Kane is here on behalf of the attorney general and is prepared to present charges in federal court. The president has always valued your friendship and support, and he wishes to spare you embarrassment and humiliation. He'd like to have your immediate resignation. There are some documents to sign, to acknowledge

— "

Kenwood crossed his arms and stood defiant. "Covering his own ass, that's what he's doing. I'd much rather hear this from the president himself."

Mandy said, "I understand." She passed a phone to him. "Feel free. I can give you a moment if you wish — "

"That won't be necessary. I want to see your faces when the president pulls your rope. You two have no idea who you're dealing with, no idea at all. By the time I'm done, honey, you'll be an ADA in Boondocks, Iowa." Kenwood dialed a number from memory. He turned away, his tone increasingly intense while Tommy and Mandy exchanged glances.

Wonder if your knees are shaking as much as mine.

In Mandy's ear, the voice of Lucy Tramanian spoke to Kenwood with an inflection of urgency, concern. The president is not available. Everyone's in the situation room, some sort of crisis with the markets. No, triggered by some sort of rogue software, a lot of chatter that it started in China, maybe Iran. Yessir, absolute turmoil. Yessir, he wants you to return immediately, explain what you seem to know about it.

Kenwood spun to look at the screen. "My God..."

Mandy asked, "Something wrong, Mister Secretary?"

Tommy pointed to the screen. "I think so. It sure looks like the markets are going all to pieces. Isn't what all that flashing red means?"

"He could have signed, Tommy. He could have walked away. But no, he couldn't take our word for it. He had to go and call the White House. Didn't trust us."

Tommy shrugged. "Maybe we could ask him again if he'd like to do what was asked."

Kenwood's face was ashen. His hands shook, out of control. He grabbed the monitor and shook it. "No, no, no..."

And calm. He sucked air in huge gulps and turned, his face contorted in a glare so icy that a chill tumbled down Mandy's spine.

"Who the hell are you people?"

"Tommy Kane. And she's my partner, Mandy Owens."

He nodded. "Halsey said..."

Tommy shrugged. "Yeah, probably so. She's not a good golfer, you know..."

Mandy said, "Well, that's not quite true. She's a excellent golfer. Just doesn't have much luck betting on her putting game."

"Yours actually."

Kenwood seemed totally crushed, rumpled. "Wha — I don't... You're the people who..."

Mandy patted the arm of the chair next to her. "Brendan, you re—ally should sit down. You don't look well at all."

Tommy said, "Wow, how about that? All the safety switches to stop a crash aren't working at all. The Dow is down ninety-four per—cent. NASDAQ, ninety-six. Dollar's down to pennies and, wow, looks like China's going to rule the world. I thought they were supposed to have some sort of safeguards on the system, you know, to stop free—falls. Oh, wait. The Mercury Five people said the application overrode those. So it's going to be a depression unprecedented in history."

Mandy sighed. "C'mon, Brendan, sit. Maybe we can help you out. Uruguay is nice this time of year. There's all kinds of little towns where a person can hide from all those nasty people looking for the guy who started it all."

Tommy nodded. "Wet teams from intelligence agencies all over the Europe, Africa, the Middle East. The people from India are — well, it's not important. But think of law enforcement. Not to mention the media. Wow, those media people, they're the worst."

"It was supposed... oh, my God... what have I done?"

Mandy patted the chair again. This time, Kenwood tumbled into it and leaned far forward, his head between his knees. In her earpiece, Lucy said, "Five minutes, tops."

"Tommy, you should get some water. I think he might be feeling unwell. Brendan, tell me. What was it supposed to do?"

Kenwood's voice fell to a mumble. "DNI had this concept. Use a foreign exchange trading application, experimental, coming out of NSA, CIA, somewhere, to rig the markets, kind of push governments into proper, you know, alignment. It's a matter of foreign policy, keep—ing spheres of influence under control."

Tommy settled on the arm of a chair opposite. "So what hap—

pened?"

Kenwood was reduced to a whimper. "Some sort of flaw, a prob—lem. But DNI wanted to go with it anyway, and we were to support it through the Fed. It was secret, off the books. But somebody in Fin—CEN got wind of it and after that..."

Tommy said, "It went south. Who was running Gillborn?"

"Private investment group, you wouldn't know them."

Oh, but we do. So well. "I see. So when the plan got leaked — "

Kenwood held his head in his hands, his fingers running hard through his hair. "We had to contain it." He nodded toward the screen. "Obviously, we failed."

"And the investors said they'd take care of it?"

Kenwood nodded and sighed. "My God. So many people, ruined. Civilization, destroyed. Nuclear war would have been better."

Mandy said, "Terrible price to pay, Brendan."

He looked up and took several deep, full breaths. He looked strangely calm, at ease. Even a faint smile. "Just curious. How did you people... Why?"

Mandy leaned forward. *Steady, strong, serene.* "I was supposed to be the ninth victim, Brendan. The people you sent came after me."

"I'm sorry."

"Wow, thanks. But you know what?" She held her arm out toward Tommy and he dropped the flash drive into her hand. "This is the file that you were after. It's not even a good file. It's corrupt. It doesn't mean anything at all."

"We didn't know..."

Mandy lowered her voice to firm indifference. "No. But what you did know is that it went from person to person to person. Just ordi—nary people. With all the fears and anxieties and problems and crises that ordinary people have, day in and day out. People who were trying to do the *right* thing, and would have been totally laughed at if they had succeeded. Because it was *nothing.*"

"Regrettable."

She leaned back in her chair. In her ear, Lucy said, "C'mon guys. Times almost up. This won't hold." *But I want to say so much more. I want to talk about Phil. And Benny.*

Tommy made a gesture with his hands. Time to cut it off. "Still time to sign, Kenwood."

Kenwood paused to consider options.

Lucy spoke with more urgency. "We're out of time. They're start—ing to track us."

Kenwood stood. "Do you think the president — "

Tommy was on his feet. "I think you're out of time. In or out, Brendan? *Right now.*"

Kenwood straightened his tie and brushed his hair with this hands. "Yes. Time to act." He took the confession from Tommy and strode to the desk. "I've got a pen here." From the drawer, he pulled a small pistol.

What? What?

Tommy spoke slowly and calmly as Kenwood waved the pistol back and forth. "Not the answer, my friend. Just no way. Put the weapon down, step away from the desk. Okay?"

Mandy's voice choked. "Tommy — ?"

Kenwood smiled. "You two people. Just collateral damage in a project that could have made the entire world safe, safe for our way of life. Safe for America. And now you've ruined it all."

"Kenwood, put the gun down. You won't gain — "

Kenwood's smile grew into a grin. He lifted the weapon. The bar—rel began to turn. "Tell the president that I was a good American, a patriot."

No no no no no no...

Kenwood pulled the trigger. A cloud of blood sprayed from the side of his head and his body crumpled, sliding off the desk and onto the floor.

In her ear, Lucy cried out. "Mandy? Mandy!"

"I'm okay."

Tommy listened to loud knocks on the door. "Yeah, but we're not. Kill the feed, Lucy." He sprang to the door and the Secret Service de—tail tumbled in. Tommy snagged the confession and tucked it into his pocked while the agents raced to the body behind the desk.

Tommy's voice went to command. "Suicide. I want this room con—

tained, right now, cordoned off. No one in or out. We're going to need our own team in, on the double. A body bag. No damn press, no local authorities. We're putting this down to heart attack, stroke, something. Move it, move it!"

The lead agent leaned over the body and picked up the weapon with a pencil through the trigger guard. "Definitely looks like a sui—cide."

Tommy grabbed Mandy's cell phone, tapped random numbers and said, "Mister President? No sir, he took his own life as soon as I gave him the news. Yessir, it's quite sad. Yes, we're all right. I have it contained. We'll make it a heart attack, spare his family. Yessir. Thank you, sir."

Mandy stood, her hand over her mouth. *I had no idea...*

Tommy's voice stayed sharp. "C'mon guys, let's go. Today would be good. Get some of the local station people to clean up the mess." He clapped his hands. "Dammit, let's move! I'll get the lady out of here. Just tie it off the second I'm out of here, okay? *Okay?* Good. C'mon, Miss Owens, let's take it one step at a time..."

In the hallway, anxious and horrified aides waited for news.

Tommy said, "Go back to your rooms, pack your bags. There's been an incident, and people from the CIA station here will be com—ing to debrief. Nobody talks to nobody, even among yourselves. It that clear?"

A chorus of nods.

Charlie and Yenchenko herded the aides away and fell in behind Tommy and Mandy.

Tommy spoke to his lapel. "Lucy?"

"Yeah, Tommy. Everybody okay?"

Yes. I'll be fine. Just need some air.

"Yeah, we're good. Tell Cesar to get a plan filed. We'll be there in a few minutes. Where we headed?"

"Grand Cayman. Walter wants to meet you there."

"We do all right?"

Lucy cackled. "Fabulous. Did a simulcast for your big shot pals, cleaned them out. Should have the funds transferred by morning."

"How'd we do?"

"An even two fifty for each, like you wanted, plus Walter's six fifty. And I even got the last of the TKA money."

Two billion dollars. Just like that. They really are that good.

Lucy said, "Okay, Tommy, I'm shutting it all down, pulling the plug. Have a nice flight, guys."

Ten minutes later the black SUV came to a stop outside the fixed base operator at Bern Airport. Karen stood on the tarmac with an umbrella, but the clouds were parting and a few rays of late day sunshine trickled across the narrow valley. All around, snow-capped peaks were cast in pink and orange hues. As they climbed the steps, the winding cry of the auxiliary power unit began. *Cesar wasted no time starting engines.*

Mandy turned to Tommy. "The stick. You left the stick with Kenwood. The file on the stick..."

He grinned. "Just a blank I picked up in Jack's Ford yesterday. Never used. That bluff cost me eight dollars."

She gasped. "An audible. You called an audible. Dammit, Tommy, I could sock you one."

"Go ahead."

Mandy made a fist, cocked her right arm and gently tapped him on the chest. "Okay, so you know how to work a story, too. Now we're even."

Four minutes later, the Gulfstream rolled down the runway to the turnaround. Outside, the fading light of Switzerland cast a glow on the fields and trees beyond. The jet turned a hundred and eighty degrees and paused for a moment. Cesar throttled up, and they were away, racing toward the shimmering mountains. Nose up. Climbing, climbing, ever higher. Gear up. Away, toward the setting sun.

CHAPTER FORTY

Halsey Island, The Exumas, Bahamas

With a platter of snacks and beverages on his right hand, Tommy stepped into bright sunshine. The offshore breeze ruffled his shirt and the heat from the decking seared his bare feet. He scampered on tip–toes to a patch of shade.

Dead ahead was the octagonal open air observation tower, the peaked roof sheltering everyone from blue-white sunshine. Matched cherry-red sofas and lounge chairs circling a round coffee table. Be–low, the tops of low trees and the freshwater pool, sparkles of sunlight dancing on the ripples. Beyond, azure sea, unblemished from horizon to horizon. Mandy and Lucy were stretched out, sponging it in. The all-time spa.

Oh, yeah. This is what they call down time. "Got nibbles, ice-colds."

Lucy said, "Hey, Tommy. We thought you fell overboard."

"Tough to do on an island. Kitchen takes a little getting used to. All the stuff is in the wrong place."

Mandy chuckled. "Poor baby. See what I mean, Lucy? It's so diffi–cult to get good help these days." She accepted a glass. "What's in it?"

"Tropical fruit juices, ice, rum. Mostly rum."

"It'll do."

Lucy focused on the view. "I was telling Mandy that this is the most incredible thing I've ever seen. And I've seen a lot of wild things, but when Walter dropped the keys in front of you on his yacht, I thought I was gonna fall over the railing."

Mandy gathered an assortment of cut fruit from the platter into a smaller bowl. "You're not alone. And he shouldn't have."

Lucy cocked an eyebrow. "So this *entire* island is all yours? Just be—cause you sank a putt?"

Tommy nodded. "All hers. Her op, her spoils."

"Damn. I'm gonna buy some clubs."

He chuckled. "I think you can afford it now. Walter thinks there ought to be a name change for the island, completely wipe Susan off the map."

Lucy stabbed a chunk of mango. "Not a bad idea."

Tommy sampled the drink and leaned back in a chair. "He thought it should be Mandy Cay."

"Love it! Oh, Mandy, it's perfect."

Mandy rolled her eyes. "And beyond pretentious. I wouldn't have any idea how an entire island gets renamed anyway."

Lucy looked up. "I can help with that."

Tommy said, "I think we ought to take a break from — "

"Aw, Tommy, don't be such a spoilsport. It's her island. Oughta have her name."

Mandy waved her off. "*Our* island. All of us. Sergei, Charlie, you especially. Your dad if he'd like."

"Really?"

Tommy said, "Really. Sergei needs a place to hang his hat. Charlie needs a place to fish where the water doesn't freeze in winter. They're already arguing down there about where to put in a new dock."

Lucy chewed a piece of papaya. "Hm. I'm sorta between ware—houses. New York is done, closed up. Allentown got bulldozed yester—day. Some sort of medical center planned for the site — which, by the way, we made a handsome profit on — and I think I've worn out my welcome in Jacks Ford. Andy needs the space. He's growing his store."

Mandy said, "That's all good. So, yes, here it is. A huge house."

"Huge is understatement. I've always thought a grass shack on a beach would be nice. Get unplugged. Kick back, read a bunch of books."

He said, "Sounds like a really good plan to me."

Lucy stabbed a strawberry. "Well, maybe a phone. Hm. Phone and a tablet would be good. Maybe a laptop?"

Mandy said, "You're incorrigible."

"A billion bucks is a lot. A billion four-point-six if you want to manage the entire pie."

Tommy sighed. "Let's not get carried away, Luce. I mean, we could spend a hundred grand a week and it would take, what, two hundred and fifty years to go through it."

"Two hundred and eighty years, nine months and seven days, ac—tually."

Mandy's eyes widened. She turned to Tommy "I'm going to say it anyway. She's really that good, isn't she?"

Lucy shrugged. "Anyway, my new little bank in Grand Cayman is bursting at the seams. But if we want to divvy it up into shares, split up..."

Tommy said, "I've got nothing against sticking together. We did well, but everybody should follow their own path. I do know that Sergei and Charlie are good with the island."

Mandy said, "And I'm good with us."

Lucy raised her glass. "Make it three. Tommy, in retrospect, I'm kind of sorry that I was pushing so hard for TKA and dressing you up like a pinstripe doll. It's not you, never was."

"It's okay. You did right by me from the get-go and I'm totally in—debted to you."

"Aw, that's nice of you to say, Tommy. Isn't it, Mandy?"

"Oh, absolutely. A roamer, a free spirit, some new adventure on every horizon."

That sounds... A twinge of unease. *Like she's cutting me loose.* "Still thinking about some sort of an article about all of this?"

Mandy said, "Yes. You know I have to try, Tommy. Back at the hotel, when Kenwood... when he... when he took his own life... Uh, okay. I admit I froze, numbed up. It was too much. I can still see..."

Tommy leaned forward and took her hand. "It *always* is. It's a ter—rible thing. The minute you can ignore seeing something like that, well, you're dead or about to be."

"But you — "

"I never get over it either. Sergei once said the same thing, as tough as he sounds."

Mandy said, "On Walter's yacht, we talked a bit about that. I was still moping around and he asked, 'well, what did you expect. Brass band? Trophy? A medal? Come, I have box full of medal, you take as many as you wish.'"

Lucy gasped. "That's terrible. What a cruel — "

Mandy cocked her head slightly left and mustered a patient smile. "No, Luce, he's right. Like all warriors, he's done what was expected and sometimes got patted on the back, but it never changes how rotten it can be."

That's true enough. But none of us cry in our beer over it.

Mandy pressed her palms together between her knees and faced Lucy.

"I've seen two people die in a few weeks. Poor little Benny, who wanted some attention, and Brendan Kenwood, who saw Benny and Phil and all the others as bugs on the path, to be stepped on and squashed. In a way, Kenwood got away with it. Especially when the White House circled the wagons and put it down as a stroke, arranged for a phony autopsy, got him buried with all the ruffles and flourishes. Don't you see? They can't admit to anything. They have to protect the secret."

Lucy drew a breath. "But Halsey, Gibbons, Eaton, Chamberlain all got theirs."

That's true, too. "Lucy did a magnificent job when she took Walter's six hundred million, used it to launch one of her great plays — best ever, I might add — boxed 'em up and nailed it shut. They lost all of HG Trading, Gibbons got wiped out on overextended leases, Eaton and Chamberlain are going to get shredded by the SEC, Halsey's lost her island — and her nerve."

Mandy picked up a newspaper from the coffee table and held it up. Across the bottom of the front page, an article under the headline, "White House plans new safeguards for banking system." And it wrapped around a photo of the president, senators and congressmen, the chairman of the Federal Reserve Bank now under consideration to become treasury secretary. And in the back row, the beaming face of Walter Campos.

"We've seen it," Tommy said. "It's the best we're going to get."

"No. It's not enough. I can't get my head around 'well done, we solved a bunch of murders and saved the planet from falling off a cliff. So should we go for a swim or have lunch first?'"

Lucy waved off Tommy's interruption. "It has to be. I mean, if you want to give a bunch of settlement money to the family and friends of the victims, fine, but..." Her voice trailed off and she was quiet for a moment. "But, yeah, I get it. You have to try."

"It's what I do, Lucy. It's about justice."

Tommy said, "You *do* realize the odds are awfully long, right? That this is possibly a dangerous idea. Look around at the people in-volved."

Mandy placed her glass on the table, next to her empty bowl. "I have to work it out. There has to be a way. You said it yourself, Tom-my. Everyone to their own path."

He sighed. *Yeah, I get it. If I was in her shoes, I'd do it too. When you get so damn tired, so damn angry that you can't walk away.* The bomb in Beverly Hills. Carter Blackmann, blowing Myra Fielding's brains out in Virginia. On Lucy's back steps, in the pouring rain, touching bot-tom. The gunfight behind the grocery store in Nassau, the metallic scent of blood washing along the wet pavement. One grubby little Central American town after another, on the run. Half dead in Vegas. More'n half dead at Doc's, in the desert, blasting away at the CIA. Blown out of a building in Beverly Hills. Just a routine job, gone side-ways. *Shoulda died that night.* The long, lonely trail of black ops, the dirty jobs, expendable, don't much care. The boozy frat parties at LSU. Puking in the alleys the next day. The night of the tornados, trying to hold on. *Hold on, hold on. Can't hold on. Just can't. Too weak. Gotta let go.* Little Petey, sucked away. Into the night. Eyes so damn scared. Gone. Momma, too. Black. So still, so damn still.

Ol' grandpap. Settin' on a hunk of house, twisted all to hell. Look, boy, ain't nothin' you can do 'bout that. You can curl up and be noth-in' or you can pull up your britches and let it go, maybe do somethin' with your life. You hear, boy? *Yessir, paw-paw, I hear, I hear.*

Let it go. *She's got to follow her own path.*

Let her go.

CHAPTER FORTY-ONE

West Forty-Seventh Street, New York City

The railing of the subway entrance was cold, but the coffee under his nose still hot from the lone deli in a canyon of diamond mer—chants. All of Manhattan had to be smiling. Holiday shopping signage was already up, but the sunshine was bright and the temperatures pushing into record status.

After ten days on the island, the city had a claustrophobic air, a grinding bite on the ear and the scent of the gutter — not quite the same as coral sand.

Well, smiling as much as usual, I guess. Images of long ago drifted into his mind. *Her name was Belle, the girl with the darkest eyes and the prettiest smile. Most everyone thought she was the loveliest in all of St. Tammany Parish. A warm Saturday night. The band began a slow tune, a waltz, "Les Grande Bois."*

Just another routine day. The markets up a few points, the politi—cians making the usual arguments, business and commerce humming along at a steady pace. Not a hint of discord anywhere, except for the major banks, anxious about potential constraints resulting from the president's proposals on safeguarding securities trading down in the fi—nancial district.

Memories swirled in again. *Just thirteen, hanging out in the bullpen, trying to fit in, when Belle came out of nowhere, put her hands on her hips. And she said, "Well now, Tommy Kane, do you want to dance or not?"*

But mostly, no one cared much about SEC investigations prodded by the attorney general, or oilfield leases that fizzled and threatened to bump up the price of gas by five or six cents a gallon. Or some big shopping malls in the heartland — everywhere west of Manhattan — struggling going into the shopping season. David Aire was working on a new spring collection, Lenny Pink's theatrical agency was booking fast for new productions on and off Broadway.

I was thirteen stupid. Clumsy. Unsure. Out of place, and believed that no girl in St. Tammany would ever want anything to do with a kid out of St. Martin, on the Teche. I tried, too hard, and blew it. Thirteen stupid. She laughed, and floated away, into a sea of giggles. The guys, they said she was like that, a flirt.

Bug expressed gratitude for an offer to join his daughter in the Ba — hamas. But no thanks. He was on a job, and, besides, he was a New Yorker, a fan of the Mets, the Knicks, the Jets, and that was that.

"I understand," Tommy had said. "You take care."

"Yeah, yeah. Anytime pal. Just forget, I got an hourly rate."

His van sped away into traffic. *Hard not to smile.*

At last, Mandy exited the skyscraper and the plaza in front. She wove through the pedestrian traffic. Assured steps, standing tall, look — ing like she owned the city. Like she was mingling with the regular folks while awaiting that big journalism prize. Cosmopolitan. Classy. Elegant. New York City to the nines. At the intersection, she paused for the light. Impatient, all business, no nonsense. When it changed, she joined the flow and, halfway across, gave a little wave.

Ol' Belle went on out west, to Los Angeles, they say. Married some rich guy, had four, five, kids, got fat and has some sort of life, no one knows if good or bad, but a life and that's probably what counts. So they said back in St. Tammany, at the country club, over silky bourbon and long cigars. Does any guy ever get over thirteen stupid?

"Hey," she said.

The voice that warmed his ears and massaged his brain.

She smiled and joined him, leaning on the railing, as relaxed as he'd ever seen her.

"Can I get you a coffee?"

"No. But I'll share." She sipped and returned the cup. "Not the same as French Market, Tommy."

"No. I guess not." He tossed the cup into a wastebasket and to—

gether they watched traffic drift by. Cabs, cars, people of all sizes and shapes.

Mandy exhaled and began to smile. "I was ready, Tommy. Best piece I've ever written."

"I know you did. You worked really hard on that article. Your meeting went well?"

She nodded. "As I would have expected. I love those guys. Great editors. Always willing to listen. Very supportive, patient. Smart guys. Really first-rate journalists. Old school, the way it's supposed to be."

Tommy took a sip. "That's nice."

She looked up and way beyond the intersection, closed her eyes and took a deep breath. "But they don't want it. A solid rejection."

"Sorry. What happened?"

Mandy chuckled. "Three of them read through the entire piece. Just a courtesy. And they were kind about it. But Jack Chandler — he's the managing editor — thought it too inflammatory, too weak on facts, too long on speculation, too many unidentified sources. He said I was naming some of the biggest names in business — the underpinnings of ad revenue — and people that are, well, too big to fail."

"That's too bad."

"The others were less charitable. They suggested I was hanging out with too many conspiracy freaks and one of them, Mike Jerome, went so far as to say it sounded more like fiction, one of those conspiracy thrillers that are so popular these days."

Tommy turned to admire her profile. "So. End of story, eh?"

Her voice softened. "Yep. Afraid so."

Does a kid from the Teche ever get a second chance?

She took his arm to pull in close and looked up at him, the promise of adventure in her sparkling eyes. "C'mon, Tommy. Let's go home."

About the Author

Geoffrey Mehl is a writer who lives in northeastern Pennsylvania, and also the author of three best-selling books on environmentally responsible landscaping. In addition to keeping tabs on life in Jacks Ford at the always humming Puffin Diner (the official headquarters of Tommy Kane and Mandy Owens), he is an avid gardener, a cooking and baking enthusiast, and a marginally-successful household do-it-yourselfer.

Nine Lives is the sequel to *Stray Cats*.

www.ingramcontent.com/pod-product-compliance
Lightning Source LLC
Chambersburg PA
CBHW070310260626
47160CB00003B/799